THE MURDER OF
ANDREW JOHNSON

THE MURDER OF ANDREW JOHNSON

BURT SOLOMON

TOR PUBLISHING GROUP

NEW YORK

THE MURDER OF ANDREW JOHNSON

Copyright © 2023 by Burt Solomon

A Forge Book
Published by Tom Doherty Associates / Tor Publishing Group
120 Broadway
New York, NY 10271

www.tor-forge.com

Forge® is a registered trademark of Macmillan Publishing Group, LLC.

Library of Congress Cataloging-in-Publication Data

Names: Solomon, Burt, author.
Title: The murder of Andrew Johnson / Burt Solomon.
Description: First edition. | New York : Forge, 2023. | Series: The John Hay mysteries ; 3
Identifiers: LCCN 2023013395 (print) | LCCN 2023013396 (ebook) |
ISBN 9780765392725 (hardcover) | ISBN 9780765392749 (ebook) |
Subjects: LCSH: Johnson, Andrew, 1808–1875—Fiction. | Murder—Investigation—
Fiction. | Conspiracies—Fiction. | LCGFT: Detective and mystery fiction. |
Biographical fiction. | Thrillers (Fiction) | Political fiction. | Novels.
Classification: LCC PS3619.O4336 M86 2023 (print) | LCC PS3619.O4336 (ebook) |
DDC 813/.6—dc23/eng/20230608
LC record available at https://lccn.loc.gov/2023013395
LC ebook record available at https://lccn.loc.gov/2023013396

Our books may be purchased in bulk for promotional, educational, or business use. Please contact your local bookseller or the Macmillan Corporate and Premium Sales Department at 1-800-221-7945, extension 5442, or by email at MacmillanSpecialMarkets@macmillan.com.

First Edition: 2023

Printed in the United States of America

0 9 8 7 6 5 4 3 2 1

To the memory of my mother,
Maxine Toor Solomon,
and to Hunter Michael Solomon,
who took her place

For God's sake, let us sit upon the ground
And tell sad stories of the death of kings.

—Shakespeare, *Richard II*

THE MURDER OF
ANDREW JOHNSON

CHAPTER ONE

―――――

SATURDAY, JULY 31, 1875

I'll confess that I'd longed for a son—what new daddy doesn't?—but I wouldn't swap a bare-knuckled champion-to-be for the tiny girl who was smiling and squirming in Clara's arms. Helen was four and a half months old, and she still had a sweetness I could smell halfway across the room. She started to squeal.

"Your turn," Clara said.

"I'm not good at this," I protested.

"Neither was I."

She had a point, although I didn't say so. I unbent from my burgundy bergère and reached across and took Helen into my arms. I began to rock her. The squealing ceased.

Clara beamed at me. She was nice enough not to tease.

"So, when's the next one?" I said, surprising myself.

"I would imagine that is partly up to you," Clara replied.

For a young woman reared on Millionaires' Row, in this prim and proper age, Clara could be astonishingly frank about the practicalities of life. We were sitting in her father's library, the rosewood shelves full of books with uncracked spines, in his Italianate mansion on suave and stately Euclid avenue, in Cleveland. This was where any American should aspire to live, even (or especially) if the money wasn't his own. Mine wasn't. I couldn't help but hear the hammering next door, from the workmen building my new house. I mean *our* house—Clara's and little Helen's and mine. Actually, I mean *his* house, my father-in-law's, Amasa Stone's. It was his wedding gift, and naturally it came with conditions. We had left New York behind, after my five happy years at the *Tribune*, and had been nesting under Amasa's (pardon me, Mr. Stone's) roof for eight weeks, four days, and . . . let me think . . . thirteen and a half hours now. But who's counting?

I worried that I'd made a deal with the devil. Not that Amasa Stone was a devil. He generally meant well, in a hard-nosed way, putting his own interests first. But that's what people do, particularly self-made millionaires in a world that worships wealth, so I tried to keep my expectations low and my disappointments to a minimum. With mixed success, I might add. My job henceforth was to administer Amasa's investments, in railroads and steel mills, in oil refining and banks, in stocks and silver, after the financial panic of 'seventy-three had nearly ruined him. (Not even Clara knew that.) My position, vaguely drawn, put me under Amasa's thumb as well as his roof. But the work itself didn't sound terribly taxing, and I figured that having my father-in-law finance our bread crusts would give me time to write my half of the epic biography of Lincoln that Nicolay and I had pondered ad nauseam over late-night brandies. Here, something was always in the larder, even if I didn't know what a larder was. How lucky was I, at what I hoped was a tolerable cost in self-respect. Everything in life had its pluses and minuses, its benefits and costs—wasn't that so? The goal was to unbalance them rightly.

Moving to Cleveland, not incidentally, made Clara happy, which she hadn't been in New York. She was too reserved, too sensible—too pure of heart, if I may exaggerate, although not by a lot—to fit in comfortably in the East. I looked across at her. The baby had taken nothing from her health or good looks. She was the kindest person I'd ever known, but it was a kindness backed by steel. She had an unruffled sort of face, unlined, not delicate but handsome, with unapologetic cheeks and a determined chin. Her hair was braided loosely into a bun, and her dark sparkling eyes could peer inside you without seeming to try. There was nothing flimsy about her; her bosom was ample enough to hide in. She was twenty-five years old, to my thirty-six, yet she was sturdy and serene—and content—in a way I could only dream of. Clara was without guile. I had enough for the both of us.

Helen was wriggling again. I was ready to restore her to her mother's embrace when there was a knock at the door, too deferential for Amasa. The butler entered. He was a black gentleman with a fringe of white hair around a lived-in face. He carried a silver platter on his fingertips as if he were a waiter at Delmonico's.

"For you, sir," he said.

A yellow envelope lay on the platter. Across the top, Gothic script announced:

𝔚estern 𝔘nion 𝔗elegraph

Amasa owned a chunk of that, too. Scrawled underneath:

Mr. John Hay, Esq.

I could guess who had sent it—Whitelaw Reid, who had been my nominal boss and boon companion at the *New-York Tribune*. The *Esquire* was his idea of a jab.

I handed Helen back to Clara and used my bone-handled pocketknife to slit open the envelope.

> My dear Hay, Andrew Johnson died this morning in
> Elizabethton, wilds of East Tennessee. The most hated
> man in America. Can you go? Reid

Can I? My wife and daughter would fare just fine without me, and my father-in-law would sputter at my gallivanting and then acquiesce. Occasionally I needed to do something absurd.

＋══＋

I caught the noon train south, toward Columbus. No trouble with the reservations, not when your father-in-law is a director of the railroad and of four or five others. I had a compartment to myself. It was paneled in mahogany, curtained in silk, upholstered in velvet, trimmed in ebony and gold, carpeted in a tapestry caressing my feet—a testament to what my pal Clemens has dubbed the Gilded Age. But what, pray tell, was wrong with gilded?

The conductor brought me the Columbus newspapers. The printers' strike in Kentucky, the anthracite coal miners' strike in Pennsylvania, the weavers' strike in Massachusetts, the shoe cutters' strike in New York— what on earth was the world coming to? I tried not to feel nostalgic for the blood and terror of civil war. At least right and wrong had seemed clear then, and the imperatives were obvious to all. Things were different now. I was a Republican to the bone, but I pined for the days when Labor hadn't loathed Capital, and capitalism hadn't been running amok. Its titans reigned as tyrants greedier than tsars. Vanderbilt was buying up railroads—Amasa's, among others—and a Clevelander named Rockefeller was busy cornering the market in oil refining. This much was clear: The pastoral America was passing. The horse's or ox's pace was giving way to the bustle of rail. Industry, enterprise, expansion, ambition, acquisitiveness, extravagance, ostentation—anything worth doing was worth overdoing.

Below the front-page dispatches on the Missouri floods and the latest in the Reverend Henry Ward Beecher's sensational trial for adultery, *The Dispatch* ran a short item:

Andy Johnson's Apoplexy.

GREENEVILLE, TENN., July 31—Ex-President Johnson received a very severe stroke of paralysis at 4 o'clock on Wednesday at his daughter's residence in Carter county. Feeling has been partially restored to his left side. He speaks intelligently, and hopes are entertained of his recovery.

Old news.

I tried to picture the dear departed. Physically, ol' Andy had a presence. He was of solid build, with a massive head, a jut-jawed face, piercing eyes, thick hair to his earlobes. He was invariably clad in the style of the old statesmen, in doeskin trousers and a black broadcloth coat. I had never seen the man smile. The last time I had seen him at all (not counting the half hour he had hovered by Lincoln's deathbed during that awful, awful night), he was drunk. That was on the fourth day of March in 'sixty-five, at the inauguration for Lincoln's second term as president and ol' Andy's first as vice president. Before the ceremony started, he had gulped down a tumbler of whisky—blaming his unfinished recovery from typhoid fever—and then another and, as he was leaving to be sworn in, yet a third. (I had this on good authority, from Hannibal Hamlin, the man whose job he took.) He was sozzled when he delivered his inaugural address, ranting at the cabinet, lionizing "the people," embarrassing everyone in sight, possibly including himself, until Hamlin prevailed on him to stop. Lincoln forgave him—of course!—but I am a lesser soul.

I stared out of the window awhile. The hills near Cleveland had slipped behind us, and the land lay as flat as a windless sea. Wood fences that used to be white surrounded fields of wheat and corn, strewn with red barns (red paint was the cheapest) and silos and stables. Once upon a time, or so I'd heard, a squirrel could scamper from the Atlantic shoreline clear to Ohio without touching the ground. But ever since the lumbermen had given way to farmers, those days were gone.

In Columbus, I picked up the evening newspapers, which had caught up with the ex-president's fate. In *The Cincinnati Daily Star*:

Death of Andy Johnson.

GREENEVILLE, TENN., July 31—Senator Johnson, after a perceptible improvement last night, began again to sink a little after midnight, and died at fifteen minutes of three o'clock this morning.

I had felt fortunate to miss most of his presidency, which an assassin's bullet began. What an unworthy successor to the Great Emancipator! Soon after Lincoln was martyred, I sailed to Europe, taking up leisurely diplomatic posts in our embassies in Paris, Vienna, and Madrid, so I followed Johnson's failures at a distance. That was close enough. Granted, he didn't smoke or swear or steal, so far as I knew, and I had never seen him spit (although I'm not alleging he didn't). He told fewer lies in a month than most politicians spoke before breakfast. Those were his good points, overwhelmed by the bad. He was a vindictive man and a worse president, a bully and a demagogue who considered compromise a sin and never forgave a slight. He bungled Reconstruction—undermining the Freedmen's Bureau, reneging on the promise of forty acres to emancipated slaves, pardoning Confederates, restoring the slavocracy to its former glory. He earned the unprecedented humiliation of getting impeached and, after his debacle of a presidency, slumped home to Tennessee. Yet even then, he refused to accept disgrace. Twice, he lost bids for Congress, but just this past winter, by the slimmest of margins, on the fifty-fourth ballot, the Tennessee legislature sent him back to Washington as a United States senator. Vindication at last!

Only now he was dead, the most hated man in America. He had divided a nation that longed for unity. He had been venomous toward his enemies, real and imagined, and had coarsened the civic discourse, wielding a truncheon in place of Lincoln's scalpel. Who on earth would go to his funeral? Would anyone?

Ah, *this* was the story I would write for the *Tribune*.

A cow outside my window flapped his dewlap in my direction, undoubtedly meant as a salute. I returned to *The Daily Star*.

OBITUARY.

Andrew Johnson was born at Raleigh, N.C., December 29th, 1808, and was, consequently, nearly 67 years of age . . .

Most of his story I already knew. He was born into poverty in North Carolina, and his daddy drowned while rescuing two rich men when Andy was three years old. Lacking even a day of schooling, Andy was indentured at age ten to a tailor, before running away. He returned only to guide his mama and stepfather west, across the Appalachians, a blind pony pulling their cart of possessions. In East Tennessee, the rugged land of Davy Crockett and Daniel Boone, he began his political ascent, from alderman to mayor to legislator to governor to congressman to U.S. senator. He was a Democrat who idolized his namesake Andrew Jackson, Tennessee's most famous son. Yet when the Southern states declared their independence, Johnson—alone among the Southern senators—opposed secession and refused to quit his seat. Accordingly, when the Union Army conquered Tennessee, Johnson was named as the state's military governor and then, in the election of 'sixty-four, as Lincoln's running mate. The voters catapulted ol' Andy into a vice presidency that was destined to last only forty-two days.

Maybe I was thinking about the stumbling pony because somehow I dozed off. Next I knew, the train was jolting to a halt, and the conductor was swinging a lantern and shouting, "Cincinnati!"

After a quick, unappetizing dinner in the depot of boiled mutton and a blotchy potato, I boarded the Knoxville train. Within seconds, I learned more than I wanted to know about the war's impact on the nation's railroads. I was consigned to a rickety car with streaked windows and straight-back seats, wondering how in blazes I would ever get to sleep.

The porter was a sinewy young negro who belonged on a football field, if the college boys would have him. He must have noticed my look of puzzlement, because he chuckled in a kindly way and asked about my destination.

"Hope you be a patient man," he said when I told him.

"Not usually," I replied.

"You not from here, suh."

It wasn't a question. "From Illinois, growing up," I said. "Now from Cleveland." I left out Providence, Washington City, European capitals, and New York, the places where I'd most felt at home.

"You been South before, suh?"

"Not much."

"It's a different world down here, suh."

"I like different worlds," I said.

He pursed his lips and managed not to smile. "Some Ah do," he said, "and some Ah don't."

"How long to Knoxville?"

"Five hours and thirty-seven minutes."

"You sure of that?" I joshed.

This time he did smile, showing a gold front tooth. He explained that most of the railroad lines running north to south hadn't been rebuilt since the war and hadn't been any great shakes before then.

"Isn't this an era of good feeling between North and South?" I said.

He smiled again as if I were joking, which I was. I inquired if I might purchase some bourbon or rye.

"Ah could oblige."

It didn't take him long, and the bourbon wasn't bad. It warmed my chest and calmed my internals. The porter also brought two pillows and a tartan blanket that no varmints had used for their bedding.

When I turned and stared out the window, my reflection stared back. I can't say that I looked my most debonair. My dark hair, center parted, lay too flat on my ghostly white head, which made my ears stick out. My face was too thin, my chin too insignificant, my features a trifle too delicate. Should I grow a beard to match my raffish mustache? I wet my fingers to tame my eyebrows. I looked tired as hell. I *was* tired as hell.

I took two deep breaths (I had learned this in the boxing ring) and braved another look at myself. Better. I was probably my severest critic—and my greatest admirer. I was pretty sure I spied the daredevil look in my eye, although I was possibly seeing it from the inside. I tried my crookedest smile, which lent a certain dash to my countenance. I had to acknowledge that women seemed not to mind it, including Clara. It would do. It would have to.

I reached for *The Daily Star* beside me. The flimsy newspaper had fallen open to page two, home to the editorials—my domain at the *Tribune*. It was a job I loved but for which I was only fitfully suited. I do not like to blame, and I mortally hate to praise. This editorial did neither.

Death of Ex-President Andrew Johnson.

The people of the United States will be astonished and shocked to hear of the death of ex-President Andrew Johnson, of Tennessee. Until last Wednesday he was in the full vigor of health. Now he had passed from among us in the most unexpected manner . . .

The word wedged in my craw. *Unexpected.*

CHAPTER TWO

I won't bore you with the night's discomforts, except to say that I couldn't have slept for more than an hour or two and that now I ached in muscles I never knew I had. I woke up with a swollen tongue and with that word rattling around: *unexpected*. That had described Willie Lincoln's death—his murder, as it turned out—in 'sixty-two. President Lincoln's loveliest son was eleven years old when he died of what the doctors, in their self-assuredness, diagnosed as typhoid fever. I figured out that Willie had been murdered, and by whom. Unexpected, to be sure, but not unsolved.

I pried my eyes open. The porter was standing in the aisle, looking as fresh as new-mown hay. He offered a chipped cup of what looked like coffee.

"Acorns," he said. Coffee had grown scarce in the blockaded South during the war. Then he laughed. "No, suh, it be coffee. Not good coffee, but coffee."

I accepted with thanks and trepidation. A sip proved that the latter wasn't misplaced.

"Forty-two minutes to Knoxville," he announced.

Outside, the dawn was gray, almost pearly. I hated this time of day. Other than buttering croissants and making babies, nothing good happens before noon. Apparently, we had passed through Kentucky and into Tennessee. I was alone in the car, which was fine with me. I needed to shave and attend to nature. I forced myself to stand, then twisted my torso in both directions and stumbled along the aisle to the rear of the car.

The door to the water closet was locked. I took the nearest seat. Someone had left the morning's *Cincinnati Enquirer*. I skimmed the front page and halted at:

> LONG BEACH, N.J., July 31—President Grant was out driv-
> ing this afternoon when informed of the death of Ex-President
> Johnson. He was visibly affected.

Yes, he probably giggled or clapped in glee. Everyone knew the two men despised each other, for reasons both principled and personal. Johnson skipped his successor's inauguration, spurning Grant's last-minute offer of a ride from the Executive Mansion to the Capitol. Grant was not an emotional man or inclined to hold a grudge, but even he had his limits.

A man was standing in the aisle, for the same reason I was. I must have chuckled because he demanded, "What's so dad-blame funny?"

"Pardon?" I looked up at a bald man with multiple chins raggedly covered by whiskers. Morning wasn't his favorite, either.

"I want a laugh, too, my friend." He spoke with a drawl that stretched to the Rio Grande. "What's so funny, huh?"

"Just this item in the newspaper about President Grant's reaction to, you know, his predece . . . well, Andrew Johnson's . . . his . . . passing."

"What about it?"

"Well, it said he was . . ."—I glanced back at my lap—"'visibly affected.'"

"So what's so dad-blame funny about that, mistuh?"

"Nothing," I said. "It just struck me as—"

"Where you from, anyway, mistuh?"

My accent—that is, my lack of one, my lack of *his*—betrayed me. "I'm from . . . uh, Ohio. Illinois, originally. Well, Indiana, *o*riginally. Southern Indiana."

"So what're ya doin' here, anyway, mistuh?" Every *mister* was meant as a dagger's thrust. Will this nation ever be repaired—be a *nation* again?

I figured it wouldn't help my case to invoke the *New-York Tribune*, that famously abolitionist rag, the late Horace Greeley's Great Moral Organ. "I'm going to Johnson's, President Johnson's, funeral," I said.

"Are you now, if you think that's so funny? You happy he's dead?"

Best to turn the conversation around. "You admired the man, I take it."

"Ya damn right I did."

"May I ask why?"

"Why would you care, mistuh?"

"I'd like to know, is all."

"Why dya think? He was a good man, that's why. A tough man, brave as all hell. You try bein' a Union man in Tennessee. When he was a-headin' here from Washington, a mob got near to lynchin' 'im—in Lynchburg."

He chuckled. "Or mebbe it was Bristol. And he was near to gettin' hisself killed in Nashville"—while Johnson served as the military governor, he meant—"and he never paid no mind. He says what he thinks, means what he says. He don't take nuttin' from nobody. He a man like any o' us. The Great Commoner, they call 'im, and he *was*. Great *and* common. Common and great. One o' us—the best o' us."

"Did you ever meet the man?" I said. "Sounds like you knew him."

"Naw, Ah never know'd 'im," he replied, looking past me. "But I always felt like he know'd me."

East of Knoxville, I entered the South. I could tell. The air felt sultry, even on the train. I swear it smelled of magnolias. This was a foreign land to me. I had been in the South before, once on a steamship down the Mississippi (until my money ran out) from my boyhood home in Warsaw, Illinois, and a couple of times visiting battlefields as Lincoln's eyes and ears. But none of those times was I *here*, immersed in a place where people would probably detest me if they knew who I was and why I had come.

The bench was hard, and the train bumped along at what I judged to be no more than twelve—at most, fifteen—miles an hour. My railroad car was empty except for a man in overalls and his wife, probably heading home from the big city. The windows were half-open; the broken shades billowed. I stared out at the pictures of poverty—desiccated cornfields, shanties in the shadow of gnarled trees, bent-over black men splitting wood. Maybe it had always been thus. Despite all the moon and magnolia, most of the South had always been as poor as Job's turkey. But now it was worse—across this vast nation, not just here. The panic set off by the collapse of Jay Cooke's New York bank (triggered by squishy railroad loans) had ripped through the economy, ruining the postwar prosperity, setting off a depression anywhere and everywhere. In Cleveland, mere blocks from Euclid avenue, I had seen children in rags and gap-toothed women selling soap. Their world—*this* world—wasn't gilded in the least.

Out the window, the countryside rose and dipped. In the distance, ridges led to rolling hills that were perfectly rounded, like a child might draw. The hills gave way to mountains toward the east.

I changed trains in Greeneville. This time I had a seatmate, a heavyset young man with scraggly blond hair and a handsome face pitted by pox. He was grinning.

"So, bub, where ya goin'?" he said.

"Elizabethton," I replied.

"No, ya ain't."

"Pardon me?" I resisted the temptation to check my ticket.

"It's Eliza*beth*ton ya goin' to. Eliza*beth*ton. So's they figger ya for a local." He had the belching laugh of a farmer after his midday meal.

"Is it that obvious?" I said. "Before or after I open my mouth?"

"Both."

My turn to laugh. "John Hay," I said, extending my hand, no easy task in the cramped quarters.

Instead of taking it, he looked at me sidelong and said, "A Yankee?"

"I suppose you could say that." Why not gamble on the truth?

This was why: "And whatcha heah fer?" he said.

The whole truth, looking him in the eye. "I am representing the *New-York Tribune,* here to write about Andrew Johnson. His life, his death, his funeral."

"The *Tribune,* huh? Greeley's rag, right? I thought he was the biggest crock of shit I ever heard of, him in that long, funny white coat." My seatmate's eyes lit up. "Voted for him, anyway."

I laughed again. I had thought and done the same, when my eccentric publisher ran as a breakaway Republican *and* as a Democrat against President Grant, the regular Republican, in the 'seventy-two presidential election—and got whupped. "Why did you do that?"

"I would vote for a three-legged ass over a Republican."

"Would that include the late Andrew Johnson?"

He met my gaze, with a twinkle in his eyes. "Yes, suh, I'd say he was a three-legged ass."

"Not four?"

"No, suh, I'd say three is jes' 'bout right."

"Because?"

"Some poor asses simply don't have ever'thin' they need, y' know? Not their fault. Jes' the way the good Lord made 'em."

"What was he missing, would you say?"

My seatmate chewed that one over, literally, targeting the tarnished brass spittoon in the aisle. At last, he looked back at me and said, "A heart."

+———+

Carter's Depot was a low brick building with a gabled roof and superfluous pillars. It was the nearest station to Elizabethton—in its suburbs, so to speak. I was never happier to arrive at a destination. Traveling for a day felt in my bones like a week.

The heat and humidity clobbered me the moment I stepped down from the train. *Clobbered* isn't quite the right word. It smothered me, melted around me like a tallow candle. That was inside the depot. Venturing outside was worse. The wick was still aflame.

I was glancing around for a hackney when I heard my name called. "Mistuh Hay!" The voice belonged to a young black fellow with a wiry build and a friendly expression. He couldn't have been older than sixteen or seventeen.

"Yes?" I said.

His face had easy features, and his skin was as smooth as porcelain and closer to white than to black. He was about my height, and skinnier, but I had a feeling he would knock me silly if we ever got into a fistfight. The difference was desire. He wasn't cocky, exactly, but the tilt of his head and the directness of his gaze suggested a lack of subservience that I guessed could cause him no end of trouble hereabouts.

"You Mistuh Hay? You the third man I ask. I'm to fetch you back to Mrs. Brown's house. She the president's daughter."

That must be the house in which Johnson died. "Who sent you?" I said.

"Mrs. Brown did."

I wondered how she had known. Oh, Whitelaw Reid must have wired, after I had accepted the assignment. But how had *he* known?

"My name is William Andrew Johnson," he said. "Folks call me Bill."

I extended my hand, and Bill hesitated before he shook it with aplomb. Maybe this wasn't done in the South. He climbed into the buggy, and I went around and squeezed in beside him, fitting my valise between my feet. A mild application of the whip persuaded the gray mare to glance back with a languid air and trot away.

The depot was shadowed on every side by forest. Through the mountain laurel, I heard a river gurgle.

"The Watauga," he said, noticing my interest. "Flows into town. We stay on the north side."

"Where's the house?" I said.

"On the river. Up and around, past town a ways." He gestured vaguely ahead and to the left. "Ain't too far."

"Who's there?" I said.

"All of 'em."

The roadway followed the river. The vegetation was lush, slathered in greenery—good bottomland. To our left, a cornfield sloped toward a tree-lined ridge. Across the river, to our right, the hillside rose to a crest. Straight ahead, a long, low, purplish mountain stood in the way. This was the western edge of the Appalachians; the mountains hemmed us in on three sides. The only escape was retreat.

"Who's everyone?" I said.

He meant the president's son and both daughters with their husbands and assorted children. "And Miz Johnson," he said.

"His widow," I said. "Is she here?" I had known Eliza Johnson years before and rather liked her.

"For weeks now. That's why we stopped off here."

"We?"

"Me and the president."

"I thought you worked for Mrs. . . . Mrs. . . ." Such a common name— why was it hard to remember? "Mr. Joh . . . the president's daughter?"

"Oh no, suh. I work . . . worked . . . for . . ."—his knuckles were white as he lashed at the reins; the mare trotted on, unperturbed—"the president."

"How long were you with him?"

"All my life. And my mama before that."

An arithmetical finger snap: Bill must have been enslaved when he was born. "What was he like, the president?" I said. "But I should tell you first . . ." I confessed to writing for the *New-York Tribune*, unsure if he'd have heard of it.

A smile spread across his face. The newspaper's reputation preceded me. "What can I tell you?" he said.

"Was he a good . . ."—I caught myself before saying *master*—"employer?"

"Like a member of the family, they treat me," Bill said. I assumed he meant this as a compliment. "Miz Johnson, she teach me to cook, even when she ailing. Mistuh Johnson always nice, ask after my ma. Lately, I hardly never leave his side. Sleeping on a pallet near his bed or outside his door."

"Why lately?" I said, but Bill seemed not to hear.

We rode in silence. The *clop-clop-clop* was soothing me to sleep. What drew me awake was Bill's melodic voice, soft enough that I had to struggle to hear it. "I'm as free as free could be," he said, either to himself or to me. Then he was telling me the story of their arrival from Greeneville, last Wednesday by railroad.

"Was he ill on the train?" I said.

"I don't ride in the same car, Mistuh Hay—"

"Oh, of course."

"But not that I could see."

"When did he fall ill, do you know?"

"Course I know. After we got to the house for dinner. Jes' about this time—same train you came. He ate hearty—so I hear from the cook—and he go upstairs and he jes' collapse. Apo . . . apo . . ."

"Apoplexy."

"That's it. That's what the doctors say."

"Was anyone with him?"

"Jes' Lillie."

"Who is that?"

"Lillie Stover. She a granddaughter, Miz Brown's girl. Her daddy was . . . well, that be Colonel Stover. He die in the war. A pretty thing, she is, 'bout to be married off to some lucky fellow. She was upstairs with her grand-pappy when he fall to the floor."

"She still here?"

A nod.

"Did she say if she noticed anything . . ."—I didn't know how to finish my sentence. I wanted to say *unexpected*—"out of the ordinary?" I had no basis for this, other than a hunch and, truth be told, a journalistic prayer.

"Cain't say, Mistuh Hay."

I had a feeling he knew what I meant. I trusted my hunch. "Did you?" I said.

Bill kept his eyes on the road and made no reply. I knew he had heard me. I looked over and saw an oversized tear roll down his cheek.

"I'm sorry I asked," I lied. He had told me a lot.

Bill was silent for a while before he turned to me and burbled, "Some-thin' was wrong, suh, I tell you. One minute he was fine, and suddenly he warn't. It warn't natural how he passed. Somethin' happen to 'im—I just knows it. Cain't say how, cain't say why, cain't say *who*." He paused, in case I had an explanation, which I did not. "But sure as day, Mistuh Hay, somebody kill 'im."

CHAPTER THREE

We followed the gravel road along the river and up into the hills. A faint breeze through the trees soothed like a salve. Bill didn't say another word. But the words he had uttered hung in the air. Had he spoken from knowledge, or was it just a hunch? Probably just a hunch. So? Hunches mattered, did they not? They could get to the core of something in a way that a logical mind failed to fathom. I was guessing that Bill regretted his outburst, but I hoped he would be thankful in time. (I've always been a bit of a dreamer.)

The roadway curved back to the river, and the buggy came to a halt by a farmhouse. The gray mare was breathing hard, ready to be rid of its burden. Bill glanced over with an impersonal smile that I interpreted as a mask of servility, as if we had never met. I was unsure how to react, so I didn't. I climbed down.

This was a beautiful spot, wild and picturesque. We were in a clearing by the Watauga's shore, shaded by river birches and willows. The air smelled fresh and fragrant—of lilac, best I knew. I took two deep breaths and listened to the river rush by. I had grown up next to a river but was spending my adulthood hemmed in by buildings. Across the Watauga, through the trees, I glimpsed a mountain—Linn Mountain, I would learn later. Holston Mountain rose behind the house.

The house itself was a poor man's idea of a plantation manse. The white planks needed a fresh coat of paint. Jutting from the center was a two-story porch with faux-marble pillars and a pointed roof. A dogtrot connected the two wings, all of it probably shrunken from the architect's fondest hopes.

I mounted the two steps to the front porch. The door was open. A woman was standing in the doorway, clad in a plain black gown with more buttons up the front than there are hairs in a mare's mane.

Even my tired eyes were transfixed. She was statuesque, like a statue is statuesque—tall, grave, exquisitely shaped, dignified in carriage. Her skin, the little I could see of it, glistened like marble. Her long tresses, a golden brown, center parted, shone from behind her mourning veil. Her face tapered, in a pleasing way, from a strong brow to an accommodating chin. But I could see that her eyes were hard and her mouth was grim—for good reason, at least to-day. She seemed distant, unreachable.

She managed a wan smile and said, "Welcome to my home, Mr. Hay. I am Mary Brown."

"Thank you for welcoming me in, at this difficult time. Please accept my sincerest condolences." I hope that didn't sound as insincere to her as it did to me. Superlatives are perilous.

She curtsied and offered her extended arm. In Paris, I would have kissed her hand. Here, I shook it. Her handshake was light but firm. I followed her through the dogtrot and into the parlor, on the left. The room had a low ceiling and a rough lumber floor. The walls were painted in marble-like swirls of beige. The furnishings looked comfortable but worn—a round table, oaken chairs with flowery cushions, an oval rug that was loosely woven, a sofa with arm sleeves that hid who knows what sorts of sin.

We weren't alone. A distinguished-looking man with a groomed, graying beard and a high-tide hairline stood by the hearth as if he owned it. This was how all prosperous men looked nowadays—you could hardly tell them apart anymore—along with their extra pounds in the wrong places. David Patterson had those, too. For that's who he was—I knew right off, somehow. I had met him once or twice during his single term as a U.S. senator, a lofty position he had attained as the then vice president's son-in-law. (This sounded uncomfortably familiar.) In his six years in office, he made not a mark on the nation's legislative trajectory, before he returned to Tennessee to manufacture woolens and flour and to tend his farm. Despite the black armband on his swallowtail coat, he looked fat and happy. Maybe that was just his vast forehead, which promised a wisdom about which I had my doubts.

Before Mary could introduce us, I stepped forward, extended my hand, and said, "Mr. Senator." Once a senator, always a senator—that was how ex-senators saw it. There was no such thing as flattering them too much.

"And you are?" he said, his gray eyes narrowing and his eyebrows contracting into a line. His handshake was stiff.

"John Hay of the *New-York Tribune*," I said, "and formerly of President Lincoln's staff. I was his assistant private secretary. I believe we've met."

"If you say so," Patterson said.

"I remember you, Mr. Hay." A woman's voice, throaty and assured, startled me. The wing chair had hidden her from view.

Mary said, "Oh, Mr. Hay, this is my sister, Mrs. Patterson. Martha Patterson."

The woman who half rose in reluctance wasn't pretty like Mary or nearly as tall. She hunched forward, wiry and taut, the picture of energy restrained—built for endurance. She wore a high-necked, long-sleeved black dress and kept fingering the dark braided hair draped over her right shoulder. She was not unattractive, but her lips looked narrow and tight, her cheekbones rigid. Her gaze had an intensity that tilted toward intolerance, suggesting the sort of person who would shush you in church. It was a face that had known suffering and how to mask it. She reminded me of someone, but I couldn't think who it was.

"And I remember you," I said.

"As you should," she said. Her voice was quiet, unyielding. "I recall that you walked right past me once without acknowledging my presence."

Ah, her father—that's who. Her voice was his, albeit an octave higher, and her inflections were his, and his East Tennessee twang. Not to mention her air of resentment.

"I must admit I don't remember," I said. "But please accept my condolences and forgive me for intruding at this time of sorrow."

Before Martha could reply, Mary jumped in. She was probably used to this. "Mr. Reid was so charming," she said, "and when he wired us about the article you were preparing, we couldn't help but agree to cooperate."

Why on earth hadn't Reid told me? "Which article was that?" I said.

Mary said, "You know, about his loving family and how we gathered around him in his final days. People need to know the truth about Daddy."

David Patterson harrumphed, and Martha, seated again, looked smug. I was desperate to sit but waited for an invitation.

"Oh yes, that article," I said. The story sounded too sentimental for Whitelaw Reid's taste. He was either liquored up when he wrote the telegram or his usual deceptive self—plausibly both. I made a show of removing my notebook from inside my frock coat and a pencil from my shirt pocket. "If you wouldn't mind, then."

Mary gestured me into a chair while she sank into the sofa. Staring into the low ceiling, she told of her father's arrival shortly before midday dinner—"Just last Wednesday," she said with wonder. "Minced veal and bran pie. Daddy ate less than his customary fill. But we were together—that was the important thing. Even Mother came downstairs." Mary pointed to the floor above. "All three of my children and my husband. Not Martha or the . . . senator here, they didn't come until—when was that, Friday night, Martha?"

"Late afternoon, I would say," Martha replied evenly.

Was there tension between the sisters? Hardly without precedent, Lord knows.

"After lunch, he went upstairs with Lillie," Mary said. "She's my eldest. A few minutes later, that's when we heard it."

"Heard what?" I said.

"The thump on the floor. Lillie shouted down to us, that Daddy had collapsed. This was in the other wing of the house. We ran upstairs, and he was on the floor and said he couldn't move. His left side. Mr. Brown—that's my husband—and my Andy, Andy Stover, a strapping boy, like his daddy was, the two of them picked him up and lifted him onto the bed. We wanted to send for Dr. Cameron—that's our doctor—but Daddy wouldn't hear of it."

"Did the doctor ever come?"

"That night," Mary said, "or was it the next day? It's all a blur. Anyway, by the next day, he was starting to feel better, and a stream of visitors started and never really stopped. The family was here, of course, most of us, and I can't tell you how many others. Daddy was just talking away, about old times, stories of politics, of high intrigue, his days as an alderman—the happier times."

"Did those include his presidency?" I said.

"I can answer that," David Patterson jumped in. "We all lived with him, you know."

"I didn't know. I lived there, too, right before you did. Slept in the room across from the president's office. Who stayed in . . . ? Just out of curiosity, mind you."

This was the journalist's tactic of arousing empathy in the interviewee. For once, it worked.

"The three girls," Mary said. "My two, and Martha's. We figured they could be farthest away from us and wouldn't burn the house to the ground. We had to keep the boys, both of our Andys, closer."

"Too many Andys," Patterson muttered.

"Was your father unwell when he arrived?" I said.

"Nothing I noticed," Mary said. "As I say, he didn't eat his usual, but that didn't occur to me until later. He looked tired, but a railroad journey is tiring. He seemed fine when he went upstairs."

Mary told me more than I wanted to know about her father's last hours—
the teary kinfolks, the sleepy grandchildren, the doctors' head shakes, the
lone candle on the side table, the shadows that gathered as eternity neared.
I took copious notes.

When Mary ran dry, I said, "Is your daughter here, by any chance? The
one who . . ."

Mary hesitated before she said, "I'm afraid not."

I took that to mean that she was but I couldn't see her.

Suddenly I had a ghoulish desire. "Could I possibly see the room in
which he . . . passed away?"

That was when the parlor door swung open and a vivacious young lady
with a cascade of golden hair skipped through.

"Lillie!" Mary exclaimed.

She wore a black frock that, despite its color, because of its sleekness,
would have caught every man's eye at a square dance. So would she. Her
face had a grace that would set anyone at ease—dimpled cheeks, an aq-
uiline nose, a dainty chin, a mouth with a mole at the edge of her smile.
I remembered reading that she had come out as a debutante. The Great
Commoner's granddaughter had joined the social elite. Was any nation
grander than this one?

Mary introduced us, and I parroted Reid's whitewashed reason for my
presence, which Lillie accepted without suspicion. I repeated my ghoulish
request, and Lillie—bless her soul!—offered to take me.

I expected Mary to veto the notion (weren't vetoes a family tradition?),
but she didn't. The Pattersons didn't seem distraught to see me go. I couldn't
blame them.

The dogtrot was airy and empty other than two clusters of hard-backed
chairs. We crossed through to the other wing of the house. The room on
the first floor had a plain dining table ringed with rough-hewn chairs that
would discourage a leisurely meal. Other than a sideboard, the room was
bare.

A narrow staircase pressed against the side wall. Lillie skipped up the
uneven steps, her skirt rustling.

Upstairs was a single room, with a wooden ceiling almost low enough
for me to touch. The mirrored dresser in the far corner was crowded with
bottles and jars, ready for a lady's use. By the mantel hung a painting of
an odd-looking man with floppy hair and a splotchy face. The bedstead,
between the two windows, was made up for the night's retiring. At its foot,
on a wooden trunk, sat a chessboard, its pieces poised for war.

"Do you play?" I said.

Lillie nodded.

"With him?"

"Checkers," she said. Tears filled her eyes. She walked to the nearer front window, facing the river.

I let her regain control and said, "Please tell me more."

"We were talking about my wedding, it's coming up in the fall, and I was hoping that he could . . . he could . . . could give me away. My daddy, you know, died in the war." She paused to compose herself, unembarrassed. "A dog was barking outside, and I turned to the window, and that's when . . . he . . . tumbled out of that chair"—Lillie pointed to the hard-backed rocking chair behind me—"and onto the rug. Just about where you're standing."

I lurched backward, as if I had trampled a grave. My calves struck the chair, and I nearly fell into it. Lillie ignored my clumsiness.

"I twirled around, and he was lying on the floor," she went on. "He was struggling to move, and his tongue . . . it refused . . . utterance. I must have screamed—I don't even remember—because . . . he didn't look right. His eyes looked so odd."

"How so?"

"I don't know, just odd. Big. The dark part." She raised her palms toward her face and spread her fingers. "Wide."

"He wouldn't let you call a doctor, I understand."

"You'd have to ask Mama about that. She was trying to convince him."

"So, you're saying he *could* talk?"

"Grandpappy had a way of making himself understood."

"Not many robberies here'bouts, I hear," Bill, the servant, said. He eased the buggy away from the house. "Or arrests for burnin' stuff down or for lewd behavior."

Apparently we were friends again—not friends, but friend*ly*. "That's refreshing," I replied.

"But murders—plenty of those."

"Mostly among people who know each other?" I said, in search of solace.

"Often."

I shivered. Dusk was settling in, and a gust whipped through the trees. The foliage concealed the Watauga, but I heard its fury.

"So, did ya learn whatcha came fer?" Bill said.

I considered his question. "I would say . . . no. Well, not yet."

"What dya want, then?"

"How old *are* you?"

Bill's face split into a grin. He was old enough to earn such a compliment and young enough to savor it.

I said, "Do you still believe he was the victim of . . . evil?"

Bill looked over at me and said, "Oh, I knows it, Mistuh Hay."

"How do you know it?"

He sighed and stared straight ahead. "I just do," he said. "I know these things."

I hoped silence would unstill his tongue, but he showed no sign of it.

"Where are we going?" I said.

"Into town."

"So I gathered. Where in town?"

"The hotel."

"Is there more than one?" I wouldn't mind charging the *Tribune* as much in expenses as I could muster.

"Same place the other fellow went."

"What other fellow?"

"Cap'n Mc-somethin'-or-nother. He come on the train with Mistuh Johnson."

"Who are you talking about?"

"Jes' what I say. Cap'n . . . I can't remember his . . . I met him on the platform, and he come wid us and we drop him off."

"At the hotel."

"Yes, suh. Called the Union, I think—actually, I know it. The Union Hotel. Owned by a doctor, a Union man, I hear. The doctor, not the cap'n—he a Reb."

"A lot of Union men around here?"

"More'n you'd think. East Tennessee don't have no plantations, the land ain't good enough, not flat enough, for cotton. No point in field slaves. Not many black folks at all. Not like west o' here. Tennessee, y'know, goes on and on, west t' the Mississippi. Here, a fellow may be for the Union and his neighbor he be a Reb, so I guess you never ask 'im unless ya wanna fight. Cain't tell a book by the cover, they say."

I wondered again: How old *was* this young fellow? Would it be impolite to ask if he had been Johnson's slave? His last name was Johnson. This implied that he must have been the former president's . . . possession . . . or his . . . How could I ask?

"And not just any doc," Bill said. "He come to Mistuh Johnson's bed, up at Miss Mary's house."

"The man who owns the hotel."

"Yes, suh. Doc Cameron's his name."

"And the man you dropped off here—a Confederate captain, you say. Do you know anything else about him?"

"No, suh, never met the man befo'."

"Had Mr. Johnson?"

"Cain't say. But he know jes' 'bout ever'body in East Tennessee."

"And everybody knows him?"

"Cain't hardly walk down the street with him and not be stopped by ever' person passin' by."

It was a moonless night. The air grew muggier as we came down from the hills. Between stands of trees, I saw scattered lights in the valley below—cabins or churches, I imagined. We descended into the valley and onto flat land and to the riverbank.

"Hold on," Bill instructed. "It ain't so deep."

The buggy rattled down the stony bank and plunged in. The river was turbulent, but my feet remained dry.

Elizabethton—pardon me, Eliza*beth*ton—was on the far bank. I would describe it as a crossroads except it looked to have a single main street, straight ahead of us, called . . . Main street. It was a rutted roadway intersected by a few lanes. The hamlet looked even humbler than my hometown of Warsaw, although probably full enough to harbor its own traditions, first families, and feuds.

Main street was lined with one- and two-story buildings. Here and there, a light flickered inside, usually on a second floor, in the homes over the shops. The raised wooden sidewalk was empty but for a gray-headed couple out for an amble. The woman, in a beflowered Sunday bonnet, waved in my direction. I waved back before I realized she was looking past me, at an old woman on the opposite sidewalk who waved back.

Bill suppressed a smile.

He halted the buggy in front of a ramshackle three-story building that seemed to list toward the right.

"Here?" I said.

"The Snyder House, that's a couple of blocks ahead, it's nicer."

"No, here is fine," I said. I was thinking of the doctor and of Captain McSomething. I grabbed my valise.

"Good luck, suh."

I hoped my grin was a wry one.

+══──══+

My hand-tooled leather valise, bloated by funeral attire, was scuffed from years of adventurous use. It was my papa's gift for passing the bar, an achievement as useless as any I'd attained. Well, not entirely. It had taught me to think in a logical manner, which studying the classics at Brown had not. For a journalist, or a detective, it was a way of thinking that guided me closer to the truth.

But only if I had the energy to think. My valise had suddenly grown heavy. I dragged it inside. I had been awake just about forever, through multiple states, geographical and emotional, and for more hours than my foggy mind could count.

The lobby was dim, and I needed a moment for my eyes to adjust. Once they did, I saw a reception desk made from a fallen tree trunk, its top half sliced away. The young man behind it had a skeletal physique, a pinched face, and oily brown hair that grew in tufts. I asked for a room.

I hadn't meant to be pugnacious, but his hard-eyed stare suggested I was wasting his time. What had I done to earn his mistrust, other than . . . ? Ah, that was it: I had opened my mouth. And maybe my valise resembled a Yankee carpetbagger's.

A gold half eagle slapped onto the desktop engaged his attention and produced a room key. My ten dollars would pay in advance for a week. I hoped not to stay that long.

"Hot water extra," he said.

I said I was looking for a "Captain McSomething" who had registered the previous Wednesday. My query earned a shrug and the suggestion to ask Dr. Cameron, the proprietor. Possibly he would be in in the morning. Whereupon the clerk scratched his pimply nose and turned away.

No bellboy was to be found, which suited me. I was relieved to be alone, in a room that wasn't moving. I fumbled to light the kerosene lamp and, beyond the billow of smoke, was sorry I had. The room seemed not to have been refurbished or cleaned for a decade or two. Neither did I.

The necessary was down the hall, and I felt lucky to make it back to my room before stripping to my drawers and easing the long, unsettling day to a merciful end.

CHAPTER FOUR

I awoke from a dreamless sleep, thinking about murder.

Supposing Bill was right. He seemed to be, about everything else. A sharp young fellow. Granted, he had no evidence, none that he would share. But he believed it, and so did I.

I mulled this with eyes closed. Some mornings, it was painful to pry them open. I listened for Helen's crying and, instead, heard horses snorting and men shouting from the street below. I wasn't home—that was for sure. Maybe Cleveland was starting to feel a little like home.

With trepidation I opened my eyes and surveyed my surroundings. Could be worse. The floral wallpaper, although faded, and the four-poster bed had a grandmotherly charm. So did the walnut armoire and the wash-bowl chipped in the rim. Heavy green drapes kept out the sunlight. If cobwebs covered the ceiling, it was too dark or my sight was too blurry to see them.

I fumbled on the side table for my grandfather's pocket watch. My fingers grabbed at . . . nothing. I couldn't have lost it, could I? Of course I could have. Then I remembered I'd left it in my trousers, which I had dropped on the floor by the bed. I reached down and saved myself from tumbling out by grabbing at the prickly sheet. With an acrobat's balance—hah!—I fished out my watch.

It was eight forty-five. I had overslept. Not that I didn't need to, but Dr. Cameron might have come and gone. I scrambled into my clothes and didn't bother with a collar, in hopes that a country doctor would forgive me.

I recognized him by the black medical bag, the kind that my father has always carried. He was emerging from what must be the office, behind the reception desk.

I called his name, and his head snapped in my direction and bestowed a professional smile. He was handsome enough for the stage. His features were so nicely proportioned that his face was saved from blandness by the sloping pompadour and the tuft of black hair that looked glued onto his chin. He had a lean build. He was half a head taller than I was and a half dozen years older. His gaze was as patient and alert as a boxer's—or as a doctor's, accustomed to deference.

I introduced myself and explained that I was interested in President Johnson's last days, meant to excuse all manner of journalistic inquiry. "Do you have a moment or two?"

"You are asking me about a patient," he said.

"I guess I am. Could you tell me, sir, the cause of death?"

"There is no secret about that. Mr. Johnson met his end from apoplexy."

"You are certain of this?"

"If it's certainty you want, go study rocks. Medicine, Mr. . . . what is your name? . . . Mr. Hay, it struggles to be a science. Think of it as an art, and a rather primitive one at that."

"I understand." Actually, I did. "My father is a doctor. But could you tell me anything more about—?"

"I have nothing more to tell you, Mr. Hay."

"—about Eliza*beth*ton and East Tennessee?" An impish thought: "What does *Watauga* mean?"

Dr. Cameron pulled a watch out of his plaid waistcoat. "Beautiful waters," he said. "I have a few minutes before I need to get to my office. My first patient is usually late."

He led me into a back room that had been luxurious once, its dark paneling and ballroom chandelier far too fancy for the present furnishings. The leather upholstery in the high-backed chair behind the desk was slashed. He waved me into a chair with a broken slat.

I took out my notebook and started with a question he'd like. "How long has your family been here?"

"Back to pioneer days, on my mother's side. My great-granddaddy was a full-fledged citizen of the state of Franklin."

"The state of what?"

"Oh yes, the state of Franklin? For a few glorious years, East Tennessee declared itself a state, the fourteenth state of the Union. It's that sort of place."

"Really? When was this?"

"Back in 'eighty-four, that's seventeen eighty-four, after the Revolution. North Carolina didn't want to protect us, out here past the Alleghenies, and we hadn't a modicum of use for them. So, we seceded and declared statehood. Davy Crockett was born in the state of Franklin. Congress wouldn't recognize us, so we declared ourselves a republic."

"You are joking."

"I am not. This is just to say, we see things our way. Nobody is going to tell us what to do. Listen, in East Tennessee we've had our share of drunks and hornswogglers and fellows on the lam, probably more than our share. But we also have our good Christians, the law-abiding and right-thinking, square-jawed men and their womenfolk who trudged across the mountains to start a new life. Andy Johnson himself once called for statehood for East Tennessee, to keep the workingman from the slavocracy's grip. Is this what you want from me, a history lesson of East Tennessee? Because now I do have to—" He started to stand.

"How hard was it to be a Union man here? I gather you were one. I have to admire your bravery." I did—why not say so?

He sat back down. "It was hard. Half the town hated us. Still does, some of 'em."

"So why did you—?"

"Because it was the right thing to do." Dr. Cameron's voice rose. "Secession didn't solve a blasted thing. It would have brought anarchy. First the South secedes from the Union, then Tennessee secedes from the South, then East Tennessee secedes from Tennessee, then Carter county goes its own way. And, in fact, even for the secessionists, secession made everything worse—did it not? It ravaged our lands, our people, our way of life. It destroyed slavery, instead of saving it."

He was making a practical case, not a moral one.

"Did you . . . I mean, did your family own any, uh, slaves?" Was *this* question impolite?

Apparently so. "This is something I prefer not to discuss," he said. Which was an answer in itself.

"Andrew Johnson did, I understand."

He palmed his watch again. "Is there anything more I can—?"

"How long have you known the family?"

"I've known the Stovers all my life. Old Carter county folks, like we are. That was Miss Mary's husband, Daniel Stover, Colonel Stover. A great man, he was. Brave as can be. Ran a squad of mountain men who blew up bridges, to keep the Rebs from attacking."

"Commendable," I said. "Had you met the president before? Johnson, I mean."

"Hadn't had the pleasure."

"But you attended to him while he was . . . conscious, did you not? Did you get some sense of him as a . . . as a man?"

"Doctors often see people at their worst, Mr. Hay. To a journalist, this serves to reveal character. But to a doctor, it reveals only pain. For the doctor to speak of it is out of the question."

"I am told that his eyes looked odd—too wide."

"Dilated? Balderdash! Who told you this?"

"I shouldn't say."

"Whoever it was is a fool," Dr. Cameron sputtered. He rose from his seat. "I cannot possibly discuss the private concerns of a patient, Mr. Hay. You have taken quite enough of my time."

"My humblest apologies, Doctor. And I appre—"

"I mustn't keep my patient waiting." Dr. Cameron brushed past me. His medical bag created a breeze.

One last try, to his back: "Your desk clerk said I should ask you about a Confederate captain who checked in here last Wednesday. By the name of Mc . . ."

Dr. Cameron half turned and said, "McElwee."

"That's the one."

"Room two-twelve."

"The man who came on the train?" I said.

But Dr. Cameron was gone.

+══━══+

The wire composed itself. I left it at the hotel desk.

REID, ARRIVED ELIZABETHTON YESTERDAY.
FUNERAL TO-MORROW IN GREENEVILLE. ONTO
BIGGER STORY. PATIENCE. HAY

Patience? I never knew a newspaperman worth his inkwell who had any. Least of all Whitelaw Reid.

I procured the spelling—*McElwee, William E.*—from the desk clerk in exchange for a greenback. For free he told me McElwee had last been seen in the hotel bar. It was a little early, I thought, but you had to find people wherever they chose to be.

There was no mistaking Captain McElwee. For one thing, he was the barroom's only patron. He stood with his back to the bar, a squat glass in

his hand, watching every step I took; no one could sneak through his de-
fenses. The trim young man had the wholesome looks of an army chaplain
untried by combat. His hair, the color of buckwheat, was neatly parted and
combed, and his unlined face fairly sparkled with health, as if he and the
Almighty were pals. A lush mustache showed his jutting chin but masked
his mouth. His eyes had a wary calm.

"Captain McElwee?" I said.

"And who the hell are you?"

The color in his clean-shaven cheeks spoke well of whisky. I introduced
myself and explained that I was writing an article about Andrew Johnson's
last days. "May I join you?" I said.

"It's a free country, ain't it?"

I agreed that it was and invited him from the bar to a table. "My treat,"
I said.

That earned me a friend, even if I spoke with an accent. He spoke with
a twang—exaggerated, I suspected, for a Yankee's ears.

I ordered a lager for myself and a refill of my new drinking chum's rye.
The gnarled waiter might have served soldiers in the War of 1812.

"You came on the train, I understand," I said. "From Greeneville?"

"I had that pleasure," he replied, "and a pleasure it was, seeing the man
up close. Glad to give up my seat for him. Crowded car, Lord knows why
everyone was headin' this-a-way, but they was. Me and my buddy Jenkins
were comin' here to . . . We'd been doin' some—"

"Who is Jenkins?" I said, pulling out my notebook and pencil. "Do you
mind?"

The decisive moment. Captain McElwee eyed the notebook, considered
his options, and decided. "He and I, we work together, for the American
Steel Association, lookin' for farmers who's a-sittin' on iron ore. He was a
captain, too, for the bluecoats, so when we tell the farmers 'bout him and
me, they got no cause to shut the door in our faces. 'Cause you cain't never
tell in these parts who was a Reb and who was a Union man. So anyways,
I give 'im my seat and we all chewed the fat awhile."

"What did you all talk about?"

"President Johnson, he talk about iron ore as the backbone of the industrial age. He ask what was happenin' in Carter county and we talk about
how we need to finish the railroad line."

"And politics?"

"Sure as shootin'. We jes' let 'im talk, and that's what he does, talk politics. He's a politician, y'unnerstan'."

"So I gathered. I've met him myself."

"Have you? Where?"

Best not to risk a mention of President Lincoln. "In Washington," I said. "I was there for a while. Why was President Johnson passing through here, did he say?"

Captain McElwee gulped his whisky, and I signaled to the ancient barkeep for another. "He tell us he was stoppin' off at his daughter's house to see his wife. Then he was headin' up to Ohio to give couple of speeches, so's to correct some statements some Radical Republican made that he didn't cotton to. And when *he* give a speech, our Mistuh Johnson, he give a stemwinder. You must know that, if you seed him up in Washington City."

"Especially with a bit of drink in him," I said.

"Speaking of which, kin I have another?" He laughed. "We lubricated ourselves a mite on the train." The barkeep completed the transaction with ease.

"A mite?" I said to McElwee.

A nod and a smile but nothing more.

"What else did he say?" I tried, still hoping for a fact worth the ink. I had been taking notes, neglecting my beer.

"'Bout the night Lincoln was shot, he'd paced the floor, wonderin' what history was gonna say 'bout 'im a hunnerd years from now."

I stopped taking notes. I had spent all that night by Lincoln's deathbed, across Tenth street from Ford's Theatre. Johnson, the vice president, had stopped by at two o'clock in the morning and left at half past. By what right should history hear his plea?

"And what else?" I said.

A lot else. Johnson had relitigated his battles with Congress over Reconstruction—didn't the man ever let an argument go?—and claimed he had never seen an appeal to commute Mrs. Surratt from being hanged for Lincoln's death.

"You must have been exhausted, just listening," I said. I was, secondhand.

"I was ready for a nap."

"Is Captain Jenkins staying here, too?"

"Naw, he left the train early. But he's why *I'm* here, at this hotel. Captain Jenkins and Dr. Cameron, they was in the same outfit in the war. Thirteenth Tennessee Cavalry. Wrong side, y'unnerstand."

"My side," I said with a smile.

"We had a nip on the train and we had a drink here, at this very table, before he went on," Captain McElwee said.

"You and . . . President Johnson."

"Yes, suh. The privilege was mine."

"And how long did he stay here?"

"Not long. A whisky or two. Doc Cameron joined us. The nicest fella. Y'know, any friend of Cap'n Jenkins is a friend o' his—that sort. All on the house."

Bill hadn't mentioned the stop—ever the faithful servant. Nor had Dr. Cameron.

"Did he look all right when he left?" I said.

"To my eyes, he did." Captain McElwee guffawed.

"And that was the last you saw of him?"

"No. I saw him that night."

"Really? Here?"

"No, suh. I'd just retired for the night when I heard a horseman dashin' up to the hotel and callin' for Dr. Cameron. He's to go to Mrs. Brown's house, to see Mr. Johnson, who had a stroke of paralysis or the like. The doc sent somebody up to my room and invited me along."

"So you saw President Johnson that same night?"

"That's what I'm sayin'. It was late."

"How did he . . . the patient seem?"

"He was hurtin'. Couldn't move good. Kinda confused. Couldn't talk so you could understand. Ailin'."

"Did his eyes look odd?"

A shrug spilled his rye. "Couldn't hardly open 'em."

"Did you ever go back?"

A pause. "Naw, don't know if Doc Cameron did neither. Anyway, he didn't ask me ag'in. He was sharin' the job with some other doc."

"Who was that?"

"Can't remember his name. He was comin' in while we was comin' out."

"Another doctor was there?"

"Yes, suh, can't *quite* . . . Y'know, name like the fella in the Bible with all the bad stuff happenin'."

That didn't narrow it down much. "Jonah?" I said.

"Naw, naw, the one that was havin' one dang trouble after 'nother after . . ."

"Job!"

"That's the gent."

"You sick?" said the skeletal hotel clerk. "Doc Cameron no good fer ya?"

The other physician in a settlement of three or four hundred bodies (and nearly as many souls) was almost as easy to locate as a rooster at dawn. It cost me a greenback's donation to the clerk's snuff-and-whisky fund.

Dr. Abraham Jobe's office was in a brick building on Main street, two and a half blocks north of the Union Hotel. The waiting room had chintz curtains and velvet-upholstered armchairs. It was empty. I heard voices behind a door, a woman and a man murmuring too quietly for me to understand. (For a journalist, eavesdropping is a necessary skill.) The woman laughed heartily. I was anxious to be privy to the joke.

A woman, presumably the same woman, emerged into the waiting room, with a grin on her masculine face. She had a square jaw and gray bangs that framed her forehead. She wasn't unpleasant to look at, but once the smile ebbed (as smiles do) her face became a model of sobriety.

"Do you have an appointment, sir?" she said.

"No, ma'am." I told her I was with the *New-York Tribune* and that I was interested in Andrew Johnson's last days. I said I had spoken with the family, meant to imply but not quite prevaricate that they had mentioned Dr. Jobe's name.

"I'm sorry," she said, "but I don't think that Dr. . . . ."

The door swung open. "Sophronia!" a man cried out. He noticed me and said, "Oh, excuse me."

"Dr. Jobe?"

He nodded before he caught himself. "What can I do for you?" he said, from habit.

The doctor's crinkly gray beard probably hadn't been trimmed since I was a bachelor. He was tall and rangy, with a long, craggy face. His dark blue eyes—nearly purple—betrayed a luminosity I found unnerving. Yet he struck me as a man you would want at your bedside, his hand clutching your shoulder, if you were frightened of the Darkness to come.

I told him who I was and described the story I was supposedly planning to write and said, "Did you know President Johnson before?"

"Most of my life," he replied. "Our families go back. Everyone in East—"

"Tennessee knows everyone else," I finished.

This drew a smile. "You have been here awhile, I gather."

"Not too long."

"And he did me a particular honor while he was the president. Twice. He appointed me a special agent for the post office, for the Carolinas, and then a special agent for Indian affairs. He was a great and good man, in my estimation."

"Then why didn't they call you first?"

"The family called their own doctor—understandably," Dr. Jobe said. "Come with me, please." He ushered me into a spacious office that smelled of stale tobacco. Behind the desk, in a heavy silver frame, hung a lithograph of Andrew Johnson.

"May I?" I said, stepping forward to examine it.

The likeness showed the late president at his most truculent—his wide face, his clenched jowls, his furrowed brow, his lips curved into a scowl, his hooded and impenetrable eyes. He reminded me of a pugilist who wanted not only to knock you down but also to stomp on you while you lay bloodied on the canvas.

"Was his end . . . peaceful?" I said.

"By all means. After his initial attack, we succeeded in reviving him. And his second attack was . . . He slipped away quietly."

"*We* being you and Dr. Cameron?"

"Yes, he was involved, a fine doctor. The Stover family—excuse me, the Brown family—physician. And I believe that we prevented a second attack—right away, I mean."

"By doing what, may I ask?"

"I can't discuss the details of the case, Mr. Hay. I'm sure you understand."

"Of course," I said. I described my father's small-town practice, in hopes of sidling into a brotherhood.

"But we did revive him, and he was lucid and his color was good and he was receiving visitors until that Friday afternoon. I was with him much of the time, and he seemed to be improving. And then suddenly he took a turn for the worse. These things happen, for reasons that medical science is unable to explain. I asked the family to telegraph his physician in Greeneville, Dr. Broyles, but he arrived too late."

"Why did you wait?"

"I saw no reason to trouble him before that. The patient seemed out of danger."

"Until he wasn't," I said.

"Until he wasn't. By then there was nothing anyone could have done."

I shouldn't be hard on a medical man for making a mistake. I have made a slew of them, although I haven't buried any victims (yet).

"When did you . . . give up hope?"

"I never give up hope, Mr. Hay. Never."

"I understand that. But at a certain point, you realized he had no chance to recover, isn't that right?"

"At a certain point," Dr. Jobe said, "one must accept the limits of what medicine has the capacity to do and put one's trust in God's will."

I tried a bank shot. "Did you notice anything odd about his eyes?"

"I cannot imagine what you mean, Mr. Hay." His back was as stiff as his diction. He knew precisely what I meant.

"Did you happen to notice if they were dilated, perhaps?"

"I . . . I really could not say."

Meaning, he could if he wished. My friend Nicolay always counseled to never assume, but sometimes you had to. "What would cause something like that?" I said.

No response.

"Have you seen it before?" I tried.

"Recently," Dr. Jobe said. I waited for him to go on and, to my surprise, he did. "In my daughter. Sally's five. She contracted scarlet fever, and I gave her belladonna."

"She's recovered, I trust."

"Oh yes, yes. She's fine now. The treatment worked. But, in the meantime, her eyes got so big—the pupils, I mean. Belladonna—that's what it does."

"Belladonna—I've heard of it. It grew wild in the woods near my hometown. My daddy warned us to keep away from it."

"And for good reason. Look, as a medicine it's a godsend, not only for scarlet fever but also for neuralgia and whooping cough. The ladies in Italy used it to look beautiful. That's what belladonna means—'beautiful lady,' in Italian. It makes the pupils big—and, well, beautiful. But like any medicine, too much is a danger. You may know belladonna by its other name—deadly nightshade."

"Yes, that's what my daddy called it. And it worked—we stayed away."

"Wisely so. Since ancient times, witches, sorcerers, evildoers of all sorts have used it for nefarious ends."

"Only in ancient times?"

"Who can say?"

"You seem to know quite a lot about this."

"As I say, it was for my daughter. I am a careful father, Mr. Hay, and a careful physician."

And a careful murderer? If he were, he wouldn't be telling me this.

"What happens if a patient takes too much of it? What are the symptoms?"

"Other than the eyes? A certain sluggishness, perhaps, some confusion. Delirium, could be."

"A loss of speech?"

"I have heard of cases. Incoherence, at least temporarily."

"How about the physical symptoms? Could a patient collapse?"

"He could. There can be a loss of balance. Even a paralysis, as I understand it. I am no expert, I assure you, Mr. Hay."

If he declared himself an expert, I would be warier.

"I would say that the symptoms sound similar to, uh, apoplexy—do they not? But I am merely the son of a medical man."

I waited for Dr. Jobe to contradict me, to tell me I was stupid or impulsive or wrong to think that his patient had been poisoned. But he didn't, quite possibly because he was wondering, too.

Did I want it as a pill or a powder or a plaster or, perchance, a suppository? The man behind the counter at the apothecary on Main street had bushy gray side-whiskers and wore a white coat that implied he knew more than I did, which I had no reason to doubt. The drawers on the wall behind him reached to the ceiling. When I couldn't answer his query, he shuffled to the rear and reached high onto a shelf, lowered three small jars, and juggled them to the counter without mishap.

I said, "Which one is easiest to . . . administer, would you say?"

"For an adult, a pill is easiest. Just swallow it down."

"For a child?"

"How old?"

I had to make something up. How old was Dr. Jobe's daughter? "Five," I said.

"And what is his . . . her . . . ?"

"Her."

"—condition?"

"Scarlet fever," I said hurriedly.

"A physician has seen her?"

"Oh yes."

The pharmacist waited for a name. "And which form did he suggest?"

"He didn't. But it sounds like I should try the powder. Just a little bit to start."

He was looking at me oddly. "How much is a little?" he said.

"How do you sell it?"

"By the gram."

"All right, I'll take . . . four grams."

I got another sidelong look—had I ordered too much or too little?—before he tore half of a newspaper page from under the counter and fashioned it into a cone. He opened the jar that contained a powder that looked like sand on a dirty beach and poured a stingy amount into the cone.

"Here, sir, is a little extra," he said. "I make this by crushing the leaves and the roots. The berries I leave alone. They're poisonous. Eight cents, please."

I handed him a silver half dime and a three-cent piece.

"Be careful how you administer it," he said.

"What do you mean?"

"It has a bitter taste. You'll have to mix it with something that tastes stronger."

"Like whisky?" I said immediately.

Another odd look. "That would work admirably," he said, "for an adult."

"Juice of a grapefruit, then," I said. "How long does it take to . . . work?"

"An hour or two, more or less."

I doubted the pharmacist was sorry to see me leave. Here I was in pursuit of a poisoning, committed by a party unknown, and I had managed to turn myself into a suspect.

An hour or two. I kept thinking: *an hour or two.* If that's what it took for deadly nightshade to work its will, then . . .

I ambled along Main street's raised sidewalk, trying to piece together a chronology. I almost collided with a lady twirling a parasol long past dark. What had Andy Johnson been up to an hour or two before . . . before what, exactly? Before he collapsed upstairs at his daughter's house, in his granddaughter's presence. That was the first time. Lillie had noticed his dilated pupils, on Wednesday afternoon. Then he had bounced back, regaling well-wishers until . . . Friday afternoon or evening. I would need to learn the exact time he fell ill once again. Who had visited him on Friday, an hour or two before that? His daughter Mary would know, or Bill. Yes, Bill. He was the better source. He was always at ol' Andy's right hand.

Always at hand. That gave me pause. A devoted servant might not be so devoted. He might have every good reason to abhor his master. Their relationship was probably like a marriage, opaque to anyone outside of it. But why, then, would he have told me that his master had been killed? In order to put me off the track?

I reached the Union Hotel without wreaking further damage to citizenry or property and lumbered upstairs to my room. I was clearly in a bit
of a trance—I had forgotten to pick up the iron key—and returned to the
lobby. I was grateful not to see Captain McElwee.

Captain McElwee—he was another . . . possibility. I suppose the correct
word was *suspect*. The former Confederate officer had traveled with Johnson
from Greeneville to Carter's Depot and then into Elizabethton. In other
words, he had been at Andy Johnson's side an hour or two—an hour *and*
two—before the former president took ill. They had shared a drink on the
train. Maybe a drink that contained belladonna. And hadn't they downed a
whisky or two at the Union Hotel? With Dr. Cameron, as a matter of fact.
Dr. Cameron, the family's physician.

First, do no harm—isn't that every physician's sacred vow? But it is silent
on what to do second.

I went back upstairs and poured myself a rye.

Why on earth would Captain McElwee or Dr. Cameron want to harm
ol' Andy? Why would anyone?

The most hated man in America? Let me count the ways.

CHAPTER FIVE

The big man wants to see you." The pale desk clerk enjoyed delivering the bad news.

"Which big man is that?" I said.

"The Carter county sheriff." He spoke with as much of a flourish as I'd seen from him. "He sent a messenger. I said I would tell you. So, I'm telling you."

"Did he say why?"

"I figger it can't be good."

I decided his service didn't merit a tip.

The sheriff's office was on Third street, by the Doe river, in a brick bunker that looked like a jail. The reception area was painted lime green (that must be cheaper than red) and smelled of old perspiration. The uniform at the desk eyed me from head to toe and told me to go right in.

Sheriff J. Dugger Pearce was a mountain of a man, and nothing so puny as Holston Mountain. By all rights, he should have upset the swivel chair in which he was sprawled, his feet propped on the desk, but somehow he stayed upright. Practice, probably. His plump, clean-shaven face managed to look both placid and mildly curious, even as his meaty hands opened and closed, opened and closed, aching for use. He showed me a toothy smile, which chilled me.

"It was mighty fine of you to stop by," he drawled, "Mistuh . . . what's the name here?" He made a show of glancing down at his desk. "Mistuh Hay."

"You sent for me, did you not," I said, "by name."

"And it was so good of you to"—his dark eyes squinted—"obey."

I smiled back, showing as many teeth as I could summon to duty. "And what can I do for you?" I said.

"Nothin', nothin' at all. Jes' wanted to make your acquaintance. I like to meet the new people in town."

"That's quite neighborly."

"We are neighborly folks heah. Known for it, I'd say. Though I cain't quite say the same for you, suh. You seem to be askin' a lot of questions here'bouts."

"That's my job. I am here as a correspondent for the *New-York Tribune*. I have made no secret of that."

More slowly this time: "You seem to be askin' a lot of *fool* questions, so I hear."

"Not all of my questions are brilliant, but they're not foolish. Who thinks they are?"

"Do you go around blabbing about who tells you what?"

"No. That's a rule of the trade."

"Of mine, too."

I had to respect that. "May I ask you a question?" I said.

"Shoot."

"Can you tell me anything about Dr. Cameron or a Captain McElwee?" I spelled it out. "Former captain, to be precise, for the army that wore gray. He's now with the American Steel Association."

"He's passed through a couple of times. Good ol' fella, best I could see. And Dr. Cameron, he's sumpin' of a hero 'round here. What do you want to know?"

A good question, that. "Are they good men?"

"Cain't speak fer yer captain. But the doc, he's the best. Ministerin' to whoever needs it. Takes barley or chickens as pay."

"All right, thank you. Anything else, then?"

"You in such a hurry?"

"I need to leave for Greeneville for the funeral. That's why I came here first thing."

Sheriff Pearce tilted his head and peered at me with a hostility that felt matter-of-fact rather than personal, which made it all the scarier. "Just one more thing. For the sake of your health, Mistuh Hay, I would suggest that you stop askin' so many questions. It's liable to land you in hot watuh."

"Of what sort?" I said.

Another ghastly smile. "I wouldn't want to imagine. You ever hear of the Ku Klux Klan?"

Indeed, I had. "They started in Tennessee, did they not?"

"Halfway 'cross the state, and it's a wide state, Tennessee."

"I thought they were gone—defeated."

A smile. "I tell ya, friendly like, they been spotted here and there. A social club, they call themselves, but they don't ne'ssarily take kindly to white boys from the North who stick their prick where it don't belong." His jaw kept moving like he was chewing, and his hands opened and closed, but his eyes were fixed on mine. "They don't hardly need no excuse to have theirselves a li'l fun." He let that sink in.

So did I. "Anything else?" I said, hoping he would interpret my croak as understated resolve rather than fear, which it was.

"No, suh." That smile again. The sheriff's office must be elective. "Jes' a friendly warning, is all. Now you kin kindly git on your way."

One such invitation was enough.

The eight-twenty train to Greeneville was mobbed with mourners. I minced along the aisle in the farthest of the rickety passenger cars, in search of a seat. Cigar smoke suffused the air. The nets above passengers' heads sagged dangerously with luggage. I was staying only for the day.

I recognized a face along the left side of the aisle and half hoped its owner wouldn't see me. My odds weren't bad, given that David Patterson's eyes were shut. The seat across the aisle was empty, and I saw no choice but to take it, rather than stand. I found myself next to an oversized lady cloaked in black. At first, I thought she was a nun—traveling on a public conveyance!—but I realized by the set of her jaw that she was in mourning.

The train started rumbling forward—backward, from where I sat. David Patterson's eyes popped open and I sensed he was staring at me. He was, and not in a friendly way. His cheeks were puffy and his eyes were ringed in charcoal. The man hadn't slept.

"Good morning, Mr. Senator," I said.

A curt nod.

"Is Mrs. Patterson with you?"

He shook his head.

"Oh," I said.

His silence must have struck even him as silly because he said, "She went last night. I had some business to finish up."

"How is she doing, if I may ask?"

"She is a strong person."

"Like her father, yes?"

"Very much."

A tinge of bitterness? "Oh—how so?" I said.

"In every way but the obvious. She is strong like him. She thinks like him. She even looks like him, a softer version. She was his favorite, you know."

"I didn't know."

"Oh yes, he told her so, in a letter he wrote before we went to the altar."

This wasn't the time to take out my notebook. It would only remind him of who I was.

"How many children are there?"

"There *were* five. Two of her brothers are gone now, one of them in the war. Only the youngest one is left. Andrew Jr.—they call him Frank."

"Where is he?"

"In Greeneville, living in his daddy's house, pretending to run a newspaper."

A loving family, I could see.

"What is he like, this Frank?"

"He's a boy, and it's time he was a man."

This was a more voluble and candid David Patterson than I had any reason to expect. Apparently, he realized it, too. I waited for him to go on, but that was all I was going to get.

My question about the two other sons' deaths brought silence and a shrug. I tried another tack, on a subject that ladies would plunk down four pennies in a newsboy's palm to learn. "How did you and Mrs. Patterson meet?" I said.

"I can hardly remember a time I didn't know her. For years—decades— I've been a friend of . . . her father's, and one of his strongest supporters. I was a circuit court judge, as you may know."

I didn't. Not the juiciest of anecdotes. Juicier would be to ask him what he thought of his late father-in-law, although an honest answer was a dream. Or I could ask about ol' Andy's enemies or the circumstances of his death—assuring the conversation would end.

Out my window, hayfields whooshed past, separated by houses and barns. It was nothing I hadn't seen countless times before. The primeval forests were gone. Humans had taken charge. Beside me, the woman in black was whimpering, or maybe she was breathing through her nose.

I turned back to David Patterson and said, "Do you live in Greeneville?"

"Ten miles up the road. A farm near Rheatown. You heard of it?"

"Can't say I have."

"We'll be passing it soon enough, the third stop before Greeneville."

"You getting off there?"

"No, not to-day."

"Oh, of course. To-night, then?"

"I can hope." An audible sigh.

"Is it a working farm?"

"By all means. Five hundred acres, a little more. We grow corn, wheat, hay, keep a few dairy cows."

"Cotton?"

"No, sir. Cotton isn't king in these parts. Nothing is. Nobody is."

"Except your father-in-law?"

That brought a small smile I couldn't decipher.

The conversation lapsed, and as I listened to my seatmate stammer to herself, I unfolded the newspaper I had bought at the depot. I read about how a Pennsylvania girl had shot a tramp, how millworkers in Fall River were still on strike, how flags in Washington City were at half-mast and the executive departments were shuttered because . . . of what I was on my way to see.

I pulled out my notebook and reprised the conversation, best I could, taking care not to look at Patterson. Then I returned to watching the landscape of low hills and heat-stunted fields.

As the train reached Greeneville, and the aisle grew crowded with mourners, another question crossed my mind. It was impolite, perhaps, but one that a working journalist had every right to ask. I left room for Patterson to step in front of me and leaned into his ear.

I thought I understood his answer but couldn't be sure.

"Really?" I said.

"Never," he repeated tonelessly. "He died without one."

Andrew Johnson's last will and testament would not be read, because there wasn't one. In my experience, the only people who died without a will were too young to believe in death (such as myself) or assumed they were indispensable or had nothing to bequeath. And Lincoln, for reasons I had never understood. Why would ol' Andy leave this earthly realm without a plan for his earthly possessions? Whatever his reason, it foretold no end of wrangling among his kinfolk—four cents' worth, I could hope, to ladies in New York.

⊹━⊹━⊹

Greeneville's railroad depot convulsed with activity. A band of brass horns and snare drums marched through. "The Dickinson Light Guard, from

Knoxville," someone whispered from behind me, "just got in on a special seven-car train." All around me, ladies in mourning gowns and gentlemen in swallowtail coats jabbered and gesticulated as if it were the Fourth of July. Which in a way it was. The death of a president was a national event. A celebration in crêpe—I made a mental note of that turn of phrase. At the depot's exit, a scrum of young men hoisted a banner: *Andrew Johnson Guards.* "The finest gents in Greeneville," my whisperer explained. The corn-fed fellows jostled one another with playful jabs to the ribs. They looked like thugs to me.

My pocket watch showed half past ten. The funeral procession was set for eleven. I followed the hoopla outside.

In the distance, church bells tolled. The morning was already clammy, a mist giving way to unfiltered sunshine. Crowds filled the roadway, growing in density and spirit the closer I got to Main street. I snaked my way through, keeping a protective hand on my tall silk hat, which was lonely among the derbies and slouch caps. Outside a saloon, men milled in the muddy roadway, and a hotel entrance bustled with comings and (mostly) goings. East of Irish street, a livery stable's entrance was clogged with rigs.

High across Main street, a gigantic American flag, with its thirteen stripes and thirty-seven stars, shined in the sunlight. I squeezed through the crowd, muttering, "The press, please let me pass. The press, let me by, please," astonished as usual that, more often than not, strangers complied.

My destination was at the corner of Depot and Main streets. The Greene county courthouse was a brick Greek-style edifice featuring a triangular pediment and a roof with a turret and dome. Crêpe streamers, black and white, encircled the turret and hung down the walls. I wormed my way up the steps, my hat still intact, and pushed my way inside.

The courthouse interior was gloomy and hushed, like a cathedral at candle-lighting. The lower assembly room, darkened with drapes, was plastered with evergreens and flowers. Portraits of Andrew Johnson hung on every wall. At the center, on a catafalque, lay a silver coffin, ornamented with silver fittings and the sinuous shapes and crossed Vs that I recognized as Masonic hieroglyphics. I was relieved to see that the lid was closed. Underneath it, I would learn, the decedent's shroud was an American flag, and his pillow was his copy of the Constitution. Sounded uncomfortable to me.

"They had to re-ice him on the way here," a slender young fellow muttered into my ear. He had been my whisperer at the depot. "In Jonesborough, halfway from Eliza*beth*ton. Was getting a little puffy, I hear."

I tried not to giggle. "Who are you?" I inquired.

He introduced himself as Adolph Ochs—"O-C-H-S"—a printer at the *Knoxville Daily Chronicle*. "Though I'm covering this for *The Courier-Journal*—that's in Louisville," he burbled. (As if I didn't know.) He couldn't have been older than seventeen or eighteen, not much taller than I was, with dark, curly hair and cherubic blue eyes that reminded me of a puppy eager for a romp. "My first news story," he said with pride.

"Mine, too," I replied, more or less truthfully. At the *Tribune*, I mainly sat back and cogitated and told the world what I thought it should think. Occasionally, it listened; sometimes, it squawked back; most often, it paid me no mind.

When I mentioned the *Tribune*, the lad's eyes grew wide. "Did you know Horace Greeley?" he said.

"All too well."

I might as well have divulged an intimate evening with Jenny Lind. "Such a hero of mine, growing up," Ochs gushed. "Was he wonderful?"

"He could be," I replied. Why puncture the illusions of youth?

When he asked what it was like to be a newspaperman in New York, I put him off for the moment. "First let's gather the news," I said, waxing wise about the practicalities in my almost-former profession. "Then we can talk."

My informant slipped back into the crowd.

On top of the coffin, a silver engraving depicted the deceased in a gilded frame. A plaque had a simple inscription:

ANDREW JOHNSON
AGED 67 YEARS

That couldn't be right. I did some arithmetic. He had been born in December 'oh-eight, and this was August of 'seventy-five. Subtracting eight from seventy-five is sixty-seven—the age he would have become in December, had he lived. Until then, he was sixty-six. I hoped his tombstone would show more affection for facts.

At each corner of the coffin, a Mason guard stood garbed in regalia that any Ottoman sultan would envy, rich with sashes, embroidered aprons, and long collars in satin and gold. Their sheathed swords stood ready for demons invisible to me. I must admit I've never understood the Masons. It's daunting, I know, to name a rich Founding Father who wasn't one. Hadn't George Washington worn a Masonic apron when he laid the Capitol's cornerstone? With their secret handshakes and self-regard, the Masons had pretty much run the nation when it was young. Ol' Andy, the striver, had been eager to join and (so Ochs had whispered) had risen in the ranks to become a Knight Templar. That sounded highfalutin to me. Now that he had passed into the temple eternal, the Masons had taken charge.

The funeral procession started around noon, once the family showed up at the courthouse. This did not include the widow, who had remained bedridden in Elizabethton, her daughter Mary by her side. The Pattersons led the way in, staring into the middle distance, Martha small but erect, beside her slumping husband. Frank, the surviving son, followed, looking callow and confused, glancing side to side, as if taking in the sights. Then came the grandchildren, the five of them, each more adorable than the last, bearing purposefully solemn expressions. They looked uncomfortable in their clothes, other than Lillie, the eldest, in a stunning black gown, gliding down the aisle the Masons made.

Eighteen pallbearers elbowed one another in toting the coffin outside to the hearse. As I stepped back onto Main street, the procession was taking shape. First marched the marshals and the Andrew Johnson Guards, followed by the Patrons of Husbandry, the Odd Fellows, and a battalion of Masons. Then came the man of the hour, in a hearse pulled by four dark horses in velvet capes laced in silver. Behind him, in a trail of carriages and wagons, rode the pallbearers and the Knights Templar, then the decedent's family, followed by Tennessee's governor and a smattering of legislators and judges and other honorables and ex-honorables. And then came the people on foot. The people. Hundreds and even thousands of them, by my unmathematical eye. Men in overalls and women in frocks. Parasols and bonnets. Blacksmiths' aprons or Sunday best. Plain folks, from the soil or the shop. Folks like ol' Andy used to be.

"We are a plain people from the mountains of East Tennessee," Martha Patterson had announced when her father inherited the presidency, "but we know our position and shall maintain it."

Maybe that was why, beyond the rumor of his atheism, Andy Johnson's mortal remains had lain in a courthouse, not in a church. The people were his principles. They were his god.

Lovely. I had something to write.

The funeral procession stretched a half mile south, from the courthouse all the way to the grave site. Every narrow, shingled storefront along the route was draped in crêpe and mourning cloth. The procession was still unwinding at the courthouse when the deceased reached his place of rest.

The grave site was on a cone-shaped hilltop that Johnson had purchased years before. I wheedled my way through the gathering crowd with journalistic entitlement. At the hilltop, I gasped at the view. In every direction you could see for twenty miles. To the east, the low mountains of the Appalachians stood higher than the clouds, stretching into North Carolina.

The funeral itself felt medieval, like nothing I'd ever witnessed. The Masons formed a circle two hundred feet across, and the Knights Templar filed in, to conduct the rites. And rites they were, full of song and prayer and—well, mumbo-jumbo isn't quite fair. The words were prayerful enough.

> *Lord of all below—above—*
> *Fill our hearts with truth and love;*
> *When dissolves our earthly tie,*
> *Take us to thy Lodge on high.*

Lodge? I couldn't tell you if there is a heaven or not—I'm unreliable on a quibble like that—but if there is, and if I succeed in wangling my way in, I don't expect to take a room in a Lodge.

The Masons re-formed into a triangle around the grave. Three times they crossed their arms upon their breasts and raised them to the sky and clapped their palms, before letting their hands fall onto their thighs. The third time they chanted:

> *We cherish his memory here . . .*
> *We commend his spirit to God who gave it . . .*
> *And consign his body to the earth.*

It felt so . . . heathen.
The Knights Templar sang their hymns:

> *Precious in the sight of heaven*
> *Is the scene where Christians die;*
> *Souls, with all their sins forgiven . . .*

Sins forgiven—all sins forgiven. Surely this counted as Andy Johnson's most desperate desire. (Mine, too.)
The Masonic choir chanted a requiem. A bugler played taps.

━━━◆━━━

I accosted a few of the plain people as they rushed past me down the hill and asked them what they loved about the deceased. They mentioned nothing about what he had said or accomplished, only about who he was. "Came from nothin'!" "Fights for the li'l feller!" "Cuz he says 'fuck ya' to the fellas runnin' ever'thin'"—that last, with a grizzled old man's uppercut and a euphoric smile.

I was putting away my notebook and turning downhill when I heard a voice at my ear. "About New York . . ." Adolph Ochs was becoming a pest, although his taut cheeks and the honesty of his ambition had a certain charm. "I work hard, you know," he said.

"I'm sure you do," I said. "But let me ask you something first, if you don't mind. You're an East Tennessean, are you not?"

"Cincinnati by birth, but Knoxville for most of my life."

"Johnson's two older sons, the ones who died—do you know what happened to them?"

"In a word, drink."

Why was I not surprised? "Is that everything I need to know?"

"No," Ochs replied. "Laudanum."

I hoped none of the mourners (or the Almighty) heard me laugh.

"For Robert, it was both," Ochs went on. He described the president's middle son as a notorious drunkard who was found dead at thirty-five with an empty bottle of laudanum by his bedside. "That happened here, in his daddy's house—you passed it on the way out of town—a year after they all came home."

"Was it . . . on purpose?"

"An accident, is what the family says. But a *bottle* of laudanum? I wouldn't inquire if I were you."

"It sounds like you did."

"In fact, I did. And I got no printable response, other than an inkwell hurled past my head."

"Full of ink?" I said.

"Not full."

This young fellow would go far.

"And the other deceased son?"

"Charles. Thrown from a horse during the war. Or maybe he fell. Presumed to be drunk."

"I begin to sense a pattern," I said.

"And the youngest son, Frank. Drink and laudanum?"

"By all accounts, none of them publishable."

"It's a whale of a story," I said. "The best ones never get published."

"But this story"—Ochs gestured up to the graveyard—"the publishable one, I'd better get started."

"*Moi aussi*," I said.

I started to construct a first sentence: *In a cathedral of the people, the Great Commoner was buried yesterday with Masonic rituals that would terrify widows and children.*

That wouldn't do.

I hurried downhill, brushing past a gentleman in a morning coat and a silk hat. I was a step ahead when he called, "Mr. Hay."

I glanced back. He was a stout man with heavy jowls and manicured gray whiskers. He looked familiar.

"You have the better of me, sir," I said.

"Forgive me." He had the affected drawl of a Southern aristocrat. His cravat was gray with blue polka dots that matched his eyes. His shirtfront had ruffles. "Edmund Cooper, sir," he said, "at your service."

"A pleasure." We shook hands warmly. I had heard of him before, but where? "How did you recognize me?"

"I have seen your tintype, Mr. Hay. And I once occupied your office."

"Of course," I said. "In service to . . ." I couldn't get the words out. I gestured with my elbow toward the hilltop. I was suddenly made aware of the heat by a line of perspiration down my spine. "And how did you like my office? I must say I still feel a sense of possession."

"It was cramped. But the location was nonpareil." I had never heard anyone utter that word before, not even in France. "Your spirit still resided there."

"Like the Ghost of Christmas Past," I said.

"Nothing so frightening. Even inspiring."

I bowed in gratitude at his white lie.

He said, "And what, may I inquire, brings you here?"

I explained my not-quite-former position with the *New-York Tribune* and asked if he had a few moments to spare. I gestured back toward the grave site, as we walked side by side. "Besides being his private secretary," I said, "were you also his friend?"

That produced a knowing laugh. "Is it your hypothesis that he had friends?"

"I am open-minded on the great issues of the day," I replied.

"Then let us sit."

He led me to a wrought iron bench, several feet off the path. Nicer to look at than to sit on, the seat dug into my . . . least vulnerable part. He sat downhill from me. As the mourners streamed by, just out of our hearing, he balanced his top hat on his knee, showing a shock of silver hair brushed back off his brow. His eyes darted about and came to rest on mine. They seemed willing to stay awhile.

"Our late Mr. Johnson had two friends, by my count," Cooper said. "Gentlemen—and I use the word loosely—from here in Greene county."

"Do you think I could see them?"

"I believe they have passed into a better world than this one." His hand swept from Tennessee toward North Carolina. Later I learned that Edmund Cooper was a rich boy who had studied law at Harvard. (I was a poorer boy who had read for the law at my uncle's firm in Springfield, which shared a floor with a lawyer named Lincoln.) "Tell me, Mr. Hay, did President Lincoln have friends?"

I laughed. As a journalist, I admired apt questions. "Seward. That's one. Let me think. Joshua Speed, I would say. That's two. Maybe Lamon, the volunteer bodyguard. It's a definitional question. I would like to think that I was one, and Nicolay, but we were more like additional sons. The question is, did Lincoln lay his soul bare to anyone? If that's what you're asking, I would have my doubts."

"Did he have enemies?"

"Millions. I would posit that Mr. Booth counted among them."

"Let me reword that," Cooper said. "Did he enjoy his enemies? Did he love having them?"

"Never," I replied. Who was asking the questions here? "It was a necessary burden of doing what he thought was right."

"Andy Johnson did. He loved his enemies, but not like Jesus did. He loved having them. He gloried in them. In his way of thinking, his enemies were a measure of his worth."

"I gather that you became one of them."

"You gather correctly. But I earned my exalted status. I daresay I deserved it." He told me the tale of the epic contest of 'sixty-nine for the U.S. Senate seat from Tennessee, soon after ol' Andy had returned from his failed presidency. Johnson's enemies in the legislature from his pro-Union past stranded his candidacy a single vote short of a majority. Cooper, by then a state lawmaker, spearheaded the campaign, which gave Johnson's opponents an inspiration. They put Cooper's younger brother, a state senator, forward for the post. Edmund jumped sides, and Henry Cooper went to Washington, while ol' Andy slinked home in defeat.

"He hasn't talked to either of us since," Cooper muttered. His blue eyes had grown moist. "And now he never will."

"But you came," I said, "to pay your respects."

"Or my disrespects." A grim smile. "Once President Johnson made an enemy, you became his enemy for life. He collected enemies. It was a point of honor with him to never make up. A matter of his manhood, I suspect. He was a prickly sort. Saw insults where none was intended. Personal loyalty meant everything, and I betrayed him. Which I did. So, my brother and I were traitors—simple as that. That was his word—*traitors*! Ghouls, hyenas, *traitors*—that's what he called people who opposed him. Like Benedict Arnold, like Judas. And people like that must be punished."

"If he had so many enemies, how did he keep rising—all the way to the Executive Mansion, for God's sake? What was his political secret?"

"I've puzzled over that for years, and I think the answer is this: It was because people—*the* people—loved him for the enemies he made. His enemies became their enemies. He was smarter than they were, and shrewder, and unrelenting, truly unrelenting, which counts for a lot in politics. But above all, he was one of *them*, and that never changed, and his supporters knew it. They would follow him into the depths of hell, even after he started to do the slavocracy's bidding, having attacked them all his life."

"With all his pardons of Confederates, you mean."

"And restoring them to positions of power."

"Why on earth did he do that?"

"Who can say? *He* never said. Probably because he hated the black man even more than he hated the planters. He thought this should be a country for white men. *That* he did say."

"So, this was his political secret—corralling the white man's rage?"

"That, certainly, and his courage—raw courage, political and physical. Don't underestimate that. He was the only Southern senator who supported the Union. You may not understand, Mr. Hay, how brave that was. Not to mention shrewd, for it brought him into President Lincoln's good graces, first as military governor here and then as . . . well, you know the rest." He looked at me with kindly eyes, aware of my continuing grief.

"Was he a bad person, would you say?" Naive questions often proved the most productive.

Cooper shook his head slowly—more in wonderment, I gathered, than in negation. "He was complicated," he said. He thought for another moment. "Actually, he was *un*complicated, profoundly so. He truly was what he was, a man of low birth. Every second of his life, he felt like a man of low birth, and he resented it, and wielded it as a cudgel, to the delight of everyone else of low birth. He was a man of the people, bearing the people's grievances and faults. Did you know he was actually born in a log cabin, to parents who couldn't read or write? They say that his first foreman taught him to read when he was sixteen—that was back in Carolina—and that the missus taught him to write. He was constantly quoting Cato and Shakespeare and Lord knows who else, always needing to be right. He couldn't stand to be wrong, to be *seen* as wrong. He always seemed so sure of himself that I came to believe that, inside, he was anything but. Can you understand that, Mr. Hay?"

"Of course." I had fled the frontier to be schooled in the East and understood the need to look better than I was, even if the attempt itself undermined the façade.

"He had no time for what he considered frivolities. I don't think he ever went to the theater or bet on a horse."

"A sense of humor?"

"None. Rarely even a smile. I must say, he wasn't a man I ever had a desire to *be.* Rarely restful inside, always in turmoil. A sturdy man, a massive head, brawny shoulders—you know all this, Mr. Hay. Yet he was dainty in his way, with curiously small hands and small feet."

Which could, by common suspicion, make a man feel . . . small. That could explain quite a lot.

"You didn't answer my question," I said. "Let me turn it around. Was he a *good* person?"

A grin. "He thought he was," Cooper said. "How good are any of us? I am a traitor. And you, Mr. Hay?" Happily, he didn't wait for an answer. "He believed in the people, and he spoke for the people, the ones that had no voice. Andrew Johnson was the spirit of democracy, in the flesh. Not a pretty sight, is it?"

"You know, Lincoln was a man of the people," I pointed out. "A log cabin, self-taught."

"And isn't it astonishing how differently they turned out? Andy Johnson resented anyone of higher birth. His life was a constant struggle against his betters, and he brooded over the evils he supposed they had done to him. He hated men who were rich, and he hated anyone who stood in his way. Tell me, Mr. Hay, who did Lincoln hate?"

"Hmm, let me think. Only one person, I'd say—his brother-in-law. The man married his sister, Sarah, and, when she was in childbirth, failed to call a doctor soon enough to save her life. Lincoln hated the man. No one else I know of."

THE MURDER OF ANDREW JOHNSON

"Please tell me this, then—why wasn't he bitter?"

What a wonderful question, and as with most wonderful questions, I had no answer. "He simply wasn't," I replied. "That's who *he* was. By nature, he tried to understand what the other fellow was thinking, so he could see things their way. It's how he was made." I decided to take a chance with Edmund Cooper. "Do you suppose that any of Johnson's enemies might want to . . . do him harm?"

"Any or all of them, I should think. Most of them, certainly, and from every stage of his life. Whether any of them *would* do him harm is something else. Need I answer for myself?" Cooper looked appraisingly at me.

I smiled—disarmingly, I hoped. "I wouldn't think that's necessary."

"If I may be permitted a question, Mr. Hay, why do you ask? Idle curiosity?"

Perceptive man. How much should I tell him? It was a journalist's strategy to press others for tantalizing details while offering the fewest possible in return.

"It is not entirely clear to me," I said, looking him in the eye, "that his death was . . . natural."

Cooper took this in without blinking. "Do you have particular reasons"—he stressed the plural—"to think so?"

He waited.

"Let us posit, for argument's sake, that he was poisoned," I began, "and died with his loving family around him."

"I was told it was apoplexy."

"So the doctors said. But suppose, for sake of argument, there is a substance that could mimic the symptoms of apoplexy and also show a symptom unique to itself—one that, in fact, was witnessed."

"Are you supposing that?"

"For the sake of argument, let's say that I am. My question is, who might hate this man so much—?"

"Or fear him."

"Yes, or fear him, that this person would not only want to do him harm but would actually do harm? Who among his many enemies . . . ?" I was getting carried away.

He half closed his eyes. His temples throbbed, and his head bobbed as if he were praying. I was watching him think. At last, he opened his eyes and said, "I understand that he died a wealthy man."

"I thought he was poor. Wasn't that the essence of who he was?"

"In public, by all means, yes. And he started out poor, no question about it. But he found his way to prosperity. Isn't that what Americans do? He made himself into a success. He was a tailor, and a fine one at that. Not the manliest occupation, I suppose—no rail splitter, he—but he was skilled with a needle. The clothes he made were handsome indeed, and of a sophisticated taste." Cooper should know, with his aristocratic polish. "He was always impeccably dressed. And clever in business, with a keen eye for land. The farm that the Pattersons live on—he gave it to them as a wedding gift."

David Patterson hadn't mentioned that, although as a new and future resident of Euclid avenue, I could understand his reticence.

"Was he a good president?" I said.

"That you'll have to judge for yourself, Mr. Hay. Who am I to say?"

That was all the answer I would get. If the answer was yes, he would have said so.

The stragglers passed down from the hilltop, as we joined in a companionable silence. I put away my notebook and started to stand. As I extended my hand, Edmund Cooper said, "Do you know what Dickens said of him? They met, you know, at the Mansion."

"I didn't know."

"Oh yes, in 'sixty-eight. Dickens was on his second American tour, when he stopped in at the White House. Later he wrote to his American publisher that President Johnson's face was one of the most remarkable he had ever seen, that it showed a strength of will and a steadiness of purpose that was not to be trifled with. Here was a man who—this, from the great novelist—who must be killed to be got out of the way."

I had to admire ol' Andy. He had made a lot of himself out of nothing, and his courage was real. He had stood up for the Union when his state was seceding and nearly paid for it with his life. But courage on behalf of detestable goals—how admirable was that? Courage to bring the slavocracy back to power, after hating them all of his life? Courage to keep the freedmen in their place. How admirable were those? A man who scorned compromise as weakness—how admirable, or effective, was that? When a man's demons contort his presidency, you can't expect to admire the results.

The story I wired to the *Tribune* was a masterpiece of treacherous balance. On the one hand, the deceased had been a bully and a demagogue and a negro hater—I was subtler, but that's what I meant. On the other hand, the locals worshiped him. Both were true, so the piece should be publishable, right? The *Tribune* was a pushover for the truth.

GREENEVILLE, Tenn., Aug. 3—There could be no more interesting and impressive evidence of the respect and affection
of the people of Tennessee toward Andrew Johnson than the
great solemn gathering of his fellow citizens to-day in the town
of his residence . . .

I've written worse. It probably wasn't what Whitelaw Reid wanted—
"Impeachment or Infamy," the *Tribune* had declared back in 'sixty-eight—
but I liked stories that surprised me. I figured readers liked them, too, even
if editors didn't. Dogs bite men every blame day of the week.

I left the hubbub and cigar smoke of the Western Union office for the
smells of honeysuckle and wild roses, even in the center of Greeneville. All
afternoon, mourners had mobbed the trains and buggies had clawed into
the roads, as the brass bands and the Masons and the plain people left for
home. By now, the town had grown as quiet as the Sabbath.

I ambled along Main street and arrived at my destination before I realized
where I was going. Andy Johnson's homestead was a handsome two-story
brick edifice that would have done a well-heeled merchant proud, especially
in its extensions at the rear. No wonder that the Union *and* the Confederate
armies had used it (and abused it) during the war.

As I tiptoed by, a candle flickered in the window. I rapped on the door
and heard a scurrying inside. The doorknob wiggled. Three or four seconds
passed before the door opened.

It was Bill—just who I wanted to see. His eyes were wide, his body stiff.

"No, suh, nobody home." He spoke quickly and louder than necessary,
for the benefit of (my guess) someone in the parlor.

"Then we can talk," I said. "May I come in?"

Bill shook his head twice. "Come back to-morrow," he mouthed, and
shut the door.

If Bill had something to tell me that he didn't want overheard, wasn't
that a newspaperman's—or a detective's—dream? To-morrow, then, it
would be.

I decided to see the sights of Greeneville, such as they were. I dodged the
muddy parts of the roadway and sidestepped the napping dogs and wandered toward Johnson's famed tailor shop, at the corner of Depot and College streets. It was a tourist attraction, and I guess I was now a tourist. The
shop was little more than a long wooden shed, unpainted and worn, over-

hung by vines. To-day it was wreathed in loops and knots of mourning cloth. A sad sight, but beautiful in its way.

Over the doorway hung a plank, with letters that looked burned in:

A. JOHNSON
TAILOR

The interior was a single worn room, maybe fifteen feet by twenty, with wooden walls and a rough pine floor. Far from the fireplace stood a tailor's table, a few cabinets, and an ancient-looking trunk. Scattered chairs of minimal comfort—and no other furnishings. I marveled: This was where Andrew Johnson's life in politics had started, a venue for debates over civic issues large and small, whether distant from Greeneville or close to home. This was a training ground for young Andy's oratorical flourishes, the birthplace of his first political campaign. It didn't look like much, but for a man of the people, wasn't that to be praised?

In the far corner, a father smacked his young son's cheek for a sin I hadn't seen, yet it was the daughter who burst into tears. The present had intruded. I was turning to leave when a hand on my chest pushed me back.

"Captain McElwee!" I declared. His blond hair was mussed, and his cravat was askew. His face was flush with a look that didn't suggest he was happy to see me.

I pushed him back, which surprised and calmed him.

"A pleasure to see *you*, Captain," I said.

At first, I thought he hadn't heard me. But his eyes came into focus and fastened on mine.

"Been looking for you," he growled.

"What for?" I said mildly.

"You askin' folks about me?"

"That's what I do—ask questions."

"Well, don't."

I shrugged and said, "Anything else? Because I have a question for you, if I may." I waited for him to take a swing at me—I was almost hoping he would, so that I could swing back—but he stood there. "On the train to Elizabethton, did you or Mr. Johnson use a flask?"

Before he could answer, Captain McElwee was yanked backward. A hand had grabbed his collar from behind.

"Please forgive my friend," a voice rumbled. Over the captain's shoulder, a face came into view. It shared Captain McElwee's blond hair and a broom of a mustache, although it was weather-beaten and showed a few days' growth of beard. "He is drowning his sorrows. I am David Jenkins," he said, extending his hand from around Captain McElwee's waist. He seemed practiced at the maneuver.

"You're the Union captain," I said.

"At your service, sir."

I introduced myself and told him I was writing about Andrew Johnson's last days and asked if there was a place we could talk.

Jenkins sighed. "I should probably return him"—nodding at his companion—"whence he came."

"I can help," I said.

He waved me off and then, with an ingratiating smile, assented. "He isn't light. But it isn't far."

Captain McElwee stumbled along willingly, a human crutch at either arm.

"What unit were you in?" I asked Captain Jenkins, across his drunken friend, by way of conversation.

"The Second Tennessee Infantry," he said with pride. "And then the Thirteenth Cavalry."

"Wasn't that Dr. Cameron's unit?"

"It was, for a while."

"Hard time?"

"You been to war, Mr. Hay?"

"Haven't." I braced myself for a look of disdain, which failed to show itself. That my efforts to defeat the Confederacy were confined to pushing paper for the president wasn't something I cared to volunteer to a Union veteran.

"I have," Captain Jenkins said. "Life was never easy or dull." I waited for details but had learned over the years that a true warrior was reluctant to recount his battles or boast of his bravery.

"Had you met Mr. Johnson before—before the train to Elizabethton?"

"Hadn't," Jenkins replied. "But I knew his son-in-law, Colonel Stover. My wife is a Stover. It's our baby son's name."

We had walked a block to Main street and waited for a hay wagon to pass before venturing across. McElwee was getting heavier. His toes dragged in the dirt.

"Here we are," Jenkins said.

The Mason House, on the corner, was a throwback to antebellum days. In the lobby, the heavy furniture and velvet drapes probably hadn't been dusted since the war. Nor had the man behind the desk. I asked if they had a room. They did.

"I can take him from here," Jenkins said.

I shifted the right half of his companion and said, "Let me ask you a question first, if I could." I didn't wait for his assent. "When your friend and Mr. Johnson were . . . enjoying themselves on the train, that morning from here to Elizabethton, was it from a flask or a glass?"

"I don't indulge, myself," Jenkins said, "but I can tell you that only a flask was involved."

He didn't ask why I cared. Maybe he knew. You couldn't add poison to a flask without endangering anyone who took a snort. Maybe Captain McElwee was in the clear.

CHAPTER SIX

M y long, long day brought on a restless night, on a mattress as soft as a swamp. I hadn't brought a change of clothes and had borrowed tooth powder and a brush at the hotel desk. I woke up feeling rotten. It was my belly, which I recognized from enduring acquaintance was connected in unpredictable ways to my mind. My mind was muddled, too, although I was used to that. The world was a complicated place, full of nuance and contradiction. Clarity didn't do it justice. It meant you didn't fully understand.

Ooh, even that shard of wisdom hurt my noggin.

Slowly, and with genuine regret, I opened my eyes. Just as I'd feared, the sunlight was far too bright. When I squinted, I could see the room all too well. The ceiling was peeling from the summer's humidity—last summer's. The air felt clammy. The wallpaper's tangle of roses was streaked with ancient leaks. The bed creaked as I leaned over to check my watch. It was seven oh six.

For my headache, I swallowed a celery and chamomile pill (more reliable than Mrs. Winslow's Soothing Syrup or Dalley's Magical Pain Extractor) using the tepid water from the pitcher on the washstand. I tried to will myself back to sleep, but the problem in my head remained. My murder investigation, if that wasn't too lordly a term, was a mess. Captain McElwee was one line of inquiry—the train ride was only one of his opportunities—but how could I learn enough about him to decide if he was a murderer? I needed a motive, which involved a man's heart. I could guess about the state of Captain McElwee's liver, but his heart was a mystery to me. How to follow up, I hadn't a clue.

Then there was the tantalizing question of Andy Johnson's last will and testament—namely, the absence of one. Any reader of the splashier newspapers could tell you that the prospect of an inheritance, or its disappearance, was a motive for murder, tried and true. How could I investigate *that*? Need

I contemplate Johnson's allegedly loving family? Heavens! I could ask each member if he or she had poisoned their patriarch or if one of their kinfolk had. That sounded promising, right?

Or I could ask Bill!

I opened my eyes again and stared at the ceiling. The cracks were without meaning, like a toddler's scribble. To figure out a motive was either obvious or impossible. Andy Johnson had no shortage of enemies who would jump with joy in seeing him gone. But acting on a motive required a particular eagerness, as well as the opportunity.

The opportunity. That was my third line of inquiry. Who had had the opportunity? Who had had access to Andrew Johnson within an hour or two of his collapse? Or collap*ses*—first when he arrived at his daughter's house and again in his final decline? That should narrow the field of suspects, from the millions to a handful or two or three. It also had the advantage of being a question of fact.

I also knew the right person to ask. Bill had told me to come back to-day. I forced myself out of bed and into yesterday's garments.

⊹═══⊹

Main street in Greeneville was livelier in the morning than late at night— not my kind of place. Rigs of various sizes kicked up dust on the drying roadway. On the sidewalk, young ladies raised lace handkerchiefs to their mouths, pretending not to notice when a man tipped his derby. Some of the younger men had the audacity to stroll along in shirtsleeves. That's how muggy it was already, at half past nine.

I took the western sidewalk toward the Johnson homestead when I passed a one-story storefront with a ragged sign over the door:

Greeneville Intelligencer

The newspaper's office sat across Main street from the home of the town's late leading citizen. I didn't really expect Frank to be in, given his bereavement and the early hour. Newspapermen, if that is what he was, aren't early birds. They catch their worms later in the day.

The door was unlocked, but nobody was in sight. Inkwells and newspapers and overflowing ashtrays covered the half dozen desks, along with glasses half-filled with what looked like urine but was probably last night's beer. I stepped around the battered spittoons and called, "Mr. Johnson!"

I heard a stirring in the back room. "Mr. Johnson, you here?"

The stirring became footsteps. The curtains parted and a young man's head poked out. Everything about the face was exceedingly regular. The undistinguished features, the flop of darkish hair, the mustache that curved down into side-whiskers that took the current style a little too far. The skin was mottled, and the eyes had a glassy look. His father's son.

From behind the curtain emerged a fellow in a collarless shirt, half-unbuttoned, and trousers that hung on his frame. His torso was slender, almost frail, hardly the broad-shouldered brawn of ol' Andy's. If I swatted at his chest, he might flutter away like a leaf.

"Are you Frank Johnson?" I said.

He lifted his eyebrows. I took that as a yes.

I introduced myself and offered my condolences and apologized for interrupting at such a difficult time. I told him I was writing a story about his father's family and last days, appealing to him newspaperman to newspaperman.

What I didn't expect was enthusiasm. The gleam in his eyes suggested that part of his willingness was liquid. It also became clear that he needed someone to talk to—to unload on. A nonjudgmental ear. My specialty.

We seated ourselves on facing desktops, our knees almost touching.

I repeated my condolences, and he looked bored, sated with insincerities. I asked how old he was.

Wrong question. "I turn twenty-three to-morrow," he said miserably.

My *congratulations* elicited no pleasure. We established that he had finished Georgetown College and then returned home at his father's behest.

"How'd you like it up in Washington City?" I said.

"Didn't," Frank said, drawling the word into three syllables. "Too many high-hatters, if you know what I mean."

"I do, actually." Those were the Easterners who believed in the cerebral superiority of the East—unforgivable, even if accurate. "I lived there myself for a while. Actually, I lived in the Executive Mansion, before you did."

Before he asked for details, I took my notebook from my breast coat pocket and said, "Tell me a little about your father—as a father."

"He was a prince of a father." He stared past my shoulder. "A prince of a father."

He said it once too often to believe. I waited for more—a vain hope. "Was he strict?" I said.

"Not if you did what he wanted." His drawl had thickened.

"And did you?"

"Sometimes."

"What happened the other times?"

"When I got caught, you mean?"

"How often did that happen?"

"Not often. He was usually too busy to bother."

"But when you did?" I said. I hadn't taken notes yet, for fear of slowing the spigot.

"We worked it out," Frank said with an impish smile. This wasn't the heartwarming story I had in mind. A juicier one, perhaps.

"Punishment involved?"

No reply.

I said, "And your mother?"

"She spent her life upstairs, in a chair, reading or doing needlework or I don't know what all."

"I knew her a little bit, up in Washington City." I didn't think it right to say how.

"There, too. She must've come downstairs twice, the whole time we lived there. Once for a party for my sisters' brats, she came out onto the South Lawn and announced that she was an invalid. Thrilled the little buggers."

"I can imagine," I said. Now, back around. "I suppose it was easier to be your parents' daughter."

"I'll say." He stared at me with dark, watery eyes. "Martha got away with anything she had a mind to, she did. Mary, too."

"What did they have a mind to?"

"You name it," Frank Johnson said. Then he turned red and sputtered, "No, not that. How dare you even think it?"

I hadn't been thinking anything. "And your brothers?"

"They're dead." Frank's eyes grew hard.

"So I understand." I figured that knowing more about their fates wouldn't help me. The only thing I knew for certain is that they hadn't murdered their father. Maybe he had murdered them—ruined them, rather. Fathers do that. Mine didn't, and I swore silently that I wouldn't, either. I pictured Helen in Clara's arms and prayed I'd be the father I would want.

"And your brothers-in-law?"

Frank's jaw tightened. "What about 'em?"

"Were they close to your father?"

"You mean the great and good Colonel Stover, the finest man in the history of the Republic, or at least of East Tennessee? Izzat the one you mean?"

"That's one of them."

"Well, the love isn't exactly returned."

"Oh?"

"No, sir. And the livin' ones, they ain't worth a donkey's turd on Church street."

Frank *was* a boy, and a damaged one, although that didn't mean his judgments were wrong.

"Not even the senator—the ex-senator?"

Frank spat and missed the nearest spittoon.

"Senator, crap. My daddy got him elected. He lived with us up in Washington City and he did whatever Daddy told him."

"Rent-free," I said.

Frank giggled. The liquid, again. "Like the rent they don't pay on their farm," he said.

"The one east of here."

"That's the one. They live on a farm they think is theirs, but it ain't." Frank laughed, and not in a nice way.

"What do you mean?"

"Ain't I plain enough?"

I wondered if Frank had peppered his banter at Georgetown College with *ain't*s, or did he reserve those for Tennessee—or for Yankees visiting Tennessee? "So, whose farm is it?" I said.

"Who do you think? My daddy's. He kept it all the time."

"Really? How do you know this?"

A smirk. "I know."

"I understand that he didn't leave a will."

"So I hear. He was about to write one. Told me so."

"When was this?"

"Just before he . . . I got there just before he slipped into . . ." He couldn't finish.

"With your sister and brother-in-law?"

A nod.

"Why didn't he?" I said. "Write a will, I mean."

A shrug.

I said, "What was it going to say, do you know?"

Frank's temples bulged—a phrenologist would have a field day—and his face compressed into a child's conception of slyness. "Who can say?" he muttered. "Who can say?"

I knew the answer to that. She was bedridden, back in Elizabethton.

I mounted the courthouse steps and went inside. The mourners were gone, but I still felt yesterday's breath of death, a heaviness in the air that carried the weight of centuries past and the ones yet to unfold. The rotunda was sunlit from the turret's windows high above, leaving the edges in shadow. It was eerily quiet, as if to announce: don't even dare to look.

A brusque man in the clerk's office directed me to the chancery court in the basement, where the real estate records were kept. I groped my way down a dank stone staircase and through an open doorway. Outlines of shelving, floor to ceiling, led into blackness. I started to wander blindly when a voice at my back made me jump.

"May I help you?"

I swiveled and saw a thin woman with a long face, her hair in a sloppy bun. She carried a smoky lantern as she navigated the piles of tomes in the aisles. At my request, she located Deed Book 35. The giant-sized volume was bound in a billowing cloth that was already becoming unglued. Its pages were curled and brown. But the smell is what I remember—of mildew, the legacy of time.

Starting on page 573, she found the land transaction I wanted. Deciphering the spidery writing by lantern challenged my eyesight.

> *Whereas, on the 4ᵗʰ day of January 1866, one Joseph*
> *Henderson filed in our Chancery Court held at Greeneville,*
> *for the County of Greene in the State of Tennessee, his*
> *Bill of Complaint against . . .*

I skimmed down the page (a journalist's privilege, not a lawyer's), past *the County aforesaid* and *all of the cases pending*. I learned that, on the fifteenth day of April 1867, one David T. Patterson had offered the winning bid on Mr. Henderson's 516 acres in Greene county and purchased it for $19,250. That was on page 574. I rubbed my eyes and was ready to call it quits. More as a lawyer than a journalist, I turned another page and found:

> *To the Clerk and Master of the Chancery Court at Greeneville,*
> *Tennessee*
>   *I do hereby transfer and assign to His Excellency*
> *Andrew Johnson all title, claim and interest acquired*
> *by me to the lands of Joseph Henderson . . .*
> *D. T. Patterson*

The price: $17,600. This was less than Patterson had paid. Was this a mortgage? A loan? The remaining two and a half pages gave no hint. Except for this: David Patterson no longer owned more than a little of the land he lived on. Apparently, his father-in-law had owned most of it. Now his mother-in-law did.

+===+

The brick homestead on Main street looked abandoned. The lace curtains revealed no light within. I knocked anyway and was surprised—pleasantly so, for a change—when the door opened as if on command. Bill stood there, smiling. He gestured me inside.

"Do you have a minute now?" I said.

Bill pointed to his own scrawny chest.

I bobbed my head and said, "If you would, please."

Bill eyed me with curiosity and led me through the house to the back porch, looking out on a vegetable garden overtaken with weeds. The parlor was out of the question, even if no one else was here; evidently, the *do*s and *don't*s of the house in which Bill had been enslaved were engraved on his soul.

I sat in a wicker rocking chair. Bill stood.

"You were with Mr. Johnson pretty much all the time, were you not? During his last days, around the clock."

Bill nodded once. His eyes held mine.

"Can you remember who visited him last Friday?"

Bill seemed to understand right away why I was asking. His eyes welled up, and he half closed them. In a monotone, he recited the names of Mrs. Johnson, Frank, the two daughters, their husbands, the grandchildren, the doctors, the friends, the neighbors, the—

"All of them?" I said.

"At one time or 'nother," Bill said.

I took out my notebook and scribbled a while. "Which ones on Friday afternoon, do you recall? I mean an hour or two before Mr. Johnson lost consciousness . . . the final time."

A furrowed brow. "Miss Mary, of course."

"And her husband?"

Bill shook his head. "He away someplace."

"All right, who else?"

"Lillie and the Stover young 'uns, they runnin' in and out. Well, tiptoe-ing, best they able. And the docs."

"Two of them? Dr. Jobe and Dr. Cameron?"

Bill's head traced a slow circle, then back around. "Cain't remember exactly who come when . . ."

"That's all right—you're doing great. Captain McElwee, perhaps?"

"That fella from the train?" he said. Bill's brow furrowed and his eyes half closed again. He was trying to picture someone. "Could be."

Hadn't Captain McElwee said he had visited Johnson just once? "Was he alone?"

Bill shrugged.

I held my breath at my next query. "Mrs. Johnson?"

Bill shook his head several times quickly, like a mutt in a downpour. "No, no, no," he said, as if he feared it was true. "She come before. And later."

"Anyone else?"

A shrug.

"Did his . . . I mean Mr. Johnson's . . . eyes look . . . wide, do you recall?"

"Uh-huh."

"Like they had looked when you first arrived at . . . Miss Mary's?"

His own eyes widened. "Yes, suh."

So, had Johnson been poisoned twice?

"What time did the Pattersons arrive? They came with Frank, correct?"

"At ten 'til five," he said. "I get 'em at the depot." That would put them back at the house by five thirty, giving them enough time to administer a poison that took effect around seven. "Was he still . . . lucid when they came? Was he making sense?"

"Cain't say for certain, but I think so. They see 'im theirselves. Kep' me downstairs all the while. And the doctor, he come, too."

"Dr. Jobe, you mean, or—"

"Them, too. But Mistuh Johnson's doc from here in Greeneville. He come on the train with Miss Martha. He the doc that Mistuh Johnson knows."

I jotted down his name.

"Were you able to see . . . the president again . . . before he started to . . . slip away?"

Bill himself had slipped away. He leaned toward the railing and stared off across the grounds. A crow was pecking at the unkempt lawn. I realized he had omitted a name from his list: his own.

I left Bill on the porch and returned through the house. The day was bright but the corridor was darkened, a tunnel that ended at the front door. I was passing the parlor when I heard voices raised—something from a man about "damn letters" and from a woman snarling . . . I couldn't make it out.

I couldn't help but look in. The instant I was spotted, the clamor ceased.

"It's you!" David Patterson exclaimed.

"None other," I replied, my wit failing me in a pinch. "May I come in?"

"You already have," Martha Patterson pointed out. She looked up from the center marble-topped table, cradling what looked like oversized playing cards—envelopes, on closer inspection. Behind her Southern solicitude was something angled and sharp.

"I came from the courthouse," I said. Martha cringed, probably thinking of what she had seen there the day before. I explained what I found, about who held the deed to their farm.

"And he gave it back," David Patterson said. "It was a mortgage that he canceled."

"I saw no evidence of that."

"It's ours," Martha said, her arms wrapped across her chest, all five feet of her standing erect. "It was a wedding present."

I knew that two-edged sword. "When did you get married?"

"In 'fifty-five," Martha replied.

"These records are from 'sixty-six and 'sixty-seven," I said.

David Patterson's vast brow turned almost purple. He took a step toward me and snapped, "Get the hell out of here! Why do we have to prove anything to the likes of you?"

An astute question, to which I had no persuasive response, witty or otherwise. Having been properly raised, I apologized for the bother and left.

Was the farm really theirs? More to the point, did I care? I probably didn't, unless it had something to do with the workings of Johnson's family (for a story) or with his abrupt departure from this mortal coil (to solve a murder *and* for a story). The ardor of their objections aroused my interest. These were possibilities worth pursuing. When somebody shoves me, I am prone to shove back. But how?

I knew the answer to that one, too. Eliza Johnson, the new widow, now the owner of the Pattersons' farm, was the only family member I hadn't seen yet. It was time to return to Elizabethton, after wrapping up a loose end here.

Dr. James Broyles's office was above a dry goods store on Depot street. I must have arrived during a midafternoon lull. He turned out to be seventy-five if he was a day, but he was a vigorous, lantern-jawed man with a shock of white hair. I wasn't expecting much in terms of useful information, so I can't confess to disappointment when he refused to give me the time of day. That is not a rib-tickler. I asked him, when he pulled out his own watch, and he tossed his head and said nothing, waiting for me to . . . well, leave. He wasn't rude or unpleasant, but he never came close to answering any of my questions, except for one: the patient was still conscious when Dr. Broyles arrived at his deathbed.

Were his eyes dilated? No reply. Wasn't that a confirmation of sorts, albeit in a contorted, journalistically (and judicially) useless way? Not even that.

I was leaving when I thought of a ludicrous question. Why not? I would never see this man again. "If you wanted to poison someone," I said, "would belladonna be your poison of choice?"

"Are you serious?" he said.

"If you wanted to make the death look natural," I replied. "Hypothetically speaking, I mean."

The doctor's weathered face split into a grin. He was human, after all. "Just hypothetically speaking, you understand," he said. "Arsenic would take too long and require many low doses. Strychnine causes muscle contractions that would be hard to conceal. Belladonna has none of these . . . drawbacks."

"How interesting," I said. "Did you see any evidence that he—"

"Good afternoon, Mr. Hay."

I was growing accustomed to being invited to leave respectable places, and I was adept at not taking it personally. But that isn't to say I liked it.

＋━━━＋

The last train to Elizabethton left as scheduled, at seven twenty-one. I made my way to what passed for a club car and ordered a bourbon. The black waiter delivered it with a gaudy smile, which depressed me—that he felt the need. Maybe he did that for everyone, for the tips. Which depressed me more, for it suggested he had concluded that servility worked. I thought we had just waged a war over that—and won. I still had plenty to learn about the human condition.

The whisky arrived, and I offered the porter what I thought was a genuine smile, man to man, but I had a feeling he preferred greenbacks. I complied, but this didn't improve my mood any. I gulped my drink, which burned going down, and picked up a *Knoxville Chronicle*. The Arkansas river was rising by a foot an hour, and Turkish troops defeated the Herzegovinian insurgents. But there was good news, too. Rivers in Ohio were receding. In Florida, at Fort Pickens, the army reported two deaths from yellow fever but no new cases for the past eight days. The aeronaut in Chicago who had vanished in his balloon three weeks back was now believed to be conducting an ingenious advertising stunt.

The fields outside my window were smattered with a late-summer beige. I thought about the Pattersons' farm. I might be passing it right now. I squinted and saw only half-grown hay. The Pattersons had been so . . . snippety. Not that I could blame them. I had barged in on them the day after the funeral. In my defense, my timing couldn't be helped; besides, I had been invited into the house. I suppose I could have passed by the parlor once I heard voices in argument, or merely lurked outside, but no red-blooded journalist would do that. All right, they were mad at me for doing my job. Did that make them murderers? God forbid. But . . . I could imagine it, barely, from David Patterson. I wouldn't put anything past him. He was an oily sort of creature—I'd say *slithery* if not for his paunch—who probably never did anything directly when there were angles to be worked. Using a poison on someone he hated or feared—instead of, say, a gun or a knife—would probably suit him. But wasn't poison a woman's weapon? A disquieting thought. Could Martha actually murder her father? She was tougher than her husband, that seemed obvious, but was she a parricide? No, no . . . no. I'd stake my fortune, such as it was, on that. She was her father's spitting image. Killing him would be like peering into a looking glass and . . . Absurd. Nor was it clear that her father's death would help, rather than hinder, their chances of keeping the farm.

I sat back and contemplated the nature of Evil. Not the lowercase variety, which happened every day and was rooted, I figured, in human neediness. No, the depraved kind that rattled the prophets and inspired preachers to preach.

I felt a poem coming on. My class poem at Brown had been impermeable— and interminable—but I had recently achieved a bit of commercial success for *Pike County Ballads,* my platitudinous poems in frontier dialect. The *Tribune* had published them first, and they had caught on.

I pulled out my notebook, just in case. I stared out the window. A blue haze hung low in the darkening sky; shadowy mountains rose in the distance. As words came to mind, my eyes drifted shut.

I don't believe in Evil,
Nor is Satan my cup of tea,

Promising, although it needed to mean something.

But evil, in its lowercase truth,
Will never let us be.

Forgive me for intruding on Saint Augustine's turf, but wasn't this trite enough to be true? And isn't that what poetry strove for—the truth? The truth was, I had never written a rhyme that deserved to be published. No Tennyson here.

We couldn't get to Elizabethton soon enough.

I rang the bell on the Union Hotel's reception desk three times before the sullen clerk appeared. It wasn't *that* late. He looked resentful as he dropped the iron key into my palm.

I asked if Captain McElwee was in. I wanted to know if he had visited ol' Andy's deathbed a second time.

"Gone," the clerk said.

"For the evening?"

"For good. Left this afternoon."

"Where to?"

"Didn't say."

With that, he pivoted toward the back office, to continue his nap.

CHAPTER SEVEN

The nightmare was amusing after the fact. It was one of those chase dreams, in which I started as the pursuer and became the pursued. The reversal occurred in a railroad yard as I was sprinting along the track, rounding a railroad car gutted by fire, its innards still smoking. I couldn't tell who—or what—was chasing me except that he or it was gaining and intended my death. I was running and running, trying not to trip over the crossties, desperate to catch my breath. I was flying headlong when I bolted upright and felt the dark air in my face. I had left the window open, in hopes of a breeze. All I got was an oven.

> 'Twas in a world of iron and dark
> That I . . .

That I what?

> 'Twas in a world of iron and dark
> That I raced beyond my fate,
> Until . . .

My heart was pounding. I take it back: the nightmare wasn't amusing at all.

⊱━⊰

"Who the hell are you?"

People kept asking me that. Maybe I needed a sign around my neck.

The gentleman (and I use the word loosely) who filled the doorway of the Stover place looked like a brute. I had seen him at the funeral. His barrel chest overwhelmed his spindly legs. His forehead was sloped like a hillside; his broad, clean-shaven chin had a cleft deep enough for maggots to breed. His face was puffy with drink or with rage, maybe both. He was the sort of fellow I've always despised, ever since that pummeling I took in the schoolyard. It was because of oafs like him that I had taken up boxing.

I had multiple ways to respond—pugnaciously, deferentially, metaphorically. I decided on the factual. My name and newspaper drew a blank, as I figured they would. But naming any newspaper wouldn't help my case.

"You must be Mr. Brown," I ventured.

"Damn right I am. I am the lord of this particular manor, whether anyone thinks so or not."

Had I suggested otherwise? I couldn't fathom why Mary had married this man, after Colonel Stover's death. Unless she had to. Or maybe she had tired of sharing her hearth with a saint.

"I don't doubt it," I said, practicing my most ingratiating smile. I had to assure him of this? "May I come in?"

"What do you want?" he said.

"Is your wife available?" Inartful utterance. "I mean, is she free for a conversation? We have met before, she and I." I hastened to add, "Just the other day, here."

"She 'xpectin' you?"

If I lied, he would find out soon enough. "No. But I think she'll see me."

"Subject?"

"Her father."

"Not her husband?" he said with a bitter laugh.

"Whenever you like."

I cooled my heels (metaphorically only) in the dogtrot. I wished I had brought a newspaper, although its four pages wouldn't have bewildered me for long. I glanced around at the sparse furnishings; the arched windowpanes bespoke a certain level of wealth. I hung my tall hat on a peg and examined myself in the looking glass. I flattened the stray strands of my hair. I didn't look like what I felt like inside. Did anyone?

The lady of the household caught me staring at myself, and I turned with a sheepish grin. Miss Mary was silhouetted against the back windows, tall and broad-shouldered, regal in bearing, swaying as if to a tune I wasn't privileged to hear. Without a word, she beckoned me into the parlor. Drawn curtains fooled the room into dusk.

My eyes adjusted to the gloom. Mary Johnson Stover Brown looked a decade older than I had seen her on Sunday. Her hair was bedraggled and her shoulders sagged. When she saw me observing, she straightened her spine—her public self.

"And what brings you back to us, pray tell?" she said.

"Two things," I said. "Three or four, actually." It was frequently a failing of mine to blurt the truth. "For my story about your father's last days, he was never in pain, would you say?"

She closed her eyes for an extended moment and reopened them. "No," she said sadly. "We have that."

"Did you notice anything about his eyes?"

"Yes, at dinner when he arrived, his eyes did look odd."

"The pupils dilated?"

She looked surprised. "How did you know? The black part almost filled his eyes."

"And how about his eyes on Friday afternoon, before he slipped into a coma?"

"I wasn't here."

"Oh?"

"This house was crowded with visitors, well-wishers, more than I could . . ." She sighed. "It's not as big as it looks, you know. My husband's parents live nearby. We went there."

"You and your husband, both?"

"Most of the time. He was even happier than I was to escape."

"Could he have come back while your father was slipping away?"

"I don't think so. Why would he want to do that?"

Best to leave that unanswered. If she hadn't been there, she couldn't know when the Pattersons had arrived. I skipped the question and decided to clothe my next one in the subjunctive, as less likely to cause offense or to get me thrown out on my ear.

"Would it be possible for me to talk with your mother?" I said.

"I should say not." She straightened up further, a geometric marvel.

"If you would be willing to ask her, I think she would agree. I knew her in Washington City." I had done Eliza Johnson a favor just before leaving the Mansion. "I need a few minutes, no more."

She gave me a sharp look and made up her mind. "I won't be a minute," she said. She climbed the staircase against the far wall.

I twiddled my thumbs—no kidding—and then in opposite directions, as my father had once taught me on a rainy Sunday afternoon. I didn't need to twiddle for long.

"My mother will see you," Mary said. She failed to keep the surprise out of her voice. "She *wants* to see you."

How nice, at last, to be wanted.

Eliza Johnson's bedroom, up the steep stairs, was a reminder of the one in which her husband had died. The low ceiling was cozy more than (by the latest lingo) claustrophobic. The double bed and the vanity with the heart-shaped mirror were familiarly arranged. Was it Andy or Eliza who had shoved the Stovers—excuse me, the Browns—out of their conjugal bed?

The widow was curled in a reclining chair, a wraith of the woman I had last seen a decade before. She wore a caftan with a lace collar and cuffs, and a matron's cap was fastened on by two gold-headed pins. A green af-ghan covered her lap—in August! It was conceivable she had been beautiful once, a woman of quiet force, the young wife who had read to her unlet-tered husband. Her nose and jowls had thickened, and her crimped hair had turned white. I remembered a smooth face with a perky nose and eyes that followed you wherever you went. Those eyes were still vividly blue and just as alert, but they had sunk into their sockets; her mouth drooped in resignation, from years of illness. Her face had character, which is what you say when you're too polite to say more.

"Please, don't get up," I said, as if she could. "I was so sorry to hear about Robert. And your husband, of course."

She reached out her hand, which felt warm and damp. "Life is heart-ache, Mr. Hay." Her voice was soft but firm. "I can't say which was the harsher blow. Robert, I suppose. It feels so . . . unnecessary to lose a child. And so unnatural, even after a war." Her corporeal self seemed to shrink.

"I have one of my own now."

"Then I needn't tell you."

I answered the usual questions. I couldn't imagine losing my child to liquor and laudanum, but Eliza probably couldn't have, either, and I didn't inquire.

"You were kind to Robert," she said. "I shall never forget it."

"I happened to know that particular policeman, and I'd just as soon not explain how." I had used my acquaintanceships with the local constabulary (not wholly in consequence of my official duties) to clear Robert's record for sauntering and loitering without the newspapers getting wise.

"It was appreciated all the same." She had a sad and far-off look. "So, what can I do for you, Mr. Hay?"

"It was most kind of you to see me," I said. "My intentions, I'm afraid, aren't strictly honorable. I'm writing for a newspaper now."

"Your sins are safe with me, young man."

"I won't hold you to that." I explained that I was writing an article for the *Tribune* about her husband's last days. "He had his loving family around him at the end?" I said.

"That, I couldn't tell you firsthand. It was the middle of the night and I was here, asleep. Mary awakened me. Have you asked her?"

"I will. But he was without pain?"

"So they say."

"When did you last see him, if I may ask?"

"The day before."

"Friday or Thursday?"

"I guess it was Friday. You lose track of the days up here."

"When on Friday?"

Eliza gave me a quizzical look. "Just after lunch and before my afternoon nap. We had a lovely conversation."

That was a little too early to have poisoned her husband, but only a little. "May I ask about what?"

"Old times. The good times." Her voice had grown distant. "Some of the bad times, too. You have a few of those, you know, in forty-eight years of wedlock."

That seemed impossibly long. I took out my notebook and said, "Do any of those memories stand out?"

Was I really writing such a story? She told me of watching with her girlfriends as young Andy and his sorry entourage had first stumbled into Greeneville and declaring, "There goes the man I am going to marry." I dutifully copied this down, smelling a tale she had told so often she believed it herself.

"I understand that your husband"—I was entering treacherous territory—"failed to leave a will."

A single nod, with wary eyes. I could see how her glance of disapproval might terrify a child.

"Why didn't he, do you know?"

Eliza Johnson's lips curled. At first I thought it was a grimace, until I realized it was her unpracticed attempt at a smile. "That was one of the things we talked about, since you asked. He had torn up a few, for one reason or another."

"Did he have another one in mind?"

No reply. That probably meant he did.

I said, "Can you tell me anything about it?"

Her smile had disappeared. I waited, counting on silence as my ally. This time, it was.

"This is not for publication, you understand that. In fact, it is not to be repeated."

She waited for me to assent, until I did.

"He wanted to leave almost everything to Frank," she said. "As the one who needed it the most, I suppose, and maybe because we had lost both other boys. He felt some blame for that—while they *were* boys, he was never . . . at hand, and by the time he was, during his presidency, when we all lived under one roof, it was . . . not Charles, he was already . . ." She lowered her head into her hands. I thought she was weeping but when she looked up, her eyes were dry and her voice was strong. "By then, it was too late. We had lost them. Leaving Frank as . . . his hope. Andrew Junior."

"Not Martha?"

This time, I waited in vain. Conceding, I said, "Did he apprise anyone else of his intentions?"

A shrug. She seemed to be tiring, and I was pressing my luck. I pressed it some more. "Are you satisfied," I said, "that your husband . . . passed away from . . . natural causes?"

Her face drooped a little but otherwise showed no change. "Are *you*?" she said. Her lack of surprise surprised me.

"I am not," I replied.

I waited. The silence was absolute, other than a tingling in my ears.

At last, she said, "I have expected it for years."

"Have you?"

She twisted her lips again.

"For any reason in particular?" I said.

"Many a reason," she sighed.

"Any in particular? Any*one* in particular?"

No reply, and this time, her silence alarmed me. Maybe she knew something, or at least suspected it—suspected *someone*. A family member, most likely. Who else would she be trying to protect? Not Mary, under whose roof she had taken her rest. Nor Frank, who stood to benefit if his father survived long enough to write a new will. This left the two sons-in-law—and Martha.

"Did you see Martha while she was here?"

"Briefly."

"She was close to your husband, was she not?"

"She was." Eliza seemed to stress the past tense.

"Do you suppose that she knew about his plans for his . . . estate?"

"I couldn't tell you, except Martha knows everything about everything. She makes it her business to."

"I suppose I could just ask her."

"I suppose you could, if you can catch up with her."

"I saw her yesterday, over in Greeneville, both of them."

"Not anymore you won't," Eliza said.

"What do you mean?"

"They're gone. He is, anyway. She's about to join him."

"Join him where?"

"Washington City. Next, you're going to ask me why, and I don't know why. I don't want to know why. Martha didn't tell me they were going. Mary did."

"How does Mary know?"

"You would have to ask her. And now, Mr. Hay, if you would excuse me. I have taken up enough of your time."

Eliza was turning back into a crotchety old lady. May we all live to be crotchety and old.

Mary was waiting for me at the bottom of the stairs, staring up at me, admiration in the lift of her eyebrows. "Did you learn what you needed?" she said.

"Some," I replied. "She said your sister is heading for Washington, along with . . . Senator Patterson. Would you happen to know why?"

"Not really. Martha said something to me before leaving here about Daddy's unfinished business. That's what she called it, and that's all I know. I wish I could tell you what she meant."

So did I.

Mary ushered me to the door. I hadn't asked one of the questions I had walked in with. I was already on my way out—what could I lose? (Dangerous reasoning.) Did she know of anyone who might wish to cause her father harm?

I did not expect her to burst into tears.

I am always nonplussed by tears, even a baby's, and certainly a woman's (and definitely a man's). Mary was truly in mourning, and I did the only kindness remaining, which was to leave her alone in her grief.

<hr />

My rental horse was nuzzling his nose against the rough oak bark. My watch said ten past one o'clock. The day was hot as Hades (I hope never to learn how hot that is) and Bellyful, by name, unaware of his contractual obligations, and unlikely to profit from them, ambled along the shaded roadway. Nothing stirred. The river, to my left, was lazy.

I hadn't gone a half mile when the road curved away from the river and I heard a scraping in the dirt around the bend. In the roadway, on a pawing roan, Mary's barbaric husband slouched in the saddle. William Brown's forehead was furrowed, and he was holding a pistol, pointed at my chest. I stroked the penknife in my pocket and left it there.

"What do you want with us here?" he said. "Why're you pokin' around where you ain't wanted?"

"I am a newspaperman, pure and simple." I held up my hands to my shoulders but no higher. "I mean you no harm."

He laughed in a menacing way. I must admit that his skepticism was well-founded. "Get the fuck out of here," he said, the curse undermining his moral advantage.

"That's what I'm trying to do," I said, "but you seem to be blocking my way."

"Am I, now? And what do you mean to do about it, Mr. Hayes?"

"My name is Hay, and I am unarmed, as you can see. As long as you wave that gun at me, there's not much I *can* do about it. But if you would put that gun away and climb down from your horse, we can settle this with a friendly conversation. Or unfriendly, if you prefer."

Quite an oration. Better than my usual.

William Brown sneered at me, thereby establishing his manly bona fides, and slowly returned the pistol to its holster. Even more slowly, and to my surprise, he dismounted. I had no choice but to do the same.

I wasn't much more than five foot two; he stood six feet at least. He was beefy, and I was . . . wiry, shall we say. *Scrawny* was probably more accurate. But strong, I hasten to add. No, really. I had been a boxer, off and on, since college; the conditioning was more brutal than the sport.

"What now?" I said. "Settle this the old-fashioned way?" I cringed at the cliché, although clichés had their charm.

I stepped toward him and raised my fists, showing the backs of my hands toward his face. I wasn't going to throw the first punch.

But I would happily throw the second punch, and I did. His punch went wild, as I figured it might, a haymaker that was easy to dodge. This gave me an opening. I stepped forward and I swung my right fist up into his chin.

It connected. I heard it. So did he. His eyes grew big, and he staggered backward but stayed on his feet.

I turned back to Bellyful, having made my point, so I heard a little too late the tromp of footsteps. The instant I pivoted, he launched himself at me. I stepped aside but not by enough, and I would have admired his audacity had his bulk not glanced off my shoulder and spun me into the ground. I gasped for breath and felt dirt in my mouth. I spit it out and sat up. With difficulty and not a little pain, I got to my feet while he was doing the same. As we came face-to-face, I harnessed my momentum and rammed a right cross into his jaw. This time, he went down. His head smacked in the roadway and came to rest in a rut.

I watched him. His head moved, but it might have been the wind. I was ready—past ready—to go on my way, but I figured the Christian thing to do was to wait until I knew he was alive. Which I was sure he was. I had never killed a man and had no plans to. And indeed, it wasn't more than a minute or two before he moaned and struggled to sit up. He could find his way home.

Bellyful was eyeing me (I felt certain) with renewed respect. I mounted and we pranced our way past the obstacles, equine and human. I hadn't ridden more than a few yards beyond the beaten Mr. Brown when I heard a scraping behind me and turned to look. My antagonist was half to his feet, waving his pistol in my direction. His hand shook. I flicked my heels into Bellyful's hindquarters and we took off. A shot rang out. It was the loudest sound I had ever heard. Did a bullet whiz past my shoulder? Bellyful must have sensed it, too, because he bolted into a gallop. I held tight to the reins.

Maybe I needed a different avocation.

What in blazes was that about? I didn't enjoy being shot at. I had once been struck in the shoulder, and it *hurt*. I barely noticed the flatlands of dried-up crops or the woodlands I was passing through. I would say that our Mr. Brown was perturbed, was he not? But why, exactly? Because he didn't measure up to the sainted Colonel Stover, whose place he had taken in Mary's bed? Understandable, but it wasn't my fault. Or because visitors had overrun his home while his father-in-law was dying upstairs? Why take that out on me? Because I was snooping into his in-laws' affairs? All right, I could understand his annoyance—or worse. But he had married into a famous family, and the press's attention came with it. Possibly his reason was more . . . tangible than that. I recalled the sheriff's warning about the Ku Klux Klan. Or—I rapped my forehead—the obvious. He had murdered his father-in-law and feared my, yes, fool questions.

That gave me pause, but only for a moment. I simply didn't believe it. William Brown was an impulsive and violent man. There was nothing subtle about him. If he had wanted to murder his father-in-law, would he have tried poison? Surely, he would have used a pistol or his hands. And he wasn't even there when the belladonna had reached its mark—definitely the second time (by his wife's say-so, should she be believed) and possibly not the first.

Maybe he had learned about his father-in-law's soon-to-be-written will, which would confer upon him and his wife nothing at all. Who else had known? Had Frank? Probably. But he had everything to lose by his father's death. This wasn't the case, however, for the Pattersons. If Frank inherited almost everything, then Martha and David Patterson had almost everything to lose, especially if *almost everything* included the land they lived on. Now they were heading to Washington, for reasons unknown.

For reasons unknown. I needed to know them. To finish Daddy's work— that sounded ominous, indeed. Didn't the Pattersons have the most to gain from Andrew Johnson's "unexpected" death? There wasn't much more I could do here. Captain McElwee was gone, to who knows where. Frank was a college-educated nitwit, who stood to gain—the world!—had his daddy lived. Mary was an angel, by all accounts, including my own; her husband was a brute, too much of one to murder by poison. (What *did* she see in him?)

I shouldn't forget the widow. In the absence of her husband's will, Eliza stood to inherit whatever he owned, apparently including a mortgage on 516 acres. There might be more than money at stake. Don't wives (and husbands) typically have a compelling reason or three to want their spouses gone? Eliza, for one, behind her helpless façade, was steely enough to act. She used her helplessness as a means of control. But had she murdered her husband? And if she had, could I prove it? *No*, was my answer—and *no*. But I was guessing.

What else could I accomplish in Tennessee? Not a lot. Two things I could think of. They would take me a half hour at most. Plus, I had a story to write.

Elizabethton near the end of a workday would not be mistaken for New York. No blinkered horses, arrogant carriages, cops with restless night-sticks, or pedestrians who strutted like the streets were theirs. Instead, a trickle of men in frock coats and derbies moseyed along the wooden side-walk, pausing to pass the time of day. Surely a saner way to live.

My first stop was on Main street. The man in the apothecary remembered me all too well. He asked after the girl with scarlet fever and was surprised at the speed of her recovery. No, he did not know of anyone who had recently purchased belladonna other than myself. He bulged with curiosity about why I cared, but I thanked him and left before he had a chance to ask.

Next was the sheriff's office, by the Doe river. J. Dugger Pearce sat behind his desk and greeted me with a belligerent smile. It only broadened when I asked if William Brown was a member of the Ku Klux Klan.

He gestured me into a chair and said, "I heah you gittin' in trouble fer askin' questions. I thought we had a heart-to-heart."

News travels fast.

"That's one way to put it," I replied. "I just had an . . . altercation with Mr. Brown, on the road near his house. And it's his house, he assures me."

"He's a sizable fella."

"But a little clumsy," I said. "He started it, and I promise you, I did nothing to provoke it."

An ugly laugh. "You done nothin' but provoke since you got here, Mistuh Hay."

"I'm only doing my job."

"That's what you call it. Others call it bein' nosy. They see it one way, you see it 'nother. The disagreement is bound to end in, as you call it, an altercation."

"As long as it ends there. I hope it won't distress you too much to tell you I'm leaving."

"We are always sorry to see anyone go. I hope you haven't found us too . . . inhospitable. That would go agin our nature."

"Everyone has been hospitable, with exceptions. But that is the case in any civilized place."

"I am flattered that you include us in that category, Mistuh Hay, as an ambassador from the . . . land of Yankees."

"I represent no one but myself."

"And Horace Greeley."

"The late Horace Greeley. I believe he ran for president under the Democratic banner and happened to defeat President Grant in Tennessee."

"A yellow dog would defeat *General* Grant in Tennessee."

"Then, I represent myself and a yellow dog," I said. Sheriff Pearce's smile had grown so broad that I wanted to smash it. "Let me ask again, if I could. Does Mr. Brown have anything to do with the Ku Klux Klan, or do you suppose he was operating on his own?"

"Better to ask him that."

"He and I had a conversation, but it wasn't exactly civil. I was under the impression that you were the sheriff of this county"—his smile vanished—"and I was hoping that you might know."

"I might at that," Sheriff Pearce said. His smile regenerated, like a flatworm. "But I wouldn't want to get into particulars, Mistuh Hay. Now, can I help you with anything else?"

"Do you know anything about Captain McElwee?"

"What about 'im?"

"He left Elizabethton—do you know where he went?"

"Is there some reason I should?"

Which didn't mean he didn't. "Or Captain Jenkins?"

"Him I know. A fine, upstanding fella, he is. From up in the hills heah. Did you know he was the first man in Carter county to volunteer? For the Union, I mean. He commanded a company of mountain men. A regular hero, they say."

"You sound skeptical."

"No, suh. Only that I cottoned t'other side. But that don't matter no more."

I didn't believe that. Neither did he.

A wire was waiting for me at the hotel desk. Was it a check and a note of encouragement from Whitelaw Reid? Ha! It came from Cleveland. I tore it open:

HELEN SICK. NO REASON TO WORRY. LOVE CLARA

Now I *was* worried. Why else would she wire me to say not to worry unless there was a reason to worry? Should I go back to Cleveland? And tell Whitelaw Reid what, exactly? That my big story hadn't come through? Nothing undignified in that. And home was where I should be. Reid was a bachelor, but he would understand. Would Clara understand if I stayed away? She told me not to worry, but she might be testing me to see if I would. Helen wouldn't care—of that I felt confident.

Dr. Cameron wasn't in. I went upstairs to wash up and tried to write a story about Johnson's family.

Early last Saturday morning, at his daughter's home here in Tennessee, the nation's 17th president passed into his eternal reward with his loving family at his bedside. But was the family truly loving?

I crumpled up the rough, lined paper and tried for the wicker waste can and missed. I started the story twice more and couldn't get it right. It sounded either simpering or nasty. The problem was the usual: I didn't know what I wanted to say. It was a family, all right, with its share (or more!) of tensions and distrust. That's what a family was. This was news? Was it anyone's business but theirs? Who gave a tinker's dam about Andy Johnson's last days? Unless, of course, they involved murder.

I considered a slug of rye but decided virtuously to take a walk instead. I was crossing through the lobby when the desk clerk called to me. "Another wire, sir—just came."

A moment of terror—Helen was worse. I grabbed for the envelope and ripped it open.

JOHNNY, BOTH OF US FINE. TRULY. PLENTY OF
HELP. CARRY ON. CLARA

If that wasn't love, what is?

CHAPTER EIGHT

At ten minutes before six, the sun wasn't awake, and neither was I. I was up and about, however, filching an apple from the hotel kitchen. The last person I expected to see was Dr. Cameron. But he was a doctor, wasn't he, and for reasons I have never understood, physicians start their days before dawn. (Is it because patients are too sleepy to fight back?) His sleek figure leaned against the sink, chugging milk from a quart bottle.

"Cain't say." Dr. Cameron was replying to my question about Captain McElwee's whereabouts. "Our guests are our guests—they go where they like. They don't need to tell us a thing. You, for instance."

So, he knew I was leaving. "Yes, shortly," I said.

"Are you going to tell me where you're going?"

"No reason why not. Washington City."

"A frightful place."

"You've been?"

"Heard tell. Rather a swamp, isn't it?"

"They've drained it some. The city has its charms."

"Every place does, I guess, if you look hard enough."

"Here, too?"

"In its way. Life goes slow in these parts, Mr. Hay. That way it seems to last longer, if that's what you're looking for. Are you?"

"I figure to take what comes—don't see much choice," I said. I wasn't sure if I meant it. "But I was under the impression that you and Captain McElwee were friends."

"That's Captain Jenkins," Dr. Cameron said. "He was here, too."

"Captain McElwee went with you, I understand, to Mr. Johnson's bedside. You didn't mention that to me."

"I suppose I didn't think to. No secret about it. He came with me more than once, as a matter of fact."

"Did he?" Captain McElwee had said otherwise. "When was the other time—or times?"

"I can't remember, precisely. Later in the week."

"But more than one additional time?"

"I'm sorry, Mr. Hay, I don't understand your interest in this. Why is this your business?"

I wasn't about to explain it.

⊹≕≔⊹

As a destination, I wouldn't recommend Carter's Depot at sunrise. Not that I would recommend anyplace at sunrise, but the railroad station was especially distressing. Voices ricocheted like the squeals of bats in a cave, and the benches still served the occasional patron as a tenement house. The floor, by its looks, hadn't been swept for a month.

Across the waiting room, the ticket counter looked lonely for attention, and I was happy to oblige. I found yesterday's newspaper crumpled on a bench. The Wyoming territory was ending its experiment with the use of women as jurors. A passenger leapt from a Pullman car in Pennsylvania and drowned in the Susquehanna. The Reverend Beecher's trial offered yet another day's delight in surrogate sin.

The train wheezed into the station from the west at seven thirty-three, twenty-one minutes late, and continued east approximately forty-three seconds later. I braved the coal smoke and scrambled aboard, in the third car back. It was empty but for a square-jawed, gray-haired banker (just a guess) and two elderly ladies in identical plaid jumpers who gossiped like schoolgirls. The train jerked ahead, and I tumbled back into my seat. The upholstery was thin and frayed. The passenger car was little more than a cage made of steel.

The roar of the train was disorienting. This was our devil's bargain in building the railroads—convenience and speed in exchange for smoke and noise, for corruption and bluster. I think it was Thoreau who observed: "We do not ride upon the railroad; it rides upon us." Outside my window, wooded hillsides throttled past, giving way to foothills and then to low, tired mountains covered in green. Purplish haze nestled in the hollows. Not so long ago, this had been the boundary between civilization and the untamed frontier. My granddaddy had crossed it, and Andrew Johnson had, too—the central event of his life.

All I wanted was sleep. My eyes drifted shut, but my mind wouldn't stop. I imagined a hooded figure slipping a vial from an inside pocket and pouring its contents into a glass of whisky. It seemed simple, really. Why wouldn't anyone want to try it? Why weren't there murders galore? Murder-*ers* galore? Maybe there were.

I opened my eyes and closed them again and tried to conjure up the hooded man, in hopes of a closer look—a mirage in my disordered mind. Might it be Captain McElwee, gone to a destination unknown? If Sheriff Pearce lifted a fat pinkie to find him, I would be shocked. Or William Brown, sitting athwart his horse, blocking my way? Or perhaps David Patterson—excuse me, Senator Patterson—who had absconded to Washington of late? I was at his heels, or (a more accurate cliché) eating his dust.

Maybe, maybe, maybe—my hooded figure remained incognito.

The railroad timetable said it took more than an hour from Elizabethton via Johnson City to Bristol, which straddled the border between Tennessee and Virginia. By the time we pulled in, I was feeling vaguely human, for no reason I could ascertain.

The gauge of the railroad tracks was wider in Virginia, so we had to change trains. The depot was a babble of conversation. Clumps of people gathered— families corralling children, laughing young men in straw boaters. I was watching a woman swat the rump of a boy of six or seven when I saw someone I knew, half-hidden by a pillar just beyond. I went over to say hello.

I wish I could report that Martha Patterson was enchanted to see me. I try to be pretty good company; I've been known to elicit a chortle now and again. (Granted, Lincoln was always ready to laugh.) But she looked as if she had seen a ghost—another cliché, I know, but an apt one. More precisely, it was she who looked drawn and pale, all because she had crossed paths with an acquaintance of dubious provenance in an unexpected venue. Even more precisely, it was the acquaintance who had crossed paths with *her*. It seemed obvious she did not want that acquaintance to know of her whereabouts—or, plausibly, of where she was going. Now I happened to know both.

"Mrs. Patterson, nice to see you," I said.

I was surprised again at how slight she was, out of kilter with her ramrod presence. Her high-necked gown and plumed bonnet were the color of an overcast sky. Her hat was made with what I could have sworn were butterflies and miniature pears. The features of her face were blunt and, like her father's, lacked any hint of humor. I reminded myself that she was in mourning. Although if I passed her at night in an alley, I would just as soon be armed.

"And you," Martha Patterson replied, deigning to turn my way.

"So, where are you heading?" In a railroad depot, this wasn't an intrusive query.

"Washington City," she sighed.

"Me, too," I said. "What takes you there?" Also a reasonable query, in a depot—wasn't it?

"To see old friends."

So soon after your bereavement—I refrained from saying. She deserved an escape. *Daddy's unfinished business.* "Is the senator with you?" I said.

This seemed to confuse her. "Oh, my husband," she said. "No, he went ahead."

"Ah," I replied, "on business?"

A pause. "Yes," she said.

"I used to live in Washington City," I said, "as I guess you did."

"Yes, for many years. While my daddy was in Congress, I boarded at school there. And again when he was president."

"You lived in the Mansion, did you not? So did I. We should compare bedrooms."

I meant this as a jest, but she turned icy again.

"Do you like Washington?" I tried.

"What's there to like?"

"A lot of things," I said lamely, mentally ruling out the humidity, the architecture, the inhabitants, the insects, the winter's mud, the summer's dust, the political corruption. "Being close to power, for one. And beautiful trees."

She was rescued from a reply when a porter began corralling the passengers toward the neighboring platform, where our Richmond-bound train awaited.

"May I?" I said, reaching for her alligator-skin suitcase, which was big enough to hold an alligator.

"No, thank you—he will." She summoned the porter.

"Which car are you riding in?" I said.

"I have a compartment reserved."

I took a seat in the nearest sleeping car—as if I would ever sleep. I stared out the window. The view was gorgeous. The train ran between mountain ridges—the Blue Ridge to the east, the Alleghenies to the west. Lost in nature, not a bad place to feel eclipsed. The wooded mountains sparkled in the sunlight.

In Roanoke, we stopped for ten minutes, time enough to buy a hambone and a beer—moonshine, more like it—from a negro hawker who scampered through the train. At Lynchburg, we turned eastward, descending into the broad plains of Virginia. I asked the porter which car had the compartments.

"Have what, suh?"

"The compartments, the ones that passengers reserve."

"No, suh. Don't have none on this train."

Aha! At times, I confess, I can be slow to learn my place, and even slower sometimes to accept it. I saw no reason, therefore, why I shouldn't wander from car to car, ostensibly to stretch my legs and—*quelle surprise*!—to encounter my dearest acquaintance.

My fortune was found in the very next car. The back of a woman's head bobbed above the fourth seat. Her braided hair, going to gray, was coiled at the nape of her neck. I strode up beside her.

"Mrs. Patterson," I said, "hello again." I decided that mentioning her phantom compartment wouldn't gain me a thing. "May I ask you a question or two?"

She glanced up at me with an ill-concealed look of contempt. "Can I stop you?" she said.

"You can certainly decline to answer."

"That strikes me as rather impolite." Martha attempted a smile but failed.

"You were raised well"—I eased into the empty seat across the aisle—"if I may say so."

She gave no indication whether I could or couldn't.

"Please tell me about your father as a father," I said.

"He was a wonderful father," she said quickly.

I waited for her to elaborate. When she didn't, I said, "In what ways?"

"In every way."

"I am glad to hear that. You are a lucky daughter." I considered telling her about Helen but decided it would arouse no empathy. "Any particular—?"

"You said one or two questions, Mr. Hay. I shall be generous and count all of your questions thus far as one. Which allows you one more."

"I was perhaps too restrained in my request," I said.

"Perhaps you were, Mr. Hay, but a more ambitious request might not have been granted." If looks could kill, I wouldn't be recounting this now. "I respect you as a gentleman and as a man of your word."

I was prepared to vouch only for the latter. "I appreciate your willingness. I know this isn't an easy time for you."

She turned and looked me in the eye at last. Some of the hardness was gone. Maybe she forgot for a moment that she despised me. "It isn't," she said.

"Let me ask you this, then: Did you get a chance to talk with your father, at the end, after you got to your sister's house?"

"Not enough," she replied.

So, she had. "What did you—?"

"That's two, Mr. Hay."

"I was thinking it was one and a half."

Was that a smile I glimpsed?

"Very well, one half more."

"What did you and your father talk about?" I said.

"Happier times," she said.

This meant Martha—and her husband—had arrived in the nick of time to slip belladonna into . . . whatever treat they had brought.

I considered asking for an anecdote or two, but I didn't want to use up her patience on a story I didn't intend to write. I had a better idea.

"You have been very kind," I said. "If I could trouble you for a third question, it would be this: Of all the people who disliked your father, who would you say . . . disliked him the most?"

"Hated, you mean."

"Yes."

She thought for a spell, then smiled slightly, set her jaw, and returned to her book. *The Mysterious Island* was Jules Verne's latest. The nation's capital was a mysterious island of its own.

⊹⊱══⊰⊹

At the Richmond depot, Martha Patterson fled into the ladies' waiting room, beyond the reach of conversation, while I found Western Union. A telegram was waiting for me, as I knew it would. John George Nicolay was nothing if not reliable. I had wired him from Elizabethton, inquiring about a spare bed.

ARRIVE ANYTIME. DOOR UNLOCKED. NICOLAY

Anything less would have amazed me.

I didn't lay eyes on Martha Patterson again before I boarded the train to Washington or after I got on, although I meandered down the aisle of all three passenger cars. They were almost empty. She must have locked herself into a WC—I pictured the desperate ladies pounding on the door. I could see her point of view. In her life, I didn't count as an advantage. But she could, as she had said, decline to answer questions. In fact, she already had. Then what was she scared of? What did she know that she didn't want known? Plenty.

And what was she doing in Washington City, anyway? What were *they* doing, so soon after their bereavement? Finishing up her daddy's business. What in satanic majesty was that? *That's* what I wanted to know.

I can't tell you a thing about the next three hours, except that the seat was unforgiving and I would have traded my favorite Irish setter for a swig of laudanum. No wonder Captain McElwee traveled with a flask. I couldn't stay awake and I wasn't able to sleep. Reading was beyond possibility.

It felt like forever before the train rattled across the Potomac river. (What an improvement over the ferry from Alexandria!) Even at this late hour, the river swarmed with boats of all sizes and descriptions. The crescent of moonlight shimmered on the water and lit up what lay beyond. Low buildings clung to the opposite shoreline—the navy yard, the arsenal, and the penitentiary, as I knew from my years here. On the higher ground beyond, along the gentle undulations, twinkles of light marked clusters of homes. The splendor of the night was to my right—the parabola of the Capitol dome, floating above the darkness and lit from within. I swallowed hard.

Long minutes of grinding and wheezing brought the train to a halt. A final snort and, suddenly, the noise ceased. The silence was jarring. I sat for a moment before I believed we had arrived. I unbent from my seat and lowered my valise from above me.

The depot was quiet. I saw no sign of Martha Patterson. I considered waiting for her to emerge but decided that stalking her wouldn't improve my standing.

The railroad depot at Sixth and B streets, on the northern edge of the National Mall, wasn't too far from Nicolay's house, just southeast of the Capitol. But I didn't relish the walk. It was awfully late and the neighborhood wasn't the safest.

I ventured outside, into the heat, and heard: "Johnny!"

The voice, I knew right away. A buggy was at the curb. Inside was Nicolay.

CHAPTER NINE

No, Johnny, I wouldn't call you a simpleton," Nicolay said. "Not for this, anyway."

That was as much of a compliment as I could expect from my oldest and dearest friend. I dispensed with the sarcastic thank-you and slid another oatmeal ball onto my plate. "I don't want to be right," I said.

"That's a first."

"But I'm afraid that I am, Nico."

"Also a first."

"That he really *was* murdered, and that his beloved son-in-law—one of his two unlovable sons-in-law—might, might, might have had something to . . ."

"As I say, I'm willing to believe it. Even if one of them hadn't beaten you up."

"No, Nico, quite the—"

"Who beat you up?" Nicolay's daughter had skipped into the kitchen.

"Nobody beat me up." I raised my right fist to my temple. "I beat . . . Never mind. Helen, your daddy is being mean to me again."

"Father, don't be mean to Uncle Johnny," Helen said.

I said, "He enjoys it."

This earned a rare laugh from Nicolay. Ordinarily, his visage captured his way of conducting himself, which was silent and methodical, Teutonic to the core. His long, gaunt face stretched from his vast forehead to his Vandyke beard. His dark, deep-set eyes had a hypnotic quality, and his quiet way of speaking commanded attention. Nicolay had drawn me into Lincoln's improbable presidential campaign—1860 seemed a million years ago—and we had shared a bedroom in the Executive Mansion, where I was his assistant. After the Ancient was murdered at Ford's, Nicolay escaped to Paris as a dip-

lomat. He eventually came home to edit a newspaper in Chicago before returning to Washington for a sinecure (my teasing description) as the marshal
of the Supreme Court. That put him in charge of the court's logistics and
security—nothing too daunting, suited to his strengths. Most folks thought
him brusque, but to the few people he cared about, he was unfailingly loyal
and kind, one of those fellows who ought to live forever, to help sweeten a
brackish world. I am not embarrassed to say that I loved him like an older
brother.

"You know, I have my own Helen now," I said to the girl who was cut-
ting into a cruller. "She is almost as pretty as you are. She will be five
months old next week. How old are you now? Let me guess." I appraised
her sweet, round face and her flouncy hair, parted in the center, which she
hadn't bothered to comb for company. I admired that, and also that her
parents hadn't forced her. Her milky brown eyes did not shy away from
mine. "I'd say . . . nine."

"Almost nine and a half," she declared.

"Yes, I can see that now," I said.

"Did you get beat up?" she persisted.

"No," I said. "Somebody tried, and I didn't let him." Telling her about
the gunshot would be bragging.

"Did you hit him?"

I admitted I had.

"In the face?"

"Helen!" Therena Nicolay exclaimed. With this new mouth to feed, she
had returned to the cast-iron stove.

"Yes," I replied.

"Did it hurt him?"

I wanted to say, *I hope so,* but settled for, "Not for long."

"Long enough?"

I had to laugh. My kind of girl. "Yes, almost," I said.

"Then what is my father willing to believe?"

Was there nothing these children missed? "Why don't you ask him?" I
said. "Nico? What do you believe? Tell us all of it, stem to stern."

"Easy enough," Nicolay said. "I don't believe anything—never did."

"Father, now you're being mean to me," Helen said. "I heard you."

"You're right, dear," Nicolay replied, trying not to smile, but falling
short. "What I believe is that President Johnson's death—I told you about
that, right?—was . . ." He couldn't finish.

I helped out: "It was not a natural event. Somebody made it happen, and we don't know who. Or why."

The look on the girl's face wasn't one of fear but of excitement. What child doesn't love a mystery? To a child, all the world was a mystery. To a grown man, too.

"Can I tell my friends?" she said.

"Absolutely not," Nicolay said. His face had resumed its customary sternness. "Do you understand?"

"Of course, Father." Helen's eyes twinkled with mischief, but I had no doubt she would obey.

It was Nicolay's idea, and a smart one. No one knew more about the goings-on in Washington day to day—the secrets, the intimacies, the disrespects—than E. V. Smalley. Better yet, he would tell me whatever he could. We were laboring for the same newspaper, he as the *Tribune*'s veteran Washington correspondent.

I flagged down a hack in front of the Capitol, which gleamed in the morning sun. At ten minutes past nine, Washington City was already sweltering. Pennsylvania avenue was thick with traffic. Buggies and horse-drawn carts and a coal delivery wagon and men on mounts vied for pride of place, as streetcars rolled along the center of the roadway. And that roadway! Smoother than I remembered, paved with wooden blocks in lieu of dirt (or mud), softening the clip-clop of horses' hoofs—except in the many, many places the wood was already rotting away, putting hoofs and carriage wheels in danger. It was everything an avenue should not be—too wide for the buildings to be noticed, a wasteland interrupted by cottonwood trees. The brick sidewalks were busy with pedestrians strolling more civilly than in New York. The pawnshops and purveyors of secondhand clothes hadn't opened their doors yet, but surely it wasn't too early for the vendors at Center Market to hawk rhubarb and wild turkeys, for the boardinghouses to put transients back on the streets, for the patent attorneys to start fleecing their clients, for the restaurants and, yes, the saloons to deliver their pleasures. "Mean, and cheap, and dingy"—that's how Clemens had once described the Avenue's purveyors of goods and beds. No Champs-Élysées, this.

The hack turned right, onto Fourteenth street. Even Willard's Hotel, my old haunt at the corner, was looking a little shabby—some gilding wouldn't hurt. The block from the Avenue north to F street was known as Newspaper

Row. On my right, a few scribes were fanning themselves on chairs along
the sidewalk, beneath the overhanging elms. Behind them, the frame buildings varied in height, like rotting teeth. The *Tribune* shared one of the
scruffier buildings with *The New York World*.

Eugene Virgil Smalley's sanctum was on the second floor. His office
was utilitarian, featuring a simple desk, a modest bookcase crammed with
books, and two hard-backed chairs. An American flag behind his desk
curled around the pole. I heard none of these newfangled typewriters; the
inkwell and the pad would suffice. The only flourish was an ivory-handled
saber on the wall behind the desk.

I pointed to it and said, "Is that new?"

"No, old. Mexican War, I think. Almost as old as I am. But not nearly
as old as you, Hay. How the devil are you? What brings you here, to our
majestic quarters?"

He waved his arm and tried to stand.

"Don't get up," I said.

"As if I could." Smalley regarded his bulk as a prank from Above.
"Mighty fine to see you, Hay."

With his lush whiskers and a hairline that recalled a beached whale,
Smalley resembled the politicians he covered. He looked startlingly like
James Garfield, the congressman from Ohio who long ago had competed
with me for Kate Chase's attentions (with an equal lack of success) and
later was tarnished by the Credit Mobilier scandal. Smalley's face was ami-
able enough, although the whiskers concealed his mouth; his eyes watched
every move I made.

We gossiped a few minutes about *Tribune* politics. The battle for control
following Horace Greeley's sudden and mysterious death had left Whitelaw
Reid in charge, to my delight but not to everyone's. I wasn't sure where Smalley
stood, nor frankly did I care. The *Tribune* was becoming part of my past.

"Was just talking about you yesterday, Hay," Smalley said. His high-
pitched singsong belied his size and reminded me, incongruously, of a
wood thrush.

"Favorably, I hope."

"For the most part."

I laughed. "As for the rest?"

"The question arose regarding your employment for Mr. Amasa Stone,
about whether you were selling your soul or not."

So, my new position was known throughout the *Tribune*. "And the verdict?"

"My interlocutor"—Smalley pronounced it in seven or eight syllables—"and I disagreed on that very point."

"And your position, may I inquire?"

"Not a word, dear Hay, shall pass my lips." He sat with an indecipherable smile.

"Then tell me, am I selling my soul dear enough?"

"I should think your soul would bring a pretty penny, Hay."

"A matter of supply and demand, I'm afraid."

Smalley complimented me on my reportage of ol' Andy's funeral. I thanked him and said, "That's why I'm here."

I explained what I knew and what I suspected and, in confidence, offered my deduction: Andrew Johnson had been poisoned by belladonna, once if not twice. It was a conclusion that his widow as well as his servant endorsed. The list of people who wanted him dead was ludicrously long, counting his political enemies and possibly his closest kin. I was about to describe the shorter list of people, those who had had an opportunity, when Smalley leaned across his desk and whispered, "Let me add to your list, then."

"Please do."

"And possibly provide a motive."

"Really?" This sounded better than I could have hoped.

"Did you happen to stop in at the tailor shop?"

"Yes, with one of my leading suspects."

"Did you notice a trunk at one end?"

"Ye-es."

"Let me tell you what was inside it, or so he told me himself."

Smalley recounted a visit he had paid to Greeneville after Johnson had hobbled home in disgrace. "It was rather an odd visit from the start. The front door of his house stood wide open, and getting no answer to my knock I entered the hall and walked through it to a rear door, which opened onto a big vegetable garden."

"I was just on that back porch," I said.

"There I saw the president, *ex*-president, with his coat off, hoeing his corn and potatoes. He dropped his hoe as I approached and gave me a polite welcome. We went to the front parlor and talked politics, and then he took me up the street and showed me his beloved old tailor shop. As he unlocked the door, he told me he had never allowed the building to be demolished, because he felt attached to it. I found its one room filled with boxes and trunks containing letters and documents. In that trunk, or so he told me"—Smalley stopped glancing around the room, so that his eyes bored into mine—"he had letters that would ruin the reputations of many of the leading Republicans in Congress. He said he meant to print them someday. I suspected he meant to use them in some sordid fashion. I suppose time cooled his wrath and he thought better of it, because I'm not aware that he ever followed through."

Smalley waited to let this sink in. It took me a moment before I blurted, "Blackmail! That's what he meant, correct?"

"That was my general understanding," Smalley said.

"Did you see the letters?"

"No. But I believed him. Andy Johnson usually told the truth, as much as any politician does."

Blackmail letters! "Any idea who they . . . whose reputations would be ruined?"

"No."

"Were they in envelopes, do you know?"

"Couldn't say. Didn't see them." Smalley reflected on my inquiry. "Why do you ask?"

"*I* might have seen them." I told him about the envelopes on the table in the parlor at Johnson's homestead, where the Pattersons had been arguing over . . . something. "That's why I came to Washington. I followed them here."

"I heard he was here. Didn't know about her."

"He came first. She arrived late last night, on the same train I was on."

"Any idea why?" Smalley said.

"To see old friends, she says. To finish Daddy's unfinished business—that's what her sister says. Now I can guess what that business is."

"That would explain it," Smalley said.

"Explain what?"

"My spies tell me that senators have been sneaking into town in the past day or two."

"So?"

"Congress hasn't been in session since March, and God knows when it will harm us again. And it's August, for pity's sake. Nobody in their right mind comes to this Hades in August, not if they don't have to."

"Have your spies asked them why they're here?"

"No," Smalley said, "I'll let you do that."

Suppose those letters still existed—I had no reason to believe they didn't. Who would throw them away? And suppose the Pattersons had, by fair means or foul, come to possess them. I had heard them arguing over letters. Suppose those really were the envelopes I had glimpsed on the marble-topped table in Andy Johnson's parlor. And just suppose, for the sake of argument, that the senators whom Smalley's spies had seen in the city were . . . Republicans with reputations susceptible to ruin. In this day and age, rife with scandal and the temptations of unearned wealth, that could mean any or all of them.

Smalley's copy of the *Congressional Directory* had divulged where the senators lived.

I walked north along Fourteenth street, a hodgepodge of stooped store-fronts and ambitious edifices. The Foundry Methodist Church, at G street, was a modest brick structure, trim yet self-assured, that plausibly housed a back channel to God. What impressed me most was what I had expected to see but didn't—hogs in the gutter, geese on the prowl, the earthly remains of weak-willed mutts, the garbage rotting at the curb. I couldn't say that the city smelled of lavender and roses, but it no longer reeked of night soil or fish bones. Almost every street boasted a green canopy from maples, lindens, or elms. Since I had spent the war years here, the sprawl of villages had grown into a city of sorts.

At I street, I turned left and found myself in the handsomest neighborhood I had seen since Euclid avenue. Smalley had filled me in about the notables who lived along here. To the left was the secretary of state's three-story mansion; to the right, the chief justice's residence and the banker George Washington Riggs's palace. The opulent Arlington House sat next to the late Charles Sumner's four-story manse. Then came a stretch of ad-joined town houses, decorated with turrets and mansard windows, most of them made from a cheerful red brick that preened with understatement.

Only a smattering of senators, by Smalley's account, were rich enough to keep homes in the capital, given how rarely Congress managed to rouse it-self into session; their dollar-pinching colleagues preferred boardinghouses or hotels. If you were a blackmailer, wouldn't you ply your wares where the money was?

Frederick Frelinghuysen, the stick-up-his-arse Republican from New Jersey, lived at 1731 I street, past Seventeenth. The four-story town house was painted the gray of a shark's snout and featured bow walls and an intri-cate brick design. The porch was small and curved. I lifted the curled door knocker and let it drop. The arched yellow door opened.

"Frelinghuysen residence!" The butler, of perfect carriage, could have gone on stage in the role.

"Is the senator in?" I said.

"Whom shall I say is calling, sir?"

I gave my name and offered my calling card—my old one, from the *Tribune*. No deception; I was still on the job.

"Is he expecting you?"

"It is unlikely." In the extreme.

"The subject, sir?"

"The death of Andrew Johnson." A mention of *murder* or *extortion* would find any politician indisposed.

The butler left me on the stoop, having closed the door—and bolted it, best I could hear. A minute and a half later, it opened again.

"The senatuh is otherwise engaged," the butler said. I cursed to myself. "But if you would care to wait in the parlor."

I would, indeed.

The butler ushered me along the marble corridor to the first door on the left. In my years of poking through people's lives, I had made a sport (I hesitate to say *science*) of examining front parlors. *Front* was the right word, for that's what it was for, the façade its occupants wished to show to the world. This parlor was elegant. The drapes were drawn, to keep out the heat. The valances, burgundy satin braided in gold, might have brightened a queen's boudoir. The chairs were French, upholstered in red velvet and with a courtesan's curves. The paintings matched the parlor's colors. The translucent marble mantel would have devoured a newspaperman's pay for a year; the gold-edged mirror above it, a second year; the carved mahogany molding over the floor-to-ceiling bookcases, a third. The bookcases were filled with the complete works of Shakespeare and Tennyson, a volume of Washington Irving, Parson Weems's hagiography of George Washington, a biography of Lafayette, a history of New Jersey, two Bibles, and a hymnal. A respectable number of the books looked read, although I doubted that the upright piano had been played since Chopin left this earth.

I was still inspecting the senator's pretensions when I got caught. I hadn't heard anyone enter the parlor, but a polite cough turned me around.

"Mr. Senator," I exclaimed.

"You are a literary man, I see."

"I aspire to be."

"Don't we all."

Frelinghuysen was an odd-looking fellow, from a famous old family (his

adoptive father and his grandfather had preceded him as New Jersey senators) that I suspected had done too much inbreeding. He reminded me of
a bird—a heron, perhaps. He had a beak of a nose and slate-gray eyes that
seemed to stare in divergent directions. His face was long and thin, from
his pompadour to his clean-shaven chin. His shirt had ruffles at the cuffs
and collar. I introduced myself and asked if he had a moment to spare.

"I can always spare a moment for a gentleman of the press," he said.
Especially the New York press, I figured, which had readers in New Jersey.
He might regret it once he learned of my mission.

"I am interested in Andrew Johnson," I said.

"I am not."

"I take it you weren't an admirer."

"Nor do I speak ill of the dead, young man."

"Even when you want to."

"Especially then."

"A fine rule," I said, by which I meant: *Fine in theory.* "And I would
never ask you to." *Unless I could persuade you otherwise.* "I am looking for
information and insight, not a diatribe. If you would speak candidly, I can
assure you that your name need not be mentioned."

"Anywhere?"

"Nowhere in print."

He gestured me into a brothel-like chair and took one of his own.

"How did you feel about Mr. Johnson's return to the Senate?" I said.
"You voted to convict him at his impeachment trial, I believe."

"Every state has a right to choose whomever they wish to represent its
citizens. The only requirements, according to our blessed Constitution, is
that he has reached thirty years of age, has been an American citizen for
at least nine years, and is an inhabitant of the state that elected him. On
every count, Mr. Johnson qualified. What he did while he was president is
old history."

"No history is old history," I said.

Frelinghuysen chuckled. "You are a wise young man," he said. "But I
have no regrets. In my considered judgment, President Johnson was guilty
of impeachable offenses. And I must say I am flattered by your attention
here. But I can't say I understand what you want from me other than to
throw brickbats at a man who is fresh in his grave."

I couldn't disagree, so I didn't. "Let me ask you, then, about more recent
history. I understand that Mr. Johnson addressed the Senate, during the
special session in March, on a matter that was dear to your heart." Smalley

had told me about Johnson's tirade against Frelinghuysen's resolution that endorsed President Grant's dispatch of federal troops to Louisiana to prop up the state's corrupt carpetbag (that is, Republican) government.

"Your newspaper will never mention my name?"

When I nodded, it was as if a veil slipped from the senator's face. His eyes came ablaze in fury. "Do you know what that man did to me, that harangue he delivered?" His voice sank an octave, into a growl. This must be Frelinghuysen's true voice, after his constituents had left his presence. "Have you had occasion to read his remarks, Mr. Hay?"

"I haven't. I shall."

"By all means, do. I assure you, Mr. Johnson used the situation in Louisiana as an opportunity to launch a philippic"—Frelinghuysen actually used the word—"against President Grant, not only for his enlightened policy on Reconstruction but for every other sin you could imagine. All of it intended to sabotage my resolution, and for no other reason than his own ill will toward the president. The galleries were mobbed with Senator Johnson's supporters, the president's detractors, and they gave vent to a rambunctious demonstration. A most unseemly display."

"I can understand your displeasure," I said.

"He was the meanest man I've ever known, and the world is better off without him." I had found the venom beneath Frelinghuysen's patrician polish. "And not a word of this shall ever appear in print, do you understand?"

"Understood."

"And I have never been so—"

How to turn off this spigot? "Let me ask you this," I said, "if I could. What brings *you* to Washington in the middle of a hot summer?" This pleasantry was actually the reason for my visit.

Frelinghuysen popped out of his seat and crossed to a table of knickknacks and shifted a vaguely Asian statuette. He turned back to me and said, "Six children. I needed some quiet."

"I have a little one, and I can only imagine what you mean," I said. Then, casually: "Tell me, have you seen the Pattersons while you've been here?"

This was *my* brickbat—and it hit, by the look of fright in his eyes. "No," he muttered.

So, he knew who the Pattersons were. And whatever it was they wanted, it seemed to rile him.

"Do you expect to see them?" I said.

No reply.

"Was there any mention of a letter?"

Senator Frelinghuysen stiffened. "By what authority do you ask me this?" he said.

He hadn't asked about the sort of letter I meant. "By the authority of the First Amendment," I replied glibly. Since when did a journalist need authority? "Freedom of the press."

Frelinghuysen looked down his nose and said, "I see. And does freedom of the press decree that anyone to whom you pose a question has a constitutional obligation to answer it?"

This point of law kept coming up. "I would admit that that's an expansive view of my constitutional . . . privilege," I said. I *was* a lawyer, despite my protestations. "But I would still like to know."

"I can't imagine why," he said. He made a show of pulling his watch from his waistcoat. "And now, Mr. Hay, if you will excuse me. I have an appointment."

By my own watch, it was nineteen minutes past eleven, which struck me as either too early or too late for another engagement to begin. But I could hardly continue to interview a man who had fled the room.

⊢━━⊣

I started to perspire the instant I ventured back onto the street. I couldn't hail a hack until Farragut Square, and by then I felt like a bucket of slop. I gave the mop-haired coachman Nicolay's address, at 230 First street, in the city's southeastern quadrant.

A truck stacked with hay bales rumbled past, and I had to repeat the address twice. The driver must be deaf. His nag probably was, too. I pointed toward Capitol Hill and hoped for the best. I knew the city well enough to avert disaster.

Barely. As we crossed Fourteenth street, I saw it coming from the corner of my right eye, which has failed to notice many a left hook. A pair of horses, spittle flying, careened in harness, dragging a buggy, all splintered, a wheel gone. It was empty, its passengers . . . somewhere on the roadway. Only by the grace of whichever god controlled the flow of traffic did my driver halt our rig an instant before the runaways bolted past.

My heart was thumping as we kept on our way. The driver was nonchalant, as if nothing of consequence had happened. In his world of silence, maybe it hadn't.

Nearing Twelfth street, I shouted, "That way!" I tapped him on the shoulder and pointed south and shouted again. The rig turned sharply and wobbled from the speed.

The air smelled like coal over the asphalt. Twelfth street was lined with two- and three-story row houses that had seen better days, interspersed with a repair shop, a run-down hotel, a grocery stand, a wood and coal yard. The "New Washington," as its evangelists called it, had not entirely paved over the old.

On the left, as we neared the Avenue, stood the stolid five-story bulk of the Kirkwood House. It was why I had asked for this route. I was surprised when Smalley told me where David Patterson was staying. I thought the hotel had already been torn down. I knew just one thing about it—well, two, counting its location, on the northeastern corner of Twelfth and Penn. The other was that Andrew Johnson had lived there during his vice presidency. It's where he was, at the Kirkwood House, the night Lincoln was shot, and it was where Johnson would have been murdered as well, had his would-be assassin not gotten soused and turned yellow. Even then it hadn't ranked among the city's finer hostelries. But it was a place without pretension, and one that a man of the people could afford.

Why would the Pattersons want to stay there, beyond reasons of sentiment? I considered alighting from the carriage and asking them point-blank. I stifled the temptation. I didn't know enough yet. Suppose I asked the Pattersons if they happened to be blackmailing some of the leading Republicans in Congress, and they laughed at me, or worse. What on earth would I say next?

+══════+

"I don't *know* anything," I said.

"That's refreshing to hear," Nicolay replied. He was carving the venison, which Therena had bought at Center Market that afternoon. The deer might have been nuzzling its fawn the day before.

Helen giggled. Smart girl, but sassy. I hoped my Helen would be the same. So far, my Helen was mostly a bowel-challenged blob of . . . I hadn't a clue, really, about who she was and what she would become. How could anyone know before she emerged? And then, it will probably have seemed inevitable.

"But I do suspect a lot," I said, "and I think I have evidence for some of it. Negative evidence, but to me that's evidence. I got invited to leave an enchanting house on I street—the fanciest furnishings, Nico. Not exactly my taste, but . . ." I forbore mentioning a brothel because of Helen's presence—and Therena's, too. "My sin was mentioning the dread word: Patterson."

"Who is he?" Helen said, sipping her ice-cold tea.

"A man who I suspect is up to no good," I replied. I figured she was old enough to discover that there was evil—even Evil—in the world. This was the city to learn in.

Therena said, "You are only doing your job."

"Bless you," I said. "Which job is that?"

"A man of many talents," Therena said. I preferred to think she was too middle western to dare sarcasm, but I couldn't be sure I was right.

"Well, thank you," I replied.

Therena had a round face, a blunt nose, wide and honest cheeks, and a bloat of black hair with slivers of gray that signaled her indifference to fashion. Her dark eyes had a twinkle, and a smile always lurked at the corners of her full lips. This evening she was wearing a brown-and-white striped dress with a bow and a white doily collar. She wasn't beautiful, unless you looked harder. Therena Nicolay seemed middle-of-the-continent to the core, a mismatch for the small deceptions of the East. (That described Clara, too.) I had grown used to those deceptions myself, and Nico had learned to work around them, to the extent that they thrived at the court. Could Therena forever remain an innocent? She had lived in the nation's capital long enough—and in Paris—that I had reason to hope that she might. Either that, or she had learned to hide her complexities even from me.

"Did Frelinghuysen tell you anything useful?" Nicolay said, passing the platter of overcooked game. The bowls of beans and yams and the tray of corn muffins had already made their rounds.

"What a funny name," Helen said.

I pronounced it twice more, and she repeated it back, and we worked through the spelling. "It's Dutch, I'm pretty sure," I said. "It almost has to be."

To Nicolay, I replied, "Not really. He showed some . . . hostility, shall we say, toward the late Mr. Johnson—who doesn't?—but I salute his candor. He didn't admit to knowing anything about any letter of . . ."—I hesitated in front of Helen—"of any sort. But he knew what I was talking about, and he didn't like it. And he apparently knew who David Patterson was. He didn't ask."

"They must have served together in the Senate."

"I can check, but his knowledge seemed recent. And I'm quite sure I hadn't mentioned Patterson's first name or that he was a senator. That was the moment in the conversation when our dear Frelinghuysen suddenly remembered a previous engagement."

"Who else did Smalley say is in town?" Nicolay said.

"Roscoe Conkling."

Silence. Even young Helen knew to be reverent. The senator from New York was the most powerful man in Congress, and possibly in Washington City.

"The biggest toad in the puddle," Therena said. "Why is he here?"

"Apparently it's my job to find out."

"You going to see him?" Nicolay said.

"Not to-day. One senator a day—that's my limit. Besides, why would he talk to me? What's in it for him?"

Not a word eluded Helen.

"Here's a way," Nicolay said. "You said that Frelinghuysen wanted to know on what authority you ask your questions. Why don't you obtain some authority?"

"Excuse me," I said, chewing. The venison was dry. "There is a higher authority than the First Amendment? The *New-York Tribune*?"

Nicolay turned to his daughter and said, "You may not have learned this yet in school, Helen, but who is the highest authority in our land?"

"You are, Father." *She* was capable of sarcasm.

Nicolay laughed. "Even higher, my dear," he said.

I blurted the answer. "Grant!"

Nicolay said, "Why not? You did this with Willie Lincoln, and the president gave you a letter of some sort, authorizing you to do . . . whatever you were already doing."

"Nobody actually read the blamed thing—oh, sorry, Helen. It could've been a butcher's list, for all anyone checked."

"Didn't matter," Nicolay said. "You had it, and they knew it."

"You're saying nobody called my bluff. But President Grant, he's the last . . . I mean, they hated each other. He's probably glad that Johnson is dead. Why would he want to help me investigate?"

"Because he's the president," Nicolay said. "Presidents stick together. They see themselves in each other. No president wants to see one of his predecessors"—a glance at Helen—"harmed. Bad for business. Maybe Grant would give you a letter of some sort. It couldn't hurt to ask him. It doesn't really matter what it says, as long as you can flash it around. Remember, Roscoe Conkling is Grant's man in the Senate, and the Senate is running the world." In the recent congressional elections, the Democrats had easily

captured the House, for the first time since before the war, as the elector-
ate's verdict on Republicans for the economic havoc, but the Senate had
remained firmly in Republican hands. "A letter would certainly help you
with him," Nicolay said.

"And with the rest of those blackguards," Therena jumped in.

I admired anyone who saw the world as it was.

CHAPTER TEN

SUNDAY, AUGUST 8, 1875

I opened my eyes and it took me a moment to remember where in the blazes I was. Nicolay's spare bedroom. In Washington City. I didn't like being a vagabond. I liked being home, wherever home happened to be. All right, Cleveland. It could be worse. A booming city. In many respects, charming. Clara was there. Helen was there. True, Amasa was there. But now home was there, and I was here. I wondered how Helen was faring. Was Clara missing me, like I was missing her? I guess I had grown used to not sleeping alone.

It took me longer to remember where I was going. To church, of all places. At nine o'clock sharp.

I made it down to breakfast by seven oh two. The dining room was empty. I tried the kitchen. Therena was managing the stove.

"Johnny!" she called. "Early as always."

"Only in error," I said.

Over blueberry flapjacks, we traded the day's gossip—namely, the red fox she had spied behind the house at dawn, Helen's stomach upset, described too vividly (did I really want to be a parent? too late), my gambling losses from last night's excursion with Smalley to the congressional faro bank.

"How much?" This from Nicolay, striding in.

I told him.

"A week's groceries," Therena said.

"I'll win it back to-night," I said. She slapped three pancakes on a plate and shoved it under my nose. "A bad joke," I added.

"What are your plans for the day?" Nicolay said.

"I'm going to church," I announced.

"Isn't that lovely!" Therena said. "There's a very nice Presbyterian church here on the Hill, over on—"

I said, "This one's at Four-and-a-half street and C. It's Methodist *and* Episcopal, so I can hedge a couple of bets."

"Isn't that President Grant's church?" Therena said.

"That's why I'm going," I said. "Smalley told me."

"You want to . . . prowl after him, you mean?" Nicolay said.

"That's not the word I would use."

"What is, then?"

"To *see* him. Maybe be seen by him. And maybe—who knows?—get a word or two in. Conning a letter from him was your idea, Nico."

"I said nothing about conning. I meant that you should go to the Mansion and make an appoint—"

"Go through the proper channels in the regular way. I definitely could, Nico, and it would take me a month of Sundays. I would rather do what works."

"That's one approach," Nicolay said. "So, tell me, Johnny, how *did* you wind up as a lawyer, trained in procedures and rules?"

"I had nothing better to do, dear Nico, until you came around. It was a wrong path, however, that I've since made right."

"Two or three times," Nicolay pointed out.

"Granted. But no newspaperman worth the ink—you know this, Nico, from your own experience—not a one of them bothers with the rules."

The Metropolitan Methodist Episcopal Church was a graceful Gothic edifice with a slender spire. It stood a block north of the Avenue, down the street from a livery stable and a bakery. The neighborhood had seen better days. The elms were haggard, and the row houses looked worn—they *were* worn—although, by the miracle of brick, still standing. A nag was dragging itself and its cart full of cucumbers along C street, encouraged by a tormentor's whip. Was nothing holy in this Age of Commerce? Such had the Sabbath become.

The church interior was a comfort despite the stone walls. Sunlight streamed into the church and separated into rays—otherworldly, in its way. The stained-glass windows showed Adam and Eve in decorous garments and Jesus with the sun at his head. Nothing to cause a doubter discomfort.

The worshippers were monochromatic—white faces, gray hair, black Sunday dress. I scanned the congregation and found President Grant in a third-row pew, sitting alongside Julia and their three children, blending in. His head was bent. I couldn't tell from the back if he was praying or bored—plausibly the former. Grant was an observant Methodist, and if it meant I could be as calm and as imperturbable as he was, I would jump at becoming a God-fearing man myself.

I took a seat in the last pew, next to a woman holding a baby who resembled my Helen, with a swirl of dark hair and a turned-up nose and a gaze that locked on mine. At the pulpit, the pastor was rollicking, mid-sermon. "And as Saul journeyed, he came near Damascus and suddenly there shined 'round about him a light from heaven. And he fell to the earth . . ." When it came to thunder and bluster, the Reverend John P. Newman gave his all. He was a round-faced, double-chinned fellow with shoulder-length hair and a booming voice that reached the back row. His spittle flew and strands of dark hair clung to his forehead. "And the Lord saith unto him, 'Arise, and go into the city and it shall be told thee what thou must do . . .'" Even the baby kept still.

Once the last prayer was dispatched and the final hymn warbled, the president shuffled back along the center aisle, his family trailing behind. I tried to catch his eye as he passed by, but he glanced neither right nor left. This was his nature and also a useful skill for any president, to ward off well-wishers' advice. He had been the same as a general—whether from obliviousness, shyness, or a focus on matters known only to him, I never could tell. Probably all of these—the usual answer.

I caught up with him outside, as his brood was squeezing into the presidential carriage.

"Mr. President," I called. I added, in case he had forgotten: "John Hay, here."

Grant glanced back and saw me and smiled a smidgen—*smiled*, the hero of Vicksburg, a man who rarely smiled at all. I felt a boyish pleasure. I had been with Lincoln at the War Department's telegraph office the night in 'sixty-two that Grant had wired about the capture of Fort Donelson, in Tennessee—Tennessee! It was the Union's first important victory of the war. Lincoln had marveled at a general whom neither of us had met. Now *he* was the president.

"I remember you, Mr. Hay," Grant said, climbing up next to the driver. His voice was musical. "A pleasant surprise."

"Thank you, sir. Good to see you."

"Do you worship here?"

"To-day I did." Hoping that honesty had its charms, I said, "I was hoping to cross paths with you."

"And so you have."

"May I speak with you sometime?"

"Of course. Come for supper, at five."

I stepped toward the curb. "I have a favor to ask"—more honesty, in a hard whisper—"regarding your predecessor's death."

Grant turned back and gave me an appraising look. "After supper, then. At six. No, make it seven."

⊢══⊣

"Not a bodyguard in sight," I reported. "Nor did he shout for the police. He actually seemed pleased to see me."

"He was coming from church, Johnny," Nicolay said. "He could hardly be rude."

We were sitting in Nicolay's backyard, abloom with daisies. The sun was hot—and welcome. After church, it felt cleansing.

"Good timing, then," I said. "But he invited me this evening. He didn't have to. I even told him in vague terms what I wanted."

"Very vague, I hope."

"Vague enough, apparently."

"He must remember you from happier times."

"The war years? Oh yes, a time of frolic and fluff."

"For you they were, chasing a woman you would never want as a wife."

"Oh?" Therena had tiptoed into the kitchen.

I explained briefly about Kate Chase, the daughter of Lincoln's treasury secretary. "She was more conniving than her daddy was," I said. "And the lucky fellow she wound up marrying was even . . . Well, he's a drunkard besides the heir to his family's mills. Oh, and a senator, in his day, the dishonorable Mr. Sprague of Rhode Island. They're living apart now, I understand. She got the three girls; he took the son. And she is consorting these days with"—I had a captivated audience—"would you care to take a guess?"

"James Madison?" Therena said.

"Too short," I replied. "Roscoe Conkling."

Nicolay grinned. I was gratified to see he wasn't too upright for gossip. "An open secret," he said.

"Seriously?" Therena said. "How do you know all this?"

"I never reveal my sources of information," I said. "Also, I like to keep track of the bullets I've dodged."

⊢══⊣

Gone from the Executive Mansion's north lawn was the bronze statue of Thomas Jefferson. The Democratic Party's founding father was a victim of a political kidnapping. As much as I preferred having Republicans in power, they had lost their subtlety.

Subtlety was dead inside as well. The Mansion's entrance hall had been turned into a patriotic circus. What used to be a simple, dignified gateway was now an explosion of flags and eagles and Union shields and even a *U.S.* (for the nation? for Ulysses S. Grant?) all painted in reds, whites, and blues. Whatever wasn't drenched in color—the wood panels, the trimming—had been daubed to charade as stonework with a twisted rope design.

"Mr. Hay, what a sight for old eyes, sir!"

It had been ten years since I had moved my notepads and undergarments out of this building, but Edward McManus—Old Edward—hadn't aged a day. Maybe his hair had grown whiter, framing his cheerful, wizened face and matching his white gloves, so stark against his spotless black suit. We exchanged pleasantries that were pleasant indeed. "The president is expecting you, sir," he said.

"Tell me, Edward, has the food improved any?"

"It's best that you're a-comin' for whisky, sir. They are upstairs in the library."

"They?"

"General Babcock."

I exhaled in a whistle. I had brought this on myself. I had told Grant I would be asking for a favor, and it made sense for him to invite his private secretary and closest aide, whose job (and privilege) was saying no. That is what Nicolay had done for Lincoln, and bluntly enough that the listener understood it was more than a hint. Nicolay, however, was a good person to his core. I had no reason to think the same of Orville E. Babcock.

The large vestibule was divided by a sash screen and decorated with portraits of this house's previous inhabitants, by name of Van Buren, Tyler, Fillmore, Pierce. Forgettable, all.

The smell of the office staircase hadn't changed, a musky blend of decades and dust with a whiff of (I'm not making this up) urine, whether from a dog or a wayward child or . . . stop me here. The staircase opened into a vestibule and then into the central corridor that was even dingier than I remembered. The bulbous chandeliers and the globes of illuminating gas only intensified the gloom.

The library was on the left, facing south. The door was open. The oval room looked as disheveled as Lincoln had left it. Dark bookcases lined the walls, as they had since Millard Fillmore's day, with what I would guess was the same selection of classics. In the center was the same or a simi-lar octagonal table, covered for all I knew with ten-year-old newspapers. I swear these were the same upholstered rockers in which the Ancient and the Hell-cat (our nicknames for the president and First Lady) had bickered and mourned. They were occupied now by the nation's eighteenth president and his . . . Iago.

Grant stood. How small he looked—how *ordinary*. This has always sur-prised me about Grant, and also heartened me, I must confess, as proof that stature was no determinant of success. He was about average height, for a full-grown American male, but he always seemed shorter than he should be. Partly it was because his shoulders were slumped and probably more be-cause he was neither a storybook general nor a commanding-looking com-mander in chief. Yet he was no pushover—that was clear. He was squarely built, compact, every inch filled with a confidence that didn't need to make itself known. He had a stolid face—indeed, an impervious face—wider and rounder than it had been during the war. His luminous blue eyes gave his presence a calm that seemed unflappable. His whiskers were grayer yet kempt, concealing more than his mouth and his chin. I took Grant for the sort of man that no other man (or woman?) could ever truly know. Great men were like that. Lincoln was. I couldn't decide, however, whether Grant was great or utterly ordinary. I doubted that he knew—or cared, really. I couldn't help but stare at the wart by his nose, a mark of the ordinariness that had endeared him to his soldiers and then to the voters. Unlike Lincoln, who was compli-cated, Grant was a simple man. It was both his strength and his limitation.

His handshake was firm yet not showy. "Mr. Hay," he said, "this is Gen-eral Babcock."

The mustachioed man in the chair leapt up and snatched my hand and shook it until mine ached. "I understand you held my job once," he said.

"Not quite," I replied. "I was only the assistant. But I know how hard the job is."

Orville Babcock was under middle height and stout. He reminded me of a walrus, with a rounder frame and a fuller face than a fellow who looked about my age ought to have. His reddish mustache was impressive indeed, arched toward the floor, but his goatee looked store-bought. His blue eyes fastened on mine then darted away, unmoored from a smile I saw no reason to trust. At last he dispossessed my hand to its healing and returned to his seat.

"Join us in a whisky?" Grant said.

"Please."

"Water?"

"No, thank you."

Babcock strode over to the sideboard. He shoved a military map aside—were they planning a war of some sort or reminiscing about the good old days?—and generously poured an amber drink into a fluted cup. He handed it to me and said, "Tell me, what was Lincoln like to work for? Was he demanding?"

Grant sat, and so did I. Babcock stayed on his feet, with a military bearing.

"Not an easy question," I replied. "He never demanded anything—so in that sense, no. But he assumed you would give him your best, and so you did. He never had to ask for it. And he recognized good work, which was the strongest motivator of all. How about . . . ?"

I gestured toward the president.

"I always do my best," Babcock said.

I swirled the Kentucky bourbon, grateful to have something to do with my hands. I stuck my nose over the glass. Strong stuff, enough to mask belladonna's bitter smell. Would I always be checking for that?

"A cigar?" Grant said. He was lighting his own, a blunt black stub I could smell before it was lit.

I declined. Babcock didn't. I wondered if he ever challenged Grant. Ah, the military instinct.

An awkward silence. I guess it was up to me to start, but I had learned always to wait for the president. This president, however, was nearly a mute—silent in several languages, as the wags had it. That was one thing I have never been accused of.

It was Babcock who said, "And what can we do for you, Mr. Hay?"

I turned toward Grant and said, "As I mentioned this morning, sir, it's about the former president's death."

Babcock edged closer.

"Such sad news," Grant said.

"It might even be sadder," I said. "I am not at all certain that it was a . . . natural event."

"What makes you say that?" Babcock snapped.

"I can't tell you everything I've learned, because I need to investigate it further. But I have good reason to believe that he was poisoned in Tennessee, at his daughter's house, so that it only looked like apoplexy."

From President Grant, no reaction. He didn't move an inch. Was he even listening? This must be how successful generals react to terrible news. Then he blinked, before resuming a pose fit for Statuary Hall.

"Poisoned how?" Babcock said.

"With belladonna, apparently. Deadly nightshade." I raised my glass, as if for a toast. "Possibly mixed in whisky."

"Suspects?" Grant had been paying close attention.

"A couple," I said. "A Confederate captain who was on the train with him from Greeneville, although I can't imagine a motive. He also visited President Johnson, Mr. Johnson, at his daughter's house, definitely once and apparently more. Also . . . his son-in-law—"

"The Confederate captain's?" Babcock said.

"No, Johnson's."

"Not Stover!" Grant said.

"No, no." The sainted Stover's fame had spread. "David Patterson, Martha's husband. The former senator." All of us could agree on the perfidy of senators, none of us having been one. "Or possibly the other son-in-law, Colonel Stover's . . . successor, if you will. It was in his house that President Johnson died, although his wife says he wasn't there at the time."

"Why would either of them . . . ?" Grant trailed off. The president still had children at home. His family was probably a happy one—that is, boring.

"He died without a will," I said, "Johnson did, your predecessor, and apparently he was about to write one, leaving everything to his surviving son. This could well have raised a few hackles, had the others learned of it." Grant had returned to marble; Babcock was listening intently. "It seems there are also blackmail letters involved. That's here, in Washington. It's why I'm here."

Babcock leaned forward. "Targeted at . . . ?"

"A couple of senators, apparently, but I don't really know, maybe more than two. Good Republicans, prominent ones."

"Which ones?" Babcock said, too eagerly for my taste.

"I don't know for sure," I said. I didn't, not for sure. Now I would play my trump card. "I have reason to believe that one of them is Roscoe Conkling."

For President Grant, the indispensable senator.

"Are you suggesting," Grant said, "that these letters had something to do with my predecessor's death?" A sharp question.

"I cannot be certain," I replied. "But the letters were originally his. This, I do know."

"How can I help?" the president said.

Delightful! I described the letter I wanted.

"Preposterous!" Babcock exclaimed. "This seems an awfully flimsy—"

Grant interrupted, "What should it say?"

⊹≒═≒⊹

I was regaling Old Edward about my five-month-old's beauty and brilliance—and her mama's—when I heard heels click on the vestibule floor and my name barked. Without turning, I knew who it was. Babcock strode up to me and said, "In here."

Just inside the Mansion's north door, the former redoubt for ushers and messengers had been refashioned (another of Mrs. Grant's inspirations) into a waiting room for the president's callers. It had silk-covered divans and wallpaper that recalled the French countryside. Babcock waved me into a corner seat and hovered over me, a greenhorn's tactic, leaving himself open for an uppercut.

"What is it?" I said—irritably, I hoped.

"The president asked me to give you a message. That you report back regularly on what you learn. You needn't bother the president about this. You can report directly to me."

"How regularly?" I said.

"Whenever you learn something of note. I'll leave the specifics to you."

"This was the president's directive?" I said.

"My job is to do what the president wants. Colonel Hay, you may consider this an order from your commander in chief."

I *may* so consider it, which implies that I may not. Why hadn't the president told me himself? In any event, I was no longer a colonel, so the president did not rank as my commander in chief.

I nodded and said not a word.

⊹≒═≒⊹

"Johnny, you would have wanted the same," Nicolay said, "*I* would have, just to make sure the Ancient wasn't ambushed."

"Maybe," I allowed, "but he didn't ask me. He told me. He ordered me."

"So, it was his tone of voice that's troubling you."

"And I don't even know if it came from the president."

"So what if it didn't? He pretty much told you it didn't. The private secretary's job is to protect the president, whether the president knows it or not. Sometimes it's better that he not know, so he can say that without lying more than necessary. You got the letter—that was the point. Let me see it."

Like a guilty schoolboy, I produced the envelope from my inside breast pocket. Nicolay removed the square notecard and read with a melodramatic flair:

THE PRESIDENT'S HOUSE

To whom it may concern:
Please cooperate with the bearer of this letter, Mr. John Hay, in his inquiries about the unfortunate death of the 17ᵗʰ president.

Yours truly,
U. S. Grant

"Old stationery, I take it," Nicolay said.

"The best kind," I said.

We were sitting in the kitchen, nursing Sabbath brandies. Therena was drinking tea. "He could not bring himself to mention his predecessor by name," she pointed out.

This brought two guffaws.

Nicolay said, "You know why he did this, don't you?"

"Yes, Conkling. To keep him in line or happy or something—whatever minuet they're dancing."

"Besides that."

"Actually, I don't," I said. "If I ever understood why people helped journalists, they would probably stop."

"It's what I said before—it sets a bad precedent. It can't be good for the presidency if its occupants keep getting killed. First Lincoln and then Johnson? That would be two in a row. What would stop some dark soul from making it three?"

I was a wild-eyed optimist, next to Nicolay, but in this case I had to agree. "I guess our revered citizenry does include some lunatics," I grumbled. "For a man who goes to church without a bodyguard and strolls down the Avenue in the evening, why tempt fate?"

"He has a good heart," Therena said.

"Who does?" Helen had wandered in.

"President Grant, dear," Therena said. "He's a good Christian. A righteous man, kind to the black folks, genuinely so."

"Not the sharpest sword in the sheath," I said. "But yes, a good man, if that still counts for something. *If,* I say. Unlike his late and unlamented predecessor, by the way."

Therena gave me a crooked look. She was too kind to criticize the deceased (or the living). I leaned toward telling the truth.

So, apparently, did Nicolay. "If Grant's heart is so pure," he said, "why has there been no end of scandals since he took office?"

"Credit Mobilier doesn't count," I said. "The news broke when he was president, but the scandal took place before that." The company building the first transcontinental railroad had earned federal benevolence by offering stock to successive vice presidents, a half dozen members of Congress, and a gaggle of judges.

"All right," Nicolay said. "How about the attempt to corner the gold market, involving his own brother-in-law, for God's sake—"

"George!" Therena admonished.

"—and the New York custom ring scandal and the Star Route scandal and the collusion in stationery sales to the Interior Department and the corruption in the Marine Corps quartermaster department and now the Whisky Ring." The *St. Louis Globe-Democrat* had revealed in May that distillers and the government's taxmen were conspiring to cheat the federal treasury out of millions of dollars, by underreporting the volumes of taxable whisky produced. "His own brother is involved—that's the rumor. His own brother! And Babcock, too."

"Really?" I couldn't say I was shocked.

"Yes, General Babcock, the crook at Grant's right hand. Thirty thousand dollars' worth, that's what I've heard."

Heard from whom? As a journalist, past or present, I didn't feel free to ask him. Nor did I doubt it was true.

I said, "This country is more corrupt than Rome under Caligula—that's what my friend Henry Adams says. Do you think Grant knows?"

"If he knows it, he won't believe it. He's oblivious, that man. His own men can do no wrong. He trusts everyone around him, and actually admires the monopolists. I am willing to believe that he is as honest as Jesus Christ incarnate."

"George!"

"But he makes the same mistake again and again, trusting people who shouldn't be trusted. And then he's always surprised. That's the problem with Grant—he never learns from his mistakes. What does it matter whether he's personally corrupt or not? His indifference tells everyone below him, everyone who works with him, that anything is acceptable. If he isn't corrupt himself, and I don't think he is, then he is naive as all hell."

"George! Helen is—"

"She's old enough to learn about the world as it is. Whatever you want to say about Andy Johnson, and there is plenty bad to say, I don't think he ever took a penny. He was an honest man."

Rarely had I seen Nicolay, as an honest man himself, so riled. He took a gulp of brandy and coughed violently. His temples turned red.

"All right, I'm off my soapbox," he managed, coughing again. He turned to his daughter and said, "And now, young lady, you need to march yourself upstairs."

She obeyed, and I followed.

CHAPTER ELEVEN

Look at this, Johnny!" Nicolay rattled to-day's *Washington Chronicle* over his coffee mug. "Machinery Hall—it's done!"

He patted a lithograph of the grand, sleek building that was to be the centerpiece of the exposition planned in Philadelphia for the spring of 'seventy-six, to celebrate the nation's hundredth birthday. "Look at this— the Corliss engine!" Nicolay sputtered. "It's so . . . so . . ."

"Big?" I helped out. "Nico, I like newfangled things as much as the next fellow."

"As the next Luddite, you mean."

Helen said, "What's a Luddite?"

Nicolay explained how English textile workers, before any of us were born into this world of woe, had taken to smashing the machines and mills that were stealing their jobs.

"I've never smashed a machine in my life," I fussed, "although I must say a typewriter tempted me once. Machines have a use, in their place. I've been known to try a stylographic pen and, yes, even a typewriter from time to time, and I will admit to a certain fondness for gas lighting and the WC." Helen sat goggle-eyed at my oration, her spoonful of porridge suspended in midair. "The Corliss steam engine, the wallpaper-printing machine, artificial teeth, they're all fine by me. Inventions are what make America great, isn't that right? We are a nation of inventors, a nation of machinery." I was gasping for breath. "But, Nico, please tell me, is this the measure of our civilization? What is the point of making a fetish out of *things*?"

"Spoken like a man of acquired means," Nicolay said.

"I thought this even when I was poor."

"And aspired to be wealthy."

"I never thought about it much—honestly. But I admit to being an

American, and that's what Americans are supposed to want, isn't that right? Prosperity. Nothing more American than that. Let us genuflect to Cornelius Vanderbilt."

"And to Amasa Stone."

"Going for the solar plexus, Nico. And, yes, to Amasa Stone." I lifted my mug of coffee. "And to material success."

Therena was buttering a corn muffin and said, "I don't believe a word you're saying, Johnny, and neither do you."

"You are a wise woman," I said. "Have I earned another sausage?"

"Yes, aimed at your head."

I pretended to duck.

Nicolay said, "What mischief are you up to to-day, Johnny, with your precious letter in hand?"

"Two powerful and poignant words," I said. "Roscoe Conkling."

"That should keep you out of mischief," Nicolay said. "But let me suggest two more words. Allan Pinkerton."

"Oh? Not my favorite words. Why those in particular?"

"I hear he's in the city, and he could be useful."

"Useful how? Like last time?" The soon-to-be-famous detective had become my unwelcome sidekick in solving Willie Lincoln's murder thirteen years before. "My recollection is that he kept getting in the way."

"Getting in *your* way, perhaps, but not in *the* way. On balance, I think he probably helped."

I couldn't deny that, as much as I wanted to. "So, what use could he be?"

"Whatever you pay him to do."

"You mean, whatever the *Tribune* pays him to do."

"Even better," Nicolay said.

＋━━━＋

In the second-floor window of a narrow building on the Avenue, between Sixth and Seventh streets, I spotted the logotype of the unblinking eye. *We never sleep*—the slogan drew my attention even on a bleary Monday morn. I had to salute the man, as much as I disliked him. Pinkerton had parlayed his service as Lincoln's protector into a detective agency that was becoming famous—or infamous.

My destination was above a homeopathic pharmacy, next door to Mathew Brady's photography studio. The staircase stank of alcohol (not the drinkable kind) and ether. At the top was a black door with gold letters nailed on:

P NKE TON
NATIONAL
DETE TIVE
AGENCY

The door was unlocked. I was greeted inside by a tall blonde, seated on the reception table, wearing last night's tight gown. She looked as startled to see me as I was to see her. She examined me, head to toe, and evidently didn't approve.

"What do you want?" she said.

"Is Mr. Pinkerton in?"

I considered this a query to be answered *yes* or *no*, but she seemed to roll it around before she replied, "What if he is?"

"Then I'd like to see him."

"You being?"

I told her. She shifted just enough.

"Will he know who you are?"

"All too well. We go back a ways, he and I."

"Do you?" she said, scanning me again. "Wait here."

She slid off the desktop and vanished into a back office.

Moments later, Allan Pinkerton was bounding toward me, his hand outstretched. "How ye, Hay?" the detective boomed.

His beard was saltier and stragglier, and he had gained a few pounds; his torso strained his belt and buttons. He looked tireder than I remembered. But he hadn't changed all that much since 'sixty-one, when he (and I) accompanied the president-elect from Springfield, Illinois, to Washington City. He had the same square face, that prominent nose, the lagoon of a hairline, and those small, dark, deadly eyes as inscrutable as the one in his logo. His face was puffier, that of the magnate he was well on his way to becoming. His headquarters were in Chicago, but his agency had offices in other cities, offering a private police force for companies that wished to quash strikes. I wondered if Amasa Stone had ever hired him.

I put the question to Pinkerton, as he ushered me into an airy room with two big windows and a chandelier. Upholstered chairs surrounded an oblong table that could fit eight irate industrialists or a tycoon's squabbling heirs. The detective sat at one end. I took a seat along the side, facing the windows, which were streaked with birds' sacraments.

"I ne'er disclose me clients," Pinkerton said. His Scottish lilt hadn't changed. "But when somebo'y pay his bills on time, tha' is me definition o' an honorable man. Congra'ulations on yer marriage."

"Thank you," I said. I could guess how he knew.

"And how is your fa'er-in-law?"

"We're living with him at the moment—and a baby."

"Yers, I take it."

I laughed. Why take offense? "That is my working assumption."

"Would tha' be a girl baby or a boy baby?"

We talked offspring for a minute or two, and Pinkerton, ever competitive, detailed his litter.

"And wha' brings ye here," Pinkerton said, "besides ol' toyms?"

Instead of holding back, which is my inclination with people I don't care for, I unloaded. He assured me we were speaking in confidence, although the lawyer in me wasn't certain, and I told him what I knew and what I didn't know and what I suspected—and whom I suspected. Uncollated information. I wanted him to make sense of it all. I hadn't. Pinkerton was a better listener than I remembered. (Maybe he, too, had matured.) That he couldn't make sense of it either was a relief of sorts.

"Aye," the detective said. "So wha' would ye want me t' do?"

I noted the subjunctive; he wasn't committing to anything yet. "Tell me what the Pattersons are up to," I said. "Who they are meeting with. Why they are here. Had they summoned the senators?"

Pinkerton nodded. I would have preferred that he take notes.

I said, "How hard would this be?" I, too, could use the subjunctive.

"'Tis anythin' possible," Pinkerton said, "fo' a fee."

<hr />

It was twelve minutes past ten, by my grandfather's pocket watch. The air was feeling sultry already. The Avenue was crowded—and noisy, with the clip-clop of horses and the rumbling of wagon wheels and the shouts of negro vendors hawking oysters and milk. The sharp, incessant jangling of streetcar bells had supplanted the omnibuses of yore. Ladies with parasols brushed by me on the brick sidewalk and didn't seem to mind if they knocked me aside. I flagged down a hack.

"Wormley's Hotel," I instructed the driver. He was a clean-shaven young fellow with slick blond hair and a cheerful face.

"My pleasure, sir."

Politeness from a hackney coachman—would wonders never cease? Nothing like my experience in New York or my memory of Washington. Was this, too, part of the capital's renewal? Boss Shepherd had had the swamps drained, the streets paved, the canals filled, the sewers buried, aqueducts constructed, gas and water mains installed, trees planted, side-walks graded, parks created, gas lamps erected, and tenements razed—all in three years' time. I had heard about his heavy-handedness in refurbishing Washington, with its pall of corruption. But it had ended any talk of moving the national capital to St. Louis or some other central, and presumably godlier, locale. Could it also have revived the local citizenry's demeanor?

My evidence was all of a coachman's three words, four syllables.

As we passed Seventh street, I admired the sparkling new Center Market, which stretched all the way to Ninth. Gone were the filthy sheds and produce stands that had drawn as many rats as customers. The new market, with its spires and ornate brick décor, looked like a railroad depot, the emblem of a city made new. Yet the old city remained. Past the *Evening Star* building, at Eleventh, the crowd in front of Samuel Lewis jewelers parted just enough for me to glimpse a sheep inside. My merriment amused the driver, but I couldn't explain why I found it heartening to know that cities—and their citizens—weren't reborn simply because a political boss had decreed it.

Wormley's Hotel stood a couple of blocks north of the Avenue, on the southwestern corner of Fifteenth and H. It was the city's fanciest (and priciest) hotel, located in the most prestigious neighborhood, just off Lafayette Square. A handsome building it was, four stories of brick in the Georgian style but with a mansard roof and dormer windows that added touches of ornament. It was owned and run by James Wormley, a black man who had been born into freedom in Washington (his father owned a livery stable) and had proved what a free man of color could accomplish. His hotel's luxuriousness and his attentiveness to customers' comforts drew European royalty and American magnates. I should know, having stayed at Wormley's myself after returning from living abroad.

I entered through the portico into a lobby as elegant as any I'd seen on the Continent. Thick carpets tickled a forest of marble pillars, beneath diadems of chandeliers. One could loll on the sofas for a generation or two.

I asked at the desk if Roscoe Conkling was in.

Was he expecting me? I allowed as how I thought he might, keeping mum about the fortune teller this would require. I must have looked presentable because the runt of a desk clerk said, "Four oh one."

The steam elevator was at the back.

"Fourth floor, please," I said. The operator, a wrinkled old man, looked me up and down, and again I must have passed muster, wherever muster happened to be that morning.

Four oh one was down the hall to the left. The carpet here, too, was lush. The door opened at my first knock.

There stood the senior senator from New York.

I found it absurd that Roscoe Conkling was considered (by those who consider such things) the handsomest man of our day. A matter of taste, I suppose. He did embody a certain brand of manly beauty, tall and slender with broad shoulders, an arrow's posture, a peacock's strut—an Apollo in appearance, a Beau Brummell in dress. He had a triangular face, from the pointed beard to the assertive nose to his trademark foppish curl hanging down over his broad forehead. His complexion was florid, and his whiskers, best I could detect, were perfumed. This morning, his paisley dressing robe revealed a yellow waistcoat and a lacy cravat held in place by a diamond stickpin. Wasn't diamond even more glamorous than gold?

The smart money saw the senator waltzing into the presidency in 'seventy-six. I hoped the smart money was wrong. I had known Lord Roscoe in his pre-nobility days, during his service in the lowly House, and I hadn't liked him then.

Conkling looked surprised to see me, as well he might. I realized he was expecting somebody else. I wondered who.

"I am sorry," I said, "but I am not David Patterson." *Or Kate Chase Sprague,* I wanted to add, but refrained.

Conkling threw back his huge head and laughed. It was a raucous laugh, which I figured had gladdened women (yes, including Mrs. Sprague) and had intimidated lawmakers of both political parties, especially his own. His pale grayish eyes hadn't joined in the merriment.

"You are smaller than he is," said Conkling. He stood more than six feet tall and commented on such things.

"But tougher."

"I imagine you are," he said. "Almost anyone is."

We stood there a moment. I waited to be invited in, when I had a sudden fear that Kate Chase was in the bedroom, wearing a . . . I didn't want to think about it, and I didn't want to see her. I was considering a quick departure when Conkling said, "What do you want?"

"I am with the *New-York Tribune,* you know," I said. "But I have a letter from President Grant."

"To me?" he said. My revelation hadn't produced the awestruck reaction

I had figured on. Probably too many missives signed *U. S. Grant* had passed under Conkling's imperial nose.

"To whom it may concern," I said.

"Oh," he said. "And why, if I may inquire, should I be concerned?"

"If I may come in, Mr. Senator, I shall be happy to explain."

"You can explain from the doorway."

I sighed. This wouldn't be easy. "I am interested in Andrew Johnson's death."

"I know nothing about it except what I read in the usually unreliable newspapers—a description, I hasten to add, that should not be construed as including your own."

"I appreciate the endorsement. . . . It seems the late president left behind some letters that his son-in-law has been showing to the interested parties."

"Am I an interested party?"

"Are you?"

"If I were, why would I want to tell you?"

I had no persuasive answer to that. *In the interest of truth* sounded laughable, even to me. *In the interest of a good story* sounded worse.

"I think Andrew Johnson was murdered," I said. "May I come in?"

That drew a reaction—of amusement, best I could tell. Conkling stepped aside.

The rooms at Wormley's were big and sunny and lavishly furnished. The Smyrna rugs drowsed on top of the Brussels carpet. This suited Lord Roscoe, who sat me down in a silk-covered chair while he stayed on his feet.

"Why do you think that?"

"I have reason to believe he was poisoned, although I am not in a position to share the evidence—yet. I suspect it had something to do with these letters that Senator Patterson . . . former Senator Patterson . . . has been . . . showing . . . peddling, if you will."

"Please suspect to your heart's delight," Conkling said. He looked unconcerned, which I doubted he was feigning, although he had had plenty of experience in doing so. "That man is a criminal."

"A blackmailer?"

"I wouldn't know about that. I am talking about when he was here, as a senator. It turned out that he and Senator Doolittle of Wisconsin were accused of graft in connection with the New York Custom House investigation. Credibly accused, I might add."

"Was this widely known at the time?"

"I knew it."

"Did the president know it?"

"We are speaking of a president's son-in-law. Who can determine with any confidence the line between what the president actually knew and what he thought he knew or carefully avoided knowing? He was not regarded as a man of impeccable character—neither of them." Conkling swept his hand across the room.

"I am speaking of something more recent," I said, "something that would be clearly a crime. Have you seen him, by any chance, in the past few days?"

"I have not."

"Has he asked to see you?"

"Next question."

Aha! "What brings you, then, to this sweltering city in August? Business or pleasure?"

"I have never recognized the distinction, Mr. Hay. I am here because I wish to be. Isn't that why you are here, too?"

He hadn't asked why I was asking these questions. He already knew.

"Then tell me this, if you would, sir." Why not plunge in? "What can you tell me about letters of . . . blackmail, if that is not too inaccurate or blunt a term, that the late president might have had in his possession? Or that his son-in-law might have in his possession currently."

"Mr. Hay, I enjoy my interactions with the gentlemen of the press, but there are only twenty-four hours in a day. You gained entry here, in my domicile, and I was ever so happy to oblige you, to talk about *your* suspicions regarding the late president's death. Would you say that these . . . hypothetical letters have any connection to our subject at hand?"

"I can't know until I've seen them," I replied more or less truthfully. "Anything you could do to help . . ."

"Even if I could, Mr. Hay, I see no reason why I should. How could it possibly be to my advantage? But if your suspicions are correct, and his death wasn't . . . as it seemed, I have a tolerably good idea as to why."

"You do?" I said. "I am listening." We agreed to ground rules by which I essentially promised on my grandmother's grave never to acknowledge that I had ever met or even heard of a man who bore the unlikely name of Roscoe Conkling. He seated himself opposite me, in a Louis XV–style chair of pale brocade, and said, "His impeachment, of course."

"That was . . . more than seven years ago." I was a wizard at arithmetic. "What on earth could that have to do with . . . ?"

"Surely you remember the passions of the day."

"I was abroad, but I've heard tell."

"Well, whatever you heard, it was worse. Are you aware of the money that was sloshing around? The patronage? The purchase of votes?"

"On whose side?"

"The seven traitorous Republicans who voted to acquit—that's where I would look first. No proof of it, but it seems likelier than not. It is your business, Mr. Hay, to find out. Do you think that Edmund Ross, the undistinguished—forgive me, distinguished—senator from Kansas, the decisive vote for the president's acquittal, do you think he wasn't purchased for patronage and gold? Hell"—Conkling's arm flung high, a pose he held an instant too long—"he was given control over every postmaster, every federal appointment, in the great state of Kansas as well as the territories of Colorado and New Mexico. Oh yes, and the commissioner of internal revenue—that was his, too. Oh, and the superintendent of Indian affairs in Kansas and in the Indian territory to the south. And also, let us not forget, a sacred treaty with the Osage tribe, which President Johnson sent to the Senate that very day."

"*And* gold?"

"That has never been proved, but where there is smoke, Mr. Hay, there is typically—or shall I say, stereotypically—fire."

"That was seven years ago."

"Resentments linger, Mr. Hay. Resentments linger. Seven years is but an eyelash in time. Surely a man as erudite as yourself"—a compliment, recast into a weapon—"can comprehend that."

Conkling stood over me, waving an unlit cigar.

I said, "Is the esteemed Senator Ross still in Washington, do you know?"

"He is not. He is back in Kansas, from what I understand, and fills the august position as foreman in the printing office at the *Lawrence Journal*. Such is the fate of a man who once held a president's destiny in his hands. How the mighty have . . ." A sigh of satisfaction. "I might point out that Kansas isn't terribly distant from Tennessee."

"But seven years later?" I repeated.

"You are too young, then, Mr. Hay, to understand. If I were in your shoes, which I happily am not, I would find out which senators who voted on President Johnson's impeachment are still in the Senate, and which of those might still feel bitter about his acquittal. I am one of those senators, incidentally."

"Still bitter?"

"Oh no, not me." He smiled placidly. "I am never bitter about anything, Mr. Hay. Never have been, never will be."

"How many of you are there," I said—"senators from 'sixty-eight who are still in office?"

"Couldn't say. I've never counted them."

"All you do is count."

His smile widened. "It's not all I do."

"When *do* you expect to see David Patterson?" I tried.

"And now, Mr. Hay," Conkling said—not even with a glance at his watch—"it is my misfortune to have to bid you good day."

At the door I turned and said, "One last question, if I could. Was . . . *Senator* Johnson, since he returned to office, disliked by his colleagues, would you say?"

This produced another of Conkling's raucous laughs and a parting handshake. I was grateful to escape without having caught a glimpse or a whiff of a temptress named Kate.

<hr/>

Call me a bowl of mush, if you wish, but the sight of the Capitol never fails to thrill me. I am not embellishing when I say a chill goes up my spine. It was not only the exquisite shape of the dome, an icy white against the azure sky, the marble glittering in the sunlight, the steps monumental in breadth yet surprisingly light. Even more striking was the Capitol's interior. It was an explosion of colors. The floors were patterned in Minton tiles, the arched ceilings slathered with golds, greens, beiges, reds, vibrant blues in intricate designs. That showman Brumidi had been free with a brush. Every square inch of the walls showed gods and goddesses, laurels and bare-branched trees, flowers and fruits, cannons and plows, parrots and insects and squirrels and mice. Audacious, in its way, but also a little troubling, in that it suggested a young nation making itself garishly grand, trying to impress . . . itself.

The secretary of the Senate had an enviable location, within an oration's reach of the Senate chamber. The office's advantages ended there. It was twice as high as it was wide, with narrow windows that barely relieved the sense of confinement. The chandelier hung low and, even in daylight, splattered sparks of light in unstable patterns across the walls.

I introduced myself to the gentleman in the corner, seated at a desk backed by dozens of pigeonholes. George Gorham, the Senate's secretary, was a trim man with a pompadour and a perfect side part. His square face and square whiskers suggested a complete lack of creativity, which suited me fine. What I wanted didn't require any.

I was curious about why Roscoe Conkling wouldn't name the senators still in office who had voted on Andrew Johnson's impeachment. Maybe he thought it would involve him, ever so slightly, in an investigation that might embarrass his colleagues. Or maybe he thought that one of them was actually a murderer—certainly he knew them better than I did. Or maybe he had merely mentioned it to throw me off the track.

In any event, I needed to compare the current roster of senators against a list of senators who had voted on Johnson's impeachment. This shouldn't be hard.

And, to my surprise, it wasn't.

From a pigeonhole in his desk, Mr. Gorham plucked a long, skinny, yellow paper with the alphabetical list of the current roster of seventy-four senators, including the one who was freshly in his grave. "A roll call from the special session in March," he said, "compliments of the United States Senate."

"I accept," I said, "on behalf of a grateful citizenry."

"And what else can I do for you?" he said.

I told him.

"I happen to have one of those, too," he replied. "I keep it handy. People ask for it."

"Still?"

He brought me another long, slender roll call with a shorter list of senators. At the top, written in pencil:

Article XI

And below:

May 16, 1868

"This was the vote that mattered," he said.

Article XI, the last of the eleven charges the House of Representatives had included in its bill of impeachment, was a compendium of every high crime or misdemeanor, political or criminal, that the House impeachers could conjure up. This strip of paper was the tally of the first Senate vote in American history on whether to remove a sitting president from office.

"The original?" I gasped.

"Not on your life," Gorham said. "That is in my vault."

I laid the two roll calls side by side and marked the overlaps on the current roll call, scribbling a *G* or an *A*—guilt or acquittal—depending on the senator's vote.

G   *Anthony, Henry B.—R.I.*
G   *Cameron, Simon—Penn.*
G   *Conkling, Roscoe—N.Y.*
G   *Cragin, Aaron H.—N.H.*
G   *Edmunds, George F.—Vt.*
G   *Ferry, T. W.—Mich.*
G   *Frelinghuysen, Frederick T.—N.J.*
G   *Howe, Timothy G.—Wisc.*
A   *McCreery, Thomas C.—Ky.*
G   *Morrill, Justin S.—Vt.*
G   *Morrill, Lot M.—Maine*
G   *Morton, Oliver P.—Ind.*
G   *Sherman, John—Ohio*

Of the thirteen senators still in office, twelve were Republicans who had voted to convict Johnson and one was a Democrat who had voted to acquit. They included none of the seven Republicans who had saved Johnson's presidency by jumping sides and voting to acquit. Only two of the thirteen were currently in Washington City, as far as Smalley knew, making themselves available for the Pattersons' . . . deviltry. Those were Conkling and Frelinghuysen, and I had spoken to both, learning more by their silences than by any utterance. Only one question mattered: Did any of these thirteen have a reason to murder their new colleague, and the opportunity to carry it out in Tennessee?

I looked back over the list. John Sherman's brother was the famed Civil War general who was close to Grant and presumably disposed to loathe Johnson. But to the point of murder? Simon Cameron's son was Grant's war secretary, as Simon had been Lincoln's. Oliver Morton was one of Johnson's sworn enemies; indeed, his comments in Ohio had drawn the former president to Elizabethton in the first place. Granted, the national legislature was no stranger to hatreds and feuds and even violence. But to the point of murder? It seemed far-fetched. As for the other senators . . .

This was hopeless. And probably pointless. I grabbed my list and fled.

+====+

The capital's hackney drivers were earning a fortune from my meanderings. Seventy-five cents from the Capitol to Newspaper Row was probably the tourists' rate. It not being my money, I have bestowed upon each driver a one-dollar bill, bearing the forbidding countenance of Salmon P. Chase, Lincoln's treasury secretary. Not many were still in circulation, and I collected them for titillation's sake—yes, he was Kate's loving and venal daddy—and to remind myself that stature and fame won't always get you past the Pearly Gates (also, that jackasses can succeed in life).

I found Smalley scribbling furiously at his desk. At that rate, he would finish soon. I retreated into the corridor and eavesdropped on the banter in the office across the hall. Something about the Washington Nationals' business agent who had absconded with all of the ball club's money, stranding the professional team in St. Louis. "They're raising dough so the team can get home," a deep voice boomed.

"So, you gonna subscribe?"

"To help these fellas play a boy's game, when my tots need new shoes? Not a fuckin' chance." A roar of laughter.

"Yeah, let those boys keep strokin' their bats in Sain' Louie." Another roar—I missed a newsroom's repartee.

"Ain't nobody worse in the National Association but Keokuk."

"So'd they ever get home? Anyone care?"

I wasn't privy to the answer because I heard my name called. Smalley was waving me in. He *had* seen me. "Whatcha got for me?" he said.

"I'm sorry, is this a bad time?"

"For you, no."

"I'll make it short." I stayed on my feet. "I had a thought, something that Roscoe Conkling put into my mind."

"Oh, Lord. I wouldn't trust him to tell ya it's raining 'til your galoshes get wet."

"He was talking about the impeachment. You were here then, right?"

"Not *here,* but on the Hill. I was the clerk for the House military affairs committee. Someday I'll make an honest living."

"My goal is the opposite."

"Seems you're further along than I am."

I had left myself open for that. "To-day, I'm not further along than anyone. Conkling is convinced, or says he's convinced, that some lingering bitterness from the impeachment—"

"That's a lot of lingering."

"My thought, exactly. But thirteen of our nation's finest were senators at the time and may be, shall we say, lingering still. Do any of them strike you as murderers?"

"All of them, I should think," Smalley deadpanned, "if an election's at stake. Felons, at any rate."

I unfolded the list, which he examined, line by line.

"I see your problem," Smalley said at last. "But somebody's missing."

"I went over the lists twice," I said.

"There's somebody missing—the vice president."

"The current . . . ah! He was in the Senate then, wasn't he?"

"And now he presides over it. And being a Radical Republican in good standing from the abolitionist state of Massachusetts, of course he voted to convict. So, you can appreciate the amusement among those of us in the gallery as we watched him, now as vice president, swear in Andy Johnson as a senator." This had occurred at the Senate's special session in March, called to approve the treaty with the Sandwich Islands. "Sworn in, I should add—and you'll enjoy this—alongside Hannibal Hamlin, his predecessor as our magisterial vice president."

"Rich in irony, even for Washington," I said. "Did Henry Wilson look like he was ready to commit murder?"

"Henry? He has iron in his blood, but I doubt he has a murderous bone in his body."

"Everyone's got a murderous bone somewhere," I said.

"You mean, *you* do."

"Well, yes," I said with a chortle. "You don't?"

Smalley's slight smile was the sweetest I could imagine from an adult male.

"I withdraw the question," I said. "Let me leave you be, to earn your daily bread." I started to turn toward the door. "Is the vice president in town, do you know?"

"I was about to tell you. He arrived last night."

"Maybe the president summoned him."

"Your wit is still sharp, Hay, no matter what anyone says."

Nicolay returned to the kitchen holding the DC city directory, opened to the Ws.

"The Washington House," he announced. "At the corner of Third and

Penn. They call themselves a hotel, but it's no Wormley's. More like a board-inghouse, and not a nice one. Maybe we don't pay these fellows enough."

"Maybe, but what does a vice president do?" I pointed out. "If one of them vanished, who would care? Who would even notice?"

"Mrs. Vice President."

"Perchance."

"Speaking of Wormley's," Nicolay said, "what did you learn from Lord Roscoe?"

"A great man, he is. That, he made clear. He pretty much admitted—by inviting me to leave when I asked—that Patterson has approached him. He preferred to instruct me on the *real* reason Johnson was murdered."

"Which was?"

"Impeachment."

"What?"

"Exactly. He says money was involved and . . . he leaves everything vague after that."

"Money is always involved."

"Aren't there still disputes of honor, settled by duels at dawn?"

"You're living in the glorious past, Johnny. These days, the duels are be-cause a man has been swindled, and I don't mean in love."

"And the human race marches on."

"Do you think Conkling is misleading you?"

"I wouldn't put it past him."

"To what purpose?" Nicolay said.

"Good question. This could be Conkling being mischievous, for his own amusement. Or a diversion, to keep me away from—"

"From the letters of blackmail, you mean."

"What else?" I said.

Nicolay sipped his brandy and said, "It would be useful to read those letters, wouldn't it?"

"I was thinking the same, Nico. I was thinking the same."

To-night, I was drinking scotch. We were both crooking the elbow when Therena rushed in, an envelope in hand. The upper-left corner showed a fearsome open eye.

"By a brass-buttoned messenger," she said. "Just now."

My watch said twenty minutes past ten.

The envelope was sealed. I fished out my pocketknife and extracted a piece of cream-colored, thick-stock paper that suggested a luxury meant to justify his fees. The handwriting was startlingly legible, assuming it was Pinkerton's.

> Hay, the Pattersons have been butterflies. Visited
> Frelinghuysen, VP, latest Conkling. Not Grant, but we
> shall keep watch. The eye never sleeps!

No signature. None was needed.

CHAPTER TWELVE

Nicolay was waving the newspaper over his hominy with cream. "The Senate seat that your friend Andy so thoughtfully vacated, there's talk in Tennessee that the governor might appoint none other than—are you ready for this, Johnny?—a gentleman with senatorial experience named Jefferson Davis."

I spilled my coffee, halfway to my lips. "See what you—?"

"Apparently, he's living these days in Memphis, so he's eligible. Assuming he is considered to have been an American citizen for nine years."

"Nine years in a row?" I said. "Wasn't it Johnson who pardoned him and made him an American again? Perfect symmetry."

"Or perfect corruption," Nicolay said. "Though I recall it was Horace Greeley, your guiding light—"

"*My*—?"

"Yes, the very same abolitionist who paid Jeff Davis's bail—did he not?"

"Only part of it," I corrected him. "I will admit that the voters chose prudently this last time." Twenty-four days after Grant trounced him in the 'seventy-two presidential election, Horace Greeley went to his Maker by way of a lunatic asylum in Westchester county, New York.

"This country will never elect a man who is plumb crazy," Nicolay declared. "Americans have too much sense."

"I can tell you weren't born here," I said. Nicolay's accent still carried a trace of Bavaria, whence he had emigrated at age five. I shook my head and added, "I daresay you are becoming an optimist, Nico. There's no call for it."

+>====+

The vice president's boardinghouse, at Third street and Pennsylvania avenue, was known for hosting Crazy Horse, Geronimo, and other Indian chiefs. The landlady had a puffy face and rimless spectacles and stank of overcooked cabbage. She sent me away with a sniff. "Seems we don't have the . . . facilities the Capitol has."

"Hot water, you mean," I said.

"And at any hour!" she said, to make sure I understood her outrage.

I stepped out onto the Avenue and stared eastward, up the hill. Through the trees, I glimpsed the peak of the Capitol dome. The day already promised a scorcher, but this didn't deter the older ladies from their bustles and corsets. The younger ladies dispensed with these restrictions in favor of shorter, ankle-length skirts (to the pleasure of the menfolk) and piled their hair atop their heads. The men in their high collars, wide cravats, and black frock coats suffered in silence. I did.

Happily, the Capitol's interior felt cool—disengaged from the country it governed. It was empty, befitting August, but I had no need for directions, and I preferred not to ask. Thirteen years had passed—thirteen and a half, applying Helen Nicolay's precision—since I had been in the Capitol basement, to interrogate the Executive Mansion's jailed gardener about Willie Lincoln's death. I doubted that much had changed.

It hadn't. The spiral stone staircase was as narrow as in a Transylvanian castle. I expected to see droplets—and I did!—shimmering down the walls. I found myself hurrying, before the walls closed in. As a boy, I had read too much Brothers Grimm.

Belowground, daylight met its match. The pillars down here were as wide as tree trunks. Arches in the vaulted ceiling bore the Capitol's weight. I was inside the hill that held the Capitol, as if I had descended into a crypt. It smelled damp from storms long spent.

The marble bathtubs in the basement hadn't changed any. A half dozen of them lined the wall, each in a cabinet of black walnut and adjoined by a toilet—that was new. Outside the nearest opening, the marble floor was wet. I walked gingerly.

"General Wilson!" I called. This was the vice president's favorite title, or so Smalley had said, earned in the volunteer regiment he had raised in Massachusetts when the war broke out.

"Come in! Come in!"

"Sorry to bother you here." I wasn't sorry in the slightest. "John Hay of the *New-York Tribune*. I also have a letter from the president, but I probably shouldn't give it to you in the bath."

"Did he spell my name correctly?"

The vice president was a presentable enough fellow, with a broad face, a strong chin, and blond hair to his shoulders. The patience in his gaze spoke of someone who was ready for whatever life threw at him.

"I'm afraid he didn't spell it at all." The water was up to his shoulders. I read the note aloud.

"The death of the seventeenth president," he mused. "I don't see how I can help you. But you may either ask a question or scrub my . . . back."

I had never made inquiries of an unclothed man before (a woman, just once, and it didn't end well), but it seemed the less perilous option.

"I understand you have recently conversed with David Patterson."

A pause. "Is that a question?"

"More of a statement, to which I gather you agree."

"I have had that . . . for the sake of argument, let us call it a pleasure. Not ten minutes ago, as a matter of fact. You might have run into him."

I was relieved I hadn't. "May I ask the subject of the conversation?"

"I suspect you know already, or you wouldn't be asking."

"Can you tell me, then, what the letter said?"

My directness didn't faze him. Raised in grinding poverty, then a cobbler by trade, Wilson was the rare Republican who was comfortable with voters in factories or saloons. He was known to bend to political breezes, except in opposing slavery and championing rights for workingmen, white and black. He wasn't the most honest of men—three thousand dollars' worth, from Credit Mobilier, eight months of a senator's pay. But he had profited even more by his easy manner. "It would be most ungentlemanly of me," he said, "to divulge the contents of another . . . person's correspondence."

"Whose correspondence?" I said.

"I can't see that it matters."

"And what was your reaction to it?"

The vice president of the United States of America submerged his head below the water. I worried that the bathtub would overflow. He popped up again, grunting, his blond strands in tangles. A burly black man tiptoed in and checked the thermometer that hung from the side of the tub, then opened the farther spigot for twenty seconds and stirred the bathwater before tiptoeing out.

"I have done nothing in my life that I wouldn't want to read in the newspapers."

"My condolences," I said. "What did he want?"

"What do such men always want? Besides that, I mean. And I have no intention of paying him an Indian head cent. I believe we came to a meeting of the minds on that." His torso bobbed higher and settled back down. "I trust that none of this will appear in your newspaper, Mr. Hay."

I knew it never would, but I didn't want to promise. "Not unless I can learn it elsewhere."

"I feel safe, then, in your hands, Mr. Hay. Should I feel unsafe, you should expect to feel the same."

"I have never been threatened before," I said, "by a man in a bath."

"I never threaten anyone. Occasionally, I need to point out the dangers."

"As a public service," I said.

"More like a private service," Wilson replied. "Now, can I help you with anything else?" When I didn't reply right away, he added, "Surely, the president cannot possibly have any interest in this."

That his vice president was subjected to blackmail? "Not directly, no," I hedged. "Tell me, sir, do you know of anyone who would want to . . . cause harm to Senator Johnson?"

"Seventy-three of them, at least."

All of the decedent's senatorial colleagues. "Plus yourself," I said.

A shrug. A brawny right arm rose out of the water. "I don't think I can help you any further, Mr. Hay."

"Did you enjoy swearing him in?"

"It is one of the duties I enjoy most."

"And this time?"

"I must admit it gave me a certain satisfaction, for a vice president to swear in two former vice presidents at once. I am not without a sense of humor. The galleries certainly enjoyed it. His new colleagues—it caught their attention."

"In a favorable way?"

"That, you would have to ask them."

"And expect a straight answer?"

A wise old laugh. "Mr. Hay, Mr. Hay. As I understand your, shall we say, creative—nay, I say trackless—career, it has wandered from law to politics to diplomacy to journalism, with a little bit of poetry along the way. In any of these fields of endeavor, does a man of the world ever expect a straight answer? The trick is to take a crooked answer and to understand how to straighten it. In this, I imagine you are a skilled practitioner."

"As you are," I said.

A throatier laugh. I noticed how thin his hair was and how speckled his scalp. He said, "I was a struggling shoemaker, my boy, who has built a career on such skills."

I didn't feel like his boy, but fathers were prone to help their sons—weren't they? "Do you know if anyone was especially upset in accepting Mr. . . . President . . . Senator Johnson back into the fold, after the . . . trauma of his impeachment?"

"Mr. Hamlin seemed a little unnerved, for a Mainer," the vice president said. "And let me tell you something about that impeachment. I can say this seven years later—and not for print. Never for print. Is that understood?"

"It is." This had better be good.

"He should never have been impeached, at least on the grounds the House gave us. What in Sam Hill was the Tenure of Office Act, anyway? That was the grounds for the whole damn venture—the excuse for it. What do you mean a president can't fire his own secretary of war without groveling for permission from the Senate? I am no lawyer, thank the stars, but the Supreme Court will never allow that to stand. Nor should it."

I nodded in tentative agreement.

"It's not even clear that law applied to Johnson," he went on. "The way it was written, arguably it applied only to Lincoln. That's who appointed Stanton to the cabinet—Johnson didn't. And the other charges—that he vetoed our laws and said nasty things about Congress—some of which might have been true, mind you. That's what presidents *do*. They have a constitutional right to veto legislation—his were mostly overridden, by the way—and to say mean things about Congress. I've said them, too, having spent eighteen blessed years here." He pointed up, either to the Senate chamber or to the celestial skies. Swinging his arm made waves.

"But you voted to convict him."

"Of course I did, and I would do it again," Wilson bellowed. He was playing to the galleries now, which meant me. I feared for my shoes, should the tub brim be breached. "Because he was a terrible, terrible president. He had never been elected in his own right and never could be. A rotten man. Wouldn't listen to anyone else, only to his own sense of . . . rectitude, to be kind. And he would never back off, no matter the cost. Yes, he was a man of principle—*aargh*. Spare me the men of principle, unless the principles are ones I agree with. He believed in the principle that whites are the superior race and, by God's desire, ought to remain so. Of what value is a principle like that? The older I get, Mr. Hay, the less I care about principle, and the more I believe in muddling through."

The vice president of the United States ducked under the water again, then came up snorting. I was starting to understand how resentments can linger.

"Unfortunately," he went on, "we are not permitted to impeach a man for being a terrible president or even a terrible person. Not according to our revered Constitution. Madison, dash his memory, made sure of that. 'Maladministration,' he called it, and the Founding Fathers in their idiocy rejected it as grounds for impeachment. So we had to impeach him for the things he had every right to do. But what damn choice did we have? For the good of the country, he needed to be thrown out of office. On his ear, preferably, or on something lower. For the good of the country, Mr. Hay, of its people. There is no higher good."

To my ear, this principle sounded a trifle dangerous, even before its proclaimer's excitement surged bathwater onto my shoes.

"I can see the emotions haven't faded in seven years, sir."

"Mr. Johnson's didn't fade, either. Have you read the diatribe he delivered in March? The man had enemies, and if what you're implying is correct, he had one too many."

"Any in particular?"

"Any and all."

This was getting me nowhere. "Do you expect to see Senator Patterson again?"

"I can't imagine why. I have made my position clear, both to him and the missus."

"Mrs. Patterson? She was here?" I pointed at the bathwater, which hid the vice president's bulk. "*Here?*"

This brought a toothy grin to his open and affable face. "I must say she had me at a disadvantage, sitting here as God made me, plus a few extra pounds. In fact, she seemed in charge of things. She is nobody's second, you understand, other than her dear papa's. And compared to the late and lamented, no one else's candle burns so bright. Including her husband's, I would imagine, but I am hardly in a position to assess a marriage." His torso half rose again. "And now, Mr. Hay, would you care to scrub an old man's back?"

I pleaded a previous engagement.

‡⇥⇤‡

Senator Frelinghuysen had also spoken of ol' Andy's diatribe, and the secretary of the Senate, Mr. Gorham, knew which speech I meant, and the date. It took him about thirty-three seconds to retrieve a thick volume of the *Congressional Record* and to find the right page. He put me at too small a table in too large a chair, so that my knees splayed. The congressional appropriators must be playing a prank.

I swooped in where Mr. Gorham's thumb had slipped away:

The President's Action in Louisiana

SPEECH OF HON. ANDREW JOHNSON
OF TENNESSEE
IN THE UNITED STATES SENATE
March 22, 1875

Mr. President, notwithstanding I have been in the habit of speaking in public for a number of years, sometimes in deliberative bodies and sometimes before the people, I confess that I appear before the Senate this morning under great embarrassment . . . My entrance into the Senate was of so recent a date and under such peculiar circumstances, that I had determined that I would not participate in any discussion during the present session of the Senate; and what I may say on this occasion I want it distinctly understood grows out of no party bias or partisan feeling whatever . . .

The sound of a musket loading.

The speech was, in fact, a tongue-lashing. The ostensible topic was Frelinghuysen's resolution in support of President Grant's military intervention in a persisting civil war. For page after boring page, he addressed the constitutional powers of the presidency versus those of Congress, recounted a "similar" incident in 1866 that happened to involve a general named Grant, and asked why General Sheridan had recently been dispatched to Louisiana, as "a man who was obnoxious to that whole people . . ."

I know the determination of that people. Their great object is to be restored back into the Union upon equal footing with all the other states, and have a fair participation in the legislation of the country. That is all they desire. But what is that to those who are acting behind the curtain and who are aspiring to retain power, and . . . would inaugurate a system of terrorism . . .

Terrorism? Who was Johnson accusing of terrorism?

. . . and in the midst of the excitement, in the midst of the war-cry, triumphantly ride into the presidency for a third presidential term, and when that is done, farewell to the liberties of the country. [Applause in the galleries.]

A third term! That's what this was about. Rumors were rampant in Washington City that President Grant was lusting—and the First Lady, more so!—for another four years in the nicest home they had known. And why not? Grant was the youngest president in the nation's history and still the hero of the Civil War. He could probably win a third term for the asking. Was this the villain that Johnson accused of terrorism, of endangering Americans' liberties? Plainly so, and to the applause of folks—voters—in the Senate galleries.

> The president of the United States assumes to take command of the state and assign these people a governor . . . Is this not monstrous in a free country? . . . It can be viewed as no other than an act of usurpation and an act of tyranny . . . I do not care whether you call him president or monarch or king . . . We have now got "army" and "power." We have got a statocracy; we have not got a democracy, and we have not got a republican form of government. How far off is empire? How far off is military despotism? . . . I would say to this emperor, I would say to this dictator what Cato said to the ambassador of Caesar:
>
> Bid him disband his legions, restore the commonwealth to liberty.

Oh my gracious! Tyranny? Monarch? Dictator? Military despotism? The end of democracy? This was Johnson's vision of a government led by Ulysses S. Grant, the mild-mannered, slump-shouldered ex-general?

Was I living in a different country from ol' Andy?

Then another question popped into my mind: Was he eyeing a return to the presidency for himself?

+➤══◄+

"The ravings of a madman." General Babcock scowled. "Why should his pitiful little speech trouble us?"

"No reason," I said. I hadn't suggested it should.

We were sitting in the office that used to be mine. What an odd sensation. It was a plain office, nothing memorable or fancy. Only its location made it grand, at the northeastern corner of the second floor, catty-cornered from the president's office. The furnishings hadn't changed—they had looked shabby when I used them. Nor, of course, had the view, or the feeling of being in the eye of every storm. His desk, like mine—I think it *was* mine—was at the north window, facing out across the lawn, to the Avenue.

"What else have you learned, thanks to the president's letter?" he asked. "Anything of value from Elizabethton?" He pronounced it correctly.

"Not much more, I'm afraid." I had collected an impressive amount of flimsy evidence, and I told Babcock some of what I'd learned about the Pattersons' blackmail letters. He pressed me for the names of the three recipients I'd visited and I mentioned Frelinghuysen, whom I had promised to protect only in print. For reasons of constitutional delicacy, I kept mum about the vice president. *Conkling?* I couldn't say, I replied, which told Babcock what he wanted to know. I hoped he would consider this fair payment for Grant's authorization, in that it put the president's late nemesis in a terrible light. You didn't get something for nothing, in Washington or anywhere else.

Babcock seemed pleased, maybe too much so—almost lit from within. He fired questions at me as if I were an inferior officer, which in a manner of speaking I was. What did the letters say? How much money did the Pattersons demand?

None of which did I answer, mostly (although not entirely) because I didn't know. I had a feeling he was collecting evidence against a dead man.

I declined Babcock's offer of a presidential carriage to return me to Nicolay's. I had a different destination in mind. I could walk.

It was ten past four. I turned right at the Treasury Department and along Fifteenth street and then turned left back onto the Avenue, which was its usual boisterous self. Bootblacks shouted, newsboys hawked, horsecar bells clanged in the roadway. Government clerks in derbies and frock coats were lining up for the streetcar or shuffling home. At Willard's Hotel, where Nicolay and I used to take our meals, men who were sharp in dress and round in torso were streaming in and out. I crossed Fourteenth street, past the Western Union office. A print shop, a paint shop, a lithographer's shop, the jeweler's none the worse for the wayward ewe, the coffee roaster I could smell across the Avenue—not every business was migrating north to F street.

By the time I reached the Kirkwood House, past Twelfth street, the crowds along the sidewalk had thinned. Ladies lifted their skirts to step over the mud. The hotel doorman, on the Avenue, was a fugitive from a Brontë novel, a white-haired gentleman in a top hat and tails. He nodded in dim remembrance, although I hadn't seen him before.

Stepping into the lobby was like entering a cavern, cool and dim. It smelled like my grandmother's attic, musty with a hint of decay. The green in the marble pillars was as dark as bile, and cigar smoke hung in the air.

The floor felt slippery, from tobacco juice, I feared, from guests with im-
perfect aim.

The desk clerk was a sallow young fellow with reddish eyes and albino-
white hair. I inquired after Mr. and Mrs. David Patterson. With barely
a glance and no questions asked, he pointed to the stairs past the desk.
"Room sixty-eight. One flight up."

The winding staircase was unlit and smelled faintly of lye. I was careful
not to trip on rips in the carpet. Room 68 was at the top, diagonally across
from the dining room entrance.

I knocked on the door. The sound echoed inside. I was about to knock
again when I heard light footsteps. A latch was unbolted, then a second,
and the heavy door swung open. I hadn't expected to see Bill.

Bill looked just as surprised to see me.

"I didn't know you were here," I said.

"Ah work for them now," he mumbled.

"Are they in?"

"She is."

"May I see her?"

"Let me check, Mistuh . . . Hay?"

I nodded. "Before that, do you know anything about some letters?"

Bill's eyes widened, and I swear his café-au-lait complexion reddened as
his gaze darted past my left shoulder.

"Senator," Bill said without a quaver. "Mr. Hay is askin' to see ya, suh."
His accent had broadened into servitude. He stepped out of the doorway,
and I took the opportunity to slide past him, inside.

David Patterson followed me out of the corridor and stalked past me and
snapped, "What are you doing here?"

People kept asking me that. I needed a clever riposte. "Can we talk?" I
said.

"Not now."

He rushed off, toward what I supposed was the bedroom. I turned back to
Bill, but he, too, was gone. I couldn't guess where. Anyway, I figured my best
choice was to stay where I was, by the door, so I practiced my social skills by
striking up a conversation with the hat rack. I more than held my own.

I didn't need to wait long.

Martha Patterson sidled into the entrance hall and extended a long, thin
hand. "Good afternoon, Mr. Hay. It is kind of you to come see us again,
and so soon."

Her sarcasm was sharp.

"It is my pleasure," I said. "Do you have a minute . . . or two?"

"The subject?"

"Your father's death."

"Still?"

"Can we sit?" I said.

The look she gave me could have sliced granite. She led me into the parlor, a pleasant though unexceptional room, with a hotel's impersonality—
busy wallpaper, a tattered carpet, a plain chandelier dimly lit. The velvet
curtains were drawn.

"Isn't this where . . . ?"

"It is."

I shivered at the memory of that night. I had been sitting by the corner
of Lincoln's deathbed when the vice president stopped in around two in the
morning, then took his leave and came back . . . here. It was in this room,
the next morning, inside these four walls, where the chief justice (Kate
Chase's daddy, shoved upstairs!) swore in Andrew Johnson as the seventeenth president of the nation that Lincoln had saved.

I said, "Where, exactly?"

She pointed to a spot near the center of the floor, where the carpet was
torn.

She gestured me into an armless cane-bottom chair, obviously hoping I
wouldn't stay long, and lowered herself into a divan.

I had debated how to begin. I thought it best not to tell her of Grant's
letter, for fear of making her mad. Should I start with the subject of murder
or of blackmail? Which would get me thrown out first?

"I talked to your mother back in Elizabethton," I said. "She isn't satisfied
that your father's death was . . . natural." I was becoming practiced at this
particular euphemism. "She had expected something like it for years."

I braced for her reaction.

"So did he," she said.

"He did?"

"Of course. He knew the nature of his enemies, how they would attack
him and hound him and how eventually, despite his best efforts, they would
succeed. So many of his critics hated him, *hated* him—he, who loved the
people, and the people loved him. This is the fate of a man who fights for
the people and never backs down. It was destined."

"Which of them would have . . . did . . ."—I couldn't voice the verb, but
I didn't need to—"do you think?"

"Any of them."

Including your husband, I wanted to say. "Any in particular?" I pressed.

"You asked me that once before, on the train."

"Not quite. I asked you—"

The double doors to the bedroom slid apart, and the good senator—the former senator—barreled into the parlor. His face had flushed; his fists were cocked. I was relieved to see both hands and no revolver.

I said, "I am trying to understand—"

"You bothering my wife again?"

"I don't think so. In fact, she just suggested—"

"I warn you—stay away from this, Hay. The next time, I will call the police."

For a variety of reasons, I doubted that. But nothing more would be learned here, and I left with my dignity intact.

In the corridor, passing the dining room entrance, I heard my name whispered. It sounded urgent. I recognized Bill's melodious voice.

The servant stepped halfway into the corridor. In the dim light, he looked dark. "I know where they are," he whispered.

"Where what are?"

"You know."

"The letters?"

He nodded quickly and held a forefinger and thumb a half inch apart.

"That thick?" I said.

He nodded.

I said, "Where are they?"

Instead of answering, he scampered away, back to the Pattersons' door.

⊹⊱≺≻⊰⊹

I needed to walk, and a pleasant walk it was. The heat had relented enough for me to enjoy the occasional breeze rather than dread it. The traffic along the Avenue was ebbing. The buggies and the streetcars had, for the moment, made peace. The shops had rolled up their awnings and lowered their blinds. The pedestrians were few—on the northern sidewalk, anyway. Across the Avenue, Center Market was still buzzing with business and the painted, snuff-chewing ladies of the evening had emerged. I stayed on my side: I would score no points with anyone, including myself, for resisting temptation.

I tried to understand what had just happened. I had been threatened by the second of Johnson's two sons-in-law. The first one had pulled the trigger and missed. This one threatened to call the police. Innocent men didn't act like that. Did they have reasons to want their father-in-law gone? Might it involve his lack of a will, or his intent to write one?

Or maybe one or the other was protecting someone else. Martha Patterson, perhaps. Would she really do harm to her father? She revered the man. And she just told me that she thought he had been murdered, just like her mother believed. Didn't this clear her of suspicion—and her husband, too? Or was it an artful deception? Let me assure you, dear reader, that being a detective (or a newspaperman) isn't as easy as it looks.

I was hurtling along the Avenue, in Nicolay's direction, counting on the Goddess of Stupid Young Men to keep me from harm. Which She did until I was crossing Four-and-a-half street and a wagon loaded with iron bars turned into my path. The driver shook his fist, and I stopped and swept my arm toward the asphalt—*after you, m'lord.*

I returned to the quandary at hand. I was willing to believe that Mary's husband in Elizabethton was simply a lout, and that he shot at me because I had knocked him to the ground. Reasonably so, I suppose, especially in the South. The Pattersons' reason, or reasons, for hostility was something else, and the likeliest was the most obvious. They were blackmailers who didn't want their crimes exposed. They were hiding the blackmail letters.

And Bill knew where they were.

I wanted to see them. I needed hard evidence of something. Even if it didn't solve a murder, I'd have a wishbone of a story, of a former president and his blackmail letters, now as a family inheritance.

And Bill knew where they were.

I crossed the Capitol grounds as if they were a church graveyard, attentive to every spot I put my feet. Dusk was settling in as I turned south onto First street. Nicolay's house was on the left, most of the way to C street. The gas lamps hadn't been lit yet. Clouds were passing over the emerging moon.

I had reached Nicolay's when a man's voice stage-whispered, "You Hay?"

I owned up to it. I turned toward my inquisitor on the crumbling brick sidewalk. In the shadows, I saw a man who was taller than I was but not by much. Best I could tell, he was bland-looking, mustachioed, and carefully groomed. I was squinting when I saw his left hand rise high above his head and slash down. It held a knife.

My right cross was quick and thwacked his chin. But my fist came back a half second too slowly. I nudged his wrist aside, so the bayonet blade missed my cheek but sliced my forearm as my assailant fell back. His head hit the brick wall that fronted Nicolay's yard and bounced onto the sidewalk and landed with a thud. A sickening sound, for which I . . . thanked God.

My forearm didn't hurt, and I scrambled onto Nicolay's porch before I passed out. The last thing I remembered was of something warm and sticky oozing down my wrist and pooling in my palm.

I also remembered thinking, *I must be getting close.*

CHAPTER THIRTEEN

WEDNESDAY, AUGUST 11, 1875

I passed the worst night of my life since Lincoln died. This time, the pain was physical, and not only in my right forearm. Every time I moved, it hurt, and the *it* kept changing. The pain traveled down into my wrist and up my arm to my shoulder, even into my chest. My stomach quavered. Nothing felt right.

Ought I consider an electrochemical bath or possibly a consultation with Madame Ross, the astrologer, for a buck and a half (four bits less for ladies)? No, no! Am I not the fellow who prides himself on summoning the nerve to step into a boxing ring? So, would I let a little scratch stop me now?

Yes. For a few minutes more, at least.

I had a gossamer of a memory—was it a dream?—of being pulled up the stairs and trying to help myself but sinking into darkness. I squeezed my eyes shut and willed the pain to subside, with limited success. I must have moaned because the door opened with trepidation. Therena considered her options and stepped through.

"Johnny, you're awake," she said.

I tried to joke but was unable to—this was a shock—find my voice. I nodded instead and tried again: "In th-th-theory."

"You in much pain?"

This time I didn't trust my voice. I shrugged, and regretted moving.

"Where?" Therena said.

I bowed toward my right arm and winced. She went to the doorway and called, "George!"

Nicolay couldn't have been far because he rushed right in. His face showed a look of concern that for some reason amused me, although for my own comfort—and his—I refrained from bursting into "Molly Malone." He leaned over me and said, "So, what happened?"

"Was . . . was hoping you could tell me," I said. "Some man . . . a knife. You saw . . . didn't you . . . him . . . isn't he . . . by the street?"

"We saw no one out there except you," Nicolay said. "Just heard a . . . it wasn't really a knocking, more like a scratching at the door, like a dog that wanted to come in."

"The . . . the . . . the sidewalk . . . did you . . . did anyone . . . ?"

"I didn't. Did you, Therena?"

She was standing at the foot of the bed and shook her head. "Probably the police did," she said.

"The police!" I said. "They here?"

"Therena ran to the Capitol and brought one back. You were the victim of a crime."

"Then you did see the sidewalk," I pointed out. My mind hadn't expired.

"I guess I did," Therena said. "I didn't see anything—anyone—there."

"He got away," I said.

Therena said, "Are you in pain?"

Yes, I wanted to scream but I shrugged instead and flinched.

"The doctor said you would be."

"He was here, too?'

"Oh yes," Nicolay said. "Where were you?"

"Where *was* I? What else did he say?"

"That you'd live."

"Two for two," I said, "so far. Anything else?"

"That you should rest," Therena said. "What *do* you remember?"

My words began to flow, and the pain receded, just a little. I told them about the man in the shadows who had called my name and lunged at me with a knife.

"You're saying he knew you?"

"No, he didn't know me, because he asked if I was Hay. But it was me he wanted."

"And you didn't know him."

"No, I don't think so. In fact, I'm sure of it. I'd never seen him before."

"Would you recognize him again? That's what the policeman asked."

"Did I answer?"

"No, you were beyond any reply. Do you think you could?"

A pain shot through my right forearm. How long until I took a pen in hand? "I don't know," I said.

"Then what did he want, do you think?"

"I think he was trying to stop me from . . . I don't know . . . doing what

I'm doing. What else could it be? He didn't try to rob me. And he knew it was dear old me he wanted."

Nicolay said, "Do you think he was trying to kill you?"

"That crossed my mind."

"Maybe he was just trying to scare you," Nicolay said.

"Well, he succeeded," I replied.

"I hope it's discouraged you," Therena said, "at least a little."

"I don't know," I whispered. I knew it hadn't.

⊢═══┤

I lolled in bed, playing hooky from the world. Therena had fashioned a sling out of a Parisian scarf. I was feeling a tad better. The pain wasn't gone, by any means. Clara would know what to do. (Didn't she always? It drove me daft.) The Giles' Liniment—and the laudanum—helped. The pain in my bandaged forearm had dulled enough to maneuver last night's *Evening Star*. The front page, badly printed—not like newspapers in New York— told of the twenty thousand dollars recovered from the Treasury Department's forty-seven-thousand-dollar robbery; the court hearing scheduled in New York on reducing Boss Tweed's bail; Hans Christian Andersen's funeral in Copenhagen. On the back page, I skipped the advertisement for MANHOOD RESTORED (I was living proof that self-abuse did not bring impotence) and scanned the booksellers' lists of their latest: *Man and Beast; Here and Hereafter; Etonian Style of Swimming; How to Live Long; The Odd Trump, a Novel*.

A cooling breeze sneaked through the window. Therena brought me breakfast—a pot of tea and a slice of freshly baked bread. I munched the bread (with raspberry jam, courtesy of the Nicolays' garden) and stared at the cracked ceiling, pondering the question I was unable to ignore: Who would do me harm?

David Patterson? Martha Patterson? They wanted me out of the way— that was evident. This was a way to do that, whether the knife found its target or not. The fear would suffice.

I couldn't prove it. I could hardly ask them. I suppose it could be one of the senators frightened that something unsavory might come to light. What had Andrew Johnson learned about Roscoe Conkling or Frederick Freling-huysen (did anyone call him *Freddie*?) or the vice president of these United States? Of the three, I would imagine that only Conkling had the . . . gall, shall we say, to order a murder. But really, you could never tell for certain. Henry Wilson seemed capable, and the most prudish or timid of men (I'm thinking of you, Freddie) might well be a brute in hiding. I had talked to them all, pleasing none.

The tea and the bread were cold and I was getting bored with this game—game, ha!—of suspects who might want to kill me. There was a knock at the door. It was crisp, more like a policeman than a Nicolay.

I was almost right. It was Pinkerton. I was actually happy to see him.

"So, wha' in the de'il happened t' ye?" he said, barreling toward the bed.

"I got knifed," I said with too much pride. I told him my tale and didn't get the empathy I apparently considered my due. I tried to describe, without much success, the man with the knife, and I urged Pinkerton to examine the brick sidewalk. I got questions instead.

"Who knew ye were heah?"

"I've made no secret of it. I'm easy to follow."

"But this fella got there before ye. Who have ye seen since ye've been heah?"

"Besides the president, his private secretary, the vice president, a couple of senators, the secretary of the Senate, and Old Edward? Practically no one. Only Smalley, the Nicolays"—I'd run out of fingers to flick—"and Lord knows who at the congressional faro bank. Oh, and you. Does that help any?"

"It might."

"Anything else I can tell you?"

"Wha' else do ye know?"

"Surprisingly little, I must say, given that I'm the one who got . . . knifed."

"None too seriously, it looks."

"Could've been worse," I said. "Things can always get worse."

"Ye aren't too stupid fer someone so young," Pinkerton said.

"Not as stupid as I used to be."

"No mortal can hope for more than tha', Hay."

I laughed in spite of myself, and paid for it in pain.

Pinkerton said, "D'ye need some help?"

"No, the Nicolays have been wonderful. Apparently a doctor saw me last night and was medically unimpressed."

"I mean as a bodyguard."

"Oh my, no. I can take care of myself."

"Aye, like last night." Pinkerton nodded at my forearm.

"Yes, like last night. I defended myself."

"Aye, and ye're in bed t'day instead o' restin' at the morgue." His lilt made both options sound enticing. "To-morrow, it may be the morgue."

"I'll take my chances," I said.

"Ye go' a daugh'er now."

Damn him for pointing out the obvious.

"Would you care for a firearm?" Pinkerton said.

"I might," I said. "Anything else?"

"Aye. Those letters. Your man Pa'erson summoned the senators by tele-gram. The vice president, too. Wires from Greeneville. So my pals at West-ern Union tell me. Which'll cost ye a bi'."

"Happy to have the *Tribune* pay. What did the telegrams say, exactly?"

"That the honorable recipient would find it to his reputation's benefit—tha' was the phrase he used—to be in Washington on August ninth or tenth. Dated the first."

That was the day after Andrew Johnson's death, two days before his fu-neral. "Any specifics?" I said. "Anything about a letter of . . . ?"

"Nae. Apparently nae need. They must o' known what it was abo't. And Pa'erson knew tha' they knew. And they did show up, pretty much provin' it."

"Any other telegrams?"

"None I know of."

"I've been thinking about those letters," I said. I had just made up my mind. "I'm going to take them."

"Steal 'em?"

"Read them, anyway. Put them back if I can."

"Are ye now?" I swear I saw a twinkle in Pinkerton's eyes. "A fellow after me heart, such as it is. And I'm gonna help ye."

"No, you won't."

"Indeed, I shall. Not an easy operation, either. They always carry those letters with 'em. *He* does."

"How do you know?"

"Seen the envelopes meself, in his jacke' pocke', whenever they go out. Been keepin' 'em in sight, y'know. We never sleep."

"Sounds exhausting. So, how can I . . . ?"

"We."

"How can I . . . ?"

An idea struck me, one that was boneheaded enough to work. I kept it to myself.

+──⊰⊱──+

I enlisted Helen in my detection brigade, and the almost-nine-and-a-half-year-old was a natural. She could catch a weasel asleep, and in her mind, this was an adventure, scouring for evidence in her own front yard. To me, too.

I was still a little rickety. The laudanum had worn off; my forearm throbbed. Helen helped me down the narrow stairs and out the front door. The heat hit me like a dragon's exhalation. I sat on the top step for a moment and caught my breath, Helen beside me. Without further dramatics, I climbed down the porch and followed the walkway and descended the brick steps to the sidewalk. Helen watched from the top.

I hadn't a notion what I was looking for, so how could a policeman have found anything—and at night? Assuming he had looked very hard. A nick in the forearm didn't deserve much time. Unless, of course, the forearm was yours.

The sidewalk was made from a peppery brick, the edges sharp and uneven to the touch. Hitting one's head against it would . . . sting. I sank to my hands—pardon me, *hand*—and knees under the assumption that I could get back up. Nothing looked out of the ordinary. As I stood, I glanced up at the low brick wall. A spot along the top looked darker than the rest. I moved to make sure I wasn't casting a shadow. I wasn't. It *was* darker. I rubbed it with my forefinger. I looked down at my fingertip.

It was pink.

I knew I hadn't imagined the altercation, but it was nice to have proof. Even so, was this evidence? I slid a thumb along the edge of the wall, which felt moist. I scraped my thumbnail and collected a sticky greenery—moss, nothing more. Farther along, I noticed a piece of . . . detritus. I extended my thumb and forefinger and, with trepidation, picked it up. It was a clotted tuft of hair and . . . was this tissue? A sliver of scalp? I realized this was . . . part of a person. And evidence! Of minimal use, perhaps, but evidence nonetheless. I inspected it more closely. The hair was dark, maybe black. The scalp was . . . I guess that's what it was. This was beyond my . . . I knew as much about this as . . . an almost-nine-and-a-half-year-old girl.

Speaking of whom, Helen was gesturing down from the walkway, pointing past me. "Look at that, Uncle Johnny," she said. "What are those?"

I saw a couple of bricks upended on the sidewalk—I had learned to step around them—and the weeds that popped up in crooked lines. The bark on the skinny poplar looked unblemished.

"No, *there*," she said. "In the street."

I stepped to the side for a different angle in the sunlight, and I saw what she meant. Drag marks. They were unmistakable, in the dry, dusty roadway. Parallel ruts, approximately a body's width. Heel marks.

They ended a few feet from the curb, as if a body had been loaded into a vehicle and carted away.

As if my attacker hadn't been working alone.

━━━

Young Helen had to urge me upstairs. I was so tired that I slumped into my bed. I must have slept, because when I opened my eyes, the afternoon sunlight slanted in. I listened to the clattering in the coal and wood yard across First street.

Man alive, I felt fine. Not totally fine, but near enough. Fit, even. I sat up—too quickly, because pain sliced through my forearm. I froze, and it passed. I swiveled to the bedside and sat for a couple of minutes before I rose unsteadily to my feet. I waited to collapse, but I didn't. My head felt clear. This was odd, because my head rarely feels clear.

A line of poetry leapt—crept?—into my mind.

> *Out of the darkness comes death.*

That didn't scan right.

> *Out of darkness comes the death*

The death. I liked that. I sat back down.

> *Out of darkness comes the death*
> *And then the resurrection,*
> *Not of the spirit, nor of the soul*
> *But of the . . .*

What rhymed with *resurrection? Indirection? Disaffection? Insurrection?* Not *forearm.*

━━━

It was dark when I next opened my eyes, so I shut them again. My forearm ached. It felt warm and wet, on my belly. I realized the bandages hadn't been changed. I felt woozy.

I had begun to consider sitting up when there was a knock at the door. It was too tentative for a policeman or Pinkerton and not familiar enough for a Nicolay. Without a word from me, the door opened.

A silhouette stood still, as if an arm was ready to sweep high before lunging . . .

I was about to cry out when the silhouette stepped forward and took a woman's shape. Therena.

"Could you change my bandage?" I said. "I don't think I can do it one-handed."

She strode over in the dark and lifted my forearm with care. She found the end of the bandage and with a firm but tender grasp began to peel it back.

"Thank you," I said.

"You are welcome, my one true love."

I jolted up. "Clara!" I exclaimed. I pulled my arms wide and yelped in pain. "What are you doing here?"

"I heard . . . what happened," Clara said.

Therena's doing.

My forearm hurt like a pig in pincers, but the vitals still worked as Nature intended.

CHAPTER FOURTEEN

What a treat not to listen for a baby in the next room. The least rational member of the household ruled it. In Cleveland, we had servants, but I wasn't used to them and didn't want to be. Nothing so important as rearing a child should be farmed out to the hired help. That said, spending a morning in bed with Clara without being interrupted was a . . . I hesitate to say *godsend* . . . well, a delight. Maybe I was already getting old—if you're lucky, thirty-six years was halfway to death—but the afterward was as gratifying as the during. Less explosive, shall we say, but deeper somehow, with satisfactions of its own.

My forearm was feeling better already.

We lay on our backs, counting the cracks in the ceiling. Upward of twenty, by my tally. Clara was turning them into constellations, and not the standard ones.

"A burlesque dancer over there," she said, pointing to a sinuous web by the doorway.

"So it is," I said, not seeing it at all. "And there's a banana."

As I rolled toward her again, a stab of pain reached my shoulder and I fell back down.

"You all right?" she said.

"Sure."

"You need protection."

"Oh? I thought we—"

"I don't mean . . . I mean somebody who will keep you safe."

"You've been talking to Pinkerton?"

"Is he here?"

"Oh yes. And getting in the way, or wanting to."

"That's his job."

"At how much an hour?"

"You paying?" Clara said. "I mean, we paying?"

"Not a greenback. But I don't want somebody following me around all the time."

"Only when you go out," Clara said.

"Oh, wonderful," I said. "And he'll be sitting on the porch while he waits for me? Therena will keep running out to give him another cup of tea. Trust me, I'll be careful."

"Weren't you careful the other night? Your Mr. Pinkerton sounds like a sensible person." Clara propped herself up on her elbow and squinted at me and kissed my nose. "And so am I."

"Cantaloupe?" Therena offered. "Straight from the icebox."

"Such a deceitful melon," Clara said.

"What?" I declared. I had never thought about fruit in moral terms before.

"No matter how much you squeeze it and sniff it at the grocer," she explained patiently, as if to a moron, "you can't tell about its insides—its texture or taste."

"Like a man," I said.

Therena, slicing the cantaloupe at the sideboard, nearly cut herself as she giggled. "Or a woman," she said.

"Or a girl," Helen chimed in.

"Nobody except day laborers," Nicolay harrumphed, "needs anything solid for breakfast other than a roll."

I was trying to twist my forearm, freshly bandaged and now free of a sling. "A roll is about all I *can* eat," I said, "without spilling it over myself."

"A cantaloupe isn't really solid, Father," Helen said. "It's mostly water."

"Sweet water," Nicolay said.

"On a good day," Therena noted.

Clara was extolling the pleasures of train travel when I heard an impatient knocking at the front door. Helen popped up from the table—we were in the dining room, now that Clara made five—and went to answer it. She came back a moment later and said, "It's for you, Uncle Johnny."

I shuffled to the entrance hall. It was Pinkerton. "I come bearin' gifts," he said. "*A* gift."

Clara had followed me out, and I had no choice but to introduce them. He raised her hand and kissed it like an Italian noble, not the working-class bloke from Glasgow. She would have followed him anywhere—in this case, into the parlor.

The curtains were parted, and sunlight dappled the room. The furniture was worn and enveloping. A game of checkers was half-played on the center table. Newspapers and magazines were scattered about. The *Harper's Weekly* cover showed a drawing of President Grant's first grandchild, circled by GRANTISM, NEPOTISM, THIRD-TERMISM, THIRD-GENERATIONISM.

Clara and I sat on a nut-brown divan that sank halfway to the floor. Pinkerton stood over us and said, "I hope ye will forgive me, Mrs. Hay," and pulled out a pistol.

Clara startled.

"'Tisn't dinky," Pinkerton said, presenting it to me open-palmed, like a dead flounder, "bu' is easy t' conceal. A twenty-two-caliber pocket revolver, goes by the name of Dead Shot. Walnut grip, square butt, six shots. It's yers." I figured he would be charging me fifty bucks for a fifteen-dollar gun. It was small, without frills, businesslike, with a short barrel and a bluish finish. There was nothing fancy about it. "It'll do," Pinkerton said.

"Do for what?" Clara said.

"Whate'er he need it fer," Pinkerton said. "Good fer card-table distance. It'll work wonders agin a knife."

This wasn't the sort of testimonial I wanted Clara to hear.

Clara's wish that I acquire a bodyguard fell on receptive ears, all but mine. I said we would talk about it later, by which I meant we wouldn't. (Clara understood; her raised eyebrow registered her objection, for the marital ledger.) Pinkerton handed over a box of cartridges and asked if I knew how to shoot. I said I did, which wasn't too much of an exaggeration. You can't grow up on the frontier and not know how to handle a firearm, although it doesn't necessarily make you a Calamity Jane.

"Also t' tell ye, the Pa'ersons they keep making the rounds heah."

"Tell me more."

"The two senators and the vice president—of those you know—and a society lady or three, at tea time. Just the missus saw the ladies."

Maybe she *is* seeing old friends, meaning she had told me the truth but not the whole truth. Not bad, for Washington City.

Pinkerton asked about my plan to steal the blackmail letters, which was something else I hadn't told Clara yet.

"Later," I assured her again. Then to Pinkerton: "You'll be the first to know if I need help."

"Will I?" Pinkerton said. He looked unconvinced, and reasonably so.

After I gave her the necessary explanations, I asked Clara to tour the botanical gardens near the Capitol with Therena while I went on alone.

"I came to see *you*, you know," she said. But she complied.

My first stop was Newspaper Row. Smalley was in, of course. He was seated at his desk, drumming a pencil, his eyes half-shut. He was thinking, I had to assume. Either that or daydreaming. Neither would bear interruption. I watched as his temples reverberated and his jowls quivered. He was composing in his mind. Watching from the outside felt like peeping.

Beside his desk was a model of the earth in a wooden base that I hadn't seen before. When Smalley's trance ended, I asked him if it was new.

"No," he replied. "Billions of years old, or since four thousand four before Christ, if it's Archbishop Ussher you trust."

Maybe I deserved that. "Do you need to write something down?" I said.

"No, it's written," Smalley said. "I'll jot it down later."

I was in awe.

He gestured me into a seat and asked after my health. How he had learned about my mishap I couldn't imagine. I replied that I couldn't jot anything down—"Legibly, at least, but I don't have anything to write, either. Yet."

"Any good leads?"

"How much do you know about Martha Patterson?"

"A little. I was here—not at the *Tribune,* but on the Hill—when she was . . . whatever she was in the president's house. Her father's hostess, I guess you would call it, while her invalid mamma was stuck upstairs. Sometimes I wondered if they stuck her up there, but probably not. She was a tough old bird and wouldn't have let them."

"Martha seems pretty tough, too," I said. "Her daddy's girl, I understand."

"Has she sunk an axe into your skull?"

"Not yet. Though she's been twirling it around a little."

We talked about daughters for a while and then I told him of my plan to . . . "I don't want to call it stealing . . ." I meant the blackmail letters that Smalley had told me about and Bill had confirmed. "I think I have a way."

When I described my scheme, he cackled so hard that his jowls shook.

"Do you think it'll work?" I said.

"Don't see why not. You've got nothing to lose."

"Unless we get caught."

"We?"

"Pinkerton wants to help. Not sure if I want him."

"He might know a thing or two. Just make sure you don't get caught, would be my advice," Smalley said, "especially if you're representing the *Tribune.*"

I hadn't thought of that. "Please don't tell Reid," I said. "How much should I tell Babcock?"

"As little as possible. What does he know already?"

I hesitated.

Smalley noticed. "Too much, I take it," he said.

"He knows that the letters exist, but I'd have to tell him, anyway. I'll need to explain why I'm asking."

"He would enjoy those letters, I should think."

I said, "A little too much, I fear."

⊬══⊣

The Avenue was chaotic with horses and pedestrians and the occasional streetcar crossing paths in patterns only an astrologer could discern. I crossed Fifteenth street, facing the Treasury building's impenetrable Greek façade. You wouldn't think the place had been robbed recently. An inside job, naturally. You had to laugh.

I continued, just beyond, to the Executive Mansion—the White House, as students of the obvious were calling it. Set back from the Avenue, it carried a dignity of its own. Unlike the Treasury, say, or the Capitol, it was modest, low-slung, understated—in accord with its current occupant's style.

Old Edward was all smiles as I strode through the door. He made me feel a part of the good old days, which implied that I was leaving my youth behind. When I told him that Clara was in town and would soon have the honor of meeting him. I worried that his grin would cleave his face.

"You'll find General Babcock in the billiard room," Old Edward said. "With the president."

"Billiard room?"

"Oh yes. The president's project. There, sir, near the conservatory." Old Edward pointed to the west, toward the greenhouse. "The president can't get enough of it, sir."

"I daresay, Edward, you are a snob."

"Oh no, sir. I speak from envy, if I may be candid with you. The president often invites his guests to play, and he does not enjoy losing. The staff, however, is not permitted to indulge."

"I am hoping the same for myself," I said.

If I had to compete at the billiards table to earn a favor, I was in trouble. I had played the game twice in my life, and not since that Saturday night (well, Sunday morning) in Providence. Let me acknowledge that I wasn't a natural.

I crossed through the marble-trimmed vestibule. Gone was the glass-walled passage to the greenhouse. In its place was a great hall that was paneled and framed by carved timbers of mahogany and oak. In the tall windows along the north and south walls, small colored panes were interspersed with clear ones. The high glass doors to the greenhouse stood open.

The top of the billiard table was as brilliant a green as a forest after the rain. President Grant was leaning over it. An unlit cigar was in his teeth, a cue in his hand, as he lined up his yellow cue ball with the red ball. A foam had formed around his lips and threatened his whitening beard. He took his shot, missed it by a whisker, and muttered under his breath.

"Yours," President Grant growled at Babcock, who was twirling his cue by the greenhouse door. Then he noticed me and said, "Mr. Hay, you can play the winner."

"That's all right," I said.

"The loser, then."

"This isn't my sport, I'm afraid."

"What is, then?" Grant said.

"Boxing."

"General Babcock's, too. Would you care to . . . ?"

Babcock gleamed with a smile that scared me half to death. The tips of his mustache glistened.

"Not to-day, thank you," I said.

"To-morrow, then," Babcock said.

This was almost literally the last thing I wanted to do. I thought about pleading my forearm, which no longer hurt very much, but I didn't want to act like a milksop. I also needed a favor from the president, which meant cozying up to General Babcock. Perish the thought.

"Then I need a favor," I declared.

"What?" Babcock barked.

"An invitation to a formal dinner here, for two."

"For you and your wife."

"Actually, no. For Mr. and Mrs. David Patterson. Or Senator and Mrs. David Patterson." For Grant's benefit: "Your late predecessor's"—whose name shall not be uttered within these walls—"elder daughter and son-in-law."

"Really?" Babcock said. "Why?"

President Grant rested the butt of his cue on the floor and twisted the chalk as he waited for Babcock to line up his next shot.

"I want them out of the way for a while," I said. "And in formal clothes—tight clothes."

"For what purpose?" Babcock said.

President Grant had stopped twirling the cue and stood at attention by the far corner of the table.

"I am here in the presence of the chief law enforcement officer of the United States," I said. "I would prefer not to confess in advance to what might constitute a crime."

"What is?" Babcock said.

"I will tell you if I succeed—how about that?"

"And if you don't?"

"You can visit me in jail."

Now President Grant was smiling, rather a pleasant sight, although I couldn't tell if he was amused at my . . . audacity or at the prospect of seeing me behind bars. This little man was sturdy, and he was confident enough to be nice—indeed, trusting (to a fault). He turned to Babcock and said, "I believe the king of Hawaii will be our guest to-morrow evening, isn't that so?" An invitation to the president's table was not to be refused.

The boxing match was forgotten—for the moment, at least.

⊰══⊱

I didn't want to see the Pattersons, and I particularly didn't want them to see me. Not yet, at least—or, preferably, ever. A dollar bill for the Kirkwood House's sullen desk clerk sent him up to their room with a message: Could Bill fetch a package from the lobby? I had purchased a vase of lilies. I figured Whitelaw Reid wouldn't mind.

This fragment of my scheme worked as intended. If only the rest of it did. Bill emerged, and the desk clerk ushered him to the back corner of the lobby. I extended my hand and shook his. I waited for the desk clerk to leave, costing another dollar. Was everyone in this benighted nation greedy for another buck? I wasn't excluding myself.

Bill wasn't half my age but was just about as tall as I was. I talked to him man to man.

"Those letters," I whispered. "Could I see them?"

A curt nod.

"To-morrow evening?" I explained that the Pattersons would be going to the Executive Mansion, in formal dress, and might—I hoped, I hoped—leave the letters behind.

Bill's face lit up.

"Would you help?" I said.

Another nod.

I reached into my trousers pocket and pulled out a gold coin, a double eagle—twenty dollars' worth.

Bill waved it away.

<hr>

"I want to," Clara said.

"You'll only get in the way," I replied.

"I'll stay out of the way."

Neither of us liked to fight (which may explain my affection for the boxing ring) but sometimes it couldn't be helped. I was confident about which of us would win.

And she did. We had gone to bed early. I was exhausted, probably the effect of getting knifed. The doctor had stopped by—he couldn't have been older than fourteen—and changed the bandage and declared me a healthy young man. I felt neither healthy nor young.

"I didn't come here to look at trees," Clara said.

"Why did you come?" I said uncharitably.

"To look at you. To look after you."

"I don't need anyone looking after me."

"I see." She nodded at my forearm, which annoyed me only because she was right.

"It . . . it wasn't my fault," I stammered. "If you . . . if you had been with me, it might have . . . might have been you who was stabbed."

Her silence conceded the point. "At least it would have been two against one," she said at last.

"And now I have a gun," I said.

Clara's eyebrows rose. "Would you use it?" she said.

I reached over to turn the wick down on the coal-oil lamp, lifting the globe with a handkerchief and blowing out the flame. I tried to picture a man coming at me while I was pulling the gun from my pocket in time. I could do that. But would I actually fire the gun, up close? How could I know, until . . . I knew?

"Try me," I replied.

"Go to sleep," Clara said.

I was a little worried that I might enjoy it.

CHAPTER FIFTEEN

I t's probably a felony, you know," Nicolay said, waving a forkful of Spanish mackerel.

"At worst, a misdemeanor," I assured him. "I would think the material has to exceed a certain value, and I very much doubt that blackmail value counts. That much I remember from reading for the law. Which is more than I can say, incidentally, for the marshal of the United States Supreme Court."

"Don't be mean, Johnny," Clara said.

"Accusing someone of not being a lawyer is mean? How did you ever get this job, anyway, Nico, not being a lawyer?"

"Ah, but I have a lawyer's mind," Nicolay explained. "And I know people who know people. By God, Johnny, you're a lawyer *and* a journalist. You claiming your hands are clean?"

"Now who's being mean?" Therena said.

"They fight like puppies," Clara said.

Therena said, "Housebroken?"

"Yes, housebroken," I said. Helen giggled. "And, besides, I'm not *stealing* anything. I am borrowing them and reading them and putting them back. Nobody will ever know they're gone."

"After breaking and entering, you mean," Nicolay said.

"Not exactly. Bill will let me—sorry, us—in."

"Bill has no claim to that room," Nicolay said, "other than being employed by its occupants. I am no expert on the law in this city, but my guess is he has no legal right to invite you in. The room isn't registered in his name."

"Because he is black," Therena said.

"Even if he were sky blue," Nicolay said. "Be careful, Johnny. This could get you disbarred."

"I was barely barred to begin with."

A knock at the front door sent Helen to her duty. She returned with an envelope and handed it to me. "A messenger," she said.

When I saw the envelope, I moaned. It was fluffy and buff-colored, the return address embossed.

THE PRESIDENT'S HOUSE

With trepidation, I unfolded the note. This couldn't be anything good. I was right. It was an invitation, but not one I hoped for.

> *Dear Mr. Hay,*
> *It would be my pleasure if you could come here at approximately*
> *4pm this afternoon. Please bring Mrs. Hay and your athletic garb.*
> *Yours very truly,*
> *U. S. Grant*

He hadn't forgotten. My stomach knotted. As I had counted on so recently, an invitation to the Executive Mansion was not to be refused.

I passed up lunch, not for lack of succulent possibilities but because of abdominal muscles that wouldn't unclench. Let me try to explain my complicated relationship with pugilism. I love it. It has changed me, strengthened me, from the inside. Without it, I couldn't have engaged as earnestly in the combat of modern life. I also fear it. It's not that I mind all that much getting socked in the kisser; it doesn't usually hurt as much as you think it will, or for as long. Even so, the prospect scares the bejesus out of me. This irrational aversion to getting punched in the face (albeit not between the neck and the waist) is probably healthy, all in all, and will contribute to my longevity. I leave it to spiritualists to untangle the contradictions.

Clara was easily persuaded to stay away. I made sure of it by telling her what President Grant had in mind. She puts up with my interest in boxing, but not happily—because she doesn't like to watch me get hit, she says. I suspect she also dislikes seeing me hit another human, because of what it reveals about me. I love it for just that reason.

My "athletic garb," such as it was, was in Cleveland. I had left home, you will recall, to attend a funeral. Nothing that Nicolay wore, athletic or otherwise, would fit me. I hadn't arrived, however, in an uncivilized country, no matter what European diplomats professed, and I found just the place I needed, on the Avenue east of the Capitol. It was a moldering shop, and an elderly salesclerk who might have clothed William Henry Harrison took me in hand. He had obviously heard just about everything in his time and saw nothing askance in my request. Past the frock coats, vests, and pantaloons, beyond the suspenders and cravats, back with the nightshirts and underclothes, he showed me the bathing shorts. I shuddered at the ones decorated with birds or sailboats and bought the only pair that came close to fitting, which was ornamented with lavender stripes. "In fashion," the clerk decreed. It came down to my knees and would require a belt, so I bought one of those, too.

I sneaked the package back into the house—the less said to Clara, the better. She was in the parlor and called out to me, "Johnny, I'm coming."

"Coming where?"

"I want to come with you."

"Why? I thought you hated—"

"I do, but I want to meet the president. I've never met one."

"I've met three," I said. "They're just people. Odd people. They get smaller each time."

"Even so," Clara declared. "After to-night, my best chance to meet him might be in jail."

"You *are* the pessimist, aren't you," I said. "I hereby bequeath to you my crown."

Thinking about trading blows with Orville Babcock, I realized, had stifled my nerves over the evening's criminal escapade. A minor benefit.

✦

"So, this is the damsel who swept you away," Old Edward gushed. "You are a lucky man, Mr. Hay."

"I couldn't disagree," I said.

Clara curtsied—practicing, no doubt—and offered her warmest smile.

"The president asked me to come," I said. "And Mrs. Hay."

"He is in the Green Room," Old Edward said.

My heart sank again—or more precisely, my bowels. That was where I had watched Willie Lincoln's embalming and had nearly passed out. I had tried to avoid the room ever since.

"So, tell me," Old Edward said as a parting shot, "what did she see in you?"

"I've wondered myself," I said. "You'll have to ask her."

Clara offered an enigmatic smile.

We crossed the wide vestibule and veered into the leftmost of the three color-denominated parlors. This one was decidedly green, from the silk wallpaper to the Oriental carpet to the pears—were they real or wax?—in ceramic bowls. I sniffed the air for formaldehyde and detected cigar smoke. I noticed something else, besides the two men huddled by the green velvet curtains, across the room: the furniture had been moved to the walls.

President Grant strode toward us. "And who is this?" he said.

"Mr. President," I replied, "this is Mrs. Hay."

She curtsied again, deeper this time—she was ready to meet Queen Victoria—and extended her hand. He shook it. An American, not a European, would he be.

"The pleasure is mine," Grant said, beaming at her congratulations for his new grandson. "And this," he said, summoning his companion, "is my private secretary, General Babcock."

Babcock inched forward like a man on his way to the gallows. But damn if Clara didn't curtsy again. Her limbs would ache to-morrow.

It occurred to me that Babcock might regret having encouraged this pugilistic exhibition. He had more at stake than I did. I stood to lose the president's favor for my investigation and newspaper sensation. (I had left Grant's authorization letter at Nicolay's house, in case I was asked to return it.) Babcock risked embarrassing himself in front of his boss and protector.

This calmed me a little, except for one thing: my calculations hadn't accounted for Clara. I would just as soon not look foolish in front of my wife—not that it would shock her.

President Grant suggested that I "prepare for combat" in the adjacent parlor. The oval Blue Room was bigger than I remembered, probably because it wasn't cluttered with furniture and domesticity like the library on the floor above. I quickly shed my frock coat and trousers and removed my linen shirt, leaving on my long-sleeved undershirt and my drawers. I slipped on the bathing shorts and pulled tight the snakeskin belt. I shook my right forearm—pain had conceded to fear—and looked in the full-length mirror. I judged myself ridiculous. I willed for this to be over, which required that it begin. Swallowing hard, I returned to the Green Room and my fate.

Rope had been laid out on the carpet in a square slightly larger than a water closet. Babcock fidgeted along the side of the room like a hen that had caught smell of a fox. I'd have thought a general would have an easier time of it. I wondered if the Confederate generals had been so timorous. Actually, Babcock was a general who had worked for other generals—for Grant, since Vicksburg—and had never led troops into battle, so far as I knew. Which was probably fortunate: the Union had won.

I looked around for Clara. She was nowhere in sight. Grant stood in the center of the ring, beaming. I blanched. He was to be the referee.

Whereupon, the president of the United States summoned us both into the ring and had us stand face-to-face. Babcock was several inches taller and at least thirty pounds heftier than little ol' me. A walrus, I tell you, but with a sinister face. His cheeks were puffy, his mustache drooped, and a glassiness fixed his stare. He wouldn't look me in the eye.

That's when I knew I had him licked.

"Now, gentlemen," the president said, stepping away, "fight fair, fight clean."

No timing, no rounds, no gloves, no rules—the Marquess of Queensbury, be jiggered.

I was used to sparring with fellows I liked, or at least didn't dislike, usually at my boxing club or a gymnasium of choice. Fighting with Babcock was something new, for me—albeit ancient. The original purpose of fisticuffs, after all, was to settle a dispute between antagonists or to provide the primitive pleasure of punching a man you detest.

Grant chopped his forearm and stepped back.

I let Babcock take the first shot, a wild one past my temple as I danced away. I had two or three years on him, and I knew what I was doing. I let him take a second shot, an uppercut that missed my chin and nearly struck him in his own mouth. If your opponent is beating himself, don't get in his way.

I backpedaled to the rope and moved forward again. My opportunity came on his third shot, a right cross that hit my nose. It set me back a step and angered me, but only enough to calm my nerves and to harden my resolve. My adversary had left himself defenseless against a left jab, which smashed into his cheek, followed by a sockdologer to his jaw. That got his attention.

I heard a shout from the doorway—"Well done, Mr. Hay!" It was Old Edward. I lifted a glove in acknowledgment, which proved a mistake. Babcock wasn't as unskilled as I had assumed. His right fist slammed into my belly and doubled me over. I felt my breakfast mackerel rising up through my chest and fought off an urge to vomit. I slipped my head to the right to avoid his uppercut.

That gave me my chance. I straightened up and twisted my torso to put my full weight behind a right cross that slammed into his mouth. He looked surprised before his lip spurted blood. I'm ashamed to say this made me madder. I drove a hard left into his midsection and a right uppercut to his jaw and was readying a left hook when Babcock fell back onto the carpet and someone in the doorway shrieked, "Stop!"

It was Clara. So I stopped.

My fingers ached, but I reached down for Babcock's hand. He glared at me from the carpet. He must have remembered who else was looking down at him—was it the president, or God Almighty?—because he grabbed my hand and squeezed it so hard that the pain shot into my forearm. I made sure I didn't show it.

+≡≡+

We took a table by the window. The saloon was on the Avenue, across Twelfth street from the Kirkwood House. From here, we could watch the hotel's entrance.

The front of the menu depicted a beer mug and a bratwurst. Below:

Wm. H. Ottman, Proprietor

Ottman. Ottman. I had seen this name recently, in the newspaper, and not in a flattering way. (Is it ever?) It was on the front page, the upper-left corner, probably in *The Evening Star*. Yes, now I remembered. The Treasury robbery! An insider *and* an outsider had been accused of larceny. William H. Ottman hadn't actually snatched the forty-seven thousand dollars in five-hundred-dollar bills—that was the insider's job—but he had deposited almost half of it in an Alexandria, Virginia, bank and had hidden other thousands in railroad stock and such. His bail had just been reduced. Maybe he was back in the kitchen right now, pissing in my whisky.

No, I could see the barkeep pouring. I wouldn't order soup.

Clara had calmed down quite a bit, for which I was grateful. She seemed close to forgiving me for enjoying my small pugilistic triumph. *Enjoying* was an understatement, and she might forgive me even for that.

My watch said six thirty-nine. The Pattersons' invitation was for seven o'clock.

Clara said, "Should we order some food?"

The vehemence of my opinion startled her. I tried to explain that we would need to move fast once the Pattersons left.

"But I'm famished," she said.

"Something fast, if you won't mind leaving it half-eaten."

"We'll have time. They haven't even left yet."

I had to admit to both.

Clara said, "Will you have something, too?"

"I'll have a bite of yours."

"Will you, really?" she said, tilting her face in mock surprise.

I laughed. "With your consent, of course," I said. "And I guess it depends on what you order."

"Calf's liver."

"You wouldn't dare."

She didn't. She ordered filet of rabbit. No soup. I ordered terrapin.

I sipped my whisky, enough to calm my nerves but not enough to dampen my senses. This required calibration, like everything else in life.

Clara's rabbit was stringy but tasty, and my terrapin was tender and sweet. Mid-meal, a landau, drawn by two white horses, pulled up by the Kirkwood House entrance. The coachman climbed down from his box and opened the door. It had gold script on the side, entangled letters too fancy to decipher. The hotel doorman swaggered out and swooped his arm along the ground, as if for royalty. In Tennessee, I suppose, that's how the pudgy ex-senator and the ex-president's daughter ranked. She was in full toilette, and both of them wore white gloves and—I was relieved to see—close-fitting clothes. Neither Martha's purse nor her corset nor the tied-back drapery of her high-necked magenta gown had room for instruments of blackmail. Nor did his cutaway coat or (unless the top popped off) his gold-headed cane. There was room inside his silk hat, but that would need to be removed inside the Mansion.

We waited awhile after the landau pulled away. I slapped enough dollars on the table to please a lesser Vanderbilt. I counted it as my contribution— that is, Whitelaw Reid's—to the proprietor's bail.

The Kirkwood House doorman wasn't surprised to see us—he had seen me here before and presumably mistook us as guests. Clara rushed up to the desk clerk (this had been my bright idea) and sputtered that the Pattersons had left something behind and asked if their servant was still in the room. We hurried past the desk and up the stairs and rapped on the Pattersons' door.

It opened. Bill stood in the doorway. I was rarely so pleased to see someone. He seemed less pleased to see us.

This confused me. Hadn't he invited me? Was Clara the surprise?

Clara ended the awkwardness by putting out her hand and shaking his. "Clara Hay," she said. "May we come in?"

We could, and we did. The parlor was lit with the slant of garish light that precedes nightfall. We stood—awkwardly, again—until Clara said, "Could you help us?"

Already, Bill was in Clara's thrall. He couldn't look away from her face. She knew it and kept her voice low and slow, to maintain the spell.

My turn, continuing her tone of voice. "Those letters," I said, "could we see them?" Bill winced. "We won't take them away. I promise."

So far, Bill hadn't uttered a sound, and he was silent as he turned—a young man of his word!—and led us through the double doors. The high-ceilinged bedroom had seen better days. The wallpaper was peeling, and there was a faint smell of . . . I don't know . . . mold. Clothes were strewn on the floor, and the four-poster bed was unmade. Had the chambermaid been lax or had her labors been undone?

Bill stationed himself in the shadows and pointed at the oversized bureau. The top was covered with shapely bottles and sloppily closed jars. The gigantic looking glass was cracked like the Nile. The front of the bureau was curved, decorated with tulips and vines painted on white. The drawer handles were golden knobs.

I tugged on the top drawer. Wood squeaked against wood, but the drawer didn't budge. I pulled harder at the left knob, which jammed the drawer more, so I shoved the edge back in. I looked back at Bill, who was nodding like a duck gone berserk. Clara stepped forward and took the right knob, and we pulled simultaneously. The drawer squealed, but we jiggled it back and forth until it slid out halfway.

At the left was a pile of Martha Patterson's unmentionables. I reached under them and felt a wad of paper. I pulled it out. A bundle of envelopes, tied by a red ribbon. I grinned at Clara.

Behind me, Bill sounded like he was choking.

"You all right?" I said, turning around.

"My grandpappy," he rasped. "They stole from . . ."

That sent me reeling. "Your . . . grand . . . your wha'? You mean Joh . . . President Johnson is . . . was your . . . ?"

Bill's eyes were wide.

"So Frank is your . . . ?"

Bill shook his head. I realized Frank wasn't old enough to have a son almost grown. That left Charles and . . .

"Robert!" I declared. That was ol' Andy's middle son, victim of drink and laudanum.

"My mama tell me, jes' before she passed."

Now I could understand Bill's devotion to the man, his grandfather, so recently buried. The envelopes felt heavy in my hand.

I hesitated to untie the ribbon. What if I couldn't tie it again the same way? I intended the Pattersons to be none the wiser—and for Bill to side-step suspicion. I slid the ribbon off, in hopes it would slide back on.

I counted four envelopes, of identical sizes. Written on the top envelope, in a feminine hand:

Senator F. Frelinghuysen

The flap was unsealed. Inside, folded over, was a piece of satiny paper curved around the borders. I unfolded it and stepped closer to the lamp. The handwriting was brazen.

My dearest Freddie,
  I enjoyed our afternoon together more than I can say, and I could see that you did, too. (Titter.) Barnabas must go to Philadelphia next Wednesday, if you wouldn't mind staying on in such heat. (Titter.) You are a most impressive man. (Titter.) Here's to us.

My very, very best,
Dana

So, Freddie he was! My first thought was: I didn't know the old fellow had it in him. My second thought: Was he a sodomite? Hard to say for sure. And my third: Anyone could have written this. There was no reason to think it was genuine. Except that Frelinghuysen had behaved as if it were. Even so, he could hardly be the first senator, or the fiftieth, to have strayed. Certainly, his wife would object. But would he pay someone—or murder someone—to prevent its being known? Yes and no, respectively, were my guesses, although they were nothing more than that. He wasn't the type to order a murder—or to do it himself. (But what type was that?)

The next envelope, in the same hand, was labeled:

Senator Roscoe Conkling

Whatever its contents alleged, Conkling and his wife were estranged. Nor would a hint of scandal come as any surprise. Kate Chase wasn't the only belle the Senate's Lothario was known to squire around. An accusation would only bolster his reputation. This made him impervious to blackmail; exposure wasn't something he would fear.

And the next:

Vice President Henry Wilson

This couldn't have been the same envelope Smalley had seen in the tailor shop—Wilson had been a senator then. Unless it was a recent repackaging, probably Martha Patterson's handiwork. The vice president has seemed convincingly blasé.

The last envelope was smaller and crumpled. It was blackened around the edges and stained across the front. A corner was torn. Upon closer inspection, it showed tiny nibble marks. From a mouse?

Bill pointed to the ceiling, to a gash near the edge, along the molding. He pantomimed climbing on the bureau, reaching high, grabbing something, and tugging it down. That was why the Pattersons were staying here, to retrieve this from the rafters! How long had it been up there? A coon's age, by the looks of it.

Only with difficulty could I read through the smudges and make out a name:

Vice President Hannibal Hamlin

Hannibal Hamlin? He hadn't been the vice president for ten years now. He was a senator once again. What on earth was this doing here? Ol' Andy must have brought it to intimidate his predecessor in the vice presidency—now his Senate colleague—and for some reason he had left it behind. The handwriting on the envelope wasn't as disciplined as the rest—more of a scrawl.

The sealing wax was broken already. I opened the flap of the envelope and pulled out a clump of foolscap, which I unfolded then unfolded again. The paper was slimy to the touch. It was torn raggedly along the left edge, as if ripped from a notebook or a diary. I smoothed it, best I could, over my palm. Spidery writing covered the page. I needed more light to read it. Near the bottom, a word—or part of a word—was larger than the rest:

Then a mark like an opening parenthesis; the corner of the page was gone.

There was a noise in the parlor. All three of us froze. The door rolled open.

"Ou'!" A growl. The accent was Scottish. Pinkerton! What was he doing here? "Get ou' this instant!"

I folded and refolded the foolscap—the right way, I prayed—and shoved it into the envelope. Clara squeezed the other envelopes through the band of ribbon. I slapped mine back into the drawer, with hers on top. Even a child would notice the tampering. We began to push the drawer back into the bureau. I braced for the squeal. By some miracle, it slid in without a sound.

Pinkerton barreled into the bedroom. "Through theah," he barked, pointing to a door I hadn't noticed, opposite the head of the bed. We followed him through the door and into the hallway and pressed ourselves into an alcove. I hoped that Bill could reorder any disorder we had left behind.

"Back heah," Pinkerton ordered. "Be still." He pressed himself into the end of the dark hallway. Clara and I did the same—just in time. Footsteps were tramping down the corridor, toward us. They stopped at the Pattersons' door.

"Such a nerve he had, and he calls himself a general"—the silhouette was Martha Patterson's—"as if I never been in that building before. I lived there, for God's sake, which is more than he ever . . ."

The Pattersons weren't supposed to return *this* early. Had dinner even been served?

"He didn't mean it like that, dear." David Patterson's diamond studs flashed in the pitiful gaslight. They must have left the Mansion long before the brandy and cigars. "And you can't let it ruin your . . ."

He trailed off as he fit the key in the door. Neither of them noticed the cluster of intruders nearby. Nor did they realize that the door was already unlocked.

+══╡+

"Another, if you don't mind," I said.

That wasn't like me, and Nicolay knew it, but without a speck of reproof he replenished my snifter.

"How did he know you were there?" Nicolay said.

"He's a detective—a real one."

"You don't do so poorly yourself."

High praise, from Nicolay. "He must have followed us," I said.

"I'm sure that sits well with you."

I sloshed the brandy around. "Can't say that Clara minded." She had gone upstairs and, I hoped, was asleep. "I'm not complaining, mind you. Pinkerton got to us just in time. He was watching the front entrance and saw their carriage pull up and rushed upstairs ahead of them."

"Is Hamlin even in town?"

"I don't know. Smalley didn't say anything, and Pinkerton didn't know. Maybe he just got here, or he didn't come at all."

Nicolay retrieved his *Congressional Directory*. Hamlin's address was listed on Maryland avenue, on the northern side of the Capitol.

"Tell me again what it said," Nicolay said.

"I didn't see much of it. The writing was hard to read, and the light was poor. The bottom was eaten away, so the page—and maybe there were other pages, and ol' Andy . . . these letters were his, right? They're the ones Smalley told me about—what else could they be? Maybe he had only one page, but there must have been two or three or . . . it was a wad in the envelope . . . so what I saw didn't make any sense, I mean from a blackmail perspective, but maybe . . ." I heard myself prattle on, and stopped.

"You had better drink that," Nicolay said.

I obeyed.

Nicolay said, "A-t-z. That's all you could read?"

"That's where the critters got into it."

"What does it mean, you think?"

I shrugged and downed my last slug of the night.

CHAPTER SIXTEEN

My head popped up from the pillow. The room was black. Clara stirred beside me. I had been dreaming, but of what? Not of the seventeenth president, I should hope. Nor of the eighteenth—or the sixteenth. Not even Lincoln had leave to invade my sleep. The apparition was fading fast. Remaining was a jumble of letters, swirling:

A T Z

Something familiar about them loomed just beyond my grasp. I let them loom and lowered my head and went back to sleep.

Next I knew, sunlight filled the room. I half opened my eyes, but the brightness hurt, and I waited before I was foolhardy again. Clara was gone, which was the usual. The mornings were hers. I preferred the late hours, when the world was quiet and the house was mine.

My watch lay on the bedside table. Three minutes past seven. I leapt from bed, naked. Ten minutes later I was pouring a cup of coffee and crowding in at the breakfast table. This morning's fare was eggs with anchovy sauce; mine was cold. Clara and Therena were in earnest conversation about infant cholera, which I gathered was killing more children—more people—in Washington than did man or beast or what the cognoscenti described as germs.

"Thank heavens I left my Helen at home," Clara said with a faraway look.

"Did you think of bringing her?" Therena said.

"Of course. But it wasn't practical."

"I wish you had," Therena said. "I'd love to meet her sometime. I am quite fond of Helens."

The Helen at the table squirmed, proud or embarrassed or both.

Therena turned to me and said, "We've been hearing about your adventure in—"

"Thievery," Nicolay finished.

Helen's ears perked up.

Therena said, "Don't be difficult, George."

"I didn't take a thing," I said. "What I didn't expect was the letter about Hannibal Hamlin."

"The worst decision the Ancient ever made!" Nicolay snapped.

"In retrospect," I allowed. "It made sense at the time, though. A Radical Republican from Maine added nothing—*nothing*—to the ticket."

I wasn't proud of my role in urging Lincoln to drop Hannibal Hamlin from the ticket in 'sixty-four and to replace him with Andy Johnson. Johnson was a Democrat and could attract Democratic votes in Northern cities as well as in the South—which he did. The election looked close at the time. How could I know that Sherman would ravage Georgia? Or that Lincoln would die so soon and that the Great Commoner would become such a wretched president? I shouldn't blame myself. Lincoln relied on no one's advice except his own (or occasionally from Seward, my mentor and his friend). If my skin seems thin . . . well, you can understand.

Helen looked perplexed.

"Hannibal Hamlin used to be important," I said.

"Actually, unimportant," Nicolay pointed out.

"True. But he *could* have been important, had he still been . . ."

Helen's confusion had grown.

"President Lincoln was . . . You know who he is, right?" I deserved the scowl I got. "He was assassinated on the forty-second day of his second term, and his vice president—the unimportant vice president—became the new president, and very important indeed. It could have been Hannibal Hamlin, but instead it was the new vice president, Andrew Johnson. And what a catastrophe he turned out to be."

"How does our hapless Hannibal Hamlin"—Nicolay paused to admire his own proficiency in speaking his adopted tongue—"figure into this?"

"I wish I knew," I replied. "I didn't get a good look at the letter before the Pattersons barged in."

"Returned to their own hotel room, you mean," Therena said.

"Yes, that's what I mean," I said. "Barged into their own hotel room.

The nerve of them. Anyway, I was reading Hamlin's . . . his handwriting, I suppose . . . and those three letters jumped out at me—a capital *A* and a lowercase *t* and a *z*. A-t-z. After that it was bitten off, except for a curvy mark—I couldn't tell what it was."

"An *e*," Helen said.

"It could have been!" I exclaimed. An opening parenthesis resembled the curve of a lowercase *e*. "How did you know?"

"I learned about him in school."

"Learned about who, dear?" Therena said.

"About the man who tried to assass . . . assass . . ."

"Assassinate?" Therena said, holding the word at a distance like a fish caught a fortnight ago.

"Yes, Mama, that's the—"

"Atzerodt!" I burst out. I envied a child's uncluttered mind. "George Atzerodt. How could I forget? The Booth conspirator who didn't go through with it. The night Lincoln was shot. He was the one who got drunk instead of assassinating Andrew Johnson. He fell down on the job."

"And was hanged, anyway," Nicolay recalled.

⊢═══⊣

"No love lost between them," Smalley said.

"I thought Hamlin loved everyone," I said. "Why should he dislike ol' Andy?"

"For one thing, the man took his place and, as it happened, kept him from the presidency."

"That wasn't Johnson's doing."

"True, but irrelevant. Hamlin didn't let it be known, but he left Washington City a humiliated—and bitter—man. His consolation prize from Lincoln was a lucrative job."

"I remember well." I had handled the paperwork. Lincoln had named Hamlin as the collector of the port of Boston, in the belief he was an honest man. Best I knew, he was. These days, however, was anyone?

"And then he quit in protest," Smalley said, "when President Johnson was giving back to the rebels everything they had lost in the war. It was either resign or sacrifice any political future in Maine."

"So, why should Johnson dislike *him*?"

"No president can forgive someone who resigns over a matter of principle. That shows the president as *un*principled. You know that."

"Nobody ever quit Lincoln that way. In my presence, Hamlin was as mild as a salamander in the sun."

"He probably wanted something from you."

"I had nothing to give him."

"Access to the president?"

"Any man on the street has access to the president."

"Not the kind a vice president craves."

I couldn't deny that. "That was Lincoln's doing, keeping him at arm's length, not mine. And the Ancient had long arms."

"Tell that to Hamlin. I'm not saying you're wrong. Only that he may not be thrilled to see you."

"Is he in town?"

"Since last night."

Ah! "Any idea why?" I said.

"You're the reporter."

+≡≡≡+

The front yard at 113 Maryland avenue, within expectoration distance of the Capitol, was barely big enough for a worm to raise a family, let alone for azaleas or tomatoes to thrive. Certainly, it was nowhere big enough to warrant hiring a gardener, whose broad back was turned toward me. He was stooped over and wore a floppy khaki hat stained by sweat.

"I am looking for Hannibal Hamlin's house," I announced myself.

"Then your wish has been fulfilled."

The gardener stood and turned around. It was Hannibal Hamlin.

"Oh, hello, Mr. Senator," I said. "Remember me? John Hay."

He squinted. I can honestly say that his face fell. He looked older and tireder than I remembered. Strands of white hair snaked from under his hat. His broad face had settled into his jowls, which in turn had sagged onto his neck; his chest had sunk into his stomach. His chin and even his nose drooped. All victims of gravity, I guess. His eyebrows, incongruously dark, sprouted in every direction. A dissipated man, past his heyday, by all the visible evidence, until he opened his mouth.

"Tomatoes can give you such pleasuh." Hamlin dragged out the words in a Down East accent that was elongated and dry. "Mo' than money or high office or the love of the people." He waved his trowel at a withered plant. "Yes, I remembe' you well, Mistuh Hay. I can't help but remembe' all you did for me."

So, he knew. Nothing was a secret in Washington City—never was, never will be. (As a journalist, I say: thank the good Lord.) But what on earth had Hamlin expected from the vice presidency—power?

"It was nothing personal," I said lamely.

"It never is," Hamlin replied. "And what can I do for you this fine morning, Mistuh Hay?"

"Could we sit someplace? I am with the *New-York Tribune* now, and I'm interested in . . . Andrew Johnson."

"My least favorite subject."

"I think I can understand why."

"Can you really?" Actually, I couldn't be sure. "Heah will do," he said. I sighed. "What brings you to town, if I may ask?"

"To tend to my po' tomatoes. And what brings you to my modest abode, if I may inquire? Or did you happen to be passing by?"

"I have become aware of some letters."

"Letters, plural?"

He knew what I meant. "Yes, you are not alone," I said. "Have you by any chance seen David or Martha Patterson?"

"I have not."

He knew who they were.

"Well, you only arrived last night, I understand."

Hamlin's face had relaxed. "You may know more than I do, Mistuh Hay. I don't know why they want to see me."

"But you came, anyway."

"I have other business heah, too," Hamlin said as slowly as maple sap. "Tell me what you know, Mistuh Hay, and I may oblige you. I may even surprise you."

"I like to be surprised," I said.

I told him about the envelope I found with his name on it, with part of a letter inside.

"You read it?"

"I tried to. But I was . . . interrupted."

"What did you see?"

"Three letters. A-t-z. The rest was torn off—bitten off, I think. Seems it was stored in the ceiling."

I waited for Hamlin's reaction and didn't get any, either because of his stoicism or because I hadn't told him anything new. My guess was the latter.

I said, "Does this refer to Atzerodt—George Atzerodt?"

Again, no reaction, which I was inclined to count as a confirmation, although unusable in a courtroom or in print.

"You know what I'm talking about, don't you," I said.

This wasn't a question, and Hamlin wasn't listening, anyway. His mind was at work, and I waited until the task was complete.

At last he said, "He told me about this letter, just before Henry Wilson swore us in. We were nearly arm in arm."

"You mean Johnson told you, this past March."

"A mere mention, so that I knew he had it, and could hold it over my head whenever he liked. As if I would ever do his bidding."

"What was his bidding?"

"He never said. No need to. Just preparing the ground, so I knew what he had. Someday the need would arise."

"What *did* he have?"

"Nothing to speak of. It was a letter to a friend I never mailed. I learned about doing that from Mistuh Lincoln." Hamlin looked up accusingly. "Write an angry letter and leave it in your drawer—wasn't that what he did? This one I wrote after his cousin came to see me."

"Whose cousin?"

"The man you just mentioned. Oh yes. I had left for Boston and then I came back here for a visit. It must have been in the newspapers—you know how they are. I was staying at Willard's when somebody knocked on the door and I let him in. He was a rough-looking fellow, but with a kindly enough eye, or so I thought. He was Atzerodt's cousin, he told me, lived in Maryland someplace. He said he wanted justice for his dear cousin George."

"This was after Atzerodt was hanged."

"Oh yes. For a murdah he hadn't committed. That was his cousin's point of view. That Atzerodt was condemned by the word of a man whose life he had spared, my aforementioned predecessah. My uninvited guest got hot under the collah, not that he was wearing one. A farmah. Kept talking about justice, justice, justice—and vengeance. 'Vengeance is mine, sayeth the Lord'—I reminded him of that."

"To no avail, I gather."

"None."

"What did he want you to do?"

"I don't know. He didn't know. Somehow he was under the impression that I still mattered." *Or ever had,* I thought uncharitably. "I told him there was nothing I *could* do. I can't say why he came to see me in the first place.

He had heard of me somehow. Was under the misimpression I had a kind heart and some influence in this world. You wouldn't make such a silly mistake, Mistuh Hay, now would you?"

I treated his jab like a joke, so I chuckled, but I had to admire his sharp-knuckled skills. "What was his name," I said, "the cousin?"

"How can I remembah? Must be going on ten years now. All I remembah is that he had testified at the trial, the conspiratahs' trial, before the military commission. It was at his house that Atzerodt was caught a few days after . . . later."

"Where was this?"

"Up in Montgomery county somewhe'. Can't remembah the name. Started with a *G*, as I recall."

"Gaithersburg?"

"Maybe."

"What did you do?"

"Nothin'. I sent the man away. But he was persuasive that an injustice had indeed been done. So I wrote a lettah to my friend, wonderin' if Mistuh Atzerodt was hanged fo' a crime he didn't commit. Then I didn't send it."

"Where was the letter?"

"In my desk drawah in Bangah. After Mistuh Johnson had the courtesy to mention it to me in Mahch, I discovered that the lettah was gone. I have enemies everywhere, Mistuh Hay, even in Bangah. I regahd them as a badge o' hono'."

Andrew Johnson couldn't have said it better. Still, something about this didn't add up. Who cared if Hamlin had once opined to a friend about a wrongful hanging? What made such a letter an instrument of blackmail? Why was it worth anything at all? There was something Hamlin wasn't telling me.

I ventured, "Was that all your letter said?"

A wry smile. I was pleased to learn that Hannibal Hamlin wasn't always dour. "Only that I was sorry Atzerodt hadn't been man enough to finish the job."

It wasn't in keeping with my allegedly journalistic role to chortle, but that didn't stop me. "That can't be worth much," I said.

"No' a penny, and I don't figyuh to pay. Mistuh Hay, my real mistake with that lettah," Hamlin whispered, "was in not mailing it. You can thank your Mistuh Lincoln for that."

So what?

So what if George Atzerodt had been hanged unjustly and his cousin was bent on revenge? Ten years later, why should I care? Did this have anything to do with Andrew Johnson's death?

Maybe not, but it was a dickens of a newspaper story. Certainly it was worth an hour or two of my time.

My footsteps echoed along the Capitol's corridors. Midsummer had left the building an empty, haunted place. The flamboyant colors covering the ceiling and walls looked subdued, like an ancient mariner's tattoos.

The congressional library was open. It filled three floors along the western front of the Capitol. The entrance was on the ground floor. I glanced up past the tiers of wrought iron balconies, clear to the skylight in the Capitol roof. Books were shelved and stacked on every side—in bookcases and in cabinets, on tables and on the floor. The fusty smell was tribute to the centuries-old power of the word.

The librarian was a slight fellow with a button nose, sandy hair going gray, and a paunch. I told him what I wanted.

"Who are you?" he said.

I told him and showed him my card from the *Tribune,* leaving Grant's letter in reserve. (Wrong branch of government.) He gave me a skeptical look and pointed me to a scuffed oval table in the center of the corridor, which passed for a reading room. I moved some books from a chair to a bare spot on the tile floor and took their place. No more than a minute or two passed before a pale hand with slender fingers entered my field of vision and deposited a volume that was smaller and slimmer than I had expected. Its brown ribbed cover looked worn. Maybe ten years *was* a long time.

The frontispiece showed nine oval photographs, arranged in an oval— the alleged Lincoln conspirators. At the top was J. Wilkes Booth himself, with his thin, craggy, handsome face, the mop of dark hair, the frown of a mustache, an expression that seemed theatrically debonair.

Just below, to the left, another likeness was labeled: GEORGE ATZE-RODT.

The drawing was almost as real as tintype. I studied it. His face looked squashed; a low-brimmed hat pressed down over his forehead. His grizzled whiskers, sunken chin, and hunched shoulders suggested a lower creature on Darwin's evolutionary scale. His hair was limp, hiding his ears. His eyes looked vacant—stricken, staring into a distance he would never traverse. His black coat was two or three sizes too large.

I glanced at the other conspirators' pictures and turned to the title page:

Complete and Unabridged Edition—Containing the Whole of the Suppressed Evidence

THE TRIAL

OF THE

ASSASSINS AND CONSPIRATORS

AT WASHINGTON CITY, D.C., MAY AND JUNE, 1865,

FOR

THE MURDER OF PRESIDENT ABRAHAM LINCOLN,

FULL OF ILLUSTRATIVE ENGRAVINGS.

It began:

THE COURT MARTIAL.

On the first of May, 1865, President JOHNSON issued
the following order for the trial of the criminals:

The trial was conducted by a military commission, which gave Johnson,
as the commander in chief, the final say. The trial transcript was slim, as I
say—210 thin pages of teeny print, recording the testimony of the witnesses. *Complete and unabridged.*

I skimmed the alphabetical index of witnesses. No Atzerodt, nor any of
the accused. Not that the tribunal lacked for witnesses—hundreds of them,
I learned on page 16. Their raw testimony to the commission staff had filled
4,300 pages, a stack twenty-six inches high, besides 700 additional pages
of arguments. The slimness of this volume, the testimony in the trial itself,
increased in allure.

I pored through the list of charges and specifications. Booth, of
course, was dead, but the other conspirators faced multiple accusations
of "traitorous conspiracy . . . in aid of the existing armed Rebellion
against the United States of America . . ." Beyond the attacks that terrible night on Lincoln and on William Seward, the secretary of state,
came this:

> And in further prosecution of said conspiracy and its traitorous and
> murderous designs, the said George A. Atzerodt did, on the night of the
> 14th of April, A.D. 1865, . . . lie in wait for Andrew Johnson, then Vice-
> President of the United States aforesaid, with the intent unlawfully and
> maliciously to kill and murder him, the said Andrew Johnson.

Kill *and* murder? Atzerodt didn't stand a chance.
On the next page, I found:

Sketches of the Culprits.

First, the culprit in chief:

John Wilkes Booth.

BOOTH was born on his father's farm near Baltimore. Like his two
brothers, Edwin and Junius Brutus, he inherited and early manifested a
predilection for the stage . . .

He is best remembered, perhaps, in "Richard," which he played
closely after his father's conception of that character, and by his admirers
was considered superior to the elder Booth . . .

I skimmed over the rest, and on page 20, I found the culprit I wanted.

Geo. A. Atzerodt

ATZERODT, who was to murder Mr. JOHNSON, is a vulgar-looking
creature, but not apparently ferocious; combativeness is large, but in the
region of firmness, his head is lacking. He has a protruding jaw, and
mustache turned up at the end, and a short, insignificant looking face.
He is just the man to promise to commit a murder and then fail . . .

After the culprits had been described came the testimony from dozens of
witnesses. A Confederate agent who had met Booth in Montreal. The man
who had sold Booth a one-eyed horse. The doorkeeper at Ford's Theatre. A
stable boy in the alley behind Ford's. A policeman who examined Atzerodt's
Kirkwood House room. An acquaintance of Atzerodt's who saw him on the
omnibus late that night. Direct examinations and cross-examinations, of
people I had never heard of. I leafed back and forth, and near the bottom
of page 29, a name caught my eye.

> . . . Mr. Hamlin was also to have been included had the
> scheme been carried out before the 4th of March. In the
> conversation in April, Mr. Hamlin was omitted, and
> Vice-President Johnson put in his place.

I could see why Hamlin might find that fateful evening a subject of fascination. Indeed, in retrospect, I might have saved his life.

At the bottom of page 29, I noticed the name of a hotel I was getting to
know.

THE MURDER OF ANDREW JOHNSON

Oops.

Testimony of Robert R. Jones

Q. You are a clerk at the Kirkwood House? A. Yes sir.

Q. Look at that paper and say if it is a page taken from the register of that hotel?
A. Yes sir.

Q. Do you read upon it the name of Atzerodt? A. Yes sir.

The clerk spelled out Atzerodt's name—much like Helen Nicolay had—and recounted how the accused had rented room 126 on the morning of April 14. Atzerodt was ordered to stand up in the dock.

Witness said: I think that is him, sir.

Q. Do you know what became of him after he took the room? A. I do not know; it was between twelve and one o'clock when I saw him that day.

Q. Do you know anything of Booth having called that day to inquire the number of Vice-President Johnson's room? A. I don't know that he inquired; I gave a card of Booth's to Colonel Browning, Vice-President Johnson's secretary.

Q. You did not receive it from him himself? A. I did not, I think, although I may have done so.

What?! Did I just read what I thought I read? I read it again, twice more. Yes, I read it correctly. John Wilkes Booth had visited the Kirkwood House the day of his ugliest deed and left a card for . . . Was it for Johnson himself or for his secretary? And what in blazes did it say?

And then the prosecutor—that idiot of a prosecutor—changed the subject. I was quivering inside—literally. I should have been a doctor like my papa to have a clue of what my entrails were up to.

I leafed furiously through the transcript, taking care not to rip any pages. It was on page 70.

WILLIAM A. BROWNING.
For the Prosecution.—May 16.

I am the private secretary of President Johnson. Between
4 and 5 o'clock in the afternoon of the 14th of April
last, I left the Vice-President's room in the Capitol, and
went to the Kirkwood House, where we both boarded.
On going to the office of the hotel, as was my custom,
I noticed a card in my box, which was adjoining that of
Mr. Johnson's, and Mr. Jones, the clerk, handed it to me.

It was a very common mistake in the office to put cards
intended for me into the Vice-President's box, and his
would find their way into mine; the boxes being together.
(A card was here handed to the witness.)
I recognize this as the card found in my box. The
following is written upon it in pencil:

Dont wish to disturb you
Are you at home?
JWILKES BOOTH

I gasped—literally. The librarian glanced up. Figuratively, I couldn't believe my eyes. The assassin Booth had left a note asking if "you" were at
home, just hours before he shot the president! Was "you" the vice president
or his secretary? Browning wasn't sure.

I had known J. Wilkes Booth when he was playing in
Nashville, Tennessee; I met him there several times; that
was the only acquaintance I had with him. When the
card was handed to me, I remarked to the clerk, "It is
from Booth; is he playing here?" I thought perhaps he
might have called upon me, having known me; but when
his name was connected with the assassination, I looked
upon it differently.

That was all Browning said or was asked. I vaguely remembered a fat
little man with sparse hair and too broad a smile. Maybe I could find him.
I mean, maybe Pinkerton could. But how could Browning possibly know
why Booth had left such a note?
The prosecution's case against George A. Atzerodt started on page 144.
The day after Lincoln was shot, the police entered Atzerodt's room at the
Kirkwood House and discovered a loaded revolver under the pillow of his
bed, which hadn't been slept in. They also found three boxes of cartridges, a
bowie knife, several handkerchiefs, a pair of socks, two collars, a brass spur,
a hunk of licorice, and a Bank of Ontario account book in the name of one
J. Wilkes Booth. Witnesses testified that instead of knocking on the vice
president's door, while Booth was murdering Lincoln, Atzerodt got drunk
and wandered by horsecar across the city for half the night, before sleeping
in a run-down hotel. The next morning, he walked to Georgetown and per-

suaded a merchant of his acquaintance to lend him ten dollars, offering a revolver as collateral. There he boarded a stagecoach that took him north into
Montgomery county, Maryland, to his cousin's house, where he was arrested
five days later, on the twentieth of April, at four o'clock in the morning.

The defense filled barely three pages. The first witness made the reason
apparent. Frank Monroe was the naval captain on the ironclad where the
conspirators were jailed awaiting trial. When he asked to submit a written
statement from prisoner Atzerodt, the prosecutor slapped him down. The
accused's lawyer pleaded with the tribunal's seven generals and two colonels
to allow Atzerodt to present a defense, but the answer was no. I was aghast
but not surprised. I was aware that the accused wasn't ordinarily allowed to
testify in criminal trials, on the grounds that the testimony would be hope-
lessly prejudiced. The same rule, I gathered, applied in military trials as well.

This reduced Atzerodt's defense to the oddest of arguments—that he
was "a constitutional coward." This was his own lawyer's description, in
presenting witnesses who testified that if Atzerodt "had been assigned the
duty of assassinating the vice president, he never could have done it." The
prosecutor first objected then relented: "If the counsel wishes to prove that
the prisoner, Atzerodt, is a coward, I will withdraw my objection." And the
counsel so proved. "He was always considered a man of not much courage,"
a witness for Atzerodt testified. Swore another: "I have heard men say that
he would not resent an insult."

Even if true, it was a defense that would never have saved his life. I
remembered from reading for the law that every conspirator is personally
responsible for whatever the conspiracy does. Even if Atzerodt had abandoned his mission, while his coconspirators accomplished theirs, I failed to
see any injustice.

I kept turning pages, looking for . . . I didn't know what. But at the top
of page 153, *this* caught my eye:

Hartman Richter
For the Defense.—May 31.

I live in Montgomery County, Maryland, and am a
cousin of the prisoner, George A. Atzerodt. He came
to my house in Germantown about 2 or 3 o'clock on
Sunday afternoon . . . and I noticed nothing peculiar
about him. He remained at my house from Sunday till
Thursday morning, and occupied himself with walking
about, working in the garden a little, and going among

the neighbors. He did not attempt to get away, or to hide
himself. When he was arrested he seemed very willing to
go along . . .

Hartman Richter. This was the man who had barged in on Hannibal
Hamlin. Germantown started with a *G*.

⊷══⊷

I tried to explain to Therena why the conspirators weren't allowed to testify
on their own behalf, but she shook her head in amazement. Helen simply
didn't believe me. "You mean, if I do something wrong, I can't tell Father
why I did it?"

"Who would know if you were telling the truth?" I said.

"But I would tell the truth," she said.

"*You* would," I said, "but I don't know about all of the . . ."

An almost-nine-and-a-half-year-old had whupped me in debate.

I looked around at Nicolay's parlor. I was getting to love this room, for
all of its clutter—*because* of its clutter. The plush chairs and octagonal tables
and floor-to-ceiling books and oil paintings of what I gathered were Therena's
Puritan forebears—the jumble felt comforting. In Cleveland, I wondered if I
would ever know clutter again.

"Suppose he hadn't been a coward," I said. "Suppose Atzerodt had gone
through with it and assassinated Johnson. We'd have had a dead president
and a dead vice president."

Therena finished, "And who would have been president then?"

"Well, next in line was the president pro tempore of the Senate," Nicolay
said. "Whoever is elected by the Senate majority. In 'sixty-five, that would
have been . . ."

Nicolay nodded across the vase of tulips at me. He was testing my met-
tle, the self-educated putting the Ivy-educated on the spot. And once again,
I . . .

"Lafayette . . . ," I tried, unable to summon anything more.

"One-third correct," Nicolay said. "Lafayette Sabine Foster. That was his
name—*is* his name. The almost-great man is still with us. Currently as a
justice on the Connecticut Supreme Court."

"Ah yes." I vaguely recalled a brittle man with a bald pate, severe features, and a perpetual frown. "If only Atzerodt hadn't been a constitutional
coward, we'd have had President Foster. He couldn't have been worse than
ol' Andy."

Nicolay said, "A spittoon would have been an improvement."

Helen giggled.

After she and Therena went upstairs to bed, Nicolay and I sipped in silence. Our friendship did not require conversation.

After a while, Nicolay said, "So, what do you make of Booth's note?"

"I wish I knew. It's . . . beyond . . . to adapt his word . . . disturbing. Any idea?"

"To see where the clerk put the note," Nicolay tried, "so that Atzerodt would know where to strike that night?"

"Atzerodt could have found out himself," I said. "He had a room there already."

"Or there's this," Nicolay said slowly. "You might recall—or maybe you had already sailed for Europe—but at the time Mrs. Lincoln believed it. Not that she ranks as a credible judge, but some of the Radical Republicans in Congress suspected the same."

"Suspected what, exactly?"

"That Johnson was involved somehow."

"What do you mean, involved? Involved in what?" My mind had lost its edge. "In the plot to . . . ? You mean, that—"

"Oh my yes," Nicolay said. "They suspected that Andy Johnson had known of the plot to kill Lincoln or, worse, was part of it."

CHAPTER SEVENTEEN

SUNDAY, AUGUST 15, 1875

I don't usually take my daytime worries to bed, but after using the chamber pot at some ungodly hour, my mind was aswirl. I kept imagining the debonair John Wilkes Booth swaggering into the Kirkwood House and inscribing a note for Andy Johnson or his right-hand man. Truly, what had Johnson known? Had it led to his death ten years later? Maybe it wasn't the blackmail letters or his family's financial jealousies.

My squirming awakened Clara, but she went back to sleep. Eventually, I did, too, and dreamed busy dreams I would never remember.

⊢═══⊣

Pinkerton met us at the door—our door. That is, Nicolay's. On a Sunday, for God's sake. And it was Pinkerton himself—such personal attention!—rocking on the porch. Precisely as I had feared.

"I hope I'm not paying for this," I said in greeting.

"Ya not. The *Tribune* is payin'. Isn't that so? No need to trouble your pretty li'l head abou' it."

As Pinkerton stood unsteadily from the rocking chair, I considered punching his self-satisfied face. The problem was, he would punch back. All in front of Clara. And he still would be paid for his time.

"So, what are you doing here?" I said.

"Any assignments fer me t'day?"

"Yes, as a matter of fact. Two. Can William Browning be found? That's Colonel Browning, the one who was Johnson's private secretary as vice president. William A. Browning, according to the transcript. I would like to talk to him. Second, is Hartman Richter alive and still in Germantown, Maryland? He's George Atzerodt's cousin, and that's where Atzerodt was captured."

"I will be sure to find ou', Mr. Hay. My most personal attention. Anything else, *sir*?"

I ignored the sarcasm. "That's all I can think of, thank you."

"Do ye . . . need a companion t'day, perhaps?"

"I have one," I said, turning toward Clara, who had stayed behind me.

"Ye have yer . . . protection with ye?" Pinkerton said.

I checked my jacket pocket, unnecessarily. "I do."

"It is loaded?"

"Of course. Are you just trying to frighten my . . . Because you're . . ." A sudden realization. "Have you been talking to my wife?"

"I never divulge who I talk to," Pinkerton said with a slight bow.

"You have been!" I turned around. "Clara?"

"I never divulge who I talk to," she said.

I sighed. *This* was a conspiracy. "Do you want to come with me to-day," I said to her, "or should I go alone?"

Clara thought for a moment and said, "I'll come."

Rays of sunlight lit up the dust in the air and lent the lobby's faded furnishings an otherworldly radiance. We were becoming the best of pals, the Kirkwood House desk clerk and myself. He was just as sallow, just as sour, his hair as colorless, as I remembered. He seemed as surprised to see me as I was to see him, on a Sunday morn, and no more pleased about it.

We had never been properly introduced.

"Are you Robert R. Jones?" I said.

"I wish."

"Would you know where I could find him?"

"Whatcha want with Jonesy?" He spread his palms on the counter, ready to pounce.

I leaned forward. "To ask him some questions," I said.

"What about?" A worthy foe.

"He testified at the trial of the Lincoln conspirators back in 'sixty-five. It's about that. I am with the *New-York Tribune*."

"Well, he don't work here no more."

I had to laugh, and I did. "So, you put me through an interrogation, just to tell me that our Mr. Jones isn't . . . Do you know where he is?"

"I do."

I waited for him to continue. His gaze didn't waver. Nor did mine. I removed my wallet from my breast pocket and extracted a five-dollar bill.

It had Andrew Jackson—no, not Johnson—on the front. I slid it onto the counter, beneath his sniveling nose. He hesitated, calculated, and decided not to press his luck with an impoverished member of the press. Behind me, I felt Clara bristle.

"He lives upstairs."

"Oh!" I said, returning my wallet to its rightful place. "Which room?"

"He ain't here."

"All right, where is he?" The desk clerk who wasn't Jonesy gazed longingly at my breast pocket. "Where is he?" I repeated.

"He's at church."

I preferred not to accost yet another man in prayer (although that's when they're the politest). I didn't need to wait long. The desk clerk pointed us out—he demanded no other remittance—and Robert R. Jones looked puzzled as he shuffled across the lobby. He looked as ordinary as his name, a Jonesy, as mild as bread dough. His wire-rim spectacles sank into a pudgy face that was the color of hemp. His frock coat had a sheen. He stood with his arms crossed, resting on a belly that stretched his shirt like a hydrogen balloon. I stepped forward the same instant he did, and we avoided a collision only because I jumped back.

Somewhere among Jonesy's ridges of flesh was a puckering of lips that seemed to be asking me my business. I introduced myself and Clara and mentioned my letter from President Grant, intending to impress him, which it did. But when I told him of my interest in the events of April 14, 1865, he stepped back and said, "I have talked enough about that. Good day."

I had foreseen the possibility and brought my wallet into view. He could not look away. I suggested that we converse in the dining room, and he followed me like a duckling. Clara brought up the rear, to make sure he didn't stray.

The dining room, upstairs, across from the Pattersons' suite, was dark and old-fashioned. Oil paintings of ballet dancers or boats filled the walls. The tables were crowded together, populated by gray heads recently in church—ladies in pastel hats, fidgety men on their best behavior. I spied an empty table in the back corner, sufficiently isolated for a financial transaction.

Clara and I ordered coffee. Jonesy asked for apple charlotte topped with whipped cream. He sat patiently, waiting for an offer.

"I am interested," I said, "in the note that John Wilkes Booth left at the hotel desk that afternoon."

I might have been speaking in Urdu. Jonesy was shrewder than I'd thought, probably out of experience and desperation.

This would cost me more than I had figured. (Doesn't everything?) I reached into my pocket for a double eagle and plunked it on the table between us; the tattered tablecloth hushed the clink. Clara looked surprised. Twenty dollars in gold could buy you a heifer.

"I told the military commission everything I knew." Jonesy's hand crept across but stopped short of the coin.

"Do you remember Booth giving it to you?"

"Not really. I never saw the man here that day, at least that I know of. I understand he's a hard man not to notice, so handsome and all. But it was a busy afternoon, Good Friday, before Easter." Jonesy's fingertips had reached the coin's edge. "The note was left on the counter."

"Who was it for—the note?"

"I couldn't say for sure. Listen, I went all over this with them."

"The military investigators?"

"Yes. I rather assume that the card was left for Mr. Johnson, but I can't be certain. Many things for Mr. Johnson went to Colonel Browning first."

"And vice versa?"

A pause. "Not really."

"And when was the card left?"

"Can't be certain as to the time, but it must have been two or three o'clock in the afternoon. As I say, it was a busy day."

"Were you at the desk the entire afternoon?"

"Just about. It was difficult to get away even for . . ." He glanced at Clara, who was staring at the double eagle. "For private matters."

Our orders arrived. Jonesy ignored his food. "The note was on the counter," he whined, "and I put it in Mr. Browning's mailbox. Tell me, what did I do wrong?" He pulled the gold coin into his fist, like a Venus flytrap.

"Nothing," I said. "Nothing at all. Can you tell me anything about this George Atzerodt?"

"What do you want to know? I put him in a room that morning, the second floor up. I don't know nothing else."

"Did you see him that day?"

"I didn't, but another clerk, Mr. Spencer, gave him his key about four or five o'clock. The key was never brought back. I don't know whether Atzerodt asked anything about Mr. Johnson or his room, but some person did ask if Mr. Johnson roomed here and if he was in."

"Someone besides Atzerodt."

"Yes, sir. A tall, rough-looking man—looked like a carpenter. I judged from his appearance that he had no business with Mr. Johnson, so I told him he wasn't in."

"Although he was," I said.

"All afternoon and evening."

"In his room or just in the hotel?"

"Couldn't say. I don't have eyes in the back of my head, you know. His key was gone, that's all I know."

"But you didn't see George Atzerodt that day."

"I told you, I didn't, not after he registered."

"Did you get any sense of him, as a man?"

"He looked like a ne'er-do-well, and I tell ya, I can spot one a block away."

Clara, who had been sitting so quietly, piped up, "Was Mr. Atzerodt a good person, do you think?"

"I registered him at the hotel," Jonesy said, swallowing his first forkful of apple charlotte along with his exasperation. Our silence worked as a prod. "He was a man like any other, a little less so. Did he look like a *bad* person? All I can tell you is, he didn't look like no vessel of virtue."

Clara and I waited through a second forkful, then a third.

Jonesy finished chewing and said, "I know who would know, if you'll leave me alone now."

"Who is that?" I said.

"The minister. The one at my church. The Reverend John George Butler."

Clara said, "Why would he know?"

"Because he was with Mr. Atzerodt when he . . . He was with him at the end."

+———+

"He's not just any Bible thumper," Smalley said.

Clara looked as if he had slapped her. Not that she was a Bible thumper herself. She was a believer, to be sure—I envied her that—but in a way that made her more tolerant of sinners, not less. (Jesus would approve.) Her problem was with Smalley himself, and I should have expected it. She had seemed unsure about him from the moment he half stood and bowed. I had raved about his ability to know everything without visible effort and the magical way he had with a pen. Maybe that's what had put her on edge, the natural equilibrium she brought to every situation; exuberance or hostility on my part invariably provoked an opposite reaction. Or maybe she saw something in his attitude that didn't trouble me. For journalists, cynicism was an occupational hazard, if not a route toward the truth.

"What I mean is"—Smalley sensed when he had caused offense—"among the city's Lutheran pastors, all eight or ten of them, he's top dog. You know, he's also the chaplain of the House of Representatives." I hadn't known. "A position like that doesn't just happen. You've got to know the right people and how to get them to do what you want."

I said, "What is he like, this well-connected reverend?"

"Smooth as silk," Smalley said. "He won't tell you a tittle more than he wants to, about Atzerodt or anything else. These fellows are as skilled as politicians. They *are* politicians. I guess they have to be. His old church set up a new church and put him in charge. Is that where you're going?"

"Yes, up Fourteenth street."

Clara said, "A minister shouldn't be gabby, anyway."

"It's their job to be gabby," Smalley said.

"Gabby about some things and not others," I tried to mediate. (Maybe I should become a diplomat.) "I hope he's gabby about the things I'm interested in."

"You mean a condemned man's last confession?" Smalley said. "I wouldn't expect a lot."

"The secret to happiness in life," I said, "is low expectations." If only it were a lesson I could learn.

I suggested a hackney, but Clara was just as happy to walk. There wasn't much to see on the way. Two churches, two hotels, a school of some sort, a coal yard, a millinery, a haberdashery, an apothecary, empty lots—Fourteenth street wasn't on any tourist's agenda. Just south of K street, among the trees in Franklin Square, I saw a scattering of low, ragged tents—for victims of the depression that the panic had touched off. A Gilded Age, indeed! Doesn't *gilded* imply that if you scrape it, the gold will peel off?

Clara couldn't stop staring. "How do they eat?" she whispered fiercely. "Do they have children? Must they steal? Where do they . . . ?"

What could I say?

Our reward lay ahead, past M street, beyond the circle that connected four roads. Memorial Evangelical Lutheran Church rose like a plea to the heavens above. The steeple was tall and as elegantly thin as a rapier. The reddish-brown stone and the Gothic spires, astride the triangle of land between Four-teenth street and Vermont avenue, gave the church a majestic look.

"Why are we going here, anyway, Johnny?" Clara said. "What does this have to do with Andrew Johnson's unfortunate—or fortunate—passing? I'm sorry, I don't see the connection."

"This man Atzerodt was the subject of one of the blackmail letters, and his cousin is looking for vengeance. I can't be sure there's a connection, but I *think* there is. Need to follow my nose."

"And a nice nose it is," Clara said.

"And even if there isn't a connection . . ."

At twenty minutes past noon, by my watch, church was ending. Buggies waited at the curb as worshippers straggled out the door. We weaved our way inside. A vestibule and a short staircase led me into the sanctuary. See-ing it, I stood straighter. The high-vaulted ceiling, the ornamental rafters that stretched across the breadth, the simple stained windows, the pews below, an immense pipe organ that God Himself might have tuned—in here, mortals feel warmed by a higher power.

At the front, below the pulpit, towering over the people gathered around, stood a man in a white robe with a green garnish. He resembled an Old Testament prophet, the kind that ought to frighten you out of sin. The Rev-erend Mr. Butler—for surely it was he—had a lush beard and a craggy face straight out of Dickens, featuring Fagin's hooded eyes and intrusive nose. He seemed accustomed to commanding all he surveyed.

The other worshippers had slipped away by the time we approached. "May we speak with you in private for a minute?" I said.

"And you are . . . ?" His voice was used to reaching the farthest pews.

I introduced myself and Clara and mentioned the *New-York Tribune*. Smalley had described the pastor as an ardent abolitionist and therefore apt to revere Greeley's Great Moral Organ. "I am interested in the death of Andrew Johnson."

"I know nothing about his death."

"I understand you were with Mr. Atzerodt during his final hours."

"His final hours on Earth—yes, I had that privilege. There is no secret about that." This didn't bode well; it was secrets I was after. "Mr. Atzerodt was a Lutheran, and he asked for clergy. So I received a request. It was my duty—and my honor—to oblige."

I was curious about who had asked him, but I couldn't see why it mat-tered. "How long were you with him?"

"I wasn't noticing the time."

"I understand, of course, that you are . . ."—I didn't want to say *forbidden,* because that would quash any possibility—"constrained from repeating his confidences. But is there anything you can tell that might shed light on . . ."

"Mr. Atzerodt's last words, on the gallows, are known to the public. So I would betray no privilege by repeating them. 'May we all meet in the other world!' May we, indeed."

"Hopefully in the same one," I said, pointing skyward.

Apparently, this was not a lighthearted matter. A sizable lady in a wide-brimmed hat crowded with peonies was waiting her turn.

"Is that all, Mr. Hay?"

"I'll wait," I said.

The Reverend Butler blessed the lady's ailing husband and turned toward the pulpit, in search of sanctuary, then back to us.

In need of my best ammunition, I figured this was a man who worshiped authority, celestial or otherwise. "Please read this," I said, showing him my letter from President Grant.

He complied, pursed his lips, and said, "My son, you could show me a letter from Saint Peter, and it would not absolve me of my obligation to keep a confidence. All men may be forgiven for what they do."

"Let me explain. I have reason to think that Andrew Johnson's recent death was an act of . . . man, not of God. And I have reason to think that his death was connected in some way"—I was edging beyond the evidence here, but preachers did that for a living—"to Mr. Atzerodt's . . . execution ten years ago, for a crime that he declined to commit."

The Reverend Butler didn't blink. God, as I recalled, was famed for His mysterious ways. "Come with me, Mr. Hay," he said, "and Mrs. Hay, by all means. I have something you might like to see."

We exited through a paneled door behind the pulpit, into the sacristy. Goblets and half-empty bottles of wine crowded a counter next to the sink. An open cabinet showed silver accoutrements for the altar. The pastor sat me down at what, to all appearances, was a kitchen table. He stepped to a bookcase by the rear door and unwedged a volume.

"Here," he said, handing me a thin book like the fairy tales my mother used to read. It was bound in a reddish fabric that was sloughing off. "I cannot vouch for anything in here. But you may sit at the table. Take your time. I have people in the front I must see." He gestured toward the two utilitarian chairs and at the book that was now in my hands. "Your question will be answered on page two oh six. The things I am forbidden to tell you, you will find some of them here."

The opening page featured an engraving of Booth. He had the fevered eyes, tousled hair, and satin lapels of an aristocratic family's wayward son. I turned to the title page:

LIVES, CRIMES
AND
CONFESSIONS
of the
ASSASSINS
LAST MOMENTS OF THE CONVICTS IN THEIR CELLS
SCENES AT THE SCAFFOLD AND
THE EXECUTION

TRUTHFUL, WILD, AND FEARFULLY EXCITING

By Dr. L.L. STEVENS
TROY, N.Y.
FROM THE DAILY TIMES STEAM PRINTING ESTABLISHMENT, 211 RIVER STREET.
1865.

Truthful, wild, fearfully exciting. In other words, gossip. My interest, exactly.

I began to leaf through and was stopped on page 44 by

LIFE AND CONFESSION
OF
GEORGE A. ATZERODT

GEORGE ANDREW ATZERODT was born in the kingdom of Prussia in 1835, and came to this country with his parents in 1844. He arrived at Baltimore . . .

It was the typical immigrant's story. His father was a farmer as well as a blacksmith, moving the family from Baltimore to Germantown— Germantown!—to Westmoreland county, Virginia, where he placed his son George as an apprentice in a coach-making business. Before the war broke out, George moved across the Potomac, into Maryland, to join his older brother making coaches in the hamlet of Port Tobacco. That was where he came to know John Surratt, who introduced him to an actor named J. Wilkes Booth.

> The manners of Atzerodt were rough and unpleasant in the extreme, his jests obscene and coarse . . . He was about thirty years of age, of small stature, Dutch face, sallow complexion, dull, dark blue eyes, rather light-colored hair, bushy and unkempt. His was the meanest face of the whole . . . looked upon as a very weak-minded fellow—in fact, was regarded a very harmless and silly man.

In Port Tobacco, having learned the secrets of the Potomac, he was invited into the conspiracy to kidnap President Lincoln on his way to the Soldiers' Home and to spirit him across the river into Virginia—the Confederacy.

> . . . The boat was capable of carrying fifteen men, and was a large flat-bottomed bateau, painted lead color, which had been bought for the purpose by Booth . . . The whole affair failed, and Booth . . . spoke of going to Richmond and opening a theatre, and promised me employment in it, in some capacity . . .

I turned the tissue-thin leaves until I reached page 206. Halfway down:

A Partial Confession.

Atzerodt made a partial confession to the Rev. Mr. Butler a few hours before his execution. He stated that he took a room at the Kirkwood House on Thursday afternoon and was engaged in endeavoring to get a pass to Richmond. He then heard the President was to be taken to the theatre and there captured. He said he understood that Booth was to rent the theatre for the purpose of carrying out the plot to capture the President. He stated that another conspirator brought the pistol and knife to the Kirkwood House, and that he (Atzerodt) had nothing to do with the attempted assassination of Andrew Johnson.

Atzerodt had nothing to do with the attempted assassination of Andrew Johnson—that's what he told his confessor, hours before the noose. In fact, there hadn't been any attempt to assassinate Andrew Johnson. Back in 'sixty-five, that is.

I started to turn back to the earlier account when a headline higher on the page caught my eye.

Atzerodt in His Cell.

Atzerodt passed the night previous to the execution without any particular manifestations. He prayed and cried alternately, but made no other noise that attracted the attention of his keeper. On the morning of the execution he sat most of the time on the floor of his cell in his shirt sleeves.

A Mysterious Visitant.

He was attended by a lady dressed in deep black, who carried a prayer book, and who seemed more exercised in spirit than the prisoner himself. Who the lady was could not be ascertained. She left him at half-past twelve o'clock, and exhibited great emotion at parting.

During the morning Atzerodt was greatly composed, and spent part of the time in earnest conversation with his spiritual adviser, Rev. Mr. Butler . . .

I was reading to Clara about the mysterious lady in black—she adored the telling detail—when the Reverend Mr. Butler, in the flesh, appeared in the doorway.

"I am just reading about you," I said.

"At your service, Mr. Hay," he said.

I grazed the open pages with the back of my hand. "It says he gave you a partial confession. How do you know it was partial?"

"I believe that was Dr. Stevens's word, not my own."

"But accurate?"

I let the question hang until he said, "Perhaps."

"So, he had more to confess?"

This time, no reply, by which I inferred the same answer, a *perhaps* that meant a *yes*. But he wasn't going to tell me anything else. I understood. He couldn't say any more—he had reached the limits of what was allowed—although, clearly, he was trying to help. I had an inkling as to why.

"Did you think that Mr. Atzerodt was innocent?" I said.

A deep sigh. "Judgment is the Lord's, my son."

This pastor wasn't my papa. "Of course," I said, "but would you happen to have an opinion?"

"It is not for me to judge."

"Then could you tell me anything, please, about this mysterious visitant?" I said.

A pause. "I am sorry, Mr. Hay—and Mrs. Hay. I couldn't say. Now if you will—"

It was Clara who had the gumption to ask, "You couldn't or you won't?"

The Lutheran pastor's forbidding face broke into a smile. I could understand why the innocent and the guilty alike might entrust him with the truth.

"In my calling," he replied, "there is no difference. And in this case, there actually is none. I don't know who she was, and if I did, I wouldn't tell you. Surely you can understand."

Unfortunately, I could.

But I had a reason for asking that transcended the prurient. If I could find the mysterious lady in black, I might learn what Atzerodt intended to tell his Maker.

<hr>

On the hutch in the Nicolays' vestibule, amid the house keys and postage stamps, lay a telegram from Elizabethton.

> HAY, NO SIGN OF MCELWEE. WIDOW JOHNSON
> SENDS REGARDS. WM. BROWN ORNERY BUT NOT A
> CRIME IN TENNESSEE. PEARCE

Maybe I had judged Sheriff J. Dugger Pearce too harshly. *Judgment is the Lord's.* But I worried for Eliza Johnson's well-being in a house where a ruffian reigned. I was hardly in a position to warn Mary about her husband. Surely she knew and had her mother's safety at heart. Maybe I could tell Martha. She would believe the worst about her brother-in-law, and rightly so. But what could she do about it from here? She could return to Tennessee, is what.

At supper, Helen's eyes lit up at Clara's mention of the mysterious lady in black. "Like in one of my books," she warbled.

What on earth was a nine-year-old reading? "Yes," I said, "but she was real."

"Then who was she?" Helen said. "*Is* she?"

"The perfect question," I said.

Nicolay beamed. He admired sharp questions as much as I did. I cut into the canvasback duck, which was dry. This wasn't the usual fare for Sunday supper but more of a feast. I was on my second helping of duck and on my third oyster patty, barely saving room for the plum cake. The five of us didn't finish half of what Therena had cooked.

"And as with most perfect questions, I don't know the answer," I continued. "But I have a notion who does. He's up in Germantown."

I told them the little I knew about Hartman Richter—his kinship with the accused conspirator and his testimony before the court-martial avowing his cousin's innocent behavior.

"I think I may go up there to-morrow, by train." I turned to Clara. "You want to come with me?"

"Let's talk later," she said.

I thought I caught Therena's quizzical look.

"I've never chased a more sensational story," I said, spreading out on the bed in a postcoital glow, ridiculously confident that another tiny life had begun. I told her of the second missive I'd received, with an unblinking eye on the envelope, informing me that William Browning was not to be found but that Herman Richter was still in Germantown and that Andrew Johnson had been assaulted last March in Washington City, details to come. "Can you believe it?" I spouted. "This is a better story than I could ever hope for."

"Is that what this means to you," Clara said, "a newspaper story?"

"Not just *a* story. It might be a series. Then people's reactions. What's wrong with that?"

"You are talking about the night that Lincoln . . . left us."

"Believe me, I am aware of that. I had a front-row seat."

"And what is the story, exactly?"

I laughed. The hard and simple question. "I'll let you know when I've got it," I said. "So, do you want to come with me to-morrow?"

"I'm going home," Clara said.

"What?"

"I've decided. I miss Helen. She needs me."

"You need her, you mean." I felt jealous—and hurt. She needed Helen more than she needed me. And I needed Helen, too. *And* Clara. Oh, brother. Was I becoming a father—and a husband—in my soul? Not enough of either, I guess, to head home yet.

Once Clara made up her mind, there was no changing it. This, I knew. "When are you going?" I said.

She had already confided in Therena, which explained the evening's feast.

CHAPTER EIGHTEEN

Who knew that a woman could pack so sparingly that we had no need for a hackney? Pinkerton showed up again at the doorstep and insisted on walking us to the station.

"Nae charge," he said.

Most of the trains heading north or west from Washington City used the Baltimore & Ohio station on New Jersey avenue, a block north of the Capitol. The depot, like most things in life, looked better from the outside. The square stucco tower and the roofline's audacious arches suggested a grandeur that entering the premises dispelled. Twenty steps down delivered us into a dingy cavern in which creatures crept hither and yon. On closer inspection, they proved to be people much like ourselves, crossing in a haphazard manner that colonized ants would mock.

Clara boarded the first-class car for the seven fifty train to Pittsburgh and then on to Cleveland. She was expected—Amasa's doing. In her lushly appointed compartment, we said our gooey goodbyes. I promised to come home as soon as I could, and she nodded, not believing a word of it. We kissed again. She seemed elsewhere—in Cleveland, already—and I left.

Pinkerton was nowhere to be seen. I weaved my way through the crowd to a ticket window and plunked down a paper dollar and a dime for a ticket to Germantown. A decade ago, Atzerodt had taken a stagecoach. But I had neither the stomach nor the available time, now that the B&O had opened a branch line up into Montgomery county. The express train, which stopped in Germantown, was scheduled to leave at ten past eight.

Amazingly, it did. But not before I had bought a *Chronicle* and found a seat on a long bench and scanned the front page. Not a smart idea. In West Virginia, a B&O passenger train slammed into a caboose and two freight cars that the preceding train had somehow left on the track. No one was killed or seriously injured, which was not the case in Missouri, where a rotten trestle gave way and sent two passenger cars and a mail car into a dry creek twenty feet below.

The item that pulled me from my seat was near the bottom of the page:

> ANDREW (FRANK) JOHNSON, son of the late ex-President Johnson, denies all knowledge of the reported insurance on his father's life, though he says he has not yet been able to look over all of his father's papers. The estate of the ex-President is estimated at between $150,000 and $175,000.

That was a lot of spondulicks. People had been murdered for less.

Something to ponder as the train steamed beyond the edge of Washington City. We passed pine thickets and cow pastures and dilapidated farmhouses. The yards were rife with pigs and geese and poorly clad children, not unlike East Tennessee. All right: the Great Commoner had died a wealthy man. His dissolute son was probably lying when he insisted that he knew nothing about anything. Unless he was telling the truth, which gave him another reason *not* to kill his father before the old man wrote a new will—*if* he had known of Daddy's intentions. Maybe no one had ever told him about the life insurance or the will-as-yet-unwritten, rendering him unaware that it was in his interest for his father to remain on this side of the Earth's crust.

The possibilities were legion, and too many of them fit the facts. But they weren't infinite. I doubted that Frank was involved—he had too much to lose by his father's death, whether he knew it or not—although I couldn't be so sure about either of his brothers-in-law. I doubted that Johnson's impeachment still held enough passion to cause his murder, but I wouldn't swear the same about the night that Lincoln was shot. A decade later, the fumes from Booth's derringer still befouled the air.

The railroad car had a newness that hadn't worn off yet. The seat cushions still had their heft, and the wood paneling hadn't been scratched, other than two pairs of letters enclosed in a heart. Sharing the car was a family with two middling-sized boys excited about splashing in the Potomac. I figured they were heading for Point of Rocks, halfway to Pennsylvania, at the end of the line.

Soon we crossed into Maryland and its rolling countryside, heading north toward a broad, flat ridge. Expanses of tobacco and fields of corn, probably to be distilled into whisky, interrupted the woodlands. So did the farmhouses and shanties. The landscape seemed milder, less dramatic—less oppressive—than in East Tennessee.

I contemplated Andrew Johnson as a family man. Little wonder he had torn up his wills. All three of his sons were drunkards, and as sons-in-law (other than the sainted Stover) he had a blackmailer and a blackguard, respectively. His elder daughter, Martha, was as tough and as smart as her daddy and shared most of his faults. I wondered if she had known about the insurance. Certainly, the Pattersons had wasted no time in taking advantage of Daddy's death. Had they, shall we say, facilitated it as well? Only Mary, the younger daughter, had escaped her daddy's shadow (praise to the sainted Stover). She had had opportunities galore, although she didn't seem the type. Was there a never-could-be-a-murderer type? I would propose Clara, although if someone looked crosswise at Helen, I wouldn't wager a penny.

Oh Lord, my head ached.

The train stopped in Rockville. The brick depot had gabled windows and a steep slate roof that reminded me of a Swiss chalet. No one alit that I could see, and no one got on.

By the schedule, Germantown was nineteen minutes ahead. I tried to think about Hartman Richter. I knew next to nothing about him. He was George Atzerodt's first cousin and had testified in his defense at the military trial. He was a man with a cause, arguably a just cause, which made him especially dangerous. He had once been aggressive (and misguided) enough to barge in on Hannibal Hamlin. I had no idea what to expect. I reached into my right jacket pocket and fondled the revolver. It felt comforting— very comforting. Allow me to nominate the Second Amendment as the most erotic in the Bill of Rights, other than the right of the people peaceably to assemble.

The train rattled into what passed for a station. The sign, freshly painted, announced: GERMANTOWN. It was nine eighteen.

The platform was a gravel landing, and the depot resembled an outhouse. The only other passenger to disembark was an old man bent over a cane. Behind the ticket window, the clerk eyed me as I walked past.

I exited into a village that hugged the new tracks—a general store, two harness shops, a carriage maker, a carpenter, a one-room schoolhouse. No livery stable, which was just as well, because I didn't know where I was going. I was relieved to see a hackney parked across the rutted road, by the undertaker's hut.

The driver was hunched over in his seat, snoring, a wiry lad with tousled red hair. I concluded that awakening him was in his interest as well as my own, and, once restored to consciousness, he agreed. Yes, he knew where the Richters lived—"off Clopper road"—and he would charge twenty cents to take me there. I climbed in behind him. The interior was cleaner than in the city's hacks.

He was the sort of driver who liked to talk whether his passenger was listening or not. This suited me fine, for I could listen or not, to my liking. For a while, I listened, and he was interesting enough, about how the soil in this country wasn't good for anything but dairy cows—"This county's the poores' in the state"—and about how the center of Germantown had moved a mile east two years back, to meet the railroad.

"So that's who plumb controls everythin', them railroad tycoons, the Vanderbilts and them like," the driver said—incisively, I thought. (Best not to mention my father-in-law.) "Ain't complainin', mind ya. Means more business for the likes of me, y'know, cartin' folks here and about. This here's Clopper road. Used to be an Indian trail. We gonna turn up ahead, onto Darnestown road. The Richters, they be a mile and a half to the west."

We passed dairy farms and cornfields and the occasional weatherworn house. A cloud of dust lingered over the roadway—another vehicle must be close ahead. After the road twisted past a copse of chestnuts, a red barn appeared on the right.

"'Tis here," he said, pointing left.

We turned into a pathway between fields of cornstalks so high that they dwarfed the rig. I feared that a rough ride would launch driver *and* passenger into the bounty of crops.

A quarter mile along sat a two-story shingled farmhouse. Chickens skittered across the yard; a hog squealed, unseen. A man in the front was unloading barrels of . . . I couldn't tell what they contained, and I didn't care to know. He was a sturdy young man with shoulder-length hair and a biblical beard. His square face had resolute cheekbones and steely blue eyes that suggested he would wait until hell froze over before offering a blanket to the unworthy.

I asked the driver to wait. He saluted at Richter and winked. This did nothing to quell my nerves.

"And what are ya sellin', my friend?" Richter said.

"Nothing," I said, climbing down from the hack. "I would like to ask Hartman Richter a couple of questions. Is that you?"

He took a step toward me, locked into my eyes, and said, "What about?"

"Your cousin George Atzerodt and what happened to him."

"What do you think happened to him?"

"I think he was hanged," I said slowly, "and I am not persuaded that it was . . . justified."

"Ain't ya now?" His brow furrowed. "Mister, who are ya?"

When I spoke of the *Tribune,* he brightened, mumbling he had been hoping to get a newspaper to take him seriously. And when I said, with trepidation, that I was carrying a letter from President Grant, he relaxed instead of consigning me to heat eternal.

"Was tryin' to git to him," he said. "Couldn't quite."

"What about?"

"'Bout what you say—justice."

"Can we go inside and talk?" I said.

Richter had a farmer's face, leathery and brown, wary yet unafraid. He pursed his lips, gave me a long look, and whispered, "Quieter out here. Tell Jimmy there to wait, or you'll have a long walk back to the station, and you're a li'l too scrawny for that."

I took his advice.

He limped a little as he led me onto the porch—probably a war wound. I wondered which side he was on, but I figured it wasn't politic (or useful) to ask. We seated ourselves side by side, in wicker chairs painted a baby blue, looking out at the corn—succulent, still growing. Maybe he would say more if I wasn't looking his way.

"How close were you and . . . your cousin?"

"Like brothers, we was. He live here, y'know, right here"—Richter jerked his thumb behind him—"for a few years, 'til he was fourteen or so. He visit here from time to time ever since. Poor George. Nothin' ever go right for him." He lapsed into silence.

"Until he met . . . Booth?"

"He need the money, and at last he had sumpin' to sell. He knew every twist of that river, all the secret places to land. Booth was promisin' him a job, and George warn't afraid of no work. He needed the wampum."

"I thought he painted carriages with his brother."

"He did that, too."

"What else did he do?"

Hartman Richter stared off across the corn.

"Oh," I said, because suddenly I understood. "He ran the Union blockade."

"That's what you sayin'."

"I am."

"And they call him a coward. Coward?!" Richter rose from his chair and blew a gob of spittle over the railing, almost into the corn. "That's a howler. You been down to Port Tobacco? Let me tell ya, mister, to row from the Maryland side of the Potomac and hide in all them little inlets, workin' the tides, keeping yer wits about ya and dodgin' the Union gunboats, sneakin' past the blockade—and then back again—and keeping yer passengers safe and yer merchandise out o' the water and out o' enemy hands, that ain't no job for a coward. It takes smarts and . . . bollocks, let me tell ya, mister. And George, he was good at it. As brave as they come."

"You mind if I take notes?" I said.

He did not.

I opened my notebook to an empty page, pulled out a snub-nosed pencil, resisted licking the point, and said, "When did you see him last?"

"Warn't long after we was arrested."

"We?"

"Oh yeah, they arrested me, too. Right here, inside, in my own parlor. They took us aboard the *Montauk*—that was the jail, and a stinkin' mess it was—and we was getting on the ironclad when we get split up. Then we was hooded and put in irons, so if ya mean *see* each other, that didn't happen no more. Later I was took to Old Capitol Prison, afore they let me go, and I never did see poor George ag'in." Richter started to rock, although the chair wasn't a rocker. "Warn't fair what they done t' him. He didn't do nothin'."

"He didn't have to do anything himself. He was part of a conspiracy, and that's enough. I'm a lawyer, and that's what the law says."

"That's just it—he warn't part of it no more. That's what he tellin' me in the police cart, on the way to the ship. He talk with Booth that night— y'know, that meetin'."

"What meeting?"

"Earlier that evenin', two or three hours afore that . . . business at Ford's." Richter stopped rocking. "All of 'em, they met at some hotel or 'nother. And that's when Booth tell him he had to kill Johnson, and George wouldn't do it. Booth got nasty, said he'd blow his brains out if he di'n't, so George he say nothin' one way or 'nother. But he warn't gonna do it, and he never said he would. He done nothin' about it but get so drunk at that hotel that he couldn't see a hole in a ladder, and he leave Mr. Johnson alone. That sound like a conspirator to you, brother?"

"Why didn't he go through with it, then," I said, "if Booth threatened to kill him if he refused?"

"As I say, he warn't no coward. He'd signed up fer a kidnappin' but not fer killin' Lincoln, and not fer killin' Johnson, neither. No, sir, couldn't do it."

"Why not?"

"He ain't no killer, fer one thing." Richter was rocking again in his four-legged chair.

"And for another?" I prompted.

"His little girl."

"What little girl? I didn't know he was married."

"He warn't, not in the church-like way."

"Oh," I said, and waited.

"Edith, her name was. Is. That's the girl. She musta been two years old then. Make her twelve now, sumpin' like that. Oh Jesus, did he love that little girl. Had her by a widow woman who had three of her own already. That little one, George sure did take to her. Didn't want her to have a daddy who was a killer. That's why."

"That simple?"

"That simple. Cain't you understan'?"

I grunted. I tried to imagine Helen as twelve years old. Impossible. I tried two years old—a little easier. She would be walking by then, maybe talking. (*My* daughter.) Would I kill for her? Only if I had to. Would I refuse to kill, in order to spare her? To make her proud of her daddy? Without a doubt.

"Do you have children?" I said.

"Three. They's why we out here on the porch."

We were sitting silently, one of us rocking, the horse snorting below, when I remembered. The mysterious lady in black! I told Richter about the unknown woman who had visited Atzerodt on the morning of his death. "Do you suppose she was Edith's mother?"

"Coulda been her, prob'ly was."

I said, "Why would she be so mysterious? Why not just . . . ?"

The rocking stopped. I waited, and received my reward: "I sayin' they warn't exactly married, 'cept by time." His rocking resumed.

"Did you ever meet her?"

"Never did, but I heard tell. Maybe she'll know."

"Know what?"

"Whatever he didn't want to take to the grave. George knew more than he was sayin' to me. I'm pretty sure of that. We got separated on the gang-plank, and there was people listenin' in."

"Any idea what it was?"

"If I could tell ya, I would. It musta been sumpin' that President Johnson didn't want known. 'Cause George didn't *do* nothin' 'cept spare the man's life, and so the man turned around and had him hanged. And jes' about the very next day, God Almighty. He say yes to the hangings and they all was told and the very next day they was hanged. What the"—he lowered his voice—"hell hurry was that? Tell me, what was the rush? Poor George musta known sumpin' that Johnson was scared of gettin' known."

"Maybe Edith's mama would know," I said, "if she's still in Port Tobacco. The widow woman. Do you know her name?"

It cost me a half eagle—five dollars in gold. Everything was cheaper out here in the sticks.

"One last thing," he said as I climbed into the hack—"and this one's fer free." I turned. "Port Tobacco, it's a mighty rough place. If yer headin' there, don't go nekkid."

He meant: take a gun.

∗

The old man with the cane boarded at the far end of the railroad car. There were only the two of us. I met him coming up the aisle.

I greeted him with, "Pinkerton's man."

"Almost," came the reply. "Pinkerton's woman."

The white wig came off, and the torso straightened, and I recognized the snuggly blonde who welcomed clients at the agency's front desk. "I could've killed you any of a half dozen times," she said, "and nobody the wiser." No smile.

Some detective I was. "Thank you for your restraint," I said.

One of us had to move aside. I slid into a seat. "But remember, Mr. Hay, you have never met me," she said, "and I have never met you."

"We have never been properly introduced," I said as she sauntered past.

∗

The desk clerk with colorless hair greeted me warily, like a rival from grammar school. I wished him a good afternoon and pointed up the stairs, toward the Pattersons' room.

"They're gone," he said.

"Gone for good?"

"No. To Philadelphia."

"Coming back?"

"They'd better. We've kept the room for them."

I wondered if they had left anything worth stealing—sorry, borrowing. "When, do you know?" I said.

"Whenever they can buy a wedding dress."

"A what? Who for?"

"Their niece is with them."

"Lillie Stover?" I said.

A nod and a dreamy look, which I could well understand.

"Did Bill go with them?"

"Haven't seen him."

"Mind if I look?"

"All right."

I went upstairs and knocked on the door. There was a rustling inside. It stopped. I knocked again.

"Who is it?"

"Bill, it is me," I said ungrammatically. "John Hay."

The door swung open. Bill looked frightened. "Cain't come in," he said. "They know you was here."

"How do they know?"

Bill shrugged. I had put the envelopes back in a hurry.

I said, "Do they know that you . . . ?"

The barest of nods.

"Are you going home with them?"

Bill's eyes fluttered shut. I didn't recall having ever met Robert, but I glimpsed in Bill's face a resemblance to his grandfather—the resolute nose, the set of his jaw, the piercing stare.

"Would you like a position in Cleveland?" I said.

Slowly, the door swung shut.

+≡≡+

"A Pinkerton lady?" Therena exclaimed.

"Yes, how about that?" I said. "Dressed up like an old man. She was good." That last, I said a shade too enthusiastically.

Therena said, "And how's Clara?"

"Haven't heard," I said. "She ought to be getting home about now."

Therena said her good-nights and left the darkened parlor. Nicolay poured two brandies, without having to ask.

"So, why is Germantown called Germantown?" he said, stiffening the vestiges of his Bavarian diction.

"A crossroads of German merchants, I would guess."

Nicolay took a sip and said, "Good guess. And what did you learn there?"

"More than I expected. How often does that happen?" I told him about the meeting of Booth's conspirators the evening that Lincoln was shot and Atzerodt's refusal to assassinate the vice president. He hadn't acted out of drink or cowardice but because of a secret daughter in southern Maryland, by a widow named Mrs. Wheeler.

"Are you going?" Nicolay said, sputtering into his drink.

"Of course I'm going." I had never considered not going.

"Johnny, is this for a story or is this for a—?"

"Nico, don't ask me hard questions. It's too late at night." The brandy felt warm going down. I said nothing, even to Nicolay, about taking a gun.

In the darkest of woods, in the deepest of nights,
By the fairest of wishes, for the sleekest of . . .

Rights? Fights? Lights? Sprites? Kites?

Damn! Poetry was so . . . confining. Maybe that was the point, to fit reality into a straitjacket. That's what my reality felt like. Lost in the dark, too many questions, not enough answers. Journalists love a good question, but you need answers to break into print.

In the darkest of woods, in the deepest of nights,
By the fairest of wishes, for the sleekest of flights.
And me in my carriage, its horses in sight,
Forever and ever, I could . . .

Were these words so brilliant (albeit meaningless) that I should relight the lantern and scribble them down? I chose sleep—and would remember them, anyway, before crossing them out.

CHAPTER NINETEEN

I slept badly. My joints ached. I felt twice my age. I had evidently grown used to sharing a bed. My pocket watch put the time at ten minutes before six o'clock, too early for civilized connections. I tiptoed through the creaking house in my dressing robe. A yellow envelope sat on the foyer floor, below the mail slot. I picked it up. It was for me.

Telegrams delivered in the dead of night never contain good news.

ARRIVED SAFELY, EASY TRIP. HELEN IS FINE. WE
BOTH MISS YOU. DO WHAT YOU MUST. LOVE CLARA

I exhaled. Do what I must or do what I want? The usual human dilemma. What I wanted was to go back to bed. What I must do was finish what I had started. All right, first the one, then the other. Decisions should be so simple.

⊬═══⊬

"I don't want to tell Pinkerton," I said, munching a bran muffin. "He'll just send somebody along to protect me. I'll never get anything out of this woman, with him hulking beside me."

"Or her," Therena said.

"Her, too," I said.

Nicolay said, "Pinkerton probably knows you're going, anyway. He *is* a detective." A real one, is what Nicolay meant.

"How could he?" I said. "Nobody knows my plans except Hartman Richter and me, and now the people at this table. Pinkerton isn't a sooth-sayer, is he? Well, is he? Helen, you haven't told anyone, have you?"

"Told them what?"

"Exactly," I said. "Nico, you haven't been out of this house since we talked last night."

"You don't trust me in the absence of evidence, I take it."

"I don't trust myself in the absence of evidence," I said. "But I do trust *you* more than that."

"A low bar, indeed," Nicolay said.

"So, you're going through with it," Therena said, "now that Clara has left."

"What's that got to do with it? If she were here, I would take her with me."

Therena said, "Would she go?"

"If I asked her nicely enough, I think she would. She's reasonably adventurous."

"I don't know if I would," Therena said.

"Then I won't invite you," I said. "Don't worry, I'll be fine."

It was Helen who looked worried. She ceased eating her muffin mid-bite and stared at me. Her open-mouthed expression mixed reverence and fear.

"I'll be fine," I told her, less persuasively than the first time. I could almost hear *my* Helen lobbing this back at me, although only if she could talk.

⊢══╣

Let me see: I was to go armed to Port Tobacco, searching for a widow who had borne a daughter without benefit of clergy. Presumably, she had found another man in the meantime, so that even a mention of the name *Atzerodt* might provoke him to . . . who knows what?

Ah, easy as plum cake.

I fingered the pistol in my jacket pocket. It felt nowhere near big enough. Even so, I preferred it to keeping Pinkerton as my sidearm.

The Baltimore and Potomac depot was on the National Mall, at Sixth and B streets. An eyesore—the tracks across the Mall, I mean—but wasn't this the price of progress? It wasn't in my nature to fret about things I couldn't change, although I have been known to make exceptions.

The depot itself was a pleasing concoction of brick leavened by fanciful ribbons of stone and a square clock tower with a steeple that reminded me of a theologically undemanding church. Inside, the station was crowded despite the early hour—men either in work clothes and slouch caps or in frock coats and straw boaters. Without meaning to, I gave a bent-over old woman an inquiring look that caused her to clutch her purse and veer away.

On the eastward train, toward Baltimore, it was hard to find a seat. I plunked myself down next to a dark-haired young man with a long face and a tic. He blinked rapidly when I addressed him. Soon, I didn't say anything, as a relief to us both.

I busied myself with the morning's *Chronicle*. The usual fare—the fighting in Herzegovina, leaky privy boxes in Washington City, a larceny of chickens, the theft of forty lead pencils from Shillington's bookstore on the Avenue. On the back page, I read of a black man's arrest in Alexandria, in Virginia, for punching a restaurant owner who insisted that he eat in a separate room.

I glanced out the window. We had passed Boundary street and continued into what used to be known as Washington county. This was countryside, wild or cultivated, beyond the reach of city ways. The hills gave way to marshy plains. Aged and dirty frame houses were scattered among fields dotted with stagnant pools; barn animals and children gadded about. We passed into Maryland and another half hour brought us to Bowie. From here, the Baltimore and Potomac's Pope's Creek branch headed south.

Bowie's depot was a wooden hut. Inside, the waiting room was edged by hard benches. In the corner, a man in overalls kept a careful eye on three restless boys.

The train into southern Maryland left on time, at five minutes past nine. It carried seven passengers and two baggage cars filled with plows and the creosote telegraph poles I had seen stacked up on the platform. The car was the standard wooden box with tan wicker seats and toilets that emptied onto the track. I checked around for someone who looked like a Pinkerton man—or woman—and saw only the farmer's brood and two elderly ladies who interrupted their conversation with pinches of snuff. Surely Pinkerton wouldn't send a pair of agents, just so he could charge me twice. (Would he?) Beyond the conductor's stand, across the center of the car, sat two negroes, a stout gentleman in his Sunday best and a hard-eyed woman wearing a calico dress and a flowered hat.

My wicker seat, lacking a cushion, was no more comfortable than a horse's spine. According to the railroad timetable, I would have three hours and ten minutes to pity my arse. As the train rattled along, I watched Prince George's and then Charles counties slip by—tobacco farm after tobacco farm, the manicured mansions of plantation owners and the unpainted shacks of ex-slaves.

I squeezed my eyes shut and thought about where I was heading. I tried to inhabit George Atzerodt's mind. Not easy. An immigrant, struggling to make a life with limited skills, admired by a famous actor for his river expertise, promised a path out of a hardscrabble life, and now the father to a young daughter he loved. Suppose he had known more about that terrible Good Friday than the authorities wanted to hear. Wasn't that possible? Plausible, even? What had he known? And why hadn't he divulged it?

Maybe he had.

"Hey, pal, where ya headin'?"

I must have nodded off, because my head jolted up. Had we stopped at a station? This man had gotten on or had moved his seat. The last thing I wanted was a companion.

"Port Tobacco," I said, to be polite.

"A cesspool," he declared. He had black hair brushed straight back from a puffy face that was plain enough for a pastor. His skin was leathery, probably impervious to pinpricks.

"How so?" I said, my curiosity piqued.

"A sinful place," he said. "Full of fighting and gambling, slave traders and blockade runners. Satan's swamp, my friend."

"My kind of place," I replied.

He didn't laugh; my sense of humor wasn't to everyone's taste. "What made it that way?" I said.

"Always was. The war made it worse. Rebels everywhere. And Union troops."

"Ports are like that," I said.

"Ain't been a port to speak of for a hunnerd years. Longer. In its day, it was big. Tobacca 'round here is the best—got traded for silk and slaves. But tobacca ruins the soil, and the silt run into the creek that come up from the river and ruined that, too. Them ships must need five or six feet of draw, y'know, and they can't sail up there no more, not without gittin' stuck. Ruined the town, nothin' like what it used to be. Ya come up, ya get silted in, ya come down. That's life, ain't it?"

I swear he wiped away a tear. History can do that to people.

"You from there?" I said.

"Pope's Creek, end of the line. By the river."

"The Potomac?"

"Ya heard of it, then." He wasn't humorless.

"That's where you're heading now?"

"No, sir. Getting off at Port Tobacco. Got business."

"What's your business?" I said.

"Salves and liniments. Good business. Always a market in a sad-eyed world. The worse things get, the more people need 'em."

My recent affection for liniment fueled our conversation for another few phrases. After that, I could think of nothing to say.

The landscape was flat, uneventful. If you admired tobacco that was half a man's height, it was for you. It wasn't for me. I slid the window open and regretted it. The wind was hot and carried the soot from the coal-fired engine, two cars ahead. I shoved the window down but not in time. A particle burned my cheek, and I brushed it away—onto my charcoal-gray trousers, leaving a black mark that only I could see. My high collar scratched my neck.

We couldn't reach Port Tobacco Station soon enough. It was a flag stop, just past La Plata, a mile or two from the village itself, or so the conductor informed me with what I took to be a smirk.

My newfound friend told me that a hackney would be meeting him and did I want a ride. Of course I did.

"You're Pinkerton's man," I said.

He asked who Pinkerton was. This time, when I laughed, he laughed along.

"If I'm paying for you," I said, "I should know your name."

He looked puzzled again and introduced himself as Smith.

"My name is Hay," I said. "Does that ring a bell?"

Evidently not.

A lean-to served as the depot. Hogsheads of tobacco were lined up beside it, ready for the train's return north. To my surprise, I must admit, a hack was waiting. My protector and I rode in companionable silence as the rolling woodlands gave way to hills. A wooded ridge in the distance reminded me of the bluffs along the Mississippi, where I had spent my boyhood days; the Potomac must be nearby. Where the road continued on toward a town called Welcome—such expectations the place must shoulder!—the hack veered south. The road narrowed, and woods pressed in from both sides, turning the day into dusk.

The village of Port Tobacco was to the right, on marshy ground. Anywhere else, it would be a neighborhood to be avoided. Here, it was the county seat. Its wooden buildings were in various stages of disrepair. Even the brick courthouse looked worn. The village square was more of a trapezoid, and the streets were rutted roadways lined with ramshackle shops. I heard the plinking away of a smithy's anvil as I passed a dry goods store, a barbershop, the *Port Tobacco Times,* a balconied hotel past its prime, a tavern. Two taverns, maybe a third. My benefactor let me alight.

On a side street, I spotted a livery stable and, just beyond, a barnlike structure with a gaping entrance and a sign over the door. A name was painted in colors long faded. I walked toward it until I could read:

J.C. Atzerodt & Bro.

Atzerodt! This must be George's older brother, John—and George, the "& Bro." And this must be their carriage-making business, whose earnings George had supplemented by running the Union blockade.

The interior was dark, but the shop was open. I stepped in.

"Mr. Atzerodt?" I shouted.

"Who is it?" came a growl from the gloom.

"I am looking for the Wheeler house."

Slowly my eyes adjusted, and I made out a man's figure near the rear. "Which one?" the silhouette said. It started to move toward me.

"How many are there?"

"I dunno. Four, five, six. Who ya looking for, anyway, bub?"

"Rose Wheeler's . . . husband. I have business with him." Sufficiently true to satisfy the journalist's code of conduct, not that I had ever learned one. As for detectives, they had no code of conduct, as far as I knew, other than to shoot before you get shot.

"What kind of business?"

So, there was a husband. "Private business."

"Cain't help ya, then, mistuh," he said.

"Are you John Atzerodt?"

"He gone."

"Do you know where I could find him?"

"Gone, I tell ya, up Baltimore way. Why do ya want 'im?"

"To ask about his brother."

"He ain't gonna tell ya nuttin'. They weren't speakin' nohow. Half the brothers was pro-Union, half of 'em rebels. Which didn't forgive arrestin' his own brother and all."

"What?!"

"You don't know that? John was a marshal for Maryland"—he pronounced it *Merrlyn*—"and got a tip. Got there too late, is all. George was done captured already."

The man remained just beyond the sunlight, presumably not by happenstance. His trousers were tucked into high boots. I could make out a scrunched-up face with eyes too dark to fathom. He was no taller than I was but slouched.

"Are you an Atzerodt?" I said.

"What's it to you?"

"May I ask you about George Atzerodt?" I said. I had nothing to lose by asking, right?

Wrong.

Out of the darkness, waist high, shined a small silver O. I recognized it as the point of a gun.

"Who in the hell are you?" he said.

It seemed potentially counterproductive at this point to boast that I carried a gun of my own. I considered my options. A letter from General Grant was unlikely to persuade a Southern Marylander that the sun rose in the east. Nor would a press card from my legendarily abolitionist newspaper. I had been asked a reasonable question, albeit at gunpoint, and I gambled on an approximation of the truth. Actually, just a sliver of it.

I gave him my name and said, "I am a newspaperman, and I think George Atzerodt was innocent."

"That so? So what's he doin' in the fuckin' ground?"

Also a reasonable question. "He was convicted by a military court, and his sentence was upheld by the president. That's what."

My informant spat on the ground, too close to my boots. I stepped forward and gambled on another fragment of truth. I said, "A mysterious lady in black visited him the morning of his . . . execution. I think her name was Rose Wheeler, and I want to talk to her, if I could."

His pistol lowered a couple of inches. I was becoming aware of the surroundings, the carriages on the sides and in the back, the rafters overhead. I started to breathe again, inhaling the sharp smell of fresh paint.

"Do you know her?" I said.

"Course I do. River scum, the Wheelers. Always was, always will be."

"Could you tell me where I can find her?"

"I might."

A half eagle sufficed.

I walked out to Cheapside street, along the village's edge. Ladies moseyed past, and I fended off their quizzical looks by doffing my silk hat, prompting a giggle or two.

The house was built arse-backward, two stories in the front with a tar paper roof sloping down to a single story in the rear. The shingles had been painted some version of white before I was born. The abode was devoid of ornamentation, unless you counted the brick chimney at the side, which I didn't.

Two small concrete steps sufficed for a porch. The gray paint on the door was blistered. I checked for my pistol and my wallet, then knocked. I heard a scrambling inside.

The door squealed open, and I was relieved to see a woman of uncertain age. She had rosy cheeks—hence her name?—two chins, most of her teeth, and straggly blond hair that showed streaks of gray. She folded her arms across her bosom, which was abundant, as was the rest of her. Her face, however, was hard—from hard living. That was my working assumption, although I had seen enough of life to recognize that my working assumptions didn't always prove true.

I could tell her that I was peddling salves and liniments, except that I had none with me. I had to hope that her . . . consort wasn't home, or that he didn't come home for his midday meal and find a strange man at the door.

"Mrs. Wheeler?" I said, trying to look as meek as I could. Again, I hazarded the truth; it hadn't served me badly so far, possibly because of its shock value. "I am investigating the death of Andrew Johnson."

She froze. I was a voice from the past, and not a welcome one.

"May I come in?" I said.

A quick but decisive shake of her head. "You have to go." She scowled. "I have strong sons."

"I need to know what Mr. Atzerodt said to you the—"

"Go away!"

"—the morning of his . . . death."

"Or I'll shout for the police."

It seems I had found the right house. "I'll pay you," I said.

A long pause. "How much?"

"Twenty dollars, in gold."

"I'll take sixty."

"Forty . . . five."

"Sixty."

The Gilded Age had seeped down into the swamp. She had me over a barrel, and both of us knew it.

"All right, sixty," I said. "It'll have to be gold and greenbacks. May I come in?"

"No."

Would Whitelaw Reid pay for admission inside? Probably not. "You did visit him that morning?"

"Sixty dollars."

"*If* you visited him that morning."

"I did."

I took my last double eagle from my trouser pocket; from my wallet, I extracted two bills bearing Alexander Hamilton's profile. I half expected her to demand a premium because the greenbacks weren't gold. She folded the bills and stuffed them up a sleeve of her dreary dress and grasped the gold coin in her fist. I would be astonished if the man of the house ever learned of their existence.

"What did he tell you that morning?" I said.

"About what?"

"About why he didn't go through with it. Was it because of Edith?"

Without a thought, she glanced behind her and pulled the door shut. She was silent, and I realized she was trembling, fighting back tears.

"It was, wasn't it?" I said.

She wiped her cheek with a pudgy hand.

"Did he say anything about what Booth . . . ? I understand there was a meeting . . . before they . . . where Booth threatened to"—this wasn't the crisp questioning I was famed for—"kill him if he didn't . . ."

"He would have hurt Edith, had he known of her." She kept her voice low, a harsh whisper. "But George never told him. Never told nobody, never. Keepin' her safe. How'd you git to know?"

"Can't say," I muttered. "But I promise not to use your name on anything you tell me."

"Can't—can't risk it." She gestured behind her. "They all I got."

"If Mr. Atzerodt knew something about what happened," I said, "why didn't . . . he say so when it might have saved his life?"

Her eyes grew hard. "And piss off the man who could save him?" she said.

I had never heard a woman curse before. "What do you mean?" I said. "President Johnson?"

She was staring at my breast pocket. That's where I kept my wallet. She put her hand out. "Twenty," she said.

"Ten, that's all I can do."

"Twenty."

I pulled my wallet from my inside pocket and extracted a stern engraving of Daniel Webster. I showed her the empty wallet. "Ten," I said.

She grabbed it and squeezed it into her bosom and snarled. "He *saw* him."

"Who did?"

"Booth did. He was heading up to his door and saw him in the dining room."

"Saw Johnson?"

"Yes, yes. At that hotel. Booth saw him—he told George this, that night. And he spouted something from Shakespeare at him—Booth did."

"At Johnson."

"Yes!" she replied as if I were a dolt.

"What did he say?"

"How do I know? Somethin' about sittin' around and killin' a king. But how can you kill somebody if you're sittin' down? I don't know. All nonsense, to me."

"But not to Johnson," I said, half to myself.

She shrugged and then gasped as she gazed past my shoulder. "Git goin'!" Too late.

I turned and almost bumped into a bear of a man I had to assume was a successor to the late George Atzerodt. He had a square jaw, a square face, a square torso, a dented derby, and an angry look on his face.

"Salves and liniments," I mumbled. "Just ran out."

I reached into my pocket and considered removing my revolver. I worried that doing so would admit what I was trying to deny.

"Where's your case?" he said. He wasn't as stupid as I had hoped.

"In my saddlebag."

I skirted past him before he could realize that my explanation made no sense. I worried about getting shot in the back, but I am relieved to report that he was gullible, or I might not be reporting this at all.

A half eagle was still in my trouser pocket, which facilitated my escape by train. Charles county was whizzing by, but I paid no attention. I knew the quotation she meant. See, a fancy education wasn't totally useless. It was from *Richard II*, and I knew it by heart. I remembered the lines before it, too, among the most self-pitying in Shakespeare.

> *Nothing can we call our own but death*
> *And that small model of the barren earth*
> *Which serves as paste and cover to our bones.*

This is King Richard himself, imagining his own grave, mourning the imminent loss of his kingdom to his cousin Bolingbroke. Then he says, so plaintively:

. . . let us sit upon the ground
And tell sad stories of the death of kings . . .

Or, in our day and place, the death of presidents. This was what Booth, the man of the stage, had recited on the day he would murder our king. And to whom did Booth deliver this . . . forewarning?

To the man who would inherit the throne.

+====+

Pinkerton was on the platform in Washington City. At first, I didn't believe it was possible, but when I walked past, he called my name and managed to look offended. I'm sure I looked flustered, because I was. How could he possibly have known I was here?

I said, "To what do I owe the pleasure of your company?"

"Ye already 'ave had the pleasure o' my colleague's company."

"I thought so. It was the man who gave me a ride into Port Tobacco, yes?"

"No, the colored man, shor' and stou'."

"I must say, Pinkerton, you are an astonishment."

The Scotsman tried not to look embarrassed. "Ye were payin' 'im," he said. "Ye should know."

"How much am I paying him?"

"All in good time, my man, all in good time."

"I'm paying for you, too, I assume."

"I'm here, aren't I? I thought ye weren't payin' a' all."

"That's my hope."

"And I understand ye a man o' wealth, anyway."

"I've heard the same about you."

"Aren't we a lucky couple o' blokes," Pinkerton said, "relyin' on people's crimes for our pleasures. I guess somebody's go' t' make money on the troubles o' the world. Might as well be us."

"I'm not getting rich off of this," I corrected him. "But I am helping you to."

Ah, Pinkerton *could* smile—at the thought of getting richer, I suppose. Yet another man of his times. Aren't we all!

He asked what I had learned in Port Tobacco.

"Not very much," I said. I wasn't ready to tell Pinkerton about Booth's encounter. I had to talk to Nicolay first. "So, what does bring you here, besides a desire to charge me a little bit more?"

"There is someone ye'll want t' talk to. That attack on Johnson in March? It happened outside the Kirkwood House. I found somebody who saw it."

"Who is that?"

"I'll take ye to her."

"No, you won't."

"Yes, I will." We reached a hackney waiting at the curb on Sixth street. "Can I give you a lift?" Pinkerton said.

"I would just as soon walk, thank you kindly."

—————

"Your charm is legendary, Johnny." Nicolay was sipping his brandy, preparing his jab. "But why after all those years of silence would she choose to tell *you*?"

"Maybe nobody asked her before. For some reason, people like to be asked." Nicolay looked skeptical. "Also, I paid her. A lot. Everything I had, almost."

"Do you believe her? About Booth reciting Shakespeare to our Andy?"

"I think I do. Why shouldn't I?"

"Because you paid her."

"Granted. But yes, I do believe her. Could I ever quote her? No. That was part of our arrangement. Could I ever prove this? I can't imagine how. If she's telling me the truth, she's telling it to me thirdhand—from Booth to Atzerodt to our lovely Mrs. Wheeler. Then to me. Not worth a lot, in court or out."

"Why didn't Atzerodt tell anyone when he was alive? It might have saved him from being hanged."

"Seems he tried, but even his jailer wasn't allowed to say anything on his behalf. Besides, I think saying anything would have assured his execution. Implicating the very man, the commander in chief, who has your life in his hands? Who arranged to have the final say on the conspirators' sentences? Who then rushed them to the gallows? Saying anything at all would have tightened the rope around his neck."

"I see your point. But he ended up with the rope, anyway."

"That, he did," I said. "And a single confidante, who as far as we know didn't say a word to another soul for ten years."

"*Assuming* she is telling the truth," Nicolay said, "why did Booth do that at all? Striding up to the vice president of the United States and reciting Shakespeare."

"I wondered about this on the trip back here, and I can think of a couple of reasons," I said. "It's possible Johnson really was involved in the plot, as the Hell-cat believed. Though I tend to doubt it."

"Partly because she believed it."

"That would be a point against it, yes. Or maybe Booth just wanted to make it look like our Andy was involved, to implicate him in the plot."

"To what end?" Nicolay said.

"For amusement's sake? To ruin the next presidency? To give Booth leverage over it, had he lived? I couldn't tell you. But that could also explain why he left that note for Johnson or Colonel Browning at the desk."

"Do you believe he was involved?"

"I think it's possible. But do I believe it? No, not really. This is what I believe. That John Wilkes Booth was an actor, to his toes, and that is what he was doing—playing a role, the role of a lifetime. In the grandest of stage manners, he was playing it to the hilt. Leaving a cryptic note at the desk, then reciting Shakespeare to the crown prince. Booth was no longer merely playing a Shakespearean character. He *was* one. He had become one. And, by God, he was going to act like one, so that the critics, the men who write history, would stand and applaud."

"Bravo!" Nicolay cried.

"All right, I got carried away," I said. "But that's what I think he was doing. It fits the evidence, and it fits his character, though it's only a hunch."

"It does make sense," Nicolay said. I felt unaccountably pleased. "But that isn't the real question, is it?"

"What do you mean?"

"What Booth was up to is interesting. But more interesting is our Andy—what he was thinking."

"You mean, after—"

"Yes, after Booth assassinated the Ancient," Nicolay said. "Johnson would have seen the note that Booth had left and remembered some fancy words he had heard from a man who resembled the tintype he was shown. What if word got out, as surely it would? Wouldn't it implicate him in the plot? He would be a dead man, would he not?"

"Politically," I said.

"At the least."

CHAPTER TWENTY

How well did Mr. Johnson know his Shakespeare?" Therena said. She stood by the stove, flipping blueberry flapjacks. I had eaten five of them—best, with melted butter. The second batch was less blackened than the first.

"He certainly quoted him enough," I said.

"He might have dipped into *Bartlett's,*" Nicolay pointed out.

I nodded. "The best of us have."

"So, where does this leave you?" Nicolay said.

"Us," Therena said.

"Where does this leave *us* in regard to the perpetrator of . . . Helen, pretend you're not hearing this"—Helen halted a flapjack on the way to her mouth and listened all the harder—"Andrew Johnson's death?"

"Still too many suspects," I said. "A list as long as . . . Helen's arm."

"Or Mama's?" Helen said.

"Yes, or your mama's," I said.

Nicolay said, "Have you narrowed them down any?"

"Some, I guess. I think it had nothing to do with his impeachment. And I don't think it was the blackmail letters, either. That's just the decedent's firstborn and her lovely husband taking advantage of their bequest. None of the recipients—the three senators and the vice president—seemed all that troubled by what they contained. I wouldn't deny that Roscoe Conkling has it in him to . . . disable, shall we say, a rival. But Conkling had handled worse. And I simply cannot imagine the good senator dispatching a killer to Tennessee to poison a colleague, even a Democrat. He would do it *here* if he were to . . . I'm sorry, Helen, I shouldn't be talking like this."

She was rapt.

Nicolay said, "Who does this leave, then?"

"Let me see," I replied. "Conceivably the Confederate captain from the train, two sons-in-law, the surviving son, the widow, possibly a devoted servant who also turns out to be his grandson"—Helen's head bobbed forward—"plus the few dozen others who happened to visit an ailing man at his daughter's house. Or someone who could have directed one of these visitors from afar. I've probably forgotten a few."

"Not that we don't love to see you, Johnny," Therena said, "but what are you doing *here*?"

"That's a"—I spared Helen the expletive, to her disappointment—"good question." I explained that I was pursuing the suspects who had been acting the most . . . suspiciously, and who happened to have the most to gain—a farm and a batch of theoretically valuable letters—by the old man's untimely passing. "Since then I've been pursuing the story wherever it took me, following my cute little Protestant nose. And, let me point out, it has led me back around to Andrew Johnson, the vice president who escaped assassination."

"Until now, you're saying—" This, from Nicolay.

"That's exactly what I'm saying."

"And you're saying that these . . . events are . . . connected."

I sighed. "I'm not saying that yet. I wish I knew for sure. Only that I started with ol' Andy and I've come around again to ol' Andy. Like a well-constructed poem, in its way. Satisfying."

"Satisfying?" Therena said, with an uncustomary sharpness. "Johnny, you have lost sight of what all this means."

She was undoubtedly right. Like Clara, Therena's sense of morals was uncomplicated and in command. Mine was a little more . . . malleable, and this . . . adventure had grown so blamed interesting. And I *was* having fun. Not that I would admit it in Therena's presence.

"Satisfying in an artistic sort of way," I hedged. "There are so many strands here. Starting with what happened ten years ago, on that Good Friday night when Andrew Johnson was *not* assassinated, as he was supposed to be. This was hours after John Wilkes Booth sought him out at his hotel and left him a note that was eloquent in its obscurity and recited Shakespeare at the man. This was followed by a trial in which the accused were not permitted to testify, even indirectly, and then the swift hanging of the man who had spared the new president's life. Then, after years in political exile, ol' Andy's triumphal return to Washington City and his tirade against his successor. And *then,* later that very same day, the attack on his person, out on the sidewalk, in front of his hotel. Then, four months later,

his death, sudden and unexpected, and the blackmail letters he so thoughtfully left behind, for his favorite child to wave in prominent Republicans'
faces. And I haven't even mentioned his impeachment or the will that was
soon to be written. *Or* the hundred fifty thousand dollars in assets that
he left for his grateful heirs. And let's not forget the attack on my person,
outside this very window"—I pointed toward the front of the house—"and
as yet unexplained."

"You probably made somebody mad, Johnny," Nicolay said.

"Seems I did. But who? There are so many strands here, is what I'm saying, and I think they're all connected somehow. Or at least some of them
are."

"Do you?" Nicolay said. "How?"

Helen's eyes were wide, and I said to her, "Can you make sense of this?"

A quick, delighted shake of her head. Helen, too, found all of this satisfying.

I asked her, "Have you ever listened to Bach?"

"Father doesn't allow me in saloons."

"Must be a different Bach. I'm talking about Johann Sebastian Bach. A
genius who wrote beautiful music, long before any of us were born. Not
far from Bavaria, if I'm not wrong"—I nodded toward Nicolay. "In his
concertos, he would compose the most exquisite strands of melody and
he would twist them and wrap them around one another and, at the end,
weave them all together into one. They're beautiful that way, even sublime.
All of my strands here can't be *un*related, can they? Well, can they? My task
is to weave them into one."

✦

"Don't you ever sleep?" I said.

Pinkerton was waiting at the curb. "Tha's wha' me wife asked me once. I
go to sleep after she does and ge' up before she does, so as far as she knows,
I'm awake all the time. The eye never sleeps—ge' it?"

"I didn't take it literally," I said.

"I'm a man o' me word."

Pinkerton refused to tell me where I could find the witness to the attack
on Johnson, to make sure he could come along. I asked if he wanted to
blindfold me first. He seemed to consider it but said, "Not necessary. Y'aren't
goin' back there alone, anyhow."

"Where's that?"

"Murder Bay."

"Oh, I've been," I said.

Pinkerton looked at me with something resembling respect. Murder Bay was the neighborhood just south of the Avenue and east of the Executive Mansion, long home to brothels and gambling dens and saloons. During the war, its streets were a lure for thieves, dangerous after dark for anyone who looked respectable, an obstacle I had skirted in the obvious way.

"Not lately," I hastened to add.

The Avenue was busy with government clerks rushing to their offices. I thought a woman was eyeing me from the southern sidewalk, probably a lady of the evening toiling after hours. In the hack, Pinkerton remained coy about the witness's identity, except to say she worked at the Kirkwood House starting at eleven o'clock, so it was best to question her at home beforehand.

We got off at Twelfth street. "We'll walk in," Pinkerton said. "Strength in pairs."

It was a different place from when I had seen it last—and better, if that was possible in this benighted world. The wooden hovels didn't stand any straighter, and the backyard privies had not migrated indoors. Gangs of youngsters, black and white—black *or* white—still roamed the streets, flinging marbles and kicking baseballs made of twine. But now the streets, paved with wood or asphalt, looked more or less clean. The mud was gone, probably because B street now covered the filled-in canal. And sewers! I saw the openings at the curb. Would wonders never cease!

"The city shu' the saloons heah, I understand," Pinkerton said. "Nae mo' liquor licenses. The gamblin' houses, too. And bawdy houses, some of 'em." He glanced over at me.

"Old times," I said.

"If ye say so."

"I do." This, I meant with nostalgia but without regret.

At last he revealed our destination, a chambermaid's residence on C street, just east of Thirteen-and-a-half. It was nice to see sidewalks and the scrawny trees that loafers in beat-up caps were holding up. I slowed, and Pinkerton sped me along.

"Don't ask fer nae trouble," he muttered.

Caution as well as courage, I gathered, belonged in a detective's arsenal.

The buildings lacked numbers over the doorways, but Pinkerton stopped in front of a two-story frame house that seemed a relic of an earlier age. Decades of coal ash had turned the white façade a ghostly gray. A second-floor shutter hung by a hinge. Two steps led to a flaking black door.

Pinkerton knocked.

Nothing.

He knocked again. Footsteps scampered and the door swung open. A little black girl with braids and a magnetic smile stared up at us, mute but unafraid. She waited patiently; most of her life lay ahead of her.

Pinkerton was flummoxed. I stepped forward and said, "Is your mama home?"

I wasn't sure the words registered, because she kept staring up at Pinkerton when a mountain of a man slipped in behind her. He was stripped to the waist and might have decked Tom Allen, had black men been allowed to fight with whites (in the ring, I mean, not in alleyways). He, too, stood silently, gazing upon us curiously as if we were creatures from Jules Verne's seas.

"Is Isabella Washington here?" Pinkerton said.

The man in the doorway stared out for another three seconds or more—maybe sound traveled more slowly in Murder Bay—before he slipped away as gracefully as he had come. The girl stayed behind. I wondered if she was deaf—although she had heard Pinkerton's knocking, hadn't she?—or if she was addled or simply too trusting for a merciless world.

A woman slid in beside her. I say *woman* because she was old enough to be (and undoubtedly was) the girl's mother, but she wasn't much taller or heftier than her daughter. She was lighter skinned, with a golden complexion. Her face had dainty features and black-rimmed eyes. She reminded me of a Balinese dancer, with a sinuous body and an unreadable face.

The mountain of a man appeared behind them.

Pinkerton's question—was she Isabella Washington, the chambermaid at the Kirkwood House?—evidently did not dignify a response. Nor did his request to come inside. I was wondering if questioning her at the hotel might provide some useful coercion when I remembered a weight in the right pocket of my trousers. Nicolay's loan. I pulled out an eagle—I was generous with the *Tribune*'s gold—and stepped in front of Pinkerton.

"I swear to you," I told her, "on the life of my baby daughter, that no harm will come to you, to any of you." I met the man's gaze. "May *I* come in?"

Isabella gawked at the gold coin I put into her hand. Pinkerton also gawked—at me. I was no longer an amateur.

Our would-be hostess stepped back from the door. So far, she hadn't uttered a word. I turned to Pinkerton and said, "You stay here."

"The hell I—"

"You . . . stay . . . here. I will come fetch you when . . . and if . . . I need you."

To my surprise, Pinkerton agreed. I was paying him, after all.

It would be kind to call the room a parlor, for it also served as a dining room and probably a children's bedroom. The furnishings were worn and simple but clean. (She *was* a chambermaid.) And the room was comfortable, judging by the corduroy-covered chair I was invited to take. Isabella chose an upholstered rocker with a high back and folded her hands in her lap. The mountain of a man stood behind her, his eyes fixed on my face. The drawn blinds in the front window spoiled any sunlight that had the temerity to sneak its way in.

"Mrs. Washington," I began, "I appreciate your seeing me. I understand that you witnessed an incident outside the Kirkwood House involving Andrew Johnson, the former president, on the night of March twenty-second." I sounded like an ingratiating prosecutor, or merely a lawyer.

"Cain't tell you the date, suh." She had a sweet voice, with a lilt that reminded me oddly of Pinkerton's. "Only the time. Three minutes past six o'clock."

I said, "How can you be so precise?"

"Might be a minute off or two. I work six to six, and then I go, right quick if I can, and that night I could. I remember that night 'cause not every night I see what I saw."

"What did you see?"

"I was leaving, as I say, and takin' off to walk back home when I was behind this noble-lookin' man standing on the sidewalk. Reachin' out toward the Avenue like he was hailing a hackney, or wantin' to and not knowin' how. I noticed because he wore a silk hat and a high-class coat with a fur collar."

"You recognized him?"

"Yes, suh, I seen 'im befo' in the lobby. And pictures of 'im, so I knew he been the president, and not the kind I liked, could I 'ave voted. But he was jest mindin' hisself when a man came out o' nowhere and leapt at him."

"Armed?"

"Think I seen a knife, but I cain't be sure." She was peering past my shoulder, returning to the scene. "He just leapt—straight at 'im."

"And did he . . . connect?"

"He musta, 'cause the man bounce back."

"What do you mean, bounced back?"

"Just what I say." The man behind her nudged forward. "Mistuh Johnson, 'cause that's who it was, he was a rock wall. Or mebbe Mistuh Johnson hit 'im—his back was to me—because the man landed on the sidewalk, 'cept he collided with a lady walkin' by. Nearly knocked her to the ground, he did, and the knife, it skitter away. Yes, suh, it *was* a knife—I remember it now. Went into the street."

"And the man?"

"He bounced back up, like a ball you can buy, and he run off."

"Did you get a good look at him?" I held my breath.

"For a second, I reckon I did. He was facin' me, 'til he run. There was something old, old about him. Naw, not his age. He a young man. But in his . . . He wasn't of our time. He looked a mite like those pictures of Jesus, not to take the Savior's name in vain, the ones in my church, with the hair to his shoulders and a beard and those eyes that . . . see right through you, if he please."

The air in the room seemed to crackle. I waited for her to go on, but the vision was dissolving.

"Which way did he run?" I said.

"That way." She pointed west, in the general direction of the Executive Mansion. She was still seeing him. "Limpin' away," she said.

+=====+

"It was him," I told Pinkerton. "It had to be."

We were walking south, by the Bethany Chapel and by the lumberyards in the long block before B street. Still no mud, and not too much dust, considering the heat and the lack of a breeze. People sat on their doorsteps and fanned themselves. A lady as wrinkled as her cloak was toting two buckets of water from the corner cistern. We ignored the pack of boys who hooted behind us, but I expected momentarily a rock that would thwack my silk hat. I noticed that Pinkerton's hand reached inside his jacket, close to his pistol, which I figured wasn't as dainty as mine.

"Do ye know how many men in this town have a limp? There was a war, y'know."

"Who also looks like an Old Testament prophet?"

"Jesus was in the New."

I opened my mouth in mock surprise.

"Jus' pointin' tha' out," Pinkerton said.

"Biblical, anyway. That narrows it down."

"A little."

"It was Hartman Richter, I tell you. It must have been. Atzerodt's loyal cousin. Who else would attack Andy Johnson in the open, on the street?"

"Ye're the one who tells me yer Andy go' nae shor'age of enemies."

"True, but for Richter, the hatred is personal. His cousin, almost a brother, got hanged for a crime he chose not to commit. Pinkerton, could you do something for me?" The detective glanced over. "Find out if Richter was in the city the night that Johnson was attacked. March twenty-second, give or take. Check the hotels. Start with the ones his cousin used."

"I am good at me job, Mr. Hay."

Pinkerton hailed a hansom cab heading east along B street, by the overgrown greenery of the Mall, and announced our destination: Nicolay's house on Capitol Hill. I climbed in. Just as the rig began rolling, I jumped down.

"Get some sleep!" I cried.

"Where ye goin'?" he shouted back.

"And send me the bill."

"For to-day, no bill." His grin made me uneasy.

Suddenly I understood: Clara was paying!

＋＝＝＋

Where I was going, I didn't want Pinkerton tagging along. I walked east to Twelfth street, checking to make sure he wasn't behind me, before I turned north, back through Murder Bay. I went bareheaded, protecting my hat in the crook of my arm, but my pursuers had gone in search of more promising targets. I passed an ironworks and a coal yard and a livery stable and shops and—hallelujah!—a police station before I emerged back onto the Avenue. I'll admit that I breathed more easily, at least until the sultry air seared my throat.

My linen shirt was sticking to my undershirt, which was sticking to my chest. Let me say this about Washington City's summertime heat. At first, it can feel comforting to snuggle into an atmosphere that resembles the heat and humidity of the human body. Womb-like, is how I think of it. But I had lived here once, for more than four years. Day after day, the heat and humidity works its way into your pores and grinds you down. It prompted Lincoln to sleep in the Soldiers' Home, more than four miles north, on higher ground, and to ride back to the Mansion every morning to work.

I crossed the Avenue to the Kirkwood House and felt a chill. I stopped on the sidewalk in front and tried to imagine a man hurtling at me. Actually, I could, and I hoped I'd have the quickness to step aside or raise my fists.

I started to enter the hotel, until I had a better idea.

＋＝＝＋

Pennsylvania avenue seemed abandoned at midday. The National Theatre was closed for the summer, of course. But the jewelry store was empty, and the Western Union office looked deserted. Even the ice company had nary a customer. Had everyone besides myself taken flight from the heat?

Smalley hadn't. He looked fresh and clean, without a bead of perspiration. His smile looked sincere but couldn't have been. Nothing seemed amusing to-day.

"They're gone," he announced.

"Who's gone?" I sank into the hard-backed chair.

"Our favorite senators. They've gone home. Back to New Jersey, back to New York—they probably shared a compartment. And to Maine."

"And the vice president?"

"He's gone, too, back to Massachusetts. Yesterday, all of them."

"Quite a coincidence. But the Pattersons aren't here." I described their matrimonial mission to Philadelphia.

"The missus went to Philly," Smalley corrected me. "The mister stayed here, making the rounds. Either the senators paid up or left him empty-handed."

+=====+

In the morning's furtive light, the Kirkwood House lobby looked as cheerless as a dowager in distress. Dust hung in the air, and the divans blended into the threadbare rugs. The desk clerk winked at me as if we were midnight chums.

"The Pattersons here?" I said.

He glanced back at the keys on the board. "Must be. Haven't seen 'em."

"Both? She's back, too?"

A crafty look invited a greenback. But the information was worth the price.

I went upstairs and glanced into the dining room, which was empty except for a man sitting alone at the back, as if ready for a snippet of Shakespeare or just a gin cocktail. He didn't look a thing like Andy Johnson.

Across the corridor, I rapped at the Pattersons' door. I was getting ready to knock again when it opened. I had hoped to see Bill and almost asked where he was. Instead, I said, "Miss Stover! You are still *Miss* Stover, yes? Not married yet?"

Lillie blushed. She had her mother's statuesque beauty with a swirl of blond hair and her delicate face. "October," she said. "We just ordered the dress. It's gorgeous. They promised they would alter it in time. Oh, I do hope they can. If they don't, I don't know what I'll do."

How long would it be until Helen gushed like this to me? Or more likely, to Clara. "A productive journey, I take it."

"Aunt Martha was such a dear to take me. We had such fun."

"Philadelphia, was it?"

"Yes, how did you know?" she said.

A misstep on my part; an insincere interest could be overdone. I resorted to Smalley's explanation.

"People tell me things," I said—usually because I asked. "May I come in?"

"Of course. My manners are frightful, please forgive me. But my aunt and uncle aren't here. They'll be back."

"Is Bill?"

A hesitation. "No," she said. "He went . . . home."

"To Greeneville?"

"Where else?"

My stomach lurched. Was I responsible for that? No—that is, not entirely. It was Bill who had suggested the . . . unauthorized borrowing. At worst, it was an invasion of privacy. Which in Tennessee was probably a hanging offense. In Washington, it was a prerequisite to success.

"I would enjoy talking with you, too," I said.

Lillie was the most credulous member of the family. I felt a little ashamed about using that to my advantage, but not enough not to.

"You know what ceremony took place in this room," I said, once we had seated ourselves in the parlor. "Your grandfather was sworn in as—"

"I wish I could have been here," she cooed.

"You were—what?—about ten?"

"Just about."

"And you came to live here, in the president's house. Quite an experience, I should think."

"Oh, it was," Lillie said. She gazed at the ceiling's cobwebs like they were tendrils of gold.

Sentimental tales of ol' Andy's loving family wasn't something I cared about anymore. Time for a segue.

"We talked at your home, if you remember, about the afternoon your grandfather . . . collapsed. That was on a Wednesday. Were you also at the house that Friday afternoon?"

No reaction, which I took as a *yes.*

"I understand that your mother and your . . . stepfather . . ."—Lillie stiffened—"were elsewhere."

"I . . ." She exhaled with a bubble in her throat. "I . . . can't remember one day from the next. I hope you under—"

"Of course, of course," I said, attempting a rescue. "Of course I understand. Friday was the day that your grandfather"—I should use the medical formality—"slipped into a coma."

Lillie shuddered.

"You were at the house?"

A single nod.

"Do you remember seeing your . . . stepfather there? Mr. Brown."

She thought about it—actually thought about it—and shrugged. "Too many people."

"Your mother?"

"Now that you mention it . . . Why do you ask?" An intelligence lurked behind that blond coiffure.

"I am trying to get a picture of your family on that . . . day." Not a lie. This next query was delicate. "And your grandmother, could she visit? Was she healthy enough?"

"Oh yes, and she did. Granny was there when he . . . passed. I think she was."

Eliza had told me that she was asleep. Why would she have lied? Or did Lillie misremember? I said, "In the middle of the night?"

"The whole family was there, gathered 'round his bed."

"And Bill?"

"Of course. He's part of the family, isn't he?" Literally, this was true. The family might have known this.

"Do you remember a Captain McElwee, by any chance?" I said. "He was on the train with your grandfather from Greeneville. Did he visit?"

"I think so. I saw him a couple of times. And the other fellow, too."

"What other fellow?"

"From the train. Both of them came."

"Together?"

A pause. "No. Different times."

"You sure?"

Lillie thought, then nodded. "They do look alike, though."

"Captain McElwee and Captain . . . Jenkins, is that right?"

"That sounds right. I met Captain Jenkins at the door and let him in and took him upstairs. My grandfather was in lively spirits and was happy to see him. Happy to see anyone."

"When was that, do you remember?"

Lillie's eyes closed and, again, she . . . *thought*. "Sometime Friday. I think. It's all blurred."

"Anyone else there that you can remember?"

"Is this important?"

"No, not really," I said.

Oh yes, it was.

The Pattersons were entering the hotel as I was leaving it. I was cordial— the words *blackmail* or *murder* never crossed my lips—and therefore was unprepared for Martha's hostility. Her eyes were as hard as onyx. I gave a disarming smile, without effect, and walked past her. What did she think I had learned? Her husband looked angrier still, and was less practiced at hiding it. His soft, round face was red with rage. When he reached into his inside pocket, I caressed my jacket.

My gun was there, and it stayed there, as he pushed past me.

A gunfight in a hotel lobby! This hardly squared with my conception of myself. But I must admit it had a certain Jesse James sort of charm.

＋═══＋

General Babcock seemed uninterested, like he was doing *me* a favor, until I mentioned how Booth had recited from *Richard II* for ol' Andy's enter-tainment. That caught his attention, as if it increased his leverage over the dear departed. Maybe it did, but to what end I couldn't discern. Great men were opaque, but so were dishonest ones. Let me guess which kind he was.

As I left the Mansion, I stopped to exchange pleasantries with Old Ed-ward. He looked pallid, hunched over—old.

"Are you all right?" I said.

His eyes watered—a grayish green. "My grandson," he said. "My daugh-ter's little boy Silas. He's ill. Very ill. The doctors say he's . . ."

I felt honored by the confidence. "What do they think it is?"

"Diphtheria." Old Edward wiped his cheeks. "Forgive me, Mr. Hay."

"There's nothing to forgive," I said, touching his elbow.

"He is my future, is all."

Now I felt the tears. Was I ready for the weight of fatherhood?

Deep breaths later, by both of us, I said, "May I ask you an unrelated question?"

"Please do," Old Edward said.

"Do you know of a man named Hartman Richter, who may have tried to see the president? In March, it might have been, the twenty-second or the twenty-third."

"A hundred people a day want to see the president. If it's the right hours, I send them upstairs, unless they look dangerous."

"This one looked—or looks—like a biblical prophet."

"Half of them look like they stepped out of the Bible," Old Edward said, "and haven't bathed since."

◆━━◆━━◆

Therena was still transfixed by Mrs. Wheeler. Was she a widow and George Atzerodt's common-law wife? "Or neither"—Therena shuddered, before saying her good-nights and shuffling upstairs.

Nicolay was more interested in Hartman Richter and whether he had, in fact, attacked the former president on the Pennsylvania avenue sidewalk. "Was there a police report?" he said.

"Apparently not. Pinkerton says it was never reported. Johnson didn't, and the hotel didn't officially know. No police showed up."

Nicolay sipped his brandy. The parlor felt even more cluttered—that is, cozier—than usual, amid the jumble of newspapers and the precisely positioned stacks of Supreme Court papers. This served as Nicolay's office at home.

"Tell me, Johnny," he said, "do you suppose your Mr. Richter knows anyone in Tennessee? What you need to find, you understand, is a connection between Washington and Tennessee—*assuming*, of course, that these attacks on Andy Johnson, on the Avenue here and at his daughter's house, were connected."

"You mean, someone who would murder a former president at Hartman Richter's say-so? Why wouldn't he just wait until the next session of Congress and try again here? He's waited ten years already. What was so urgent?"

"It was urgent for somebody," Nicolay pointed out.

That gave me pause. "Besides, *my* Mr. Richter, as you call him, strikes me as the sort of man who would insist on doing the dirty work himself."

"Something admirable in that, I guess," Nicolay said. "What do you know about this Captain Jenkins?"

"Next to nothing. I met him in Greeneville, after the funeral. A nice enough fellow, it seemed."

"Ah, a dead giveaway," Nicolay said. "Union Army?"

"Indeed. First man to volunteer in Carter county, so the sheriff told me. In the infantry, then the cavalry, as I recall."

"A brave fellow—and agile. Do you think the sheriff knows more about him?"

"No doubt. In Carter county, everyone knows everyone, as they keep saying. But why would he tell a Yankee like me?"

"Because you asked?" Nicolay said. "Or because he believes in the rule of law?"

"You *are* the optimist, Nico," I said.

CHAPTER TWENTY-ONE

THURSDAY, AUGUST 19, 1875

"Any words of wisdom, Helen," I said, "before I go out into the world?"

She grinned. Children love to be treated as adults. "No," she replied, already wise enough to say nothing when she had nothing to say.

"These are wonderful," I told Therena. She had been kind enough to fry me two eggs, laid that morning in a neighbor's yard. (At the market, eggs cost two bits a dozen.) "I think I could tell the difference, blindfolded."

"Let's try, Uncle Johnny!" Helen said, popping out of her seat.

"Too late," I said, "half-eaten. Tell me, Helen, do you plan to be a detective someday? Or, heaven forfend, a lawyer?"

"No, no," Helen replied. "I'm going to be an artist."

Therena, standing by the stove, beamed.

"Ah, a truth teller," I said. "No loftier calling. What sort of artist?"

"I paint," Helen declared.

"What do you paint?"

"Things." She shrank back in her chair, nine years old again.

"I'd love to see them sometime."

No reply. I had embarrassed her. I had made a friend for life, but I wasn't trusted enough to be vouchsafed a glimpse of her oeuvre.

At the Western Union office at Fourteenth street and the Avenue, the clatter of telegraph keys and the scrape of machines and the whoops of customers who had just learned (I'm speculating) of a birth or an inheritance created a cacophony that embodied the Industrial Age. Would the world ever be quiet again?

It was five minutes before ten o'clock. I sent off my wire to Sheriff Pearce and stepped back into the heavy, hot air, thankful that my next destination

THE MURDER OF ANDREW JOHNSON

was only a few doors away. The seats along Newspaper Row were mostly empty. To-day was even more womb-like than yesterday, and the day was young.

Smalley was clad in a high collar, frock coat, and a polka-dot cravat, looking as cool as a lily at Easter.

"What's new?" he said, smiling. He must have just filed a story he fancied.

"This and that," I said. I told him what I had learned in Port Tobacco—a plausible reason why George Atzerodt and the other conspirators had been hanged without delay—and the telegram I had just sent off to Sheriff Pearce regarding Captain Jenkins's visit to Johnson's bedside.

"Have you thought about looking for your Captain Jenkins here?"

"How can I? He's in Tennessee."

"There must be records about him here—military records. Over at the War Department. I think they've all been collected by now, and they're stored . . . someplace. Maybe they'll turn up something useful."

"Worth a try, I guess. But why would the War Department let me see them? For old times' sake? I'm just a—"

"You have a letter from the commander in chief. I can help, too. I happen to be acquainted with the war secretary. Unfortunately, I was also acquainted with his daddy. So were you."

Oh no. Simon Cameron, Lincoln's first war secretary, had been incompetent and corrupt. And now his son Don held the post, thanks to his daddy's influence as a senator from Pennsylvania and his friendship, or what passes for one in Washington, with Grant. It was yet another example of the president's piss-poor judgment of men.

I started toward the War Department, already undone by the heat. I was tired of walking, tired of Washington, tired of my garments adhering to my skin. I was definitely tired of Andrew Johnson. A terrible president, a terrible person, beloved by his voters and (maybe) his family and loathed by everyone else. To whoever had murdered the man, my congratulations and thanks.

But why would a former Union Army captain bother? It didn't make sense. Andy Johnson had been a Union man, too. Something about Jenkins was nagging at me.

I crossed Fifteenth street and turned right. Devil to Andy *Jack*son for ruining the Avenue's vista, by placing the Treasury building directly between the Capitol and the president's house. I quickly turned left, back onto Pennsylvania avenue. Along the wide sidewalk, a government clerk in a high collar and a derby was nearly swept aside by a man with long gray whiskers and a gray cloak, by looks a Southern aristocrat who had forgotten which side lost the war. Devil to Andy *John*son for letting him forget.

The Executive Mansion looked forlorn somehow. I blamed the clouds that had crept across the sky. Under the portico, a horse snorted and pulled its brougham away. I stared up at the bedroom I had shared with Nicolay, the second and third windows from the left. The curtains were drawn.

Just past the Mansion, I came to the brick bunker that had housed the War Department since the Era of Good Feelings. I used to accompany Lincoln there late at night, to the telegraph office, to read the freshest battlefield reports. The building, painted the color of lead, was currently under siege by the flamboyant new building that was rising behind it and would soon take its place. The State, War, and Navy Building, made of granite and vibrantly gray, was a circus of Frenchified styling, slapdash with fussy columns and mansard pretensions. I loved it. Washington *was* changing. All over the city, flat brick was giving way to bay windows and ornamental rooflines. This was the nation's capital, wasn't it, so why shouldn't it reflect the gaudiness that defined (and deified) this shallow, glittering age?

The noise of construction was near to deafening. Dust was everywhere, and I kept my distance, hoping to keep my frock coat black and my collar white. I passed between the Doric columns and ducked into the doomed building's Avenue entrance. I was surprised not to see a guard, and a wee bit concerned. What if I were an unreconciled Confederate or, worse, a Democrat?

But I wasn't.

The interior looked and smelled as if it had seen better eons. It hadn't been painted and probably hadn't been cleaned since its demise was ordained. The central corridor was deserted—befitting, I suppose, a nation at peace.

The secretary's office was on the second floor, at the east end, beyond the portraits of the many nonentities who had sat behind its desk. Like father, like son, except that J. Donald Cameron was a drunk. That hadn't stymied his ascent.

The secretary's office, too, was unguarded. I entered a huge, high-ceilinged room with walnut walls and baroque chandeliers. An array of gigantic American flags diminished the man who sat behind the massive, empty desk. Don Cameron was staring ahead, at nothing I could see, his eyes rimmed in red—so early in the day. His flaccid hair, precisely parted, lay flat on his scalp. His face was unblemished—he had never known war himself—and his mustache was a janitor's broom that highlighted his receding chin.

He seemed not to recognize me, which was probably just as well. My name seemed to jostle a hidden memory, because he half rose and extended a hand.

"And what can I do for you?" he said, probably for the hundredth time that week.

I made my request—requests—and handed him my letter of introduction from his boss (by which I meant his president, not his daddy). He unfolded it and barely glanced at its single sentence, which suited me fine. I figured the less said about its contents, the less I would need to lie.

"We don't have the Confederate records, you know," Secretary Cameron said. I had asked for Captain McElwee's records as well. "Eventually, we will."

"But the Union records?"

Cameron hesitated. Should he agree without exacting a price? I was certain that's what he was pondering, so I flicked my wrist, snatching Grant's letter between finger and thumb.

"My pleasure," he said.

"I am much obliged," I replied.

Insincerity was the glue that kept this city going.

On my way out, I said, "Are you kin, by any chance, to a Dr. Cameron in East Tennessee? That's Dr. James Cameron, in the town of Elizabethton."

"I should say not," the war secretary said.

I walked halls that were living on borrowed time. The gas lamps in the corridor were dim or broken. The judge advocate general's office, across the building, was also in disrepair. The dust on the counter and the floor looked aged. A clerk at the back was annoyed at my interruption—possibly, at my existence. I didn't take it personally.

The clerk was as wide as he was tall. When I told him I was conveying Secretary Cameron's orders, I swear I detected a snicker from the rear doorway.

"Yes, sir!" the clerk said with a salute that I interpreted as mockery. How could he know that Lincoln had made me a colonel, although the nearest I ever got to combat was listening distance from the first Bull Run?

I requested the two sets of military records. Laboriously, he took down their names.

"For this Hartman Richter, what was his unit?"

"I don't know. In Maryland, if he served."

"*If* he served?"

"Yes. I don't know if he did. That's what I'm trying to find out."

The clerk glared. "All right," he said, "this David Jenkins. What was his unit?"

"Thirteenth Tennessee Cavalry, I think."

"You *think*?"

"Yes, I think. Try that first. Please. In an infantry, too, I *think*."

The clerk pursed his lips, so that his eely mustache twitched.

"All right," he said. "Come back Monday."

"Monday?" I pulled out my letter from Grant, by now begrimed from Republican fingertips. As he read it, his eyes grew wide. In this building, if not beyond, every military man (of which the war secretary wasn't one) worshiped the heroic general who was now the commander in chief. The clerk's posture lost its slump. Shoulders back, chest out, eyes cast down toward his spit-polished shoes, he mumbled, "Don't go nowhere."

"No plans to," I said.

It didn't take him long. "Nothing on Richter," he announced.

"Does that mean he wasn't in the military?"

"Unless it was misfiled."

The clerk had a military mind that understood the world in black and white. My favorite color was gray.

"No other place to look?" I said.

"You tell me, my friend."

"How about the other one?"

"Come with me."

He led me down to the basement, keeping five or six steps ahead, presumably so as not to breathe the same air. Which I soon understood because, in the basement, despite the ductwork that crisscrossed overhead, there was no air at all. Every wall was crammed with Woodruff file boxes, the tall, wooden, surprisingly elegant banks of drawers. A brilliant contraption, really. Each drawer could hold a thousand pages, triple-folded; a movable board at the back pushed the files forward, without injuring the documents themselves.

The Union's army files filled the far wall. The identifying card on each drawer was crisp. Toward the right side, at knee level, Tennessee filled only two drawers, no surprise for a state that had left the Union. I pulled out the top one, *A to Mo*, and leafed toward the back: *Jackson . . . James . . . Jeffers . . . Jeffres . . . Jenkins, David B.* I yanked it out and saw a second folder also labeled *Jenkins, David B.* I carried my booty to a pockmarked table along the wall.

Why on earth had the clerk demanded to know his military unit when the files were arranged alphabetically? Military thinking.

I unfolded the file into a triptych. The top page of the folder read:

Jenkins David B.
Co F, 2 Tennessee Inf.
<u>Sergeant</u>

On the next page:

Company Muster Roll
for <u>Pay to Dec. 31, 1861</u>
Remarks: <u>Age 30.</u>
<u>Enrolled Sep. 23, 1861</u>
<u>at Camp Robinson</u>
<u>for 3 years or during</u>
<u>the war.</u>
<u>Mustered on Oct. 26</u>

Then came muster roll after muster roll, every four months, each of them signed illegibly, authorizing the sergeant's pay, the amount unspecified, surely a pittance. Then a remark in 1863: *Transferred.* Followed by an announcement of his good fortune:

Head-Quarters, 2d Regiment E. Tenn. Volunteers.
Rogersville Tenn. October 31, 1863
I, David B. Jenkins, have the honor to make application for
discharge as an enlisted man, in the Second Reg't E. Tenn. Inf.
Volunteers, to accept a Commission as 1st Lieut. in company C of
13th Reg't Cavy E Tenn. Vols.

The Thirteenth Regiment Cavalry in the East Tennessee Volunteers. The second triptych covered Jenkins's service in the cavalry. It comprised a pile of company muster rolls, at a first lieutenant's unspecified pay, until his mustering out on July 3, 1865. That was weeks after Appomattox. The day of his discharge, he was promoted to captain. So, in a sense, his rank was honorary, rather like my colonelcy (except that Jenkins had actually served). But it gave him leave to be addressed as Captain Jenkins for the rest of his days.

Otherwise, the file had nothing of interest, other than the unit's designation. The Thirteenth Tennessee Cavalry. This nagged at me. Someone else had served in it, too. Had I already reached the stage in life when, in order to commit something new to memory, I had to forget something I already knew?

I was refolding the triptych and staring vacantly at the nearest wall of file boxes when the answer sprang to mind. (How *does* that happen in the tapioca of the brain?) I had been stumbling with Captain Jenkins along Depot street in Greeneville when he mentioned he had served in the Thirteenth Cavalry with . . . Dr. Cameron. I was sure of it. That would be James Cameron. James L., as I now recalled. (But what if I needed to remember the capital of Herzegovina?)

I rushed back to the Tennessee file box, *A to Mo,* and riffled through the early *Cs. Cabot. Cachette. Cain. Callahan. Cameron*!

Cameron, Alexander J.

Cameron, James M.

Not *L*. (The capital of Herzegovina was Mostar.)

I yanked the triptych from the drawer and clutched it like a toddler's hand as I returned to my seat. I sat too quickly and struck my left knee on the table and yelped. After the pain subsided, I examined the cover.

Cameron, James McLinn
Co <u>B</u>, 13 Tennessee Cavy.
<u>Assistant surgeon</u>

McLinn. That's why I thought it was *L*. This was the man I had met.

I leafed through pages of company muster rolls. Cameron had mustered in as a physician on October 20, 1861, at age twenty-seven, and received a monthly stipend, the size unspecified. I couldn't tell from the spare, official account which battles he had seen, what horrors he had known, how many limbs he had sawed and bullets extracted and bellies sliced open then stitched shut, how many sheets he had pulled over eyes that would never reopen.

I turned every page . . . 1861 . . . 1862 . . . 1863 . . . 1864 . . . and the pages stopped. The war wasn't over yet, but Dr. Cameron's was. I wondered why. I pushed up on the next-to-last page and a small yellow square of paper fluttered out and settled onto the table. On it was a scrawl that was written in a different hand. You could describe it as haiku, if you stretch the definition:

Court-martial.
MM-2890
8/4/64

A court-martial? Of Dr. Cameron? This wouldn't have been done lightly. The Union Army needed every doctor it could dragoon. On what grounds, I wondered. The bare-bones record gave no hint. Had he been convicted? I had to assume so. His military record ended there.

Now I remembered something else that Captain Jenkins had told me, that he and Dr. Cameron had served together—"for a while."

<hr />

Don Cameron was obstinate, like weak men can be. No, I could not be privy to any information about a soldier's court-martial, especially an officer's, not for fifty years after the defendant's death—or some such nonsense. I was confident he was making this up. He didn't know of any rules, and he didn't care. Brandishing President Grant's holy script only made him more unyielding. I thought of bribing him but figured I couldn't afford it. Secretary Cameron simply needed to be in charge—to be *seen* as being in charge.

By this time, he was standing and waving his arms. He wasn't much bigger than I was, but softer, head to toe. He wouldn't last fifteen seconds in the ring. I wondered how long he would last in this job.

I said, "Would you accept a direct order from the commander in chief?"

"I am not in the military chain of command."

"How about a direct order from the president? Or possibly a request."

"You are aware, Mr. Hay, that the Tenure of Office Act remains in effect. The Senate must approve a cabinet officer's removal."

Yes, that was definitely spittle that I noticed on his delicate chin. I was transfixed: Would it drip onto his waistcoat?

"Who said anything about . . . ?" Then I realized this was his way of reminding me (and himself, probably) that his daddy was still a power in the Senate. And that the Senate still ran the capital. It was my impression that the president, too, still wielded a smidgen of influence. But the question remained: Did I have enough influence with the president?

I watched in fascination as a droplet of spittle grew longer and thinner and, like a depleted balloon, floated down onto the war secretary's lapel.

<hr />

The storm was sudden and hard. I read later that the sewers in George-town overflowed, causing backups in cellars that smelled nothing like hy-acinths. In the president's zoo in Lafayette Park, the prairie dogs would have drowned, had he not already removed them because of the stench. I thought of myself as fleet of foot, but dashing from the War Department to the Executive Mansion next door left me in a state of dishevelment that caused Old Edward—dear, diplomatic Old Edward—to giggle. He di-rected me to the gentleman's room with a hairbrush and a sponge.

"How is your grandson?" I managed.

"Recovering." Old Edward sparkled.

General Babcock wasn't in, and I can't say I was sorry. I sat in the wait-ing room upstairs, long emptied of its petitioners and office seekers, until I saw the president's door crack open. I leapt up.

I couldn't tell if President Grant was pleased or annoyed to see me. I have never known a man, including Lincoln, who was harder to read. *Taciturn* didn't do him justice. *Impassive* was better. *Deceased* wasn't entirely off the mark. The calm and self-reliance that had made him a superb general, one who didn't flinch from decisions in the world as it was, had proved an imped-iment as president. People in Washington played by nastier rules than Grant, so pure of heart, was used to. He wasn't a bad president, by any means, not like the man he'd replaced. Grant was true to the freedmen and stood up for negroes' rights, and he was suitably tough on the vanquished South, even while turning a blind eye to the corruption by his family and friends. Was he honest himself? I had no reason to doubt it. A naif in a den of thieves, he was, guileless and trusting to a fault—and I do mean *fault*. A president needs some guile, some suspicion, if he intends to accomplish much of anything in this viper pit of a town. As a failure himself in business, Grant admired the tycoons and the crooks—often one and the same—and his countrymen did, too. Such was our moral state, I would say. Crab about it all you like—men will be men, mortals were mortal. Yes, the veneer of civilization was thin, and Grant's shell was thick. The man seemed oblivious. He fit the times.

"Good afternoon, sir," I said as brightly as I could.

He nodded and stared. My move, still.

"May I see you for a moment?" I said.

He waved me in, making me feel at least as welcome as the man off the street. The president's office wasn't as dreary as I remembered from Lincoln's time. The gloomy wallpaper was gone, along with the wartime maps, al-though the furnishings looked older than ever. Despite the heat outside, a fire was ablaze in the fearsome marble hearth, presumably so Grant or his advisers could destroy any document of which they disapproved. The president gestured me into a seat at the long narrow table with a green baize top. He sat at the head.

He waited. Although he hadn't spoken a word yet, he controlled the conversation. As I suppose he ought to, as the nation's chief magistrate in his private domain.

"I . . ." *Need* seemed overwrought. "I . . . am hoping to see the papers pertaining to a court-martial of a Union . . . soldier . . . a doctor, actually. It took place in Tennessee in 'sixty-four."

The president's countenance tilted up, and his blue eyes came alert. I suspected he saw more—always—than he was letting on. "Why?" he said. At last, a word, a single syllable.

"This was the doctor who attended your . . . predecessor. It might be connected to his death. I could use your help."

President Grant moved his head back and took my measure . . . not of my soul so much as my worthiness. I hadn't a clue as to the calculations that such a judgment entailed, but they took him a few moments. He wasn't a man to be hurried.

"How?" President Grant said.

"Another letter, perhaps? Or another . . . sentence?" I pulled out the manhandled letter, which I carried almost everywhere like a talisman. "I should mention that Secretary Cameron was . . . hesitant to give me permission."

President Grant reached for the letter and walked to his desk and sat down. He took up a dip pen and held it over the page, waiting. I dictated a sentence, and he wrote it, followed by his initials. Then he handed the letter back and, without a word or a gesture, returned to his work. He was deaf to my thanks and good wishes. He didn't need them.

✦

"Two words," I replied.

Smalley said, "You are joking."

"No. Two. *Why* and *how*. A syllable each."

"You are quite the interviewer, Hay. Any news in those two words?"

"Not yet," I admitted. "Both words were questions. But I got what I wanted."

"Which was?"

"An addendum to my letter of authorization. I composed it myself."

"May I see?"

No reason why not. I had been flaunting the letter all over the city. Smalley's eyes widened as he read it. This wasn't a man who was easily impressed.

> *To whom it may concern:*
> *Please cooperate with the bearer of this letter, Mr. John Hay, in his inquiries about the unfortunate death of the 17th president.*
>
> *Yours truly,*
U. S. Grant

> *p.s. This includes military documents that are not secrets of war.*
> *USG*

"This wording leaves many a possibility," Smalley said. "It opens the way for all kinds of . . . of . . ."

"The word you are searching for is *mischief.* But I told him I would use it for this one thing only, and that's what I shall do."

"You are a man of honor, Hay." It sounded like an insult. "And our president is a credulous fellow. It's not exactly a letter of authorization, you understand. It's a request for cooperation."

"A request from the commander in chief."

"Requests can be denied. It's not an order, either."

I said, "It has done wonders for me so far, is all I can say."

"Is our favorite war secretary aware of this?"

"He knows about the letter but not about the postscript, and I see no reason to tell him. I plan to show up at the War Department annex in the morning—that's where those records are kept—and show them this and hope it works. It will. Even if the good secretary finds out, he won't try to stop me. And disobey his boss's wishes—why would he want to do that? He's all bluff, anyhow."

+⟩═⟨+

I was tired and cross. The sun was out again, oppressively so, glaring from above. Here, down below, the ladies along the Avenue drooped beneath the weight of their gowns, and the horses seemed to be trotting under duress. I lunged between a streetcar and a wagon full of watermelons to reach the southern side of the Avenue and hailed a hack.

It was one of those spacious ones, drawn by two horses and with seating for four. I was willing to splurge (on the *Tribune*'s dollar) to get back to Nicolay's by dinnertime. The driver was a corn-fed young fellow with rosy cheeks and a hearty manner. Yes, sir, he would take me to Capitol Hill, with the help of his trusty nags, Andy and Abe. He smiled as if he had uttered the wittiest jest outside of burlesque. He was bucking for a tip, and even on my own dime, I would have obliged.

I stepped up onto the passengers' seat, its thin black cushion stiffened by years of rain. The driver applied his whip like a drizzle, and as the carriage began to roll, a man leapt onto the step and pushed me across the seat. I noticed his knife, low against his waist, pointed upward at my face.

I threw myself to the left. Before I could reach for my pocketknife or the pistol in my pocket, a whip cracked above my head. It flicked *his* face, my assailant's, and then it poked into his chest, like a policeman's nightstick. He tumbled backward, out of the carriage, onto the Avenue, looking as astonished as I was. The driver swiveled back and, without a murmur of distress, jerked his whip at the startled horses. The carriage hurtled away.

Only then did I start to tremble.

✦

"Was he trying to rob you?" Therena said.

"I don't know," I said. "It never got that far. But what else could it be?"

I knew otherwise, of course. The man was out to kill me. I was almost sure I had seen him before, outside of Nicolay's house, also with a knife. I knew vaguely what he looked like—like no one in particular. I didn't know who, and I didn't know why. The only reason that made sense was that I was intruding into things that he or his overlord wanted left alone.

"Please don't tell Clara," I said. Therena had her back to me, although she had finished heating up my mock turtle soup.

"She's my friend."

"Mine, too," I said. "It would only upset her, and there's nothing she can do about it from Cleveland."

"I'm not so sure," Therena said. She turned and I was surprised to see streaks of tears on her cheeks.

"Hire Pinkerton, you mean," I replied. "Yes, I already know about that." I figured Therena did, too. "Seems that Pinkerton's man—and it was a man this time—was across the Avenue when this happened, busy hiring another hack to follow me. He wasn't even looking in my direction."

"*I* would want to know," Therena said.

"I'm not sure if Nico would want to tell you," I said.

Nicolay was silent—no fool, he.

What I didn't say was that life involved risk. You might die any day of the week. Getting out of bed in the morning meant taking risks, and *not* getting out of bed risked bedsores. No one got through life without taking chances.

I said, "Look, I'm not trying to tell you what to do—"

"Of course you are," Therena replied, quite reasonably.

"All right, but I just don't see the point in upsetting her when she's a thousand miles away."

"Three hundred and seventy-three miles," Helen said.

I had forgotten she was there. The family had already supped by the time I got back.

"Three hundred and seventy-three, then," I said. "I still don't see the point."

Nicolay said, "Why would he attack you in the middle of the Avenue? So many witnesses. Policemen nearby."

Almost as soon as the carriage had sped off, I had asked my heroic driver to halt it, until Pinkerton's man could rush across the Avenue and a police-man lumbered to the scene. Neither of them had learned a blessed thing.

"Maybe he figured it was the best chance he had," I said, "if he'd noticed Pinkerton's man nearby."

"So, what happened to Pinkerton's man?"

"I guess his eye was getting some shuteye. By the time he realized what was going on, it was too late. So this is what Clara—by which I mean Amasa—is paying for?" I shouldn't let my sourness show. "And even with that, the man who attacked me got away. There's something about having a lot of shocked people around that means that nobody steps forward to do anything. Maybe they didn't see. Maybe they didn't want to see. And maybe he counted on that. Thank God for the driver. The double eagle was all I had—hope it was enough. I owe him my life."

Not the cleverest thing to say.

"Therena, really," I said, "there's no point in telling her. I'm going home soon, anyway."

This was when I realized that I was ready to—how much I wanted to.

I believe, I do, in evil,
Though I'd rather hold to good.

The lamp flickered. Should I turn it up or turn it down? I left it alone. Everything in life was precarious.

Oh, go to sleep, Hay. Put yourself out of your misery.

I closed my notebook and returned it to the doily atop the bedside table and leaned over to turn down the wick. The light was sputtering when I thought of another line.

From the angels to the devil . . .

Evil and *devil* didn't rhyme, but on paper they did. I had a glimmer of a fourth line. I could attach this quatrain to the four-line treatise on evil I had written in Tennessee and wire them both to Whitelaw Reid, for publication, coyly signed with my initials. They just might be banal enough to catch on.

I tried to turn the lamp back up, but the flame sputtered and expired. I vowed to remember the fourth line in the morning. Something on the order of: *Everything is true,* ending in *should,* or maybe *could,* to rhyme with *good.* It was a conclusion so profound, how could I forget it?

CHAPTER TWENTY-TWO

I forgot it.

I shouldn't have been surprised, and I can't say that I was. This had happened more than once, forgetting what I had promised to remember the night before. Usually, whisky was involved, but not this time. And usually, I decided that whatever it was wasn't good enough to remember. Probably this time, too.

Then I remembered the other extenuating factor: someone was trying to kill me. That was bound to put a damper on everything else.

I didn't mean to be flip, because I was trying to allay my all-too-reasonable fears by being, well, flip. Often, that sort of self-deception worked. Not this time. But that didn't excuse lolling in bed.

At breakfast, each of the Nicolays assessed me on the sly, like an asylum's lunatics might judge a newcomer. Therena grasped my shoulder and asked how I had slept.

"Not badly," I said.

Nicolay recognized a falsehood by instinct. (How irksome that must be in Washington City.) He said simply, "How are you doing?"

"I'll be all right." That was more of an admission than I cared to make. Blame it on Nicolay's sincerity.

Bolstering my faith in insincerity.

The messenger from Western Union was climbing to the porch as I was leaving. The envelope had my name. I tore it open. It came from Elizabethton, Tennessee.

CAPT. JENKINS A LOCAL HERO, BELOVED BY ALL.
CURRENT WHEREABOUTS UNKNOWN. PEARCE

Nobody was beloved by all, neither in Washington nor in East Tennessee.

Another messenger caught me at the curb, carrying an envelope embossed with an unblinking eye. No greeting, no signature; none was needed.

> Richter stayed at the Kirkwood House on March 22 and
> 23. Apologies for yesterday. No charge. Godspeed.

It takes strength for a man to apologize. I can't admire men who won't.

+————+

"You sure?" the driver said, once the hackney had halted.

The War Department's annex was in the swampiest part of the capital, near the Potomac shore. Boss Shepherd's miracles aside, the river was still fragrant with last night's sewage and last season's carp. I heard a goose and a gander honking. Over the low hills of Virginia, the flats blurred into the river and the gloomy sky, a tableau of beiges and grays such as Frenchmen in the know were calling *impressionism*. I climbed down.

The judge adjutant general's clerk had proved as good as his word. I showed off my letter from the commander in chief with its addendum. The épée-thin clerk with a mustache to match had the court-martial papers in hand. With a grimace that passed for a smile, he pointed me to a desk of rotting wood. I checked around my feet for rodents and was pleasantly surprised.

The documents stood at least an inch thick. A faded red ribbon, threaded through two slits at the top, was tied into a bow.

Proceedings
Of a General Court Martial which convened at Greeneville, Tenn.,
on August 4, 1864, in the case of Doctor James McLinn Cameron,
13ᵗʰ Tenn. Vol. Cavy., by virtue of the following orders, viz.:

I found the list of charges a few pages in:

Charge 1ˢᵗ: Espionage.

Luckily, I was seated. I had met the man. He was a well-knitted fellow with an easy manner. Hardly a spy. All right, I knew this was nonsense. What on earth did a spy look like, especially in a civil war? The daintiest ladies had smuggled military secrets in their crinolines, knowing that their persons were safe from search. Espionage might have meant nothing more than a whisper to your brother behind the outhouse. In any event, spying for the Confederacy wasn't necessarily a badge of dishonor in Tennessee.

And maybe, just maybe, he was innocent.

I read on:

Specification: In this, that Doctor James McLinn Cameron did inform the Confederate authorities as to the U.S. army's plans for destroying rebel-held bridges in East Tennessee and did act to prevent those plans from effectuation.

This did sound serious. I turned the page and was grateful yet again I wasn't upright.

Charge 2nd: Desertion
Specification: In this, that Doctor James McLinn Cameron left his post for hours at a time, not long before U.S. army planned to destroy rebel-held bridges in East Tennessee.

This raised my suspicions. Dr. Cameron was in the cavalry, which didn't blow up bridges. That would be the infantry's job, or that of a band of marauders, such as the sainted Colonel Stover had led. I let the papers fall to the desk. *That* was the connection. Dr. Cameron was the Stovers' doctor, which would explain how he might have learned of bridge-burning plans that, conceivably, he could have revealed to . . .

Still hard to believe but . . . not implausible.

To each charge, and to each specification, the defendant had pleaded not guilty.

The testimony was disjointed and circumstantial, but detailed—and damning. Dr. Cameron had been seen hobnobbing with Confederate officers in the lobby of his father's hotel, on an afternoon he was assigned to duty, a day before rebel soldiers repulsed a nighttime attack on a Holston river bridge. Eleven days later, a witness noticed Dr. Cameron speaking in "a suspicious manner" to a known Confederate spy on the wooden sidewalk outside of his office. In what way suspicious? Leaning forward, hand hiding his mouth, in a hush. The next day, a bridge across the Pigeon river survived a Union attack.

Dr. Cameron, allowed to testify, insisted that each time he had merely been dispensing medical advice—and was honor bound to say no more about it.

I might have believed him the first time or even the second, but the third episode beggared his claims of innocence. Another whispered conversation in another Confederate's ear, with "Clinch river" overheard distinctly. Two days later, a nighttime raid on the railroad bridge across the Clinch river was met with an ambush.

Dr. Cameron's best defense would have been: He was too stupid, too obvious, too handsome to mask himself as a spy. Instead, he offered nothing but a stubborn denial he had done anything wrong. By the time I finished reading, I would have voted to convict.

I was skimming the concluding arguments—nothing that hadn't been said—when I heard a shout from behind.

"Mr. Hay, you need to leave!"

Without a thought, I coughed and cleared my throat to conceal the sound of yanking the last two pages from the red tape. I stuffed them down the front of my doeskin trousers, which taught me something about myself: my instincts were those of a thief.

"Who says?" I replied.

That confused the clerk. "I do," he said.

No, someone had told him to.

"Secretary Cameron?" I said.

The clerk blushed—unpracticed at lying.

Why would Don Cameron care? Because I had gone over his head? Or maybe he and the spying doctor from Elizabethton *were* related. Maybe one of them had murdered a former president, and the other one felt compelled to protect him. But even if this were the case, what was their motive? Why would either man commit such a crime? This made no sense.

I rose and half turned, to hide the bulge in my pants. "I know you are only following orders," I said, "but can't I just finish, please?"

"I am sorry, no," he said, although his unbent posture eased a little.

"Very well. Do you want this back?" I prayed that the missing pages hadn't left any trace.

"I shall take care of it. Now, go."

"Why such a hurry?" I said. "I only had a few pages more."

"Now," he said. "Or do you want me to call for reinforcements?"

"I'm going, I'm going," I said. This fellow would need reinforcements. "Please follow me," he replied as if inviting a courtesy.

The air outside was hot and viscous, like split pea soup, which I dislike. The miasma, the source of so much disease, wasn't green so much as dun-colored. Was there a sun behind that haze? A gray gull swept out of the clouds and vanished back into them.

I hurried away from the river, northward along Fourteenth street. I shared the muddy curb with a jittery goose and a feral cat, neither of which intended to let a human pass unimpeded. I kept to the roadway, as the pages of transcript were digging into my . . . well, digging in. I looked for a place to relieve my inconvenience. A shipping office, a blacksmith and wheelwright, two lumberyards, a laundry, a warehouse that smelled of last fall's hay—none of these looked like an inviting place to pull a rabbit, so to speak, out of my trousers.

I wondered—once again—if I had committed a felony. I hoped that depended on the value of what was taken, which in this case, by any objective standard, was negligible. But this probably wasn't the case. In any guise, theft was frowned upon (didn't the Ten Commandments say something about that?) even if committed by a detective or a journalist. Or, certainly, by a lawyer. I had read of a sneak thief who stole a pair of pants from a shop on Fifteenth street and was sentenced to six months in jail. A cabbage thief got thirty days. To be honest, stealing a military document from the War Department sounded flagrantly worse than filching vegetables. Though only, I hastened to add, if I got caught.

Neither the formidable Bureau of Engraving and Printing, just south of the Mall, nor the Agriculture Department across Fourteenth offered hope of a respite. I considered ducking inside a weeping willow on the Mall when I saw a likelier spot. Just to the northwest, the marble obelisk honoring the city's founding father was a stump—a factory chimney with its top broken off, as my pal Clemens mocked it. Construction of the monument had stalled when the money ran out. At the moment, it looked a sickly white against the gloom, its base surrounded by hideous sheds, piles of lumber, and heaps of rocks.

I crossed the spongy grounds, sidestepping pools left by the storms. No wonder I was alone here. The court-martial transcript was stabbing my thigh. Wetness crept down my socks. Was that blood trickling down my leg, or perspiration? I wished to consider no other possibilities.

A thunderstorm felt imminent. I limped behind a mound of granite and marble shards and found a ledge that jutted enough to sit on. I planted my feet in the muddy ground. With a few wiggles, a deep dive, and a whimper of pain, I freed my contraband.

The pages were stiff and crumpled—no wonder they hurt! I hopped off the ledge and lay them on top, one page spooned inside the other. I took meticulous care in flattening them with my hand on the semifinished marble, warmed by the sun. I picked up the top page and read:

> *The Court was cleared for deliberation, and after mature consideration upon the evidence adduced, believing it to be a malicious prosecution, does find the accused as follows:*

To 1ˢᵗ	*charge*	*Not Guilty*
To 1ˢᵗ	*specification*	*Not Guilty*
To 2ⁿᵈ	*charge*	*Not Guilty*
To 2ⁿᵈ	*specification*	*Not Guilty*

> *And does, therefore, acquit him.*

Acquit? That couldn't be right. The military judges had heard the same testimony I had read. Something potent must be in the pages I hadn't been permitted to see. But malicious prosecution? I couldn't imagine what this meant. Surely this counted as a miscarriage of justice—even, of military justice! Why on earth had this happened? Had money changed hands? Who bore responsibility for letting a guilty man go free?

The next page listed the nine judges of the military court—two lieutenants, three captains, two majors, a colonel, and a general who served as the chairman.

I skimmed down the list and recognized a name—the chairman's. I blinked several times. Were my eyes playing tricks? The verdict was signed by someone I had come to know all too well, who at this very moment was probably seated in his office—my office.

> *Orville E. Babcock*
> *Brevet Brigadier General*

I ignored the traffic, and I was fortunate that the traffic did not ignore me. A coachman shrieked at me as I crossed B street south, saving my life or at least a limb or two. It was dangerous to think while I walked. It was dangerous to think, period. I had been searching for a connection between Washington City and East Tennessee. I had found it, in a favor that was eleven years old.

But how did all of these pieces fit together? It was a jumble—*I* was a jumble. I pondered the strands. (Ode to Bach.) An assassination that did not occur. A hanging, swift and arguably unjust. An attack on a president-turned-senator, thwarted, this past March. Oh yes, and those letters of blackmail. And now, the court-martial of a Confederate spy (alleged!) who, years later, treated ol' Andy in his last . . . illness. Acquitted by the man who now stood at President Grant's right hand.

At Grant's right hand!

That stopped me in my tracks. Happily, I had reached the other sidewalk. Bile climbed into my throat, and I swallowed it down, leaving its sour, sharp taste. I felt dizzy. A man wearing a felt hat and a frayed swallow-tail coat cursed at me as he veered past. I felt his beery breath on my neck.

I was on Fifteenth street, alongside the president's park, which was empty of people and cows. I staggered over and squatted against the wooden fence. The nausea had passed, and in its place was a feeling just as intense. I couldn't identify it at first. The muscles in my arms were in spasm, my forehead burned, and sweat rolled down my spine. It wasn't illness I was feeling but fear. Fear for my country. No, don't laugh. Are we only as good as the leaders we choose? Lord help us if that is true. Nobody could match Lincoln—I understood that, in my head if not in my heart. But to slip so precipitously in character and craft . . . The Ancient's successor, Andy Johnson (mea culpa!), was mean and unforgiving, a president who disunited a nation that was struggling to repair itself. His successor, the hero of war, had a good heart and a blind eye. But what if his eye wasn't so blind? What if he *knew*? What had he known?

Nothing. I prayed for this. *Nothing, nothing.* I wasn't a praying man, but this time I actually prayed. I prayed for Grant to be ignorant.

But wait—what did I *know*? I knew that Grant's right-hand man had once done an inexplicable, possibly profitable, kindness for the doctor who would attend Andy Johnson on his deathbed in Tennessee. That was all I knew. This could well be a coincidence or an irrelevancy. Or maybe Dr. Cameron *was* innocent.

Or maybe the explanation was the evident one, that General Babcock had called in a favor from Dr. Cameron, presumably larding it with a threat of exposure, in exchange for committing a murder. But why?

I prayed again, this time for the country I loved.

I swallowed, breathed deeply, opened my bleary eyes, and pushed myself away from the fence. When you're knocked down, you've got to get up. This was the main rule I knew, in boxing as in life.

I had an errand to run before I braved the Executive Mansion. Western Union was in a lull before lunchtime. I was fifth in line, behind a skinny pastor who kept scratching his arse. This gave me time to compose my follow-up telegram to Sheriff Pearce, inquiring about Dr. Cameron and his war record. Should I mention the court-martial? I considered what the Western Union operator in Elizabethton might tell his wife that night over catfish and corn, and what she might repeat to her whist partner the next morning. Was there anything useful I could ask that the sheriff would be willing to answer?

I quit the queue.

It was also time to quit stalling. I needed to do what I needed to do. I barged out of Western Union and nearly collided with a horse, which was minding its own business, tied up at the curb. "Pardon," I said and patted his rump and stepped around him. I crossed Fourteenth street, zigzagging between rigs, fancy or rickety.

The doorway of Willard's Hotel was clogged with fat gentlemen in silk hats. I skirted them and remained otherwise unaware of passersby, who parted to let me through. Up ahead, the Treasury building was gray; the sidewalk was gray; the sky was gray; the world was gray; my mind was gray. What else was new?

I returned to the question at hand: What should I ask General Babcock, and how should I ask it? I hadn't reported to him in a couple of days. Maybe I should start with an apology for that (and expect the same response I got from the horse) and . . . make my report. I would tell him what I had learned in Murder Bay and, by the way, in a War Department warehouse. And see what he says.

I was feeling almost buoyant once I reached the Mansion's door. Old Edward lit up, as usual, at seeing a face from the past.

"Babcock?" I mouthed.

Old Edward's thumb pointed up.

This time, I ignored the portraits of unmemorable presidents—how many more would the next centuries bring? On the staircase, my footsteps echoed. The building seemed empty. It *was* August.

General Babcock was in, behind his desk—*my* desk. I tried to sneak up like a . . . spy. He heard me, in the doorway, and pivoted with a sneer that he softened in case the intruder was the commander in chief. When he saw it was me, his scimitar of a mustache drooped. I figured he was still furious at me for knocking him down in front of his boss. It wouldn't help to remind him that the fight had been his boss's idea.

"Is this a bad time?" I said.

"They all are," Babcock replied. "I needn't tell you that."

"As good a time as any, then?" I took his silence as assent. I would begin with the most provocative item that did not implicate him.

"Andrew Johnson was attacked just last March, on the sidewalk outside of the Kirkwood House."

"You told me."

Had I? "I have spoken with an eyewitness who described the man who attacked him. He looked a lot like Hartman Richter. That's George Atzerodt's cousin, the one in Germantown."

Babcock looked unsurprised. "Who was the eyewitness?" he snapped. "What's her name?"

Her name? Babcock knew. But how? Who could have told him? No policeman had come. The Kirkwood House doorman, perhaps. Or . . . suddenly I pictured it . . . Richter himself. Why not? After assaulting Andrew Johnson on the sidewalk at Twelfth and Penn, and noticing a witness, he was seen limping away, heading west. Quite possibly to the Executive Mansion, where he barged in on Babcock as he had on Hannibal Hamlin. Yes, yes! Everything fit. The strands were weaving into one. "You saw him, didn't you?"

"Saw who?" Babcock said, evading my gaze.

"Hartman Richter."

"I don't know who you're talking about. I've never met the man."

"He came here, didn't he, and he told you."

"Told me what? You're talking in riddles. Now if you—"

"About attacking Andy Johnson outside his hotel."

"Look, Hay, I have too much to do here to—"

I had better ask what I came for before Babcock sent me away. "Do you remember a doctor named James Cameron, from Eliza*beth*ton"—I exaggerated the pronunciation—"Tennessee?"

Wait, wasn't that the pronunciation Babcock had used once before? Was it my imagination, or had his eyes gone blank?

I pressed on. "You presided over his court-martial, in Greeneville, Tennessee, in 'sixty-four. He was acquitted."

"How could I possibly remember that far back?" Babcock's lips pursed.

I realized that President Grant hadn't told his private secretary of the new sentence in my letter.

"I didn't have a chance to read all of the court-martial transcript"—I paused, to no reaction—"but the parts I did read showed that the evidence against him was strong."

"But not strong enough to convict," Babcock said.

His eyes were no longer blank but cold, like a cobra's. This was the true Orville Babcock—I had reached bottom. He did remember. But why would he, eleven years later? The implication was unmistakable: the acquittal had created an obligation that he had recently cashed in.

"Have you been in touch with him since then?" I said. "Recently, perhaps?"

"What are you accusing me of?" Babcock said. He knew that, too.

"I haven't accused you of—"

Slowly he turned and slid open the top drawer of his desk. I remembered what I had kept there.

I drew my gun first, grateful that it didn't snag in my coat pocket.

He drew his gun second. It was bigger than mine. He also knew how to use it. But I couldn't believe he would shoot, not inside the president's sacred shelter. Besides, the distance between us was short, and my chances of firing a lethal blow were almost as good as his were. Good enough, anyway, to dissuade.

"Gentlemen!"

Both of us jumped. Neither of us pulled the trigger—thank the Lord for that. We hadn't noticed the president.

"What in blazes is going on here?"

The stern whisper was, for Grant, a shout. His query could not be ignored.

Silence, until Babcock . . . I swear he squeaked. "Merely a difference of opinion, sir."

"About what?" Grant demanded.

I broke the silence this time. I had to know.

"About whether Andrew Johnson deserved to be murdered," I said. "General Babcock seems to think so. I am not so sure."

"The hell he did!" Grant thundered. "What kind of bunkum is that?"

+≈—≈+

"And you believed him?" Therena said.

"Either Grant is a consummate actor," I said, "and nobody has ever ac-

cused him of pretending to be anyone other than himself—or he was telling the truth."

"Or what he thought was the truth."

"That's good enough. What matters to me is what Grant knew, or what
he thought he knew."

"What's the distinction?" Therena said.

"None, I guess," I said. "You should be a lawyer, Therena. I have a law
license that you're welcome to borrow, if the authorities don't take it away."

I had started on brandy early to-night, out of necessity, while young
Helen was still finishing her gingerbread. So far, I was drinking alone.

"Grant hates death," Nicolay said, "like all military men. He saw too
much blood in the war. They say he won't even eat rare meat."

"What *did* he know?" This, from Helen.

"Nothing," I said, "and thank God for that. I'm satisfied that he was
genuinely outraged and that he knew nothing about what Babcock was
up to."

"Hail to ignorance," Nicolay said.

"The president's strong suit," I said. "I must say Babcock did look a little
frightened, and not at me."

"Despite your weaponry," Nicolay said.

Helen's eyes were wide.

I said, "He was frightened of the president. I can't imagine he ever told
Grant what he had done."

"That's his job," Nicolay said, "protecting the president."

"And leaving him in splendid ignorance, yes?" I said. "It's just what you
would have done, Nico."

"Wouldn't you?" Nicolay went to the kitchen cupboard and returned
with a snifter. He poured the brandy and savored the aroma before taking
a sip. "But not to the point of murder," he added.

I peered into my friend's gaunt face and considered his adoration for
Lincoln. "If you say so," I allowed.

"I will ignore that," Nicolay said. "You are persuaded that Babcock was
behind all this, I gather."

"I am. This is what I think happened. Grant took Johnson's return to
the Senate as a personal insult, and Babcock took it as a political threat,
an obstacle to Grant's chances for a third term, a rallying figure for the
opposition, maybe a candidate himself. He has a certain following that
could never be shaken. Babcock's job is to eliminate the president's political threats, by any means necessary. That, as you say, was his job. And he

didn't do it only to protect the president. It was also to protect himself. This Whisky Ring business looks serious—doesn't it, Nico?"

"Very. People are going to prison, distillers and government officials alike."

"And so Babcock needs a president in his corner for another four—well, five—years. I am sorry, Helen," I said. I wasn't sure what I was apologizing for—mostly, I guess, for the world we had built and would bequeath her. "A third term for Grant would also help our gilded Babcock to get richer, quicker. Which may, by the way, explain how Dr. Cameron in East Tennessee achieved his acquittal. He bought it, or his daddy did, from the general in charge. Why should we assume that Babcock's affection for the gilded life began with the Whisky Ring?"

"So," Nicolay said, "you think General Babcock contacted Dr. Cameron, who owed him a favor of sorts."

"That's exactly what I think," I said.

"I don't understand," Helen said.

"Bravo, Helen," I replied. "Let me try to weave our concerto. Andrew Johnson, the former president, now a member of the august Senate, delivered a speech last March that lit into President Grant as a tyrant, an evildoer, a man desperate for a third term in office. This upset General Babcock—he's the president's right-hand man, like your father used to be. But a bad egg, unlike your father. That night, the former president Johnson was attacked on the sidewalk, on the Avenue at Twelfth street, by a cousin of the man who was supposed to have murdered Johnson the night that President Lincoln was shot. You with me?"

A tentative nod.

"Atzerodt—you're the one, Helen, who remembered his name. He decided not to murder Johnson that night because of a little girl named Edith, his daughter, and he was . . . hanged for it, anyway." How awful to reveal the world's wickedness to a child. "Still with me?"

Helen was withholding judgment.

"So this cousin—remember him?—barged into the Executive Mansion and couldn't get to the president—he told me that—and he must have found General Babcock instead. That's what gave General Babcock the idea. Maybe it emboldened him. He could solve his political problem—be rid of it for good."

"Or for evil," Therena said.

"Or for evil. So when he learned—who knows how?—of Andy Johnson's travel plans to Elizabethton, his plan sprang into action. He knew someone there—a doctor, no less—who owed him a favor and, better yet, had no choice but to obey. If he refused, Babcock could expose his court-martial and the allegations of espionage, which was bound to alienate half of the town, maybe more. For a doctor in a small town, it behooves him to keep everyone happy." This, I knew all too well from my father's struggles. "The situation was perfect. Somebody else would fix Babcock's problem, far away from Washington City, in a way that no one would ever suspect."

"Until you," Nicolay said.

"Thank you, Nico." I meant it. Then a thought made me ill. "I should have known it!" I sputtered.

"What do you mean?" Nicolay said.

"I should have known!" I managed not to swear. "Eliza*beth*ton—that's how General Babcock pronounced it. It's a tiny place, and he had heard of it. I remember him saying it, and he knew how to say it correctly. I realized that to-day. I should have realized it then."

"Don't be hard on yourself," Nicolay said. "You did figure out—"

"And something else, now that I think about it. The first time I was attacked, down by the curb here, I had just been with Babcock and told him I was staying with you. He knew where to find me, or to have one of his men find me. One of his less competent men, fortunately."

"Thank God for incompetence," Therena said, offering the theological perspective.

"Come to think of it, both times I was attacked in Washington City, it was right after seeing him. The time on the Avenue, too."

"He's a bad man," Helen declared. She was young enough to see the gist of things. "He should go to jail!"

"Only if I could prove it," I said, "which I probably can't. I can ask Pinkerton to search for telegrams, but the chances of finding anything explicit . . . If there were letters, they're now in ashes."

"Then have this Dr. Cameron arrested," said Therena. She ought to be a prosecutor, not just a lawyer.

"On what evidence?" Nicolay said.

"There must be some," Therena said. She pointed to the gingerbread cooling on the stove top. "Johnny, you sure you don't want a piece?"

"You're twisting my arm," I said. "A small one."

She cut too generous a slice.

"The doctor certainly had plenty of opportunities," I said, "to slip belladonna into ol' Andy's whisky, first at his hotel on the way in from the depot, and when that didn't work, at his patient's bedside. And then, as the attending physician—how convenient!—he declared the cause of death to be apoplexy. The symptoms are similar enough, other than the dilated eyes—which Dr. Cameron, by the way, kept denying. He got downright testy when I suggested it. But he knew what I was talking about. I can see that now."

"So, arrest him," Therena said. "He could implicate General Babcock."

"He might at that," I said, "but to quote your husband, on what evidence? I can't imagine he would ever confess. The glasses Johnson drank from were washed, so I don't see any material evidence we could find that would . . ."

Therena said, "So you're saying that neither of them will ever be . . ."

"Not unless I can—"

"While Mr. Atzerodt was hanged for a crime he didn't commit"— Therena was livid—"as part of a conspiracy he tried to pull out of."

"That seems about right to me," I said with a sour laugh. "On this earth, that is what passes for justice. Wouldn't you agree, Nico?"

"This is what I don't understand," Nicolay said. "Did Johnson know about Booth's plot beforehand? Was the Hell-cat—it pains me to ask this—but was she right?"

"It depends what you mean by 'know,'" I replied.

Helen seemed puzzled. Therena groaned.

"No, I mean it—"

"You usually do," Therena said.

"Let me try to explain," I persisted. "Booth delivered his lines from *Richard II*—assuming, of course"—I nodded at Nicolay—"that Booth actually did do that and wasn't just bragging to Atzerodt. But assuming he did, orating to his audience of one, Johnson would have no way of knowing what he was hearing or why. Here was a comely young stranger spouting from the restaurant doorway some words that ol' Andy might—or might not—have recognized as Shakespeare. And even if he had, would he have understood what Booth was trying to say? So, did he *know* about the plot ahead of time? Is that what you're asking? Honestly, I don't think he did. But later, after the Ancient was killed, and Johnson learned of the note Booth had left at the Kirkwood House and recognized him as the man who had spouted . . . something at him, he had good reason to panic. People would *think* that he had known. Which, in fact, they did, and not only the Hell-cat. *This* was what he was worried about—that people would suspect that he had known of Booth's plot, even if he hadn't. It was a political problem he needed to be rid of. And he found a cold-blooded solution—a military commission and a quick hanging. He could never let the word get out about his literary encounter that very afternoon, Good Friday, with one John Wilkes Booth. The note that Booth left at the hotel was damaging enough. That did become known at the trial, but the prosecutors never pursued it, probably in fear of a vengeful president, and no one could ever explain it, so the world forgot."

I maneuvered my fork through the gingerbread, which—beyond expectations—tasted as good as it smelled.

Across the kitchen table, Helen peered at me with shining eyes.

"Wait a minute," she said. She slipped away and headed upstairs. Therena called after her—this was a violation of household rules—but Helen's rules were her own. I could see that, even if her parents couldn't. I hoped I would wax so wise someday about my own Helen.

"So, what are you going to do," Nicolay said, "with everything you've learned?"

"I am going home," I announced. "Already packed."

"How about all of the—?"

"I've got nothing, I tell you. I've seen letters of blackmail that I don't have in my possession and that parties on all sides will deny. Beyond that, what I know, or think I know, doesn't amount to breakfast for a flea. I can't prove a thing against Babcock, and Grant would never believe me if I could. Babcock won't admit to anything, and I would be astonished if Dr. Cameron did, either. I'll be almost as shocked if Pinkerton can turn up hard evidence. I've got nothing, Nico—nothing. Unless I rhapsodize about Johnson's last days, with his loving family around him, I don't even have a story to write, not one that any reputable newspaper would publish. The only thing I've got is . . . the truth. You know, Nico, I try and try and try to learn what's true in the world, despite the obstacles and best efforts of people who don't want me to know. And when I finally figure it out, if I do, nobody gives a . . . damn. Sorry, Therena. But nobody does. People don't want to know. They prefer their fictions. Maybe our friend Clemens is right, that truth is stranger than fiction because fiction has to make sense. Truth is also better, simply better, no matter what anyone says. It's more reliable as a guide to how the world works."

How would I explain my failure to Whitelaw Reid, considering the money I'd spent? I could remind him that not all stories pan out and that this one cost less than a drunken evening at Delmonico's. Better yet, I could regale him with my misadventures during a drunken evening at Delmonico's.

I remembered my brandy and imbibed too large a gulp and came near to choking. "I've got a train ticket," I managed. "For to-night."

"What time?" Therena said.

I pulled my watch from my waistcoat. "Nine seventeen. We have time."

"When do you get to Cleveland?"

"God knows when to-morrow."

Therena looked crosswise at my blasphemy. "Will Clara meet you?"

"Yes, with the little one, Helen, I hope. There is nothing in this hot and dusty world that compensates for the loss of her society."

Therena said, "We've certainly grown used to having you here, Johnny."

"I cannot thank you enough for—"

We were rescued from sentimentality by Helen's return. She was clutching a small wooden frame. She sidled up to me, eyes downcast, and thrust it forward—a gift. I turned it over and saw . . . Clara. That is, a portrait of Clara, an impression of my beloved in small, deft brushstrokes suggesting a wry smile, a wise gaze, a self-possession in her brow.

Or maybe that's just what I saw there. It was time, past time, to go home. That meant Cleveland now. If gallivanting was a joy, it was a joy of my youth. For me now, having a wife and a child and a home being built meant something deeper, a connection to generations gone and yet to come. All of this was a train ride away.

AFTERWORD

On July 31, 1875, at around 2:45 in the morning, Andrew Johnson breathed his last. The former president was at his younger daughter's house near Elizabethton, in East Tennessee. The doctors blamed his death on two successive strokes—apoplexy, in the parlance of the day.

In my story, he was poisoned. As far as I know, this is fiction. But I would argue that it is plausible. Seven years and five months after leaving the presidency in disgrace, Johnson had no shortage of people who wanted him gone.

As in my other John Hay mysteries, the most outlandish plotlines are based on fact. For one thing, Johnson really did claim to possess letters that he said "would ruin the reputations of many of the leading Republicans in Congress," as E. V. Smalley, formerly a *New-York Tribune* correspondent, wrote in *The Independent* magazine in 1900. Smalley had interviewed Johnson after his presidency in his famous tailor shop in Greeneville, Tennessee, where the letters were stored, although the names of intended recipients have never come to light. Smalley's recounting in my story is almost verbatim.

Most intriguingly, John Wilkes Booth actually did leave a note for Andrew Johnson or his private secretary at the Kirkwood House, with the wording I've cited, on the afternoon of the day that President Lincoln was shot. This was revealed at the conspirators' trial but has never been satisfactorily explained. (I have conflated the editions of the trial transcript printed in 1865 by two publishers in Philadelphia and a third in New York.) Mary Lincoln and some Radical Republicans in Congress believed that Johnson was involved in, or at least had foreknowledge of, Lincoln's assassination. A House Select Committee on the Assassination of President Lincoln was established in 1867 to investigate "many persons holding high positions of power and authority"—including Johnson, presumably—but never issued a report, probably because no proof was found. The committee's investigative files have vanished, other than two innocuous depositions stored at the Library of Congress in the personal papers of the committee's chairman, Representative Benjamin Butler, a Massachusetts Republican.

It is also true that George Atzerodt, who refrained from assassinating Johnson, had secretly fathered a two-year-old daughter, Edith, with a Mrs. Wheeler in Port Tobacco, Maryland. She was likely the "mysterious lady" in black who visited Atzerodt on the morning of his execution, as described on page 206 of *The Trial of the Conspirators at Washington City, D.C., May and June, 1865, for the Murder of President Abraham Lincoln,* published in 1865 by T. B. Peterson & Brothers in Philadelphia (and not in *Lives, Crimes and Confessions of the Assassins,* put out the same year). The Reverend John G. Butler, a leading Lutheran pastor in Washington, attended Atzerodt in his final hours. The Kirkwood House desk clerk's recounting of events to Hay is verbatim from his affidavit to the military commission's investigators. My account of the conspirators' meeting on the evening of April 14, 1865, when Atzerodt tried to withdraw from the conspiracy, is taken from confessions he made during his incarceration, suppressed by the military authorities but found years later among his lawyer's papers; by at least one account, it was mentioned during the trial.

I haven't altered anything in the historical record of the Lincoln assassination, but I have added to it in two ways to offer what I hope are reasonable explanations for lingering mysteries. There is no evidence that Booth actually saw Johnson at the Kirkwood House on April 14, much less recited Shakespeare to him, although the then vice president was on the premises most of the day. Also, whatever Atzerodt might have confided to his cousin or to the mysterious lady in black remains unknown.

Other than the cause of Johnson's death, my depiction of his last days is accurate. Captain William E. McElwee, who gave up his train seat for Johnson, joined in a conversation I've taken almost verbatim from his recollection in 1923. McElwee stayed at Dr. James Cameron's hotel in Elizabethton and accompanied him to the former president's bedside. Dr. Cameron served in the same Tennessee cavalry unit as Captain David B. Jenkins, who had a baby son named Stover, his wife's maiden name; their military records are correct, other than Dr. Cameron's court-martial, which I've invented. My list of visitors to Johnson's deathbed, except for Jenkins, is factual. Dr. Abraham Jobe's recollections of Johnson are nearly verbatim from his autobiography. I have accurately described the land deed records for the Pattersons' 516-acre farm. Amazingly, there was talk that Jefferson Davis, who was living in Memphis, might fill Johnson's vacated Senate seat. Charles Dickens's assessment of Johnson is nearly word for word.

My description of Johnson's funeral is taken from news accounts and from *The Masonic Text-Book of Tennessee,* published in 1888. The opening sentences I've cited in the *Tribune*'s coverage are verbatim, although the reporter is unknown. The funeral was, indeed, Adolph Ochs's first news story, twenty-one years before he purchased *The New York Times,* and Horace Greeley was the budding journalist's boyhood hero.

David O. Stewart's *Impeached: The Trial of President Andrew Johnson and the Fight for Lincoln's Legacy* describes the patronage and possibly bribes that benefited Republicans who voted to acquit Johnson of the impeachment charges in 1868. The former president died without leaving a will, having torn up previous ones, although I have concocted his intentions for another. He did have "small hands and feet," according to a recollection in *Century Illustrated Magazine* decades after his death by Benjamin C. Truman, his onetime private secretary.

The major characters in my story are all real, and I've kept to the known biographical facts. John Hay had just left the *New-York Tribune* (which still used a hyphen) and moved to Cleveland with Clara and baby Helen. I have borrowed phrases and sentences from his letters. General Orville E. Babcock, President Grant's private secretary and closest aide, was soon to be indicted in the Whisky Ring scandal and acquitted on Grant's good word. Henry Wilson was known to bathe in the Capitol basement, and the U.S. senators lived at the Washington addresses I've used. David Patterson was accused of graft while he was a senator. William H. Ottman, the proprietor of the saloon at Twelfth street and Pennsylvania avenue, was an accomplice in the Treasury robbery. Robert Jones was a desk clerk at the Kirkwood House in 1865 who testified at the conspirators' trial; the hotel chambermaid, however, is fictional. Johnson's servant William Johnson's death certificate named Robert Johnson, the ex-president's middle son, as his father. Robert died from an overdose of liquor and laudanum.

I have relied on biographies of Andrew Johnson by Hans L. Trefousse, David O. Stewart, Annette Gordon-Reed, and Brenda Wineapple, among others. I found descriptions of Washington and the 1870s in numerous books and contemporary travel guides; in *Harper's Weekly, The Atlantic Monthly, Lippincott's, Potter's American Monthly, Every Saturday,* and other magazines; and in newspapers, mainly *The Evening Star* and the *Washington Chronicle.* The incidents I've portrayed on the city's streets—the sheep in the jewelry store, the carriage accidents—derive from newspaper accounts. To the extent known, I have placed stores and other landmarks in their actual locations. The newspaper quotations are verbatim, although the editorial I've attributed to the *Cincinnati Daily Star* actually ran in the *Cincinnati Enquirer*. *The New York Times* described cantaloupe as a "deceitful" melon. I have retained the lowercase use of *street, county, and negro,* and the hyphenation of *to-day, to-night,* and *to-morrow,* which were common at the time. Many historians say the Gilded Age started around 1877; others place it earlier, in the prosperity that followed the Civil War. *The Gilded Age: A Tale of To-day,* a novel by Mark Twain and Charles Dudley Warner, was first published in 1873.

I have taken liberties, however, for the sake of my story. There was no report that Johnson, as he was dying, had dilated eyes, the hallmark of belladonna use. I have invented Robert Johnson's expunged arrest and Hartman Richter's run-ins with Hannibal Hamlin and Orville Babcock. Kirkwood House had recently been razed, its furnishings sold at auction, so Johnson resided at the Imperial Hotel during Congress's special session in 1875; there is no evidence he was assaulted. President Grant spent August 1875 in New Jersey, Rhode Island, and Buffalo, not in Washington. The Hawaiian king had visited Washington the previous December. Bowie, Maryland, was called Huntington City until 1880.

Also, Babcock's office in the White House was next to Grant's, in Nicolay's old office, across the waiting room from where Hay's had been. I have tweaked 1875's chronology. Jules Verne's *The Mysterious Island* was already being serialized in *Scribner's Monthly* but would not be published as a book in the United States until December. Donald Cameron became Grant's war secretary nine months after my story ends. There is no evidence that John Hay was a boxer—although he was a published poet—and I have imagined his interior life and rhetorical style as more of my own.

I have made up most of the scenes and dialogue, but I have tried to portray accurately the events and tenor of the time—what Lincoln scholar Michael Burlingame calls "emotional history." My goal is for readers to feel like they're there.

ACKNOWLEDGMENTS

Trying to make the past come to life requires assistance, and I've been fortunate to find it.

In researching my story in Tennessee, I am grateful to Joe and the late Shirley Taylor for guiding me around Elizabethton and to their daughter, Jessica Taylor of *The Cook Political Report,* for instructing me in the town's correct pronunciation. June Pinkston at the T. Elmer Cox Library in Greeneville tirelessly answered my questions and hunted up materials. I am much obliged to Dr. Daniel Schumaier for showing me the house in which Andrew Johnson died and for answering my follow-up questions. Thanks also to Joe Penza, the archivist at the Elizabethton / Carter County Public Library; Johnny Blankenship, the Carter County circuit court clerk; Ronald A. Lee at the Tennessee State Library & Archives; and the special collections staff at the University of Tennessee's library in Knoxville, home to Andrew Johnson's papers.

In Washington, too, librarians were a joy to work with. At DC's public library, Jerry McCoy helped me in countless ways, consulting documents the pandemic put off limits. Meg Kuhagen in the U.S. Senate library and Dan Holt and Heather Moore in the Senate Historical Office went out of their way to assist my research. So did Sarah Hedlund and Jane Sween at the Montgomery County (Maryland) Historical Society's Jane C. Sween Research Library and Special Collections. At the National Library of Medicine's history division, Dr. Stephen J. Greenberg was delightfully creative, and Crystal Smith was cheerful and efficient. The Library of Congress's staff, as always, was unfailingly helpful.

Thanks also to the Reverend Karen Brau at the Luther Place Memorial Church in Washington; Elsie Picyk and Carin Diggle at Port Tobacco Historic Village; southern Maryland railroad historian Vince Cipriani; Mike

Mazzeo, vice president of the Charles County (Maryland) Historical Society; Deanne Blanton and Andrew Brethauer at the National Archives in Washington; Sid Oakley of the Bristol Historical Association; and Sister Mada-anne Gell VHM at the Georgetown Visitation Preparatory School. I appreciate the assistance of novelist and former Alexandria, Virginia, policeman Mark Bergin; Hannah Byrne at the Smithsonian Institution; Jesse Kraft at the American Numismatic Society; Bill Barrow at Cleveland State University; and Matt Rutherford at the Newman Library in Chicago, where Orville Babcock's papers are housed.

I am especially indebted to five people who offered careful and thoughtful readings of the manuscript: James M. Cornelius, the former curator at the Abraham Lincoln Presidential Library and Museum; Celeste Carruthers, a University of Tennessee, Knoxville, economist; my college friends Steve Morgan and Joel Altschul; and Jessica Taylor.

I could not have written this trilogy without the enthusiasm and wise guidance of Claire Eddy, my editor at Macmillan's Tor Forge. It wouldn't have seen the light of day without the excellent services of Ron Goldfarb, my literary agent, and his former associate, Gerrie Sturman.

Friends have helped in all sorts of ways. Warm thanks to Bill O'Brian, Jonathan Rauch, Marshall and Joan Wolff, Candace Katz, Dan Shapiro, Rich Cohen, Kirk Victor, Dean Roemmich, and Julie Abramson. I am grateful beyond words to my loving wife, Nancy Tuholski, for somehow keeping this enterprise afloat.